THE CLEANER, THE CAT AND THE SPACE STATION

THE SHANTIVIRA BOOK ONE

FAY ABERNETHY

First published in 2021 by
Fay Abernethy
c/o autorenglück.de
Franz-Mehring-Str. 15, 01237 Dresden, Germany
www.fayabernethy.com

German National Library Cataloguing in Publication Data
A catalogue record for this book is available from the German National
Library (*Deutsche Nationalbibliothek*). More details available at
http://dnb.d-nb.de.

Cover design and illustration © Patrick Knowles
www.patrickknowlesdesign.com
Formatting by BB eBooks Co., Ltd. www.bbebooksthailand.com

ISBN: 978-3-949516-01-6 (ebook)
ISBN: 978-3-949516-02-3 (paperback)
ISBN: 978-3-949516-03-0 (hardcover)

Paperback edition

This book is dedicated to all those who, for whatever reason, have left the country of their birth and made their home elsewhere.

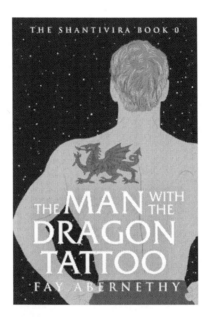

Get your FREE no-obligation download from
www.fayabernethy.com today.

Yours to keep, forever!

PART ONE

1. THE STRANGEST GRAVE
HANNA, JUNE 2013

H ANNA SQUATTED IN the dirt beneath the bridge, barely registering the noise of the midsummer night traffic beyond the Regent's Canal. She wouldn't be cleaning hotel rooms in the morning, so much was clear.

Her existence had shrunk to waves of pain, the fear of the coming wave almost worse than the pain itself. There was no room for thought when giving birth: only instincts, reactions. Eventually, after a mighty final spasm, the pain stopped. The relief! Oh God, the relief! Carefully, Hanna gathered up the slimy bundle and investigated.

A boy. Much smaller than babies were supposed to be and strangely floppy. Why wasn't he moving? Why didn't he cry? She held him to her face, but she could feel no breath. She clutched him to her chest with the last of her strength. Samuel, she'd call him. He should have a name, even though his life was over before it had started.

Female voices. A white-tiled bathroom. Strong arms holding her upright. A warm shower. Pink water swirling down the plughole. Gentle hands shifting the miniature corpse from one arm to the other. Samuel. Hold him tight. Never let him go. Sleep.

Hanna woke in a king-size bed made up with freshly laundered bedding: dainty blue flowers on a white background. Tiny Samuel lay on the pillow next to her, swaddled in a soft red blanket like any other newborn. She was relieved to see her plastic bag of belongings on an armchair in the corner. Apart from a persistent ache in her abdomen, she felt considerably better.

She lay still for a minute, relishing the sensation of being warm, clean and comfortable. Then she rolled over and blinked in disbelief as she took in the woman sitting silently at her bedside. In all the years Hanna had spent surviving in London's underbelly, she'd never met anyone who looked like this. Hanna stared at the delicate features, silver skin and long, lime-green hair. She ought to be frightened, but giving birth to Samuel had left her uncharacteristically passive, anaesthetised by postpartum hormones. She was just too exhausted to be scared. Anyway, the woman's expression was so kindly Hanna knew at once that this was a friend. Wherever Hanna was, it was a place of safety.

She tried to speak, but her tongue stuck to her mouth. Understanding immediately, the silver lady poured her a glass of water from the jug on the bedside table. Hanna sat up and gulped it down gratefully. Then she tried again.

'Where am I?'

'Marylebone.'

'Still London then. Why is your skin that colour? I mean, if you don't mind me asking.'

'I'm a Sayari. My home planet is at the other end of our galaxy. My skin is this colour because our sun emits more radiation than yours does. My name's Irion.' She

4

held out her hand for Hanna to shake. 'And you are?'

Hanna drew her arm out from under the covers and reached for Irion's hand. It was warm and slightly rubbery, as if made of neoprene. 'Hanna. Are there…um…lots of aliens in London?'

Irion's face remained serious, but her ears waggled violently, making Hanna want to giggle. 'I suppose that depends on who you define as an alien. Hanna, you're very welcome here. You're safe with us.'

And intuitively, Hanna felt she was. Whoever and whatever Irion was, Hanna knew she'd help her with the urgent task ahead. 'I have to bury my son,' she said. 'As soon as possible, somewhere I can visit him regularly. Not a cremation: a burial. That's how we do it where I come from.'

'Where do you come from, Hanna?'

'Gambella. In Ethiopia. The thing is, I don't have any papers. I'm not supposed to be here.'

Irion nodded gravely. 'We guessed as much. We looked through your things to see if there was anyone we could contact about you, but we found nothing. Leave it with me. I've been living here illegally for years myself. I have an idea; I just need to clear it with my boss.'

'Do you have anything to eat? I'm so hungry.'

The ears waggled again. It seemed to be an expression of amusement. 'Of course. I'll go and get you something.' Irion stood up and left the room, her thin white robe swishing around her ankles.

Grateful for the chance to weep in private, Hanna picked up Samuel and held him to her. He was cold and stiff now. Her tears splashed onto the little face and she rocked back and forth, howling as she allowed the grief to engulf her.

SOMETIME LATER, HANNA had cried herself out and was investigating her surroundings. She was in a basement flat in one of those posh old central London houses. Her room was larger than most hotel bedrooms, with a fitted pale blue carpet and heavy curtains which matched the bed linen. Everything was spotlessly clean, the en suite bathroom white and modern. The dark wooden furniture – a bed, drawers, a desk with a green leather top, chairs and a wardrobe – appeared to be antique. The wardrobe was a massive, carved affair which dominated the room. She opened it curiously, but it was empty save for some padded coat hangers and lavender sachets, the bare shelves lined with scented paper.

The window faced the front of the building and, outside, mossy stone steps led up to the pavement. Beyond the black railings she could see the legs of passers-by and, behind them, a row of mature trees. Hanna undid the latch and the sash slid up with reassuring ease. She could leave anytime she wanted.

Fresh air flooded in and she was reconnected with audio London: footsteps, the background hum of combustion engines, screeching brakes and the occasional siren, overlaid by the sound of the summer breeze rustling the leaves above her. She could smell exhaust fumes and the sharp tang of vinegar as someone walked by eating fish and chips.

Food. Exploring had distracted her, but she couldn't

suppress her hunger forever. Unfortunately, she didn't yet have the courage or the energy to leave her sanctuary in search of something to eat. How long was Irion going to be?

A knock at the door. At last! Hastily, she jumped back into bed before calling, 'Come in!'

A short, stout woman entered with a tray. 'Hello, dear. How are you feeling? I'm Mary. I've brought you some shepherd's pie.'

This woman's appearance was so conventional, so British-Establishment, Hanna wondered if her conversation with the silver alien had been a hallucination. She studied her. Steel-grey hair. Boring brown skirt. Woollen stockings. Lilac cardigan. Saggy boobs like a shelf halfway up her chest. Hanna found it hard to judge the age of white people. They all looked so old, like papery ghosts. This one could well be past retirement. Presumably there was a matching husband around somewhere too. Hanna imagined a snowy-haired gentleman with sunken cheeks and brown lace-up shoes, who wore a shirt and tie even while watching TV.

In all her years in London, Hanna hadn't had much to do with the people she thought of as 'The Natives'. The English whose ancestors had been content to remain on this moist and chilly island, generation after generation. They surrounded you wherever you went, but were separated from you by an invisible crust of unconscious privilege.

'Where's the other lady?' she asked. She half-expected the woman to reply, 'Who?'

'Irion's gone to find a place for your laddie, there,' said

Mary, nodding at the red bundle on the pillow. 'Have you given him a name?'

'Samuel. After my little brother.'

'Lovely. Names are important.' Mary passed her the tray and sat down by the bed.

'How did you find me?' asked Hanna, starting to eat.

'Kitty found you. She saved you; you'd almost gone the way of Samuel there.'

'Is Kitty…like Irion?'

Mary laughed. 'Oh no! Nothing like Irion! But she's not human, if that's what you mean. You'll meet her later. Don't judge her until you've had a chance to get to know her. None of us here are what we seem. Not even me.'

Hanna raised her eyebrows in a silent question, but Mary was not to be drawn.

'Why don't you tell me your story, dear?'

Between mouthfuls, Hanna related how, five years ago on her fourteenth birthday, an 'Auntie' from the orphanage had brought her to London on a tourist visa for a 'holiday'. The 'Auntie' had left her in a big house with some people who'd seemed nice enough at first – until they took her passport and forced her to work as a cleaner. She never saw the 'Auntie' again.

Hanna ran away as soon as her English was good enough. She lived under the radar, surviving by cleaning hotels for cash. Through her work she met other illegal immigrants, who helped her find somewhere to stay and taught her how to avoid getting deported. She had no immediate desire to return to Ethiopia; even if she'd had the money and documents to get there, she had nothing to go back to. Her life was in Britain now.

'And Samuel's father?' asked Mary, gently.

Hanna pursed her lips and shook her head. She wasn't ready to talk about *him*.

Mary didn't press her any further. Instead, she took her hand and squeezed it. 'I promise you Hanna, whatever surprises you experience here, you are safe. Stay as long as you want. You're clearly a strong person, and you will be strong again.' She stood up and took the tray. 'Rest now, until we know more about the funeral. One of us will be back when there's news.'

HANNA LAY DOZING, digesting the first warm meal she'd had in weeks. She hadn't heard the door open, but she was suddenly aware of a presence beside her. Opening her eyes, she found herself face-to-face with the most beautiful white woman she'd ever seen. Narrow, dark eyebrows framed symmetrical features in a pale, heart-shaped face. Straight black hair hung loose to her waist. Only the woman's eyes gave her away. The emerald irises glowed with an unnatural sparkle and the pupils were vertical black slits, like a cat's. Another alien.

'Hey,' said the woman, barely moving her cherry-red lips. 'How are you doing?' Slender, black-nailed fingers held out a tiny blue-and-gold casket for Hanna to take. 'I'm Kitty. I'm so sorry about your son.'

'Thank you,' said Hanna, accepting the coffin. 'You're the one who found me?'

Kitty nodded. 'You're lucky I happened to be passing. May I?' Closing her eyes, she reached for Hanna's hand. Warmth spread up Hanna's arm and across her body, making her feel stronger and more alert. The pain in her abdomen faded entirely.

'The infection that caused the miscarriage has gone now,' said Kitty. 'I've healed the physical damage for you. But I can't ease the grief, you'll just have to get through that one day at a time.' She released Hanna's hand: the energising inner glow remained. 'We've found a place for Samuel. Get ready and the others will take you there.'

Then, before Hanna could reply, Kitty vanished. Hanna stared at the now-empty chair by the bed. How was that possible? What else was Kitty capable of?

WHEN THE KNOCK on the door came an hour later, Hanna was dressed in black and had shaved her head. Although she knew this was the proper thing to do, she felt strangely light-headed without the familiar weight of her braids to ground her. Clutching the miniature coffin, she followed Mary and Irion out of the flat into an unexpectedly institutional hallway lit with low-energy light bulbs. The scuffed beige linoleum and skirting boards were evidently subject to heavy traffic. A fire safety notice hung on the wall, next to a fire extinguisher and a red 'break glass, press here' alarm unit.

Mary opened an inconspicuous door which Hanna assumed was a cupboard. Cool air blew into her face and an abrupt drop in temperature made Hanna shiver. She was entirely unprepared for what confronted her: a cavernous hall, dotted with spherical white pods the size of small cars. These were connected to each other by a web of thick cables criss-crossing the white floor.

Mary was already striding ahead towards a large column at the centre. 'Come on,' she said, looking back at Hanna and Irion. 'They're waiting for us.'

'It's OK,' said Irion, taking Hanna's hand and tugging her gently over the threshold.

Hanna gazed all around as they crossed the brightly lit space. Was this one of those iceberg basement conversions billionaires had to house their swimming pools and staff quarters? Surely even they weren't this big? And what were those pod things? Why was it so cold?

Mary was waiting for them in a cylindrical lift. All white, like everything else.

Hanna whispered, 'What *is* this place?'

'This is the *Shantivira*,' said Mary, pronouncing it 'Shanty-*veer*-a', with the stress on the second-to-last syllable. 'It's the space station which protects the Earth. The door we came through is a teleport linking our cellar to the training deck.' The curved doors of the lift slid open and they stepped into another circular space, bordered by numbered doors around the perimeter.

Irion said, 'This is the accommodation deck.'

But Hanna wasn't listening. Her brain was still wrestling with the words 'space station' and 'teleport'. She followed Mary numbly past an enormous curved swimming pool to a gap between the doors. There was a hatch set into the wall, which Mary opened with a practised spin of the wheel handle. It swung inwards with a rush of cold air and Hanna was suddenly blinking in intense sunshine. Once her eyes had adjusted, she almost dropped Samuel in shock.

Directly ahead of them was a vast swirl of blue, green

11

and white, suspended against an inky velvet background. The Earth! Was it real? Was that Africa she could see? There was no platform beyond the hatch. No airlock. They were facing directly out into – Space. Space with a capital 'S'.

'Magnificent, isn't it?' said Mary, and stepped out over the edge.

Hanna yelled and grabbed at Mary's cardigan, fully expecting her to float away. But she was too slow. She shut her eyes tightly, not wanting to watch Mary die.

She felt Irion place a gentle hand at the base of her spine. 'Hanna,' she said, 'it's OK. Open your eyes.'

Mary was crouching on the wall outside at right angles to them, extending her hand back towards Hanna with an encouraging smile. 'Take my hand, Hanna. It's perfectly safe.'

Hanna did as she was told and Irion caught her around the waist, lifting her smoothly over the edge onto a white metal surface. The hatch which, seconds ago, had been a door in a wall was now a trapdoor at their feet. Huh?

'Always tricky, the first time,' said Mary cheerfully. 'The gravity generators allow us to walk on any surface we like up here. We're on the outer hull of the space station now.'

Irion patted her arm reassuringly, and they followed Mary through a gate and across a farmyard, glossy brown chickens scattering at their approach. A farm? In space?

Hanna kept stealing glances up at the Earth. How could the sky be black and sunny at the same time? *Was* it the sky, or were they still underground in some huge film set?

'But how can we be in space?' she demanded. 'We don't have space suits on. We shouldn't be able to breathe. This can't be real.'

'We're in one of the *Shantivira's* biomes, protected by layers of magnetic shielding,' explained Mary. 'You can't see the shields, but you're right, there'd be no air up here without them. This is where we generate the atmosphere for the rest of the facility. The crew also grow their fresh food here.'

'People *live* here?' said Hanna.

'About two hundred fighter pilots, plus the support staff and their families.'

'Fighter pilots?'

'Ready to protect the Earth from alien invasion,' said Mary, as if this were obvious.

'Oh,' said Hanna, not knowing what to make of this. 'Right.'

THEY CONTINUED WALKING, past greenhouses, fishponds, across fields with grazing cattle, taking a direct line towards a forest on the horizon. How far were they going? She didn't have the right shoes on for this.

'Would you like me to carry that for you?' said Irion, indicating Samuel's casket.

Hanna shook her head. The cloth-covered box in her arms was all that connected her to reality. No way was she letting go of it. She struggled on, the heels of her only good pair of shoes sinking into the mud. Soon they reached the wood, a dirt track leading them into dim, fragrant coolness under a mottled green canopy.

The track wound between ancient trees, past tangled undergrowth, swarming anthills and mossy, rotting tree trunks sprouting bizarre fungi. The air tasted tangy and moist and wherever Hanna looked, the whole place was vigorous with life. Beetles, spiders, birds. Four different kinds of butterfly. A ginger streak of squirrel above and machine gun bursts of woodpecker somewhere to her right.

Finally, Mary stopped on the edge of a clearing with a straw-roofed hut at the centre. A man stood next to it: a stocky white man not much taller than Hanna, flicking intently through the pages of a small, leather-bound book. A black jaguar sat motionless beside him. Hanna froze, her instincts telling her to back away slowly before the predator saw her.

Irion put her hand on her shoulder and whispered, 'It's all right. It's only Kitty. She often takes that form when she doesn't feel like talking. She won't hurt you.'

As they crossed the grass, Hanna noticed the hole which had been dug in preparation. She remembered why they'd come to this strangest of places and her throat clenched into a painful knot. The man was introducing himself, welcoming her, but she couldn't respond. It was as if he were on the other side of a triple-glazed window and she couldn't hear him. Instead, she began to cry again, wailing loudly and persistently, her grief a wall of sound blocking everything else out. Hanna recalled her parents' funeral, back in her village when she was ten years old. At the time, she hadn't understood why the adults had made such a racket. But it was oddly cathartic.

The man gave up speaking and guided her to the

graveside. He helped her place the colourful little casket into the ground and, when Hanna's sobs subsided, read some suitable words from the Bible. She couldn't say afterwards what they'd been, but they had sounded appropriate.

Then he produced a sapling, a Wanza tree, she noticed with a spark of recognition. When had she last seen one of those? She helped him plant it carefully in the hole above the coffin. As she scraped the soil with her bare hands, watering the roots with her tears, she imagined them growing, encircling Samuel in an eternal embrace.

2. THE WEEKLY MEETING
JOE

J OE RESTED AT the side of the roof-top pool, looking out over the twinkling carpet that was Essoona at night. The city lights stopped abruptly at the water's edge, outlining the broad curve of Essoona Bay with a chain of gold. Out at sea, the black void was punctuated by occasional dots of brightness: ships waiting for permission to dock and spacecraft coming in to land. To the north, Joe could see the lighthouse flashing steadily, six times a minute, simultaneously warning shipping of the rocks at Kallio Point and guiding incoming pilots towards the large spaceport on the edge of town. A cool breeze brushed his forearms and he pulled them back into the water for warmth, reaching a decision. There would be no better moment.

He turned away from the view and watched his brother-in-law's pale torso bobbing in the opaque green water. Aldeman floated peacefully, his black hair swaying under the surface like a mermaid's. Wisps of steam rose into the starlit darkness. Essoona's public baths were almost empty at this time of night.

Joe reached out with his foot and touched his boss's hand. Aldeman's eyes snapped open and he flipped over, swimming a few strokes to where Joe waited.

'What is it, little brother?'

Time to get it off his chest. 'You know…how I'm an adrenaline junkie?'

'Remind me, "junkie"?'

'Addict. It's just an expression. I'm bored, Aldeman. Being the captain of the *Shantivira* isn't the challenge I thought it'd be.'

'But you have only been in the job four years! Rohini did it for twenty-five!'

'I don't have her patience,' sighed Joe. 'Since I've been in charge, we've deflected precisely seven probes and one single alien spacecraft before it entered Earth's atmosphere. Apart from constant training exercises, we fill our days tracking down space debris and dematerialising it. It's not enough. I need a job that gets my heart pumping. You haven't got a cohort of interstellar ships looking for a new commander, by any chance? Or, how's your personal pilot these days? Is she as good as I was? Are you thinking of replacing her anytime soon?'

Aldeman grinned. 'Sorry, Joe. I miss your company on those long trips. And I do not deny you got me out of a few tight corners. But I need you on the Earth.'

'What's the point, if the world doesn't even know we're there?'

'All my sources, including you, tell me that most humans are not ready for that knowledge yet. And yet they also tell me the probability of the Earth being invaded by a hostile species increases with every day that passes. What does Mrs Llewellyn have to say about this?'

'Kitty thinks I should wait until my contract is done

17

before considering what to do next. But neither of you understand, you Syenitians. You'll never feel the pressure of time like we humans do. I'm forty-three. I've got maybe twenty years of active service left in me before my body starts packing up. If I'm lucky. And there's so much to see out there! So many adventures to be had! No wonder I've got FOMO!'

'FOMO?'

'Fear of missing out.'

Aldeman chuckled. 'You are a warrior in peacetime, Joe. You were bound to find it hard. Be patient. Build your friendships, consolidate your team. Enjoy the time with your wife. I put you where you are with good reason and I believe it will pay off. Thank you for keeping me informed, but for now I ask you to persevere.'

Joe felt a wave of frustration building. He ducked his head below the surface in an attempt to hide his disappointment. Then again, he'd expected no other response. Of course he'd complete his contract, but he wanted to have something more interesting, OK, yes, more dangerous, set up for the day it finished. Something to look forward to. This conversation was only the first step of what would have to be a concerted and persistent campaign. Working with Syenitians was often like banging your head against a polite but immovable wall, but they weren't unreasonable. They just had a horror of acting too quickly.

Lungs empty, he resurfaced. With wet hair, the night air felt several degrees colder.

Aldeman gave him a sidelong glance. 'Supposing you left the *Shantivira* when your five years are up? Who would you suggest as your replacement?'

'Kazembi.'

'Nkosi's wife?'

'That's right. Thandiwe will be in school by then. Before you ask, Yisheng doesn't want the job. He'd rather stay as second-in-command and support a young captain with his experience and wisdom, although he phrased it more modestly than that. You know Yisheng. But Kazembi is the ideal choice. She has a real knack for getting people to want to do what she wants them to.' Joe's mouth twitched. 'Like you, brother.'

'An important skill, Captain Llewellyn, which has served me well. Then let us discuss this again in a year's time.'

Joe knew he'd get no further today. At least he'd broached the subject. 'As you wish, my lord,' he nodded respectfully. 'Actually, there's something I left out of my briefing earlier.'

'Your wife's latest adoptee?'

'So you've heard.' Joe smiled wryly, unsurprised. 'Kitty found her, but it's Irion who's adopted her. It seems she's always wanted to be a mother. If the girl's story wasn't so tragic, it would be rather sweet.'

'A child burying her child. Immensely sad. I am glad you could help her.' The glacier-blue eyes were wells of compassion.

'I didn't help much. She was like a howling zombie. I've never seen anyone so young consumed by grief like that. Not even during the Troubles. It touched me proper, I have to say.'

Aldeman reached out underwater and held Joe's

shoulder, a comforting grip, firm and warm. Joe grasped the arm affectionately in return. Aldeman made hundreds of difficult decisions every day, but however much you might disagree with him, there was no doubting his empathy for all living creatures.

'Humans are one of the most resilient species I have ever come across. I am sure she will bounce back. Keep me updated on her progress. And her reaction to the *Shantivira*. From what I understand, she boarded the space station with no psychological preparation at all?' Aldeman raised a charcoal eyebrow, informing Joe of his disapproval and that Joe would be held responsible for any negative repercussions.

'There was a time constraint, my lord. I won't bore you with the details, but I can assure you the girl is being closely supervised.'

3. TWO UNEXPECTED PROPOSALS
LUCY

L UCY DREW IN great lungfuls of pollution-free air, relishing the tangy scent of wet ferns and peaty Dartmoor soil. Apart from the reedy whine of the wind, they were surrounded by silence: no traffic, no electronic intrusions, only the thud of hooves and an occasional creak from her saddle. The track was so narrow, she could barely see her feet. The horses swam in an emerald sea.

Why didn't she do this more often? It was such a contrast to her dusty, grimy-windowed office on the industrial estate in Telford, where she spent long hours achieving other people's goals. She'd thought engineering was a creative profession, but she'd become trapped in the corporate machine, ticking boxes and fulfilling targets for profit-hungry shareholders. Job satisfaction: zero.

She should have gone into renewable energy, or robotics, or biomedical engineering. Somewhere she could have made a positive difference to people's lives. But, at twenty-seven, it was almost too late for her to switch industries. Not if she wanted to have children and still have a career to return to afterwards. All her experience was in the automotive sector, and that was where she'd be most likely to get another good job. But her heart wasn't in it anymore.

She tried to look on the bright side. Spending the weekend at her parents' house in Devon meant she could escape the cramped shared house in Shrewsbury, and her housemates and their boyfriends unwittingly reminding her of her newly single status. Not that she wasn't better off without Jude. She'd felt unconsciously for months that their relationship wasn't working, and known it for certain when he'd assumed she'd be delighted to 'invest' all her savings in his nebulous new business venture. Money she'd painstakingly scraped together towards a deposit for a house. She was about halfway there now, as long as she gave up any notion of buying somewhere close to her parents, or indeed anywhere at all in the south of England.

Her refusal had cooled Jude's ardour perceptibly. A week later, she'd found him in the bath with that slinky little tart Katie. How long had *that* been going on? What shocked her most was the sense of relief she felt. Anger too, but more with herself for wasting two years of her life on that loser.

If only her mum and dad hadn't moved away from Marlborough when her dad had retired from the RAF, leaving behind the house she'd grown up in. The guest bedroom in Topsham was just that – a guest room – not the familiar cocoon in which she'd spent her adolescence. That was long gone. She had no sanctuary to retreat to now. Lucy felt rootless, as if she didn't truly belong anywhere.

On the plus side, she was meeting Alice in Exeter tonight. Amazing that the energetic medical student she'd once shared a house with was content to live so far from the rest of her family in London. Falling for solicitor-farmer Pete had shifted Alice's priorities. Pete's upbringing on his family's farm rooted him so deeply in the local community, it was unthinkable for him to live anywhere else.

Lucy envied him his certainty about where he belonged, but the idea of spending the rest of her life in one place made her shiver. Perhaps she should take some time out and go travelling? She could go back to Karlsruhe and see if she could resurrect her German. Weird to think she used to speak it fluently. She sighed, remembering how exhilarating it had been to communicate easily in a foreign language. Use it or lose it. Maybe she could apply for a job in Germany?

FIONA, THE RIDE leader, reined in and gazed westwards. 'Uh-oh, look at that!' A solid bank of cloud was racing in their direction. 'That wasn't in the forecast this morning!'

Minutes later, deadening fog surrounded them.

'Don't lose sight of the person in front of you,' called Fiona's disembodied voice back down the line of horses. 'But don't get too close, you don't want to get kicked. The main thing is for no one to fall off.'

'How do you know where we're going?' asked one of the riders nervously.

'I've got a compass and a GPS thingy. If we get separated, the horses should find their own way home. We'll be fine.'

At that instant, a sheep exploded from the undergrowth, directly in front of Lucy. Silvertone shied violently, galloping flat-out away from the other horses into the mist. Lucy lost a stirrup and slid precariously in the saddle, the ground a thundering blur below, too close for comfort. Knotting her fingers in the steel-grey mane, she clung on for dear life.

At last, the mare began to slow, puffing and blowing. Lucy managed to right herself and regain control. The initial panic was over, but Silvertone was still jumpy. Lucy patted her neck, waiting for her own pulse to return to normal. As far as she could see was – nothing. A white out. The moist silence was eerily total. As she peered in all directions, trying to get a fix on any kind of landmark, Lucy wondered if this was what it was like to be deaf. She looked at her mobile. No signal. Of course not.

Without warning, Silvertone wheeled around and began cantering through the fog. Her ears pointed firmly forward and there was a joyfulness to her gait, which she punctuated at intervals with a communicative whinny. This time they were heading towards something, not running away from it.

A shape loomed out of the mist: a black horse with neither saddle, bridle nor rider. A fairytale cascade of wavy mane failed to disguise its muscular build. Its dark coat absorbed the flat light, giving the impression of a horse-shaped hole in the whiteness. Lucy had never been afraid of horses but there was a wildness to this one, an aura of independence and power, which made her uneasy.

Silvertone screeched to a halt, throwing Lucy inelegantly onto the mare's neck. The horses performed an equine greeting, blowing into each other's nostrils and speaking in soft whinnies and whickers. Close up, Lucy could see iridescent green eyes burning behind the stranger's forelock. The pupils were vertical, like a snake's. She'd seen eyes like that before somewhere, but she couldn't for the life of her remember where.

The horse vanished without warning. In its place stood an extremely tall woman with long black hair and the same sinister eyes as the horse. She moved gracefully, like a dancer, and her medieval red dress accentuated her regal posture. She smiled broadly, displaying yellowish, elongated canines: slightly curved and barely hidden by her lips. Lucy jerked back in alarm.

'Lucy Cooper! Great to meet you at last. I'm Kitty.'

'W-What are you?' Lucy stammered. 'How did you do that?'

'I mean you no harm, please don't be frightened,' said Kitty. 'How did I shape-shift? I don't know. I've never understood how it works.'

'How do you know my name?'

'I've been watching you. I've waited weeks for the chance to speak with you alone.'

Lucy surreptitiously gathered up her reins, preparing for a quick getaway. Kitty spotted the movement and raised her hands in frustration.

'Look at me, Lucy, I can't meet you in a public place! And you'd feel even more threatened if I approached you in your home. Out here, if you don't like what I have to say, you can just ride away. I have an invitation for you from my boss. He's as human as you are.'

'Couldn't he just e-mail me?' said Lucy.

'What I need to tell you should be said in person. And how you handle meeting me is part of the test.' Kitty moved in front of them, stroking Silvertone's nose. 'You're in no danger, Lucy. I'll not stop you if you want to go.'

'Then get out of the way!' shouted Lucy, kicking Silvertone's girth violently. But Silvertone stood stubbornly where she was, happily nuzzling the woman's velvet sleeve.

'I could guide you back to the stables and we could talk on the way. This is the only chance you'll get.'

'My only chance for what? And what test?'

'To start with, how you react to meeting an alien,' said Kitty, adding, 'Not doing too well so far,' in a murmur loud enough for Lucy to hear.

'You're an alien? Like, from outer space?'

Kitty grinned, revealing her predator's teeth again. 'Well, I wasn't born here. But I've lived here longer than any human has. Earth is my home. I consider myself a naturalised citizen.'

Lucy considered for a moment. If this…person was going to attack her, it probably would have already happened. And she hated the idea of failing a test, whatever it might be. Curiosity edged up her field of galloping emotions, overtaking fear and confusion by a nose. 'All right,' she said. 'Take me back to the stables and tell me what this is all about.'

Kitty smiled up at her. 'Attagirl.' She folded her arms behind her back and started walking. Only then did Lucy notice that her feet were bare below the hem of her dress. Silvertone moved too, keeping Lucy's knee level with Kitty's shoulder.

Kitty spoke without turning round. 'I come from a planet called Syenitia, many parsecs from here. My mother's people, the Syenitians, are one of the oldest known intelligent species. They travelled all over the galaxy, exploring and building trade alliances. There was even a settlement here on Earth for a time, about twenty thousand years ago.'

'What happened to it?'

'It was abandoned. They couldn't breed here. Syenitians aren't very fertile. They don't need to be, because their lifespans are so long. But every single pregnancy here ended in a miscarriage.'

Lucy remembered the abortion she'd had in her first year of university, a sadness she carried even now, eight years on. Not the same as a miscarriage, but still a lost child to be grieved for. She found herself sympathising with the Syenitians, whoever they were.

'Where is this settlement? Can I visit it?'

Kitty laughed. 'Not without a submarine! Sea levels are much higher now. It's long gone.'

'So you have no evidence? You could be making all this up?'

Kitty turned and looked her in the eye. 'I could be,' she winked. 'Actually, traces of my people are evident in your folklore. If I say "Elf" to you, what do you think of?'

'Elf? I suppose…pointy ears.'

'Check.' Kitty swept back her hair to expose a pointed ear.

'Woah! Freaky!' Briefly forgetting her fears, Lucy leant down and examined it. 'I can't see a join; it looks really real!'

'What else?'

'Um, green hats with bells on and stripy tights?'

'Not Christmas elves! The other kind.'

'Floaty dresses and into trees and flowers and stuff?'

'Syenitians believe all life is sacred and we try to live in harmony with the natural world. What else?'

'They're magical. I'm sorry, I don't believe in magic.'

'Even though you just saw me change from a horse into a Syenitian?' said Kitty. 'Don't answer that. I don't believe in magic either. I think there's always an explanation, even if it's too complex to understand. I'm only half Syenitian, biologically. Normal Syenitians' teeth and eyes are like yours, and they can't shape-shift. They're no more magical than you are. But think about how they must have appeared to the locals back then, with all the technology they brought with them.'

'OK, I accept your point. But what are you then? What's the other half that's not a Sai-yeh-what-was-it-again?' asked Lucy.

'Syenitian. That's a story for another day.'

OK…probably something unspeakably nasty, then. Lucy considered for a moment. 'What about other fairytale creatures? Fairies, dwarves, witches and dragons and the rest?'

'People invent them to explain things, don't they? Stories are collective knowledge, older than religions and longer lasting. I've never seen a fairy, have you?'

Lucy shook her head and Kitty continued, 'Little people are just humans with dwarfism. Witches were women who dared to voice an independent opinion. Dragons are so rare; no wonder people think they're a myth.'

'And vampires?' asked Lucy.

Kitty laughed. 'Yeah. They might actually be my fault. Although I don't understand where the whole blood-drinking thing came from. That's not how I feed at all!

Anyway, we digress. I must tell you about the Alliance.'

'The what?'

'Syenitia's long-term strategy is to actively form part-nerships with other space-faring civilisations. It's a founder member of the Galaksi Alliance: a union of intelligent life from around thirty or so different planets. We work to promote peace, trade and the exchange of ideas throughout the galaxy. When a planet joins the Galaksi Alliance, it gains access to the technology of all the other Alliance planets, in return for peace treaties and trade agreements.

'Syenitia's population has been decreasing for thou-sands of years. The rise and fall of many peoples are documented in our archives: we've accepted that our civilisation won't last forever. But we're not willing to sacrifice the progress we've made. We're always on the lookout for species with similar attributes and values, who might be capable of continuing our work when we're gone. Humans are one such species. You're so fertile and adaptable, and there are so many of you. Your potential is huge. And you're physically similar to us, which means we have a natural affinity for each other.'

'I thought you said you lived here? Do you never watch the news? Living in harmony with nature and promoting peace is really not our thing.'

Kitty laughed. 'Not yet. But either you'll work it out or head for extinction even faster than my people. Syenitians live for thousands of years. They take the long view and are permanently optimistic. I'm not sure they're right, but I have my own reasons for wanting humans to survive.'

'But why are you telling me all this?' said Lucy, getting

impatient. 'You said your boss had an invitation for me?'

Kitty nodded. 'This is a dangerous time for the Earth. You're constantly sending signals into space – advertising this luscious planet to any passing spacecraft – but you can't flee it or defend it without outside help. Luckily, you're well off the main trade routes. But the risk of invasion only increases with time. The Syenitian Council has designated this planet as a nature reserve, so you can develop without outside interference, but only Alliance members recognise that status.'

'A nature reserve?' spluttered Lucy. 'Did you even *ask* us if we wanted your help?'

'We have a small base in orbit with human fighter pilots on standby,' continued Kitty, ignoring Lucy. 'The *Shantivira*. Its purpose goes beyond protecting the Earth. So far there's not been much to protect it from. Our other objective is to train human ambassadors, so that when the time comes, your planet will have its own representatives who understand the interstellar community and speak its common language.'

Lucy attempted to digest the information. 'That's a huge investment. What's in it for the Syenitians? Why bother?'

'This planet's greatest resource is its intelligent life,' said Kitty. 'My people might not be able to settle here, but we would still benefit from an association. If we don't get in first, some other species will, and they are unlikely to be as sympathetic or well-intentioned. This planet is a treasure trove. Once word of its existence gets out, there will be wars to win control of it. If humans want a say in the future of their planet, then they'll have to form strategic alliances early on. But that's all far off. Syenitians like to think ahead.'

'What does all this have to do with me?'

'Haven't you guessed?' Kitty turned to face Lucy and said formally, 'I am inviting you join our training programme.'

Lucy's mind whirled. Impulsively, she gathered up the reins and mercilessly kicked Silvertone into a gallop, only allowing her to slow once Kitty was safely a hundred metres behind them.

Could it be true? Or was the woman insane? Those teeth could be faked. Those eyes could be contact lenses. It could all be a hoax.

Except. The black horse had been there, she hadn't imagined it. And it had disappeared right before her eyes, to be replaced by Kitty. Lucy couldn't conjure up a rational explanation for that.

Silvertone halted to nibble at a bush and Lucy didn't urge her on. She just sat, waiting for Kitty to catch them up. What if it were true? She had to know more.

Now Lucy remembered where she'd seen those eyes before. A black cat had been turning up at her house recently, never staying long, never eating anything; it simply liked to sit on people's laps and be stroked. Bizarrely, it always appeared in time for *Strictly Come Dancing*, which she and her housemates often watched together. They called the cat 'Magic' because of its weird eyes. Thinking about it now, they were less peculiar on a cat than on a horse. Or a person.

White-hot fury overtook aversion and doubt. How dare she! Kitty had been eavesdropping as Lucy grumbled about her job, the whole Jude drama and God knew what else. Seriously creepy. Lucy turned in the saddle, psyching herself up to tell Kitty where she could stick her invitation. But the moor behind her was empty.

Silvertone pricked up her ears; whinnying, she began trotting purposefully down the hillside. Soon Lucy could hear it too: hooves on a road. More than one horse, and voices too. Moments later she was back with the others, being bombarded with questions.

'What on earth happened to you?' exclaimed one of the ladies.

'We waited for ages!' said her friend. 'We were so worried!'

'Are you OK?' asked Fiona. 'You're not hurt?'

'I'm fine,' said Lucy. 'I stayed on and Silvertone found the way back.'

'Thank God you're all right. That sheep came out of nowhere!'

Lucy reassured her, 'Really, I'm fine. We're not even going to be late back.' It was true. She felt she'd lived a lifetime in the last hour, but that was all it had been – not even a whole hour.

THE WEEKEND PASSED in a blur of social obligations. Her mum couldn't understand her breakup with Jude. 'Such a nice, well-mannered man. So charming.' When he wanted to be, thought Lucy, dourly. Generally only in front of other people. Why had it taken her so long to realise it was all an act?

The train journey back to Shrewsbury was Lucy's first

chance to think about the alien spy. She was still too angry with Kitty to make a rational evaluation, but her gut feeling told her not to have anything to do with it. Perhaps it was a great opportunity, but it just didn't feel right. It might all be a wind-up. Unless she'd imagined the whole thing?

By the time the train pulled out of Bristol, her churning thoughts had subsided. OK, it had been the weirdest weekend, but at least she'd learnt something new. It ended there. She'd update her CV and find another job somewhere down south, closer to her ageing parents. She wasn't ready for the commitment a mortgage represented yet. It would be better to rent for a few more years.

She put in her headphones, letting her mind drift with the music as her eyes roamed the passing landscape. The leaden sky became a heavy squall of rain, leaching all colour from the world. Her eyes tracked the paths of the water droplets from one side of the window to the other.

At Cheltenham Spa, three men in black suits and ties waiting on the platform caught Lucy's eye. They had no luggage, not even a laptop. Odd, she thought, wearing work clothes on a Sunday. The youngest of them looked like a night club bouncer, all muscle and no neck. The others weren't far off retirement. One was short, overweight and balding, pink skin stretched over his face like a sausage ready for piercing. His craggy-featured companion was taller and in better physical shape. A shock of snowy hair topped crevices formed by long exposure to life. Not someone who smiled often.

The train pulled away and Lucy was about to resume her daydreaming when the doors to her almost-empty carriage hissed open. The three men from the platform made a beeline for Lucy's table: the bouncer trapping her in her window seat, the older men sitting opposite.

What was this? She flicked a glance at the emergency brake. She'd have to stretch past the fat man's shoulder to reach it. Would they stop her? How would she explain afterwards why she'd wanted to stop the train?

Sausage Face spoke. 'Lucy Cooper?'

Lucy didn't feel like cooperating. She said nothing, just studied the thin, greasy hair draped across his scalp, imagining how much more ridiculous it would look if brushed the other way to hang down over his ear.

The man pulled an envelope from inside his jacket. Stubby fingers spread the contents on the table. Photographs: close-ups of Lucy in the canteen at work, Lucy riding yesterday, her father filling his car with petrol and her mother working in their garden. Fear spiked Lucy's heart.

He said, 'You have been approached by an extremely dangerous and violent individual. A demon responsible for countless deaths. You are only alive now because it wants to use you. It sees you as a pawn; cannon fodder; a snack.'

Lucy looked at the men, gathering her thoughts. He could only be talking about Kitty. Was Kitty a murderer? Possibly. Be honest. Probably. Somehow that didn't bother her as much as the fact that Kitty had been spying on her. Just like these people had.

'So?' she countered. 'What does that have to do with my parents?'

'This creature and the organisation behind it must be

stopped. It has told you a pack of lies to enlist your cooperation.'

Lucy leaned across the table. 'What did "it" tell me? What do *you* know about it?'

'It recruits impressionable young humans to serve the Syenitian Empire. You don't have the slightest idea what you are getting yourself into, my dear. It doesn't care whether you live or die. It wants to control this planet because it considers…it considers the human race,' the man's face flushed puce and his chins quivered with indignation, 'to be a…a *delicacy*!'

Lucy restrained herself from sniggering at his pomposity. This was no joke. The guy was obviously outraged by Kitty's very existence. Did she really eat people? Surely not.

'You still haven't told me what this has to do with my parents.'

The other man opposite, the one with eye bags you could carry your shopping in, took a more conciliatory tone.

'We want you to spy for us, Lucy.' His accent was foreign – Spanish? 'You are in an ideal position to access the information we need. We know the creature got to you first and has started the brainwashing process.' Bushy eyebrows met in a frown. 'We understand you are reluctant to help us. But the fate of our planet is at stake. We must discover what the Syenitians intend to do with the Earth, so we can mount a defence.'

'Who are you?' demanded Lucy.

'My name is Nestor. I lead the Anti-Alien League. We are a top-secret organisation; if the Syenitians found out about us, they would wipe us out like that!' He slammed his hand down on the table top, making Lucy jump. 'I do not relish pressuring you, Lucy, but it is for the greater good. Yes, we know where your parents live. Sometimes the ends justify the means. By assisting us, you will be keeping them safe and helping protect humanity from an existential threat.'

He stood up and the others rose with him.

'Goodbye for now. We will be in touch.'

They trooped out of the carriage, leaving Lucy in her seat. Her hands trembled as she put the photos away in her bag. Yesterday she'd been afraid of Kitty, but Kitty hadn't threatened her in any way. The fear had been Lucy's own, primeval impulses enhanced by the mist and the deserted moorscape.

Who was telling the truth? She wanted to believe Kitty, but her visitors' zeal had been genuine. She'd never forgive herself if anything bad happened to her parents. Did this mean she had to take up Kitty's offer after all? But as a spy? She quailed at the thought.

A HAND-DELIVERED A4 envelope awaited Lucy when she got home from work the next day. In the privacy of her bedroom, she ripped it open to find a pack of printed paper with a handwritten letter on top.

Dear Lucy,

I must apologise for the way I approached you. I didn't pitch it right. I'm sorry I scared you. But I'm not ready to give up on you just yet.

Here are some more details so you can make an informed decision. The next step would be an assessment weekend on the Shantivira — for you to get to know us and for us to see if you're a potential pilot. You can meet the team and tour the base.

You have one week from today to call me on the number below. Until you do, I will not approach you in any form. This is your decision and that decision is final. If you do not initiate contact, we'll leave you alone. The same applies after the assessment weekend. If you decide against joining us, we won't contact you again.

Warm regards,
Kitty

So she could just not call the number and it would be over. Only, what would the anti-alien guys do to her parents?

Lucy flicked through the rest of the paper. Joining the *Shantivira* was a five-year commitment, the first half spent training and the second half as a duty pilot on the space station. The first year would be in London, learning 'Kawaida', whatever that was, with some simulator training. Her eyes widened when she saw the second year would be spent flying real spacecraft on Syenitia, with 'Courses in the theory of space travel, spacecraft mechanics and maintenance, troubleshooting, emergency repairs, navigation, marksmanship, etc.' Serious stuff. Ah, here was an explanation of the Kawaida thing:

Kawaida is the official language of the Galaksi Alliance. It is widely used by intelligent life forms across the galaxy. Kawaida is also the language of the *Shantivira*. It is essential you learn it quickly, so you can communicate with your colleagues. If you fail the language exams at the end of the first year, your contract will be terminated.

Lucy breathed a sigh of relief. That could be a way out. If those men in black were going to pressure her into this, she could fail the first year and say, 'Sorry, I didn't make it through to the next year.' She could handle a year of language lessons and simulator training. It might even be fun! Here was another interesting bit:

Your contract will be terminated with immediate effect if you publish information about our operation on the internet or anywhere else (don't think we won't find out). If we consider you to be a serious security risk, we will relocate you without notice to a non-Earth location and leave you to fend for yourself for the rest of your life.

Well, that would be another way to get out of it, although the consequences were pretty dire. Perhaps not. All in all, it looked almost too good to be true. A generous salary. They provided a cover story for your absences and a device which let you call home any time, no matter where you were. They emphasised you were free to leave the programme whenever you wanted, you just wouldn't get the large bonus everyone received after five years' service.

Lucy spent the next few days procrastinating. She still seethed with anger about being spied on by Kitty. She'd like to see her again, just to get it off her chest. And she was curious to see this space station. She could have a look and still not join the programme. She might fail the assessment anyway. She wondered how the anti-alien league would react if she did. How were they watching her? Who had taken those photos? What else did they know about her?

At work on Thursday, a bouquet of yellow roses was delivered to Lucy's desk. The flowers were dead, the slimy rotting stems stinking sweetly of decay. Confused and revolted in equal measure, she pulled out the stiff black envelope wedged between the crispy petals. It contained a single sheet of printed paper.

YOU HAVE NOT MADE THE CALL YET.
MAKE THE CALL.
YOU HAVE 24 HOURS.
DO NOT DIVULGE OUR EXISTENCE OR YOU
WILL REGRET IT.
AAL

Her stomach flipped. They'd hacked her phone? Bastards! What did the bouquet signify? That she was dead if she didn't do as she was told? Or her parents were? Fury, fear and frustration jumbled her thoughts. What should she do? Telling Kitty wasn't an option, not that Lucy trusted her enough to consider it. She felt powerless. How dare they treat her like this?

With trembling hands, she pulled out her phone and searched for Kitty's contact details. Waited as the number dialled.

'Lucy! How lovely to hear from you!' Kitty sounded genuinely delighted. 'Are you coming to see us, then?'

'Um, yes, I'll come.'

'Funny, I had the feeling you weren't going to go for it. I'm so happy to be wrong. Would this weekend be all right?'

Bloody hell, that's quick, Lucy thought. She answered, 'Yes, that would be fine,' in as calm a voice as she could manage.

'Great. Meet me at Bodbury Ring by Church Stretton at 7 a.m. on Saturday. Bring an overnight bag and wear comfy shoes.'

The next day, Lucy received another hand-delivered note.

GOOD. DO NOT FAIL THE ASSESSMENT.

AAL

What would happen if she did? What could they do? It would be too late then. Maybe she should make some harmless blunder and get herself labelled as a reject.

4. THE SWIMMER

HANNA

T HE DAY AFTER Samuel's funeral, Irion showed Hanna how to scan her palm print on the teleport door, so she could visit the cosmic oasis whenever she felt like it. In the forty days that followed, Hanna went every day. She would sit for an hour or so, gazing at the Earth and the stars, sometimes crying, mostly silent.

The house was a language school, Mary told her. Twenty human trainee *Shantivira* pilots lived on the upper floors, studying Kawaida, the lingua franca used by space-travelling species. Hanna began doing odd jobs around the school to earn her keep: cleaning, shopping, helping in the kitchen. She stayed out of the students' way, observing them in furtive fascination as they crossed the hallway to the dining room at lunchtimes.

They seemed so confident and happy, chattering away in the singsong alien language they were learning. As if they all belonged to one big family – although they clearly didn't. According to Irion, they were deliberately selected from countries with different languages, so they had to use Kawaida socially as well as in lessons.

One student in particular caught Hanna's eye. A head taller than the others, slender yet athletic, he always wore a pair of heavy black and silver boots, despite the summer heat. His skin was the same ultra-dark tone her father's had been, and although he had no scars to indicate which tribe he came from, his face suggested an East African heritage. She found herself loitering near the classroom when their lessons finished, hoping to catch a glimpse of him. She imagined how good his skin might smell. How could she find out more about him without embarrassing herself?

In the afternoons, Irion helped Hanna with her English, patiently encouraging her through pages of exercises until she could speak and write with confidence. Mary focused on improving Hanna's numeracy skills. In the evenings, she went next door to Mary and Irion's flat, where they would cook together and tell Hanna stories about the *Shantivira* and Irion's home planet, Sayari.

Again and again, Hanna loved to hear the story of how Mary and Irion had met. Looking at her now in her cardigans and lace-up shoes, Hanna could never have guessed at Mary's life story. Forty years ago, she'd been part of the first generation of pilots on the *Shantivira*. After her contract finished, she went travelling, visiting as many of the Alliance planets as she could. By the time she got to Sayari, her spacecraft needed a complete overhaul. Mary fell head over heels in love with the mechanic overseeing the work: Irion. They married soon after and Mary settled on Sayari. But when her father died, Mary returned to Earth to care for her increasingly frail mother. Irion came with her and together they took over the Dunia School of Language.

For the first time since coming to the UK, Hanna had

time and energy to spare for leisure. She spent much of it at the local library, devouring information with a newly acquired thirst for knowledge. She explored London, taking long circular walks and visiting all the free museums and art galleries she'd heard of but never been to.

Slowly, her grief softened around the edges. It stopped being overwhelming and became a natural part of her: something she carried permanently, but that no longer paralysed her, as long as she made time for it each day in her green sanctuary on the *Shantivira*.

Sometimes Kitty sat with her, always in her jaguar form, which precluded any pressure to make polite conversation. The first time she appeared, Hanna had to force herself to remain still – her heart in her mouth – centimetres away from jaws capable of crushing a deer's skull with one bite. As the days passed and nothing happened, Hanna gradually relaxed. Soon she found the mute presence positively comforting.

One afternoon, Hanna plucked up her courage and tentatively reached out to touch the black fur. To her surprise, Kitty pressed herself against Hanna's fingers in return, nuzzling her wrist with her head. Her fur was wonderfully thick and soft. Hanna rubbed her under the chin and the jaguar closed her eyes with pleasure, emitting a growly purr. Hanna laughed out loud and threw her arms around the creature's neck, burying her face in her flank. The laughter turned to tears, which Kitty licked away tenderly with a sandpaper tongue.

In the days that followed, Hanna began to speak to Kitty in Nuer, her mother tongue. She had no idea whether Kitty understood, but she shared every thought, every memory that surfaced as they sat there: about her childhood, helping look after the cows, how beautiful Ethiopia was, about the people in her village and how she'd lost her family. Things she hadn't spoken of since coming to the UK half a lifetime ago. Feelings she could never express in English. Kitty lay motionless, her front paws on Hanna's lap.

Eventually, Hanna found herself able to speak of Mr Ahmed, her former landlord and Samuel's father. Now she thought about it, she didn't even know his first name. She'd known he was a creep when she'd taken the room, but after her last place got raided by the immigration authorities she hadn't had much choice.

In brief, factual sentences, she described how he'd waited until she was ill and off work so he could get her alone in the small room she shared with five other women. How he'd lain on top of her, forcing himself inside uninvited. How he'd whispered in her ear, 'Scream all you like, there's no one here.' But she couldn't make a sound; couldn't put up a fight; couldn't believe what was happening. Her body betrayed her, responding to the situation with an alarming passivity: immobilised by fear, all she could do was wait for it to be over. Her stomach still squirmed every time she remembered how, when he'd finished, he'd kissed her on the forehead and tenderly tucked the covers around her.

On discovering Hanna's pregnancy, his primary concern was to ensure his wife wouldn't find out. He stuffed Hanna's scant possessions into a plastic bag and threw them into the street. With nowhere else to go, Hanna became a homeless person.

When she finished speaking, the jaguar stood and rested her heavy head on Hanna's shoulder, nuzzling her cheek to cheek. Hanna could have sworn Kitty was crying.

THE WEEKS PASSED. Hanna's days became so full it got harder to fit in her daily trip to the *Shantivira*. But she wasn't ready to give it up, so she decided to squeeze it in before breakfast.

Her route from the language school took her past the swimming pool on the accommodation level. This was one of the backup water and oxygen reserves for the space station, Irion had explained, saying Hanna could swim in it any time she liked. Hanna was too embarrassed to admit she'd never learnt to swim and didn't even own a swimming costume. Instead, she'd made a noncommittal noise and changed the subject.

That morning, on her way back, a lone figure was ploughing up and down – the first time she'd seen anyone in there at all. A serious swimmer, wearing fins and goggles. Her heart turned a somersault as she recognised the black and silver boots at the poolside. It was him! Overwhelmed by shyness, she hurried by before he noticed her.

For the rest of the day, she kept having flashbacks about the powerful shoulder muscles pulling the swimmer smoothly through the water. Without admitting the reason to herself, the next day she went to the *Shantivira* at the same time – for purely practical reasons, because she was so busy. Nothing to do with him. Would he be there again?

He was! This time she took a closer look as she passed. His upper body was like an athlete's, but there was something odd about his legs. Despite the fins, they seemed too short: not in proportion with the rest of him. She didn't want to be caught staring, so she scurried home without being seen.

The next day she was more honest with herself. Yes, she wanted to see him again. But how could she fantasise about a man when she was still grieving for her son? What kind of person did that make her? True, six weeks had passed since Samuel's death, but it was unseemly to be experiencing…lust, yes, this must be what lust felt like, when she'd so recently lost yet another member of her family.

When she got to the glade, Kitty was waiting for her, now a familiar friend. Hanna absent-mindedly stroked and rubbed the black flanks as she tried to articulate her feelings of guilt and the pressure of the other uncertainties building inside her. The jaguar remained silent as always, but the act of speaking her thoughts out loud helped Hanna realise it was time she found a path forward. But doing what? How long could she stay with Irion and Mary? They'd said 'as long as she wanted', but no one ever meant that, did they? She needed to earn some money; she'd been dependent on them for long enough.

Kitty padded beside her as she walked back across the fields to the teleport. That was unusual. Normally she just turned and disappeared. They reached the accommodation deck and Hanna's heart yo-yoed in her ribcage as she saw the swimmer doing his lengths.

Without warning, Kitty took off: accelerating from

zero to black streak in less than a second. Hanna screamed as the jaguar sprang from the poolside towards the man in the water. He stopped and looked up as the black shape grew and turned grey in mid-air. It splashed down heavily right beside him and he disappeared from view. A huge wave slopped out of the pool and across the surrounding tiles.

Hanna ran to the water's edge in horror, wondering who she could call for help. Then she saw the joyful flick of a dolphin's tail and, to her amazement, the swimmer burst out of the water, holding onto the dolphin's dorsal fin. He grinned at her and yelled in Nuer, 'Come on in, the water's lovely!' Dolphin-Kitty raced away down the pool, towing him alongside.

Hanna couldn't believe her ears. He spoke Nuer! And Kitty – could she turn into any animal? Now they had turned and were heading back towards her. Kitty still had her reptilian green eyes, bizarre in the head of a dolphin. As they approached, the swimmer let go and swam towards Hanna. Pulling off his goggles, he said in a low, melodic voice which made her trust him immediately, 'What are you waiting for?'

Hanna knelt at the edge of the pool. 'I can't swim,' she admitted shyly.

'I'll teach you. No problem. And today you can hold on to Kitty.'

'But I don't have a swimming costume!'

'Wear what you're wearing,' he twinkled at her mischievously, nodding at her shorts and T-shirt. The dolphin swam up beside him and opened her mouth wide, emitting a series of loud chirps. 'Kitty agrees with me,' he

47

said, putting his arm across the creature's back. 'You can have my towel afterwards.'

How could she refuse? She couldn't. Thank goodness she hadn't put on her white T-shirt that morning. 'OK.' She kicked off her flip-flops and slid into the water, grabbing at the man's arm as she did so.

'It's cold!' she squealed.

'You'll get used to it in a minute.'

'What's your name?'

'Hassan. You're Hanna, right? From Gambella?'

She nodded. 'Where are you from?'

'Juba originally, but I mostly grew up in Uganda. Now, hold on here with both hands,' he said, indicating Kitty's dorsal fin, then added in a louder voice as they pulled away from him, 'and don't let go!'

They surged through the water, Hanna's legs either side of the undulating grey body. She laughed out loud, filled with physical joy. Her smile stretched so wide, her cheeks cramped. She couldn't remember having this much fun since leaving Ethiopia. Brilliant! Kitty made a few circuits, then returned her to Hassan.

She let go of the fin, her fingers bloodless and numb from holding on, and gingerly felt for the bottom with her feet. Kitty flicked her tail, drenching them both, and vanished. Hassan stood up – strange, he didn't seem as tall in the water – and guided her to the side.

'Right, hold on there, keep your arms straight. Now, I'm going to lift you up so you're horizontal.' He placed one hand gently on her stomach and raised her slowly through the water. 'OK, keep your legs straight and practice kicking. Good!'

Hanna concentrated, trying to follow his instructions and keep her face out of the water at the same time. But her mind kept writhing like an eel on a hook: HE, the swimmer, object of the most intense crush she'd ever had, was talking to her, holding her, he spoke Nuer, Kitty must have told him about her…told him what?

'Relax, it's supposed to be fun. That's it, well done! I'll bring a float tomorrow, that'll make it easier.' Hanna continued kicking until Hassan took his hand away and her feet sank to the bottom like stones.

'All right, let's try one more thing before I have to go to lessons. Have you ever floated on your back before?'

Hanna shook her head.

'Do you want to try? I won't let you sink, I promise.'

Hanna wasn't sure, but she didn't want him to see she was scared. Also, she really wanted him to touch her again. 'OK.'

This time, he had one hand at the base of her spine and the other on the back of her head. 'It's about letting the water hold you, letting your ears go under the waterline but still breathing through your nose and mouth. Don't tense up so much, I've got you—'

Slowly, he lowered her head. But it was too much for Hanna. The sensation of water entering her ears made her spring up with a jerk, banging heads with Hassan as she did so.

'Argh!'

'Ow!'

They both stood clutching their foreheads in pain. 'Sorry!' cried Hanna, mortified, but Hassan was laughing, a deep, infectious belly laugh. A giggle burst out of Hanna, which made Hassan laugh all the more. Now she couldn't stop. She reached for the side of the pool for support, doubled up with mirth. Hassan did the same, laughing so hard he was struggling for breath. Minutes later, when their laughing fit had finally subsided, Hassan flipped himself elegantly out of the pool, removing his fins with practised ease. He reached back down to pull Hanna up.

'Where are your feet?' she asked, staring at his legs. Both ended in stumps halfway down his shins, long-healed scars snaking all the way up to his thighs. She cursed herself for her tactlessness. The question had just slipped out.

'Left them in Sudan,' he said matter-of-factly, although Hanna noticed he switched to English. 'South Sudan, as it's called now.'

'A landmine?' Hanna switched to English too.

'When I was ten. I was lucky. My little sister caught the full force of it. She was there one minute and gone the next, like that.' He clicked his fingers. After a moment's silence he continued. 'When my mates joined the army, they wouldn't take me and my crutches. It broke my heart at the time – to be left behind, you know? I had nothing, no one. Then Kitty found me and sent me to a foster family.'

'Is that a hobby of hers, do you think?'

'What, rescuing people? Perhaps. She told me your story.' He placed a hand on her arm. 'I'm sorry about your son,' he said. 'Kitty hates it that there's so much suffering in the world and that there's so little she can do to change it, despite her powers. I'm sure we're not the only ones she's helped.'

He pivoted away from the water and dried his legs carefully. He reached out for his boots and showed them to Hanna. 'These are my feet. They connect with the nerve-endings in my stumps so I can operate them just by thinking about it. That's why I'm allowed to swim up here. I can't take them outside school because they're alien tech. On Earth, I mean. It's fine up here or in Essoona.'

Essoona, Hanna knew from her evenings with Mary and Irion, was the capital of Syenitia, the planet where the *Shantivira* had been built. Hassan sounded so casual about it, as if he went there every weekend.

He grinned and pulled on the boots. 'Plus, up here, the pool is never crowded and it's free!' He sprang up energetically. 'Come on, let's get you home before you freeze,' he said, wrapping his towel around Hanna's shoulders.

HANNA'S LIFE TOOK on a new rhythm. Early each morning, Hassan gave her a swimming lesson. Then she'd daydream about him for the rest of the day while she did her chores. He introduced her to the other students, in particular his blond-dreadlocked best friend, Aussie Ozzy. Hanna spent so much time in their flat, Irion joked that she and Mary never saw her anymore. For Hanna, it was like a window had opened wide onto the world and she was sucking in as much of the fresh air as she could. Meeting people, building friendships, trying out new things…she felt as if her life had finally started.

Irion and Mary had started paying her for the work she did in the language school. She saved most of it, unsure of what the future held. But as she had no living costs, she permitted herself to buy fabric.

Ever since coming to London, Hanna had been fascinated by all the different people. She liked to watch them and imagine their life stories – where they came from, what they were doing in London – but what interested her most was what they wore. She was constantly soaking up influences and sources of inspiration; she had notepad after notepad of sketches and notes. Hanna had had a passion for dressmaking ever since the orphanage had taught her to sew. Now, finally, she had the time and resources to realise her ideas.

She borrowed Mary's sewing machine and started experimenting. Her style was distinctive: full, knee-length skirts and dresses with mismatched panels of eye-watering colour to combat the London grey. She began to receive requests from some of the students and before long her creativity was earning her extra money. Could this be her future?

But a dark cloud loomed on the horizon. In the safety of Mary and Irion's kitchen, Hanna broached the dreaded subject one evening during the summer holidays.

'So, when do you need me to move out?'

Irion dropped her fork. 'Move out?'

'I heard your big boss is coming to visit. The leader of the Syenitian Council? Someone told me he's the most powerful man in the galaxy. And he always stays in the basement flat? He's not going to be too happy to find me there, is he? I've started looking; I'm sure something will turn up soon.'

Irion's eyes were suddenly moist. 'No,' she whispered,

a heart-broken syllable. Mary reached across the table to take Irion's hand.

'Are you happy with us, Hanna?' she asked.

'I've never been happier,' she replied honestly.

'We are immensely fond of you, you know. It's true, you can't stay in that flat forever, but you don't need to worry about Aldeman. With you in mind, he arranged his visit this year to coincide with the holidays. We're putting him in Hassan's flat, actually. Ozzy is going home to Darwin that week.'

Irion put her arm around Hanna's shoulders. 'It's all sorted,' she said. 'Please don't leave us.'

'He knows about me?'

'Aldeman knows about everyone with access to the *Shantivira*,' said Mary. 'He's looking forward to meeting you.'

Hanna wasn't sure how she felt about this. Her survival habit of avoiding authority was so deeply ingrained, the idea that someone so important was aware of her existence was unsettling, to say the least.

Irion gave her an affectionate squeeze. 'You're part of the *Shantivira* family now, Hanna. Whatever direction you end up taking, you'll always have us to fall back on. This is your home – if you want it to be.'

Mary added, 'We should formalise your living arrangements, though. It's time.' She gave Irion a questioning look and Irion nodded enthusiastically. 'We've been discussing how we can best help you in the long term,' Mary continued. 'I even looked into adopting you, but that's not possible under UK law because you're already an adult.'

Hanna was astounded. Was Mary serious? She had no idea she meant that much to them.

'We'll clear out our spare room for you. It's yours. Then you'll always have a base to come back to, whatever you decide to do.'

Hanna's vision blurred with tears. She jumped up, clumsily knocking over her chair with a crash as she threw her arms joyfully around Mary and Irion.

'Thank you, thank you!' she croaked, barely able to squeeze the words past the lump in her throat.

'The most important thing we have to do is to get you legal,' said Mary, giving Hanna a motherly kiss on top of her head. 'I've been doing some research and the situation is...complicated. If they find you, they will lock you up and deport you, end of story. We can't have that. And our organisation naturally wishes to avoid scrutiny from the terrestrial authorities.

'Now, it would be relatively simple to get you an Ethiopian passport; Kitty's already tracked down your birth certificate. Then it's just the visa which is tricky. We could put you on a student visa like we do for the students, but that wouldn't work in the long term. And it won't help you if you wanted a job outside the language school.'

Mary shook her head, lips pressed into a thin line. 'They make it dreadfully difficult. We can't adopt you, so we can't bring you in as a family member. You haven't lived here long enough to argue against being sent back to Ethiopia. Employing you as the school chef is a no-go for now, because you're not old enough to prove you have the experience. There aren't really any other legal options to let you stay longer than six months, as far as I can make out.'

'But there are illegal options,' added Irion with a humorous twitch of her ears. 'The easy way would be to get you a fake UK passport and create you a digital history – the computer on the *Shantivira* loves doing that kind of stuff. Then you'd be free to live and work anywhere in Europe as an EU citizen.

'But Ethiopia doesn't recognise dual nationality, so you'd have to choose. Once you're in the government system, there's no chance to start over, unless you're willing to take on a whole new identity.'

'What will it cost?' asked Hanna, her mind whirling.

'Money is only numbers in a computer. Don't worry about the expense.'

What should she do? Did she want to pretend to be an English girl forever? What if she needed to go back to Ethiopia one day? What about her siblings, wherever they were?

'I need time to think. I want to talk it over with Hassan. And Kitty.'

'Take all the time you need, my love.'

5. WELCOME TO THE SHANTIVIRA
LUCY

A S LUCY CRESTED the hilltop, she saw Kitty sitting on the grass by the ancient hill fort, looking towards the Wrekin in the distance. The air was clear and still, promising heat later in the day. Lucy suppressed her nervousness by rekindling embers of the fury she'd felt after their last encounter.

Kitty got up to greet her. 'Good morning!' She held out her hand for Lucy to shake, as if this were a perfectly normal business meeting. 'Is there anything you want to ask me, before we go? I won't see you much this weekend.'

Lucy seized her chance. 'You spied on me in my own house! For months! How dare you violate my privacy like that? What gives you the right?'

She met Kitty's gaze head on. To her surprise, Kitty looked away in shame.

'I have no right,' she said quietly. 'Your anger is entirely justified and I can only hope you will forgive me one day. Stalking a target, remaining hidden – it's in my nature.' She looked up again. 'But you never would have known about it if I hadn't approached you last weekend. How else can I find potential pilots? I need to learn more about you before I risk revealing myself.'

'But why me? What's so special about me?'

Kitty hesitated. 'You've noticed how my eyes are different to yours, right?'

Lucy nodded.

'Well, I don't perceive the world the same way you do. Every living creature emits life energy, and I can see it. Humans in general radiate it. You all look like angels to me. But some people shine more brightly than others. Like you.'

Lucy sniggered. 'Angels? I'm here because I look like an angel to you?'

'You're here because, having found you, I took the time to get to know you. You care deeply about the people in your life. You're more interested in harmony than personal gain. You're curious, self-confident, opportunistic and adventurous. You always think several steps ahead. You have a talent for languages. You're unattached and ready for a new challenge. Your hand-eye coordination and spatial awareness are well above average. And there's an aggression in you which I hope to harness. A darkness. You need that to be a good pilot. I certainly see you as a pilot rather than a diplomat.'

Lucy remained silent, stunned by this unexpectedly frank assessment.

'Anyway, we should go,' continued Kitty. 'The others are waiting.'

'Others?'

'Hold my hand and close your eyes.'

Lucy's ears filled with a rushing sound, as if she'd dived into a swimming pool. Instinctively, she held her breath. When she inhaled again, she sensed the air around her had changed: she was no longer outside. She opened her eyes to find herself high on a mezzanine overlooking a huge quadrant-shaped hall, filled with rows of what looked like giant conkers in prickly green shells. The curved wall was one enormous opening, through which Lucy could see the Earth, a blue-green half-moon. She clutched the railing, mesmerised.

Kitty touched her hand, breaking her trance, and Lucy realised they were standing by two men. The older one, in a dark green hoodie and ancient frayed jeans, sat on the railing, seemingly oblivious to the drop behind him. He had short blond hair and a deeply lined face, as if he'd spent much of his life outdoors. Cornflower blue eyes twinkled as he jumped down to welcome Lucy with an easy smile. He reminded her of her dad: that touch of the military in the way he held himself.

His companion was taller, with the lean physique of the permanently active. Chestnut hair curled on the collar of his softshell jacket. He was gazing round the hall like a puppy seeing snow for the first time.

'This is Captain Llewellyn,' said Kitty, indicating the older man. 'He's in charge of the *Shantivira*. And this is Felix; he's also being assessed this weekend.' Kitty looked at the captain. 'Shall I tell Tima you're ready for her?' He nodded, still smiling. To Lucy and Felix she said, 'Good luck you two. See you tomorrow afternoon.'

With that, Kitty sprang over the railing and disappeared. Lucy and Felix both yelled and ran to look over it, expecting to see her falling. But she was strolling down the wall with her hands in her pockets, heading for the floor below.

Amused at their surprise, the captain said, 'Loves a dramatic exit, does our Kitty.' His accent was distinctly Welsh. 'It's the gravity generators, see? They generate a field from all the fixed surfaces of the station. It means we can walk on the walls and ceilings. So,' he said, leaning back on the railing, 'the plan is for you to spend today on the simulators learning to fly a *Tumba*.' He pointed to the conker-objects in the docking bay below. 'That's one of those things down there. You can have a look round the *Shantivira* too. Then I'll take you out in Essoona this evening and bring you back here for the night.

'Tomorrow you'll have a written exam. You can do yours in German, Felix, don't worry. Then Kitty will return you to your pickup point.'

Felix asked, 'What's Essoona, Captain Llewellyn? A kind of spaceship?'

'Call me Joe,' said the captain. 'Essoona is the capital of Syenitia.' He winked conspiratorially. 'I'm going to take you to see some normal aliens. Kitty doesn't count, she's been with us lot too long. Do you like seafood?'

As Lucy and Felix shared a puzzled glance, a petite figure in a navy-blue flight suit stepped out of a nearby lift. A bob of black frizzy curls framed intelligent dark eyes and a hooked nose. Lucy felt suddenly tall, despite her average height.

'Ah! Lucy and Felix, this is Tima. She'll be your instructor today.'

'Hey!' she said. 'Welcome to the *Shantivira*.' After shaking hands, she gestured towards the lift. 'Please come with me.'

Joe called after them, 'Have a brilliant time! See you

later!' The lift doors closed and he was gone.

Tima smiled up at them. 'We're going to have a great day today.'

The lift doors opened onto a vast, windowless hall with harsh electric lighting. Large white spheres clustered in groups, connected by thick, multi-coloured cables.

'This is the training deck,' said Tima. She led the way to a kitchen area, where a table was set with coffee and biscuits. 'Let's get to know each other a bit before we start. Me first. I'm Fatima Rahimi. I've been working here for nearly fifteen years – I've never had a "proper job" on Earth. I was born in Iran, but my family moved to Malmö when I was eight, so I grew up in Sweden. My mother tongues are Farsi and Swedish, but I also speak English, Spanish, Syenitian and Kawaida.

'I met my husband when I was studying biochemistry in Uppsala; he's from Malmö too. He's a commercial diver now, so he's away a lot working on the oil rigs. We have three children: Johan, who is nine, Sofia, who is seven and Sören who is five. Sören was actually born here on the *Shantivira*. You might meet them later; they like to help out on the farm at the weekends.'

Felix interrupted, 'On the farm?'

Tima smiled. 'I'll show you later.'

Lucy asked, 'So you live in Sweden? But you work here? And you bring your children?'

'Sometimes. There's so much for them to learn here. I only work three days a week, and we have a lot of help from their grandparents. My cover story is that I work from home; we have a personal teleport set up from here straight into our cellar. See that door?' Tima pointed to a door in the opposite wall of the hall.

Lucy and Felix nodded.

'Once you're authorised, you can walk straight through it into the basement of the language school. It's a point-to-point teleport for particular bio-signatures. It won't work without authorisation – it would just look like a cupboard.'

Lucy said, 'So what does your husband think about all this?'

'When we got married, we agreed to support each other wherever our careers took us. Björn loves it up here.' Tima put down her coffee cup. 'So that's me. Why don't you tell us about yourself, Felix?'

Putting down his coffee cup, Felix said, 'My name is Felix Freitag. I am coming from a place called Nesselwang in the Allgäu region of Bavaria. I did my diploma in Business Studies in Munich, with a year on an ERASMUS exchange in Lyon. I planned to work in our family sawmill business, but I travelled for half a year first. When I got home, I realised I wanted to see more of the world before settling down.' He chuckled. 'But I never expected to see as much of it as we saw just now!'

Lucy adapted the introduction she used on business trips. 'I'm Lucy Cooper, from the UK. I'm a project manager for a company producing sub-assemblies for vehicle suspension systems. I studied Mechanical Engineering in Birmingham, and I also did an ERASMUS year, in Karlsruhe.'

'*Also, du sprichst Deutsch?*' said Felix.

'*Nicht wirklich. Ich habe viel vergessen,*' Lucy apologised. 'I'm not sure why I'm here. I nearly didn't make the call,' she said, admitting as much as she could without mentioning the AAL.

'You can trust Kitty's judgement,' said Tima. 'She's been selecting our pilots since the beginning. It's not often she gets it wrong.' She stood up and led them to a pair of the oversized golf balls. 'These are simulators for the *Tumba*-class fighters you saw upstairs. They're ergomorphic: the seats and controls adapt to your individual form. Which is lucky for me, because that means there's no minimum height requirement,' she laughed.

'Real *Tumbas* are cybernetic organisms – the shells are grown on Syenitia and they have a basic level of consciousness. They're alive kind of in the same way that a plant is. These simulators aren't; they're only a seat with software attached, networked together so we can simulate dogfights or fly in formation.'

As Tima spoke, a door on each of the spheres was opening slowly downwards with a pneumatic hiss.

'They're voice-operated. I've set up this one in German for you Felix, and this one in English for you Lucy,' said Tima, pointing. 'Here's a helmet each and a clean balaclava for hygiene. In you hop. Don't be shy.'

Lucy climbed the steps. The simulator was a cramped, dimly lit space containing a single saddle-shaped seat with a narrow backrest and headrest. It didn't look particularly comfortable. The moment she mounted, fitting her feet into the loops on the floor, she heard mechanical whirring beneath her.

The space lit up, showing stars and a semi-circular Earth on a 270° screen, edged by a colourful panel of lights and buttons labelled in a script Lucy had no hope of understanding. She shrieked as a harness snaked over her chest and hips, securing her to the growing and changing saddle.

Tima poked her head through the door. 'Everything all right? I know, it's weird the first time. If you feel you need to get out, press the button on the front of your harness.'

She disappeared and the door closed slowly. Lucy felt a stab of adrenaline. She was about to learn to fly.

In Lucy's earpiece, Tima's voice said, 'To be a good pilot, you need the *Tumba* to become an extension of your body. If you want to go forwards, lean forwards. If you want to accelerate, lean forwards more. Lean backwards to slow down, or stop, or reverse. If you want to go left, turn your shoulders to the left. To go right, turn your shoulders to the right. Try it, have a play.'

Lucy leaned forwards ever so slightly and felt the *Tumba* begin to move. A display appeared, seemingly outside the window, showing changing green luminous characters. A speedometer? She leaned forward further and the characters changed faster. She tried a turn. Wow! It was responsive! She turned to the right, more slowly this time. She threw her weight backwards and felt herself decelerating. Then forwards again, then a left-hand spin. This was fun! By pulling against the foot loops she could make the *Tumba* dip downwards, and make it go up by pushing away from the floor. She found she could loop the loop, fly in a spiral, and come to a sudden halt, all by moving her body.

A twisting red tube appeared on the screen. Tima's voice said, 'Your next task is to follow the red tube, as fast as you dare. There are a few of these: they get harder and harder, so be prepared.'

Full of confidence now, Lucy plunged into the tube, accelerating all the while. Uh-oh! The turn ahead was sharper than she'd anticipated. She flung herself backwards, but it was no good; the wall was coming for her. A yell escaped her as the whole cabin shuddered violently with the impact. One of the characters on the head-up display started flashing red.

Tima's voice exclaimed, 'Steady Lucy! Your shields are at fifty per cent, you can't afford another crash like that! OK?'

'OK!' Lucy grinned, enjoying testing the limits. All the same, she slowed down and flew more prudently. By the time the door hissed open again, her body was quivering from the unfamiliar form of exercise.

They returned to the table where sandwiches and a jug of water awaited them. Ravenous, Lucy filled her plate.

'So what did you think?' asked Tima.

'It's like skiing,' said Felix, between mouthfuls. 'You lean the way you want to turn and it follows like it's part of you.'

'Is it always that physical?' asked Lucy. 'I mean, if you're going long distances, don't you get saddle sore?'

'There's an autopilot for long distances. It can be tiring, but less tiring than sitting in one position for hours at a time.'

After a short break, Tima offered to show them the rest of the *Shantivira*. 'Bring your bags, you can leave them in your cabins. The *Shantivira* is shaped like a hamburger, where the bread is bigger than the burger,' she said, as they followed her to the lift. 'Today you'll see four of the seven levels.'

When the lift doors opened, they were on the same level as the *Tumba* fighters. Close up, they gave off a pleasantly verdant scent. Beyond the spiky shells she glimpsed the hemispheric Earth outside: no simulation this time.

'This morning, you were up there,' said Tima, pointing up at a railing Lucy recognised. 'This is the main level, where everything happens. It's divided into quadrants. This is Docking Bay 1 and directly opposite is Docking Bay 2. Each holds around a hundred *Tumbas*.' Tima pointed to a curved window at the apex of the quadrant. 'That's the control room.'

Inside the control room, a heavyset, bearded man with shoulder-length hair stood as still and tall as a statue, betraying no emotion as he stared through the glass at Lucy. Was that a Syenitian? Weren't Syenitians supposed to be friendly? Unsettled, Lucy quickly followed Tima through to the next quadrant.

'This is Docking Bay 3, for larger ships and maintenance,' she was saying. 'The sickbay is here too.'

Lucy gaped. In front of them, resting on six jointed legs, was the most elegant machine she'd ever seen. A shimmering turquoise dragonfly spacecraft with translucent wings. Not a harmless insect: heavy-duty weapons protruded from each side of its thorax. Three seats were faintly visible inside the transparent dome head. Behind it, a much larger spacecraft dominated the docking bay: black, shiny and beetle-shaped, also with six legs. Craning her neck, Lucy saw gigantic doors in its belly.

Tima pointed at the smaller craft. 'That's the captain's, it's called the *Pride of Essoona*. A *Korento*-class ship, very fast. Joe lives on board. The hull is coated with a solar panel skin, that's what gives it that lovely colour. It was a wedding present from his brother-in-law. The big beetle is the *Koppakuoria*, our cargo transporter.'

Before they could ask any questions, Tima walked back past the control room to the opposite quadrant. Lucy looked for the bearded giant, but the room was empty.

They followed Tima through to a dining hall as large as the docking bays. Instead of an opening into space, the outer curved wall of this segment was an enormous window, with a deep window ledge perfect for sitting on.

They could see far into the Milky Way from this side of the *Shantivira*. Never in her whole life had Lucy seen so many stars: a heart-stoppingly beautiful plume of glittering, glowing smoke, stretching into infinity. Felix caught her eye and they beamed at each other. However this weekend turned out, it was worth it just for that view.

It was lunchtime and people sat in clusters throughout the hall, although most were near the window. No one paid the visitors much attention.

'Nice view, isn't it?' said Tima. 'This is the canteen and this—' she pointed at a sectioned-off area nearby, '—is the kitchen.'

A hair-netted head poked out of the serving hatch. 'Hello Tima, were those sandwiches enough for you?'

'Yes thanks, Maneewan.' Tima turned to Lucy and Felix. 'This is Maneewan, the boss of our catering team. She keeps us all in order.'

Maneewan's crow's feet danced. 'That'd be right!' she

laughed. 'I'll send someone down with drinks and snacks at around four, OK?'

'Great, thanks.'

'Right, must get on. See you later, Tima.' The head withdrew.

'I thought everyone on the base spoke Kawaida?' said Felix.

'They do,' replied Tima. 'Maneewan was speaking English for your benefit.'

'What's the food like?' asked Lucy.

'Mostly curry, mostly vegetarian. Never boring. We grow as much of our own food as we can, but we don't have the resources to keep much livestock. We try to follow the Syenitian principles of sustainability. Meat is a once-a-month treat, and then we eat all the animal, including the bits we in Europe would typically throw away.

'Right, let's go upstairs to your cabins. You can leave your stuff there. Then we'll go out and see one of the biomes.'

Felix recalled their earlier conversation. 'Is that where the farm is?'

Tima nodded. 'That's right.'

The lift doors opened onto a large open space, with numbered doors curving away around the circumference of the space station. 'This is the accommodation level,' said Tima. She handed them each a key. 'Lucy, you're in seventeen. Felix, you're in nineteen. When you're done settling in, I'll be waiting for you through that door there.' She pointed past an Olympic-sized swimming pool, curved to fit the shape of the deck, to a white submarine-type hatch in the wall.

'It's not locked. Come up when you're ready. Oh,' she added, 'press the green button to open the toilet and the red button to close it. Don't be long, we've got a lot to get through this afternoon!'

Lucy's room provided an immediate sense of sanctuary. It was more like a cosy cabin on an old-fashioned sailing ship than her idea of a room on a space station. The wood-panelled walls, wooden floorboards and furniture gave off a pleasant, calming scent. It was a red-hued wood she hadn't seen before, with the dark patina that only came with age and frequent use.

The wall opposite the door was all window, with a captivating view of South America partially veiled by clouds. Plain furniture lined the right-hand wall: a table and two chairs, drawers, shelves, a built-in wardrobe. On the left was an overly long bed, at the foot of which a sliding Japanese-style screen opened into a tiny, brightly lit white bathroom.

Lucy dumped her rucksack on the bed and went to investigate. It was the size of a shower cubicle; it even looked like a shower cubicle, except for the small sink protruding from the back wall. Where was the loo? Then she saw the red and green buttons Tima had mentioned. She pressed the green one and sprang back as the base of the shower silently retracted, uncovering an oval-shaped hole with foot rests on either side. Lucky she hadn't been standing in the shower! Cautiously, she stepped onto the footrests and squatted. The white plate sealing the hole slid away and she felt a cool breeze from below. Afterwards, Lucy stepped out of the cubicle and pressed the red button. The shower base reappeared, but there was no sound of running water. She hoped it wasn't broken.

As she washed her hands and re-did her ponytail, she reviewed the day so far. Seeing the Earth from space was amazing, of course. That Felix was a nice, straightforward guy. She had the feeling he said what he meant and meant what he said. Not as attractive as Jude, but then her tastes had always tended towards older men. And the *Shantivira*? Gut feeling? It all seemed too easy: the friendly people, the simple-to-operate spacecraft – what was she missing?

With a jolt, she remembered the 'DO NOT FAIL THE ASSESSMENT' note. She'd got so caught up in learning to fly, got so distracted by all the new sights, that she'd forgotten her plan to make a mess of things. But flying had come so naturally to her, she didn't think she *could* mess it up now without raising suspicion.

What had Kitty meant about there being a darkness in her? Did she think Lucy had it in her to destroy another intelligent being? Did Kitty think she might *enjoy* it? The idea scared Lucy even more than the thought of being shot down herself.

And who had the unsmiling presence in the control room been? He didn't exactly fit the cosy image they were selling. Neither did Kitty. Her indisputable beauty didn't change the fact that she was clearly some kind of alien predator. She'd said she was only half Syenitian. So what was the other half?

The AAL thought Kitty was a demon who wanted control of the planet so she could eat the people on it. Did that apply to all the Syenitians? Horror froze Lucy's lungs, leaving her breathless. What was worse? Killing aliens or being eaten by them? Perhaps the AAL had a point. People needed to know what was going on up here.

Resolving to find out as much as she could about the *Shantivira*, for herself as much as for the AAL, Lucy took a last look at the Earth out of the window and left the cabin. She skirted the pool and headed for the hatch as instructed. After one turn of the wheel, the heavy door swung inwards with an ominous creak, and Lucy stared into—

Space.

Huh?

6. THE TEMPERATE BIOME
LUCY

WHY WAS THERE no airlock? Was this a test? Lucy imagined her body floating away the minute she stepped over the threshold, irretrievable and forever silent. Would that be a good way to die? She didn't want to find out.

Holding her breath – her knuckles white on the door-frame – she gingerly poked her head out and saw muddy footprints on the otherwise spotless exterior of the space station. What had Joe said about the gravity generators? That they could walk on any surface they wanted?

She got down on her hands and knees, parallel to the hatch, and reached for the outside wall: first with a hand, then a foot and a knee. She shifted her weight across, quickly pulling through her other leg and arm, and there she was, kneeling on the snow-white surface. Close up, the metal had a pearlescent quality. It looked more like something used for making jewellery than for heavy-duty construction.

The view back through the hatch was disorientating, a surrealist optical illusion. Walls and floors in the wrong places. Enough. Don't think about it. Get going and find the others. Lucy stood up and hauled the hatch closed with a practical rope fixed to the outer door handle.

She followed the footprints to a gate in a wooden fence, beyond which she was relieved to find Felix and Tima standing in a farmyard, chickens pecking contentedly by their feet. Tima was having a discussion in Swedish with three children in boots and anoraks. Behind them, an orchard stretched away into the distance, the ground between the trees thickly planted with a jumble of different crops. The sun shone brightly in the black sky. On the horizon, conical towers poked out of the ground at intervals. Lucy crossed the yard to Felix and whispered, 'How is this possible?'

Tima turned back to them. 'Please excuse us. We were discussing exactly when Johan and Sofia are going to get round to doing their homework. This is Johan, Sofia and Sören. *Säg hej till Lucy och Felix.*'

'Hej, Lucy och Felix,' chorused three voices. Then the children ran out of the yard, shouting and laughing.

'They're off to play in the forest, since they've done all their jobs,' said Tima. 'When they're here, they have to collect the eggs, clean out the rabbits and do whatever else the biome managers ask them to.'

Lucy thought Tima was utterly irresponsible. If *she* ever had kids, she wouldn't let them anywhere near an alien military facility, even if she did work there. *Especially* if she worked there.

Felix asked, 'How can we breathe? How can there be an atmosphere?'

'None of our spacecraft would survive long without a shield generator and the main space station is no different,' said Tima. 'The biomes are triple-shielded: each hemisphere is double-shielded with static shields, and then there's the main operational shield which covers the whole *Shantivira*. That can be thinned in places to let ships in and out.

'The biomes maintain the atmosphere for the *Shantivira*. This is the temperate biome, and on the other side of the docking bays is the tropical biome. Without the plants and trees, we'd quickly run out of oxygen and get carbon dioxide poisoning. The shields filter the sun to simulate the Earth's atmosphere, so the plants don't all burn and freeze.'

They passed a series of ponds, each with a fountain at the centre. 'That's our fish farm,' said Tima. She opened a gate and led them across a field, past some cows. The cows stopped eating to stare at them.

'What are those white cones?' asked Lucy, pointing at the towers.

'Those? You know the *Tumbas* you saw down in the docking bay were spiky on the outside? Some of those spikes are thrusters for moving the spacecraft, some are part of the cloaking system, and the others belong to the weapons system – that's where the dematerialisation beams come out. Those cones are the same thing for the main space station, on a bigger scale.'

'Cloaking system?' said Felix.

'Of course,' said Tima. 'Someone would have noticed us up here long ago if the space station weren't cloaked.'

'So, the weapons don't blow things up, they make them disappear?' said Lucy. 'Do they reappear somewhere else?'

'No. They're gone forever. It only works in space,

though. The beam absorbs the target's intrinsic energy and converts it to power which the spacecraft can store. You can't go round blowing things up in space – we have enough problems with space debris as it is. The Syenitians convert matter directly into energy, without burning it.'

'What, even metal? Or stone?' asked Felix.

'Well,' said Tima, 'all matter yields energy, but organic matter is an exponentially richer power source than inorganic matter. Something to do with the complexity of the molecular structure.'

Maybe that's why the Syenitians want the Earth, thought Lucy. There can't be many planets with such abundant life. Out loud she said, 'Isn't that kind of cannibalistic? You're basically powering your spacecraft with your enemies' remains. As they die.' She turned to Felix. 'Don't you think that's grotesque?'

Awkward silence. Felix said, 'Well, yeah, I suppose, when you put it like that—'

'It's quick, Lucy,' interrupted Tima. 'If you get hit, you're just gone. There's no time to feel anything.'

'But—'

'Do you think it's better *not* to harness your enemy's energy?' said Tima. 'Do you think it's better to waste that energy out of respect for your target? Even though the debris would create a problem which might result in loss of life elsewhere? Even though extra fuel would have to be sourced from much further away?'

'I just think it's kind of brutal. And yes, I do think it's disrespectful to the victim.'

'Nature *is* brutal. But pragmatic. In the natural world, everything is recycled and reused. Syenitian tech just emulates that. The Syenitians have the greatest respect for life, especially intelligent life. But in space warfare you can't bury people or cremate them.'

'Have you ever dematerialised someone, Tima?' asked Felix.

'Twice.' Her eyes flashed with displeasure at his question. 'Both times I prayed for the target's soul for months afterwards.'

Touched a nerve there, thought Lucy. But she clearly believes she's doing the right thing, working here. She must utterly trust the Syenitians or she wouldn't let her family up here.

'So do you grow biofuels as well?' said Felix.

'No. Food is the priority. But the generator converts all forms of waste into energy. Even our toilets feed straight into the generator, so don't drop anything important down them!' said Tima, smiling again.

Beyond the fields, Lucy could see tall trees. 'The Wild Interior,' she muttered, half to herself.

'Each biome has a wild zone at the centre to promote biodiversity,' said Tima. 'Otherwise we wouldn't have enough insects to pollinate our crops.'

Inside the forest it was dark and cool, a microclimate. 'How old is this space station?' asked Lucy. 'Some of these trees must be hundreds of years old.'

'They are. This isn't the *Shantivira's* first mission. She's an antique. If you maintain them well, Syenitian ships can last for five or six hundred years. Judging by the trees, I reckon the *Shantivira* is more than four hundred years old, although she's only been called the *Shantivira* for the last forty years. They wanted to use a name from an

Earth language because the crew's mostly human.'

'An Earth language?' said Felix. 'I assumed *Shantivira* was a Kawaida word. What does it mean?'

'It's Sanskrit,' replied Tima. 'As far as I understand, it means "the strength to choose the path of peace".'

Huh? thought Lucy. Funny name for a space station able to wipe out its enemies at the touch of a button. Was it some kind of sick joke?

They crossed a clearing dotted with beehives and soon reached an open space with a thatched gazebo at the centre, its rough wooden posts dark with age. A sapling grew next to it, not a variety Lucy recognised. Inside, woven grass matting covered the floor and a stone fountain made a pleasant trickling sound.

'This is our *Ohimo*,' said Tima. 'It's a centre for contemplation. Syenitians aren't religious, so temple is too grand a word. Some of us use it as a mosque, or a church or a temple or whatever, and others come to be alone with their thoughts.' She glanced at her watch. 'Look at the time! We'd better get on.'

Back indoors, a woman in a lab coat was waiting for them by the lift. Tima introduced her as Hagar, the *Shantivira's* medical officer.

'I need to give you a check-up before you go back on the simulators,' she said. They followed her to Docking Bay 3, where she led them past the dragonfly ship and the monstrous beetle to the sickbay – a series of rooms along one of the walls. Hagar pointed to a row of seats.

'If you'd like to wait here, Lucy, this won't take long.'

Ten minutes later, Felix reappeared and it was Lucy's turn. Hagar recorded her height, weight and blood pressure, and took a blood sample. Then, after she'd tested Lucy's vision and hearing, Hagar handed her a glass of water and a little green pill.

'What's this?' said Lucy.

'You'll be eating out on Syenitia tonight. This is against the bacteria shock. Stops you getting an upset stomach.'

Bacteria shock? Was that a thing? Lucy took the pill and swallowed it.

Hagar returned them to the training deck, where Tima demonstrated the *Tumba's* weapons system. Back in her pod, Lucy was ready for the automatic harness this time. Red and green rings were scattered across the display: red were targets and green were friendly. Fuel gauges down the left-hand side: three large circles filled with different coloured slices, like pie charts.

The top circle was the weapons fuel cell, the centre one powered the *Tumba* and the lowest was a reserve, half full. Tima had explained that, when flying for real, excess energy was discharged to the *Shantivira* on docking. If one cell got too low, the other cells redistributed their energy.

Right then, Lucy thought, let's give this a go. It was a simulation – no need to involve her conscience just yet. She said, 'Targeting,' and focused on a red ring. 'Lock on.' Now the target had a double ring around it. 'Fire!' The ring filled with red and vanished. Easy peasy. The coloured portion of the upper circle on the left grew slightly.

Soon there were only green rings left. In the following tests the targets sped up until Lucy felt almost dizzy.

'OK, you've got the hang of the basics,' came Tima's voice. 'Now comes flying and shooting at the same time.'

The screen changed to show a dense cloud of asteroids. 'Fly through this asteroid field as fast as you can and dematerialise the red-ringed targets on your way. Points will be deducted if you shoot at an unmarked asteroid. Good luck.'

Lucy took a deep breath. OK. Go.

She hurtled forward, past the first asteroid, around the next, below the one after that, trying to keep her path as direct as possible. She spotted the first red ring, some distance away and blocked by other asteroids. She waited for a clear line of sight. Targeting. Lock on. Fire. The red ring filled and disappeared.

Lucy refocused on the rest of the screen. Shit! She flung herself to the right, narrowly avoiding a monster asteroid. She could see the next red ring ahead, no, there were three in a row. Aaargh! She got two but missed the last one. She looked ahead: nothing coming. She swivelled around in her seat and grinned as the whole cockpit rotated with her. Now she was flying backwards. Targeting. Lock on. Fire. Done.

She swung back again, enjoying herself now. Rocketing towards the next target, she spun 360° and obliterated it as she passed, without losing speed. Time seemed to slow as she threw herself around her cockpit, blitzing target after target with increasing confidence. Only when the simulation ended did she realise how hard her heart was pumping.

'Well done, both of you! Right. One more test to go.'

The screen flickered. Right in front of Lucy was another *Tumba*, so close it filled her entire screen.

'This is where we pit you against each other in a dogfight,' said Tima. 'The test won't finish until one of you has been dematerialised. Remember, this is just a simulation, not real life! Good luck.'

'Be the hunter, not the hunted.' Lucy heard her dad's voice in her head. She said, 'Targeting,' but Felix was already accelerating away. She gave chase, firing as she went. He wove erratically from side to side, making it hard for her to follow. She felt sure she'd hit him a couple of times, but he kept going.

Felix changed direction abruptly and came straight at her. She swerved, but his shot must have connected, because the whole cabin trembled. One of the characters on the left-hand side of the display change from green to yellow and a robotic voice said, 'Shields – at – sixty-three – per cent.'

Breathing hard, she rotated her craft until she could see Felix. She reversed rapidly, firing all the while. Again his *Tumba* swung from side to side and she wasn't sure if her shots had connected. She threw herself forwards into her harness and gave chase. He was fast, but she was faster. Now she had him. 'Targeting. Lock on. Fire!' But nothing happened. She tried again. 'Fire!' she shouted. Why wasn't it working? A tsunami of dread surged through her stomach as she realised what had happened. Oh God. She was so dead.

In the thrill of the chase, she'd forgotten to check her fuel cells. Two were empty and the third was on twenty per cent. Ahead of her, Felix turned, coming in for another attack. She pushed away from the floor with her legs, as hard as she could, sending her *Tumba* out of his path, but she knew it was over. They were in open space; there was nowhere to hide. Two seconds later, the little *Tumba* shook violently. As the computer voice was saying, 'Shields – at – three – per cent. Warning! Warning!' the spacecraft shuddered again and the screen went blank.

The control panel dimmed and all went quiet. Lucy was trembling. She pulled off her helmet and balaclava and wiped her sweaty forehead on her sleeve. Had she failed the assessment? Was that good or bad?

As she climbed out of her simulator on shaky legs, Lucy saw Felix jump down from his, beaming with delight. He came over and shook her hand, saying, 'Well fought.' Lucy grinned despite herself and felt better. They crossed the hall to the table, where Tima was waiting with the promised refreshments.

'Lucy. Why did you fail?'

'I didn't watch my energy levels and I blew all my energy on missed shots.'

'That's right. Although you're not lacking killer instinct. You're itching for a revenge match now, aren't you?'

Lucy smiled thinly and nodded. 'Yeah.'

Tima turned to Felix. 'How did you win, Felix?'

'Um. By not shooting until I was sure I could hit something?'

'Partly. Your evasive manoeuvring was excellent, or you wouldn't have survived for so long. So,' she said, looking at her watch, 'you're due to meet the captain. Any more questions before you go? Lucy?'

'Have I failed the assessment? I mean, because I lost the dogfight?'

'We look at your performance across the whole weekend. We'll decide tomorrow afternoon whether we want to train you. But you did well in the dogfight. Sometimes you learn more from losing than from winning. You won't make the same mistake again, will you?'

Lucy shook her head. Behind them, Joe came out of the lift.

He said, 'Are you ready to cross the galaxy and see some aliens?'

Lucy and Felix exchanged an apprehensive glance and nodded. They thanked Tima and followed him into the lift. He tapped the touchscreen and scanned his palm.

'How long will the journey take?' asked Felix.

Joe winked. 'We're already there.'

The lift door slid open to reveal a wooden door, richly carved with stylised plants and insects intertwined in flowing curves.

'Are you ready?' Without waiting for an answer, Joe pushed it open.

7. AN EXTRA-TERRESTRIAL EXCURSION

JOE

J OE ALWAYS RELISHED this moment with the new recruits. He stepped into the ornately tiled stairwell and peered out of the window, checking the weather. The silver-barked trees around the pond were swaying in a stiff breeze, but the ground was dry.

'This is Dunia House,' he said, observing Lucy and Felix's confused expressions with quiet amusement. 'We use it as an unofficial embassy for Earth on Syenitia, accommodation for our second-year trainees and any visitors who prefer to lodge with other humans. We'll just say "hi" before we go out.' He led the visitors along the beeswax-scented corridor, giving them time to get used to the different gravity. He never got tired of the spring it put in his step.

There were four people in the sunny, wood-panelled lounge: Qingqing in an armchair, reading a Chinese newspaper, Hassan lying on a sofa, watching a video on his *zana*, and Traian, cross-legged on the rug by the fireplace, experimenting with different chords on his guitar. Dipesh snoozed in another armchair. One hand dangled limply above a paperback book on the floor, next to bags of shopping. Joe resisted the temptation to give his colleague a rude awakening and greeted the three students with a silent wave.

Seeing Hassan reminded him that Kitty was taking Hanna to Addis Ababa today to get her new passport. As he escorted Lucy and Felix down to the entrance hall, he reached out to Kitty with his mind. As always, their telepathic conversation was in Welsh.

Hey, how did it go?

All done. She had to wait for hours, poor love.

What happens now?

She's staying with Senai's family while she waits for her tourist visa application to go through, then she'll book a flight so she can arrive 'officially' in the UK. Once she's back, we've got six months to get her on a course to study something or other so she'll qualify for a student visa.

OK, good. Has Tima given you her report on the potentials yet? I need to know how they did so I can ask the right questions.

I'm on my way to her now. Give me fifteen minutes.

DOWNSTAIRS, JOE PULLED some coats out of the hall cupboard. Green for Felix, blue for Lucy and grey for himself.

'It gets chilly in the evenings here. People won't stare at you if you wear these.'

The coats were of a thick, stiff fabric, with a soft lining in a paler shade. The sleeves were so long they covered their fingers completely, making gloves unnecessary. Felix put his on and pulled up the hood.

'You look like a gnome!' laughed Lucy.

Joe pushed on the swan's neck door handle to open one half of the grand front door and ushered them outside. The street was lined with buildings five or six storeys high: solar panels glinting on the upper levels, the foliage on the lower levels rustling in the wind. A strip of grass and shrubbery shielded pedestrians from a wide, busy cycle track and a road, the two carriageways also separated by grass and flowers. The identical vehicles travelled fast and almost noiselessly, some individually, others in platoons of four or five. Joe appreciated the lack of air pollution, but the sophisticated transport network could never match the thrill the throaty roar of his motorbike gave him every time he started its filthy petrol engine.

A humming shadow made them look up. Lucy and Felix ducked as a vivid green tram passed overhead, hovering just a few metres above the transport pods.

'Damn, we've missed it,' Joe cursed. As he led them to the tram stop, he explained that there were three 'layers' of trams running on set routes. 'There aren't any buses, only trams and pods. Almost no one has their own transport pod, but most people have a bike or scooter of some kind.'

They climbed the steps to the second level of the tram stop, where Joe bought a white bottle of steaming *saiju* from one of the kiosks. He took a swig and sighed with satisfaction.

'The first one of the day always tastes the best. Want to try?'

Lucy declined. Felix took a cautious sip.

'Not bad. What is it?'

'*Saiju*,' said Joe. 'Like tea, but with more pep. They serve it in these deposit bottles for commuters.'

While they waited, he used the 3D hologram tram map to show Lucy and Felix their destination. The tram pulled in and, once on board, Joe glanced around at the passengers in their carriage. Most were pale-skinned Syenitians with long, straight hair, wearing thigh-length, V-necked tunics over their trousers. Learning to tell the males from the females had taken him years. There were some furry Grookas, a couple of Sayari and a large group of three-eyed Mhasibu at the end of the carriage, all wearing identical brown suits. There must be a finance conference on, thought Joe. He couldn't imagine Mhasibu travelling for pleasure.

He made sure Lucy and Felix sat facing the rest of the carriage so he could observe their gobsmacked expressions. No one paid the slightest attention to the small group of humans. At the next stop, an elderly Wadudu got on and sat in the seat next to his. A pair of leathery-brown hands pulled out some knitting and got to work. Another hand held an audio-phone, into which she talked non-stop in a series of clicks and whistles, and a fourth clutched the handbag on her lap, underneath the knitting. Joe saw Felix catch Lucy's eye and Lucy covered her mouth with her hand, suppressing a snigger.

As he watched them, he felt Kitty's consciousness poking at his, requesting contact. He opened up their connection and waited.

Hi, love. So, Felix's flight skills are pretty average, but he took everything in his stride. He seems to accept things as they are without thinking too hard about them. Calm and relaxed. Based on what Tima saw today, he'll never head the pack in a combat situation, but that's not why I picked him. He's a potential diplomat. He enjoys connecting with people, that's where his talent lies. Excellent interpersonal skills, loyal, obedient, unflappable, physically resilient. With the right training, he could be a real asset to us in twenty years or so.

And the woman?

Entirely different. Not diplomat material; her emotional intelligence is too limited, but she's a natural pilot. Tima said she saw straight away that Lucy loves flying. But she also reckons Lucy's having severe doubts. She has a more active imagination than Felix; she's thinking further ahead than he is. I admit, I messed up our first meeting. Bloody Dartmoor mist. Not the first time it's caught me out. I was surprised she made contact at all.

OK, thanks for the heads up.

Tima will give you a more detailed report tomorrow, while they're doing their exam.

Right. You coming to Nkosi's birthday party later?

S'pect so.

OK, see you then.

Good luck with your meeting. You still don't know what she wants?

Nope. God knows how small-fry like me got onto her radar. But I trust her less than I'd trust a Mwongo.

Kitty giggled. *No, me neither. She's never forgiven Aldeman for being chosen to lead the Council. She's made screwing him over her life's mission. Tell me everything later.*

Will do. Bye, love.

He broke the link and tuned back in to Felix and Lucy's conversation.

'Have you ever been to Munich?' Felix was asking.

'Years ago,' Lucy nodded.

'Don't you think these buildings are like the ones around the University there? Kind of *Jugendstil*?'

'Art Nouveau, you mean? Yeah, kind of.'

It was true, Joe thought, the buildings in Essoona were beautiful: all those carvings and paintings of plants, animals and insects around the entrances and windows. The Syenitians had a habit of making artistic statements on every available surface.

Joe wondered if they'd been discussing the *maalaus* while he'd been talking to Kitty. Newbies were always surprised by the Syenitian approach to public art. He smiled, remembering that Kazembi and her daughters had done one for Nkosi's birthday. Perhaps he could have a look at it later.

He looked out of the window and saw they were approaching the city centre. He stood up as the tram slowed and said, 'This is our stop.'

'I can smell the sea!' exclaimed Felix, as they disembarked at the bustling tram intersection; a three-tiered pentagon surrounding some tall trees.

'You can,' said Joe, pointing eastwards. Their tram pulled away, revealing a misty blue horizon beyond the city rooftops. He handed back his *saiju* bottle at the kiosk and returned to Lucy and Felix. 'Right, well, we don't have lots of time, so we'll just do a whistle-stop tour.'

They took the stairs to the ground level and stopped in the doughnut-shaped space below the tram stop. 'This is the *Määritelmät*, the fish market,' said Joe. 'It's been here in some form or another for tens of thousands of years. There's nothing to see now, but a cool thing to do is to come early in the morning and look at all the weird sea creatures.' He led them out to the Jokivarsi, where spacecraft hovered above the boats in layers, as if in an invisible multi-storey car park.

'The Soon Estuary is an informal short-stay spaceport in the city centre,' said Joe. 'There's a big spaceport on the edge of town for those who need to land.' He nodded at the spacecraft above. 'They all have someone aboard, keeping the craft in the air.'

'Why?' asked Lucy. 'Don't they have autopilots?'

'Of course, but it's a safety thing. Hovering takes fuel. If the owner doesn't return in time and the fuel runs out, well,' said Joe with a grin, 'the lawyers will be happy, but no one else.'

They strolled along the riverbank for a while, looking at the different boats and spacecraft. Then Joe turned abruptly into Ruokakuja, a tiny street rammed with food stalls, restaurants and bars all jostling for space, pumping a cacophony of exotic aromas into the air. He bounded up the steps at the end of the alley two at a time and waited at the top for Lucy and Felix. Despite the gravity advantage, at this point on his standard tour prospective trainees often panted as if he'd made them do fifty press-ups. Physical fitness wasn't a critical entry requirement for the *Shantivira*, but there was no harm in testing them. Fortunately, these two weren't too out of breath. A good sign.

'This is Kalakaivo Square,' he said. With the late afternoon sun glinting on the glossy black stone of the imposing official buildings, it was a good time of day to show off Essoona. Tourists clustered around the fountain at the centre of the square. He let Lucy and Felix watch the locals criss-crossing the white flagstones for a few moments and then pointed at a gap between the buildings in the opposite corner, 'We came via the scenic route, but we could have just gone up to Level Three at the tram station and come out over there.'

He turned to the building on their right, his personal favourite: a multi-storey structure with two symmetrical halves. A gigantic white marble relief carving stretched from ground level to the roof, showing two naked Syenitians holding hands: one male, one female. The two grand entrances didn't even reach their knees.

'That's the public baths. Separate doorways for men and women. Syenitians love bathing, it's a spiritual thing for them. No one has a bath tub in their flat; if you want a soak you have to come here or go to one of the neighbourhood bathhouses. It's a social activity; most people go at least once a week. These are the Law Courts,' he continued, indicating the grandiose building on their left, 'and opposite are the Council Chambers. That's one of the most important buildings, apart from the Library, which we'll see in a minute.

'The Council Chambers are the administrative headquarters for the planet, and also the Syenitian branch of the Galaksi Alliance. The Alliance has no fixed headquarters; it moves from planet to planet depending on who is the current president.'

'A rotating presidency?' said Felix.

'That's right,' said Joe. 'The head of the Syenitian Council represents Syenitian interests at the Alliance Assembly, which meets four times a *mwaka*. As a founder member, Syenitia is very influential within the Alliance.'

'*Mwaka?*' asked Lucy.

'A galactic year,' answered Joe. 'Based on what we on Earth call Planck time, so it's the same for everyone. About 300 Earth days, roughly.'

He pointed to the far end of the square, where green roof tiles glistened like fish scales above dark wooden walls. 'Over there is the *Ohimo*, you saw ours before, right? The walls keep out the noise.'

Lucy was more interested in the colourful panels covering the base of the Law Courts and the Council Chambers. 'What are they? We saw loads from the tram. There's graffiti everywhere you look.'

Each was about two metres high by three metres wide. Many were cartoons, some were lifelike paintings and others were full of text in Syenitian or Kawaidan script, which of course neither Lucy nor Felix could read, Joe reminded himself. Probably just as well.

'They're *maalaus*,' Joe said. 'A kind of public art form. The city awards a prize for the best one each month, assuming you enter the competition. The only rules are that they're not allowed to advertise products or services, and they must be painted on location. You're not allowed to prepare it in advance and then paste it on. These ones here are political criticism and comments on one of the trials taking place in the Law Courts.'

They crossed the square to the fountain: a carved column of writhing sea creatures, each spraying a jet of water out of its mouth. The wet black stone made them look almost alive. A group of orange Tarumbets with elongated heads were having their photo taken in front of it.

Felix held up his phone. 'Come on, let's take a photo of us.'

Joe shook his head. 'Sorry, that's not allowed.' Seeing their disappointment, he relented. 'All right. How about, I take a picture of you both on my *zana*, and if we take you on then I'll give you both a copy?'

Lucy and Felix stood before the fountain and Joe pulled up the camera function on his *zana*. He was amused to see Felix put his arm around Lucy's shoulders while she put her arm around his waist. Had Kitty been matchmaking again?

Joe said, 'We won't go into the *Ohimo*; you're only supposed to go in for contemplation. Most of the roof is a skylight, so it's a nice place to go when it's raining. Which it does a lot here.'

He led them to an adjoining square behind the Council Chambers, dominated by a forbidding tower at the far end. At the centre stood an ancient white tree, its twisted boughs propped up with supports.

'This is Kirjasto Square,' he said. 'Opposite us is the Planetary Museum of Syenitia. That's a good place to start if you want to learn about the Syenitians. Behind it is the Extra-Syenitia Museum, with all sorts of oddities from across the galaxy. Another one for a rainy day. That fortress there,' he said, pointing to the dark skyscraper, 'is the Library.'

'It's huge!' said Felix.

'The Library isn't just somewhere you borrow books. It's the Ministry of Knowledge. An archive of all the data on the planet, including all the Syenitians' information about other civilisations and their histories. Rumour says there are as many storeys below ground level as there are above it. It's also where they keep the main servers for the planet. The waste heat warms all the surrounding buildings, including the baths. It's a very powerful institution. Some would say too powerful.'

A peal of bells rang out across the square, drowning out Joe's voice. Perfect timing. He grinned and strode towards the source of the din – a circular, single-storey building opposite the Library. From all around, Syenitians and the occasional alien were making a beeline for the great wooden doors, where a crowd was forming as they waited to enter. There were no *maalaus* or graffiti here. Instead, the exterior was decorated with a white stone relief of life-sized Syenitians, holding hands and facing away from the viewer.

When the bells died down, Joe said, 'This is the *Laulaahaalia*, which translates as "sing together". It's an ancient custom – the spiritual experience of singing in a group. There's no audience, it's all about the participation. Sing "la-la-la" and you'll be fine, all right?'

They reached the steps and their view was obscured by the crowding Syenitians, all at least two metres tall, who swept them through the doors and into a round hall. A glass dome spanned the diameter, providing an uninterrupted view of the cloudless sky above. People took their places in the colourful spiral on the marble floor, holding hands to form a long, coiled chain.

Joe scanned the room. No sign of his contact. He took Lucy's hand and that of his unknown neighbour. Surrounded by tall people, there was nowhere to look but up at the sky and the high white walls. The hubbub died down. All was still.

A single voice at the centre began to sing. Vertical text in different colours scrolled down the walls and, as it did so, people started singing different choral parts, one circle after another joining the soaring melody. An old favourite; Joe knew it by heart. He waited for the text matching the floor colour under his feet to appear, then launched confidently into his rich baritone, head back, eyes closed, worries momentarily forgotten. Above them, the blue sky gave way to dusk, stars pin-pricking the twilight one by one. By the time the choir stopped, night had fallen: the only light coming from a myriad of stars.

The dark mass of bodies was briefly silent, then low-level lighting flickered on and the sound of chatter filled the hall. Lucy and Felix were smiling from ear to ear, slightly overwhelmed by the intense experience, Joe suspected. Through the crowd he spotted a blue-robed figure approaching. Ah, there she was.

Dalian lowered her hood, uncovering long white hair braided in complex twists. How long did it take her to get ready in the morning? They bowed to each other, and Joe introduced Lucy and Felix.

'This is Councillor Dalian, Syenitia's Defence Minister. She welcomes you to Essoona. You don't have to say anything – she doesn't speak English – just smile and bow.'

He switched to Syenitian. 'Good evening, my lady. To

what do I owe the honour of this meeting? I was astonished when your secretary approached me.'

'I might be in a position to assist you, Captain Llewellyn. It has come to my attention that you seek alternative employment.'

Fuck. How did she know that? A spy at the bathhouse? Was that why Aldeman had been so unforthcoming? Had he suspected an eavesdropper?

'My career aspirations are a private matter, my lady. May I enquire how you acquired this information?'

He knew she wouldn't answer, but it was worth asking.

'We are having difficulties in the Quturjuuk system. They are suffering from repeated Ranglatiri raids and need more permanent assistance with their defences. I am seeking volunteers for a support garrison. In particular, a commander. Are you interested?'

Well, yes, thought Joe. Right up my street. She must know that. But what was her game? It wasn't her usual style, this direct approach.

'I'm contractually bound for the next twelve months, my lady.'

'But afterwards?'

'I'd like to see more details before making any commitments, my lady.'

'You shall have them. I bid you a good evening.'

They bowed again, and she departed in a swish of velvet.

8. NO RISK, NO FUN
LUCY

T HEY FILED BACK out to the square, now illuminated by lights set into the flagstones. 'Right, we'd better be off,' said Joe. 'Stay close and don't get lost.' He led them behind the square into a maze of twisting streets which got narrower and darker by the minute. Lucy began to feel nervous. She couldn't see many Syenitians; most people seemed to be aliens of some kind. Like her. Where was Joe taking them?

Before she could ask, Joe ducked down an alleyway and drew back a thick, brown curtain, which hung in a semicircle protruding onto the street. In front of them, another brown curtain completed the circle. They pushed their way through and emerged in a low-ceilinged, no-frills drinking establishment. White paper lanterns gave off a soft light, making the nooks and crannies at the edges seem all the darker.

Out of the thirty or so people Lucy could see, only a couple were native Syenitians. Joe led them past the bar to a table at the back, where they had a good view of the rest of the pub and the entrance. Music played in the background, but Lucy couldn't hear it properly over the babble of voices.

'This is the Nakymaton bar,' said Joe. 'It's one of my favourites, because no one looks at you twice, wherever you come from. Essoona isn't as cosmopolitan as Aldina, but it does have a large spaceport, so there are always people from all over passing through. It gets a bit rough sometimes, but you'll be safe with me.'

'Where is Aldina?' asked Felix.

'Three hundred kilometres up the coast. It's Syenitia's second city, where they do all the shipbuilding. Historically, they built ships for the sea, but nowadays it's mostly spacecraft.'

The waiter came and Joe ordered *saiju* all round. This time it came in a pot, with little handleless cups.

'The Syenitians have a strong naval tradition,' said Joe. 'Syenitia is mostly water, separated into two oceans by a narrow band of land running all around the planet. There aren't many other landmasses, apart from some remote islands. The east coast is the most populated, that's where we are now. The west coast is more of a backwater because access to it is blocked by a ridge of mountains.

'Syenitia is smaller than Earth and further away from a sun, so their years are longer. That's why they're so tall – they have less gravity. There's a flip side to that: humans are stronger because our muscles have developed to overcome more gravity.'

While listening, Lucy observed the rest of the pub's clientele. On several tables they were playing a game with small bowls of marbles arranged in a circle. As she watched, the entrance curtain twitched and a cloaked figure entered the bar, the person's face obscured by a deep hood. The figure approached their table with confident strides.

Joe grinned and stood up. 'Lucy, Felix, I'd like you to meet a good friend of mine. This is Aldeman.'

Long, pale fingers appeared from the folds of dark green fabric and pulled down the hood. Lucy took in a clean-shaven, square-jawed face with a humorous mouth and turquoise eyes under fine dark eyebrows. His ears were pointed, like the other Syenitians she'd seen that afternoon, and his black hair was scraped back into a thick plait that reached his waist. Lucy guessed he was around the same age as Joe.

'*Hei, Pikkuveli!*' He greeted Joe by holding his hands up vertically, at right angles to his outstretched arms, palms facing outwards. Joe lifted his arms in the same way, and they touched hands while maintaining eye contact. Lucy noticed they each wore a plain white ring on their right thumbs.

Aldeman removed his cloak and placed it neatly over the back of the chair next to Lucy's. Underneath, he wore a simple grey woollen tunic over a midnight-blue shirt. The overall impression was expensive yet understated; aristocracy attempting to travel incognito.

'Newlings!' he said, bowing solemnly to Felix and Lucy. 'Welcome to Essoona.'

He smiled, with a mischievous glint in his eyes. Lucy had a flash of intuition that this man was both charming and dangerous.

'How are you finding your first trip away from your planet?'

Lucy and Felix answered simultaneously.

'Amazing!'

'Awesome!'

They told him about what they'd seen and done so far and ended up talking about the graffiti.

'But it is not graffiti as you know it, is it?' said Aldeman. '*Maalaus* are a constitutional right of expression: to communicate ideas and emotions through the medium of painting. Children are taught it at school. Your public art is created by corporations trying to sell things. Is that better than an individual expressing their opinion?'

They were interrupted by the waiter bringing mugs of beer and a dish piled high with crispy-fried insects. Lucy shuddered as Aldeman and Joe attacked them with gusto, eating them by the handful as if they were crisps or peanuts.

'You two not want any?' asked Joe with a wink, a leg poking out of the corner of his mouth.

Aldeman laughed. 'Try one, they are tastier than they look.'

Felix rose to the challenge first. 'It's not that bad, actually,' he told Lucy. 'Kind of crunchy and salty.' He pushed the bowl towards Lucy.

Trying not to think about what she was doing, Lucy picked up one of the cricket-like creatures and put it quickly in her mouth. Felix was right, they weren't bad at all. They had a kind of nutty, shrimpy flavour. She reached for another one.

'So, what you do for a living, Aldeman?' she asked, trying to change the subject away from insect eating.

He leaned towards her conspiratorially. In a low voice he said, 'What do you think I do?'

Was he flirting with her? Teasing her?

'Um. I have absolutely no idea. Don't take this the

wrong way, but you don't strike me as the respectable upstanding citizen type.' She guessed wildly. 'Are you perhaps some kind of space pirate? Or a secret agent for the Syenitian government?'

Aldeman threw back his head, roaring with laughter as if this was the funniest of jokes. '*He* is the pirate,' he said, pointing at Joe. 'Come on Joe, show us what monstrosities you are carrying today.'

Sheepishly, Joe extracted a small but mean-looking weapon from a holster at the base of his spine and put it on the table.

'What's that?' asked Felix.

'Plasma gun,' said Aldeman. 'Standard space cowboy equipment. And this is supposed to be a weapons-free establishment! What else are you hiding, little brother?'

Sighing, Joe pulled an opalescent blue knife from the shaft of his boot. A pair of intertwined snakes formed the handle, which glinted in the soft light.

'And?'

A set of knuckledusters and a short stick emerged from the pocket in the front of Joe's hoodie. He held the stick horizontally above the table and pressed a button at the centre. Lucy jumped as the stick rapidly increased in length, growing into a solid-looking staff about two metres long. For all his twinkly charm, it seemed that Joe wasn't someone you wanted to get into an argument with.

'What can I say?' Joe grinned as he swiftly returned each item to its hiding place. 'Old habits die hard.'

'I would report him to the authorities, but Joe and his little collection there have saved my skin more times than I like to think about.'

'Have you known each other long?' enquired Lucy.

'He's my brother-in-law,' said Joe. 'That's why his English is so good. He's one of the few Syenitians who speak an Earth language.'

'So, is that what those rings are on your thumbs? Wedding rings?'

'You don't miss much, do you?' chuckled Joe, draining his beer and signalling to the waiter for another one.

'Are you married to a Syenitian, Joe? Or is he married to a human?' asked Felix, nodding at Aldeman. Joe smiled and said nothing.

Information dead end, thought Lucy. Perhaps she could ask again when he'd had a bit more to drink. She turned to Aldeman, determined to discover something useful.

'So what do the Syenitians want from the Earth?'

'I am sure Kitty explained what the Galaksi Alliance wants from humankind. Knowledge transfer and trade. And the hope that humans might help spread peace through the galaxy one day.'

Some hope, thought Lucy. Interesting he knows Kitty. Did he work with Joe as well as being related to him?

Felix said, 'So, if you can all teleport everywhere, why do you need spaceships?'

'We can't all teleport everywhere,' said Joe. 'Anyway, it's no good for transporting a lot of stuff at once. Only those involved with the *Shantivira* know about teleportation. You need a demon to make it work, and most Syenitians think demons are an ancient myth. Kitty and Rowan prefer to keep it that way. If Kitty goes too far away from the Earth, the teleports on the *Shantivira* stop working. Inconvenient for the staff, but the space station is still operational.'

'Who's Rowan?' asked Felix. 'Is Kitty a demon?'

'Kitty and Rowan are twins,' said Aldeman. 'Their mother was a Syenitian like me, in fact, her family are ancestors of mine. Their father was a space spirit. The sisters are a unique half-breed, able to move through space and modulate their size and shape at will. In their original forms they are several hundred metres high. We call them demons for want of a proper scientific name. Our archives are extensive, but there are no other recorded cases of space spirit hybrids with any species.'

'What's a space spirit?' said Felix.

'What do they eat?' said Lucy simultaneously, remembering what the man on the train had said.

Aldeman paused. 'Two questions, one answer. The universe was created with a certain quantity of life energy. As gravity pulled matter together to form stars and planets, some of this life energy coalesced into celestial spirits. These developed consciousness and roamed the universe, unaffected by radiation, lack of gravity, or the vacuum of space.

'Over time, life energy mixed with matter. As it became concentrated on planets, there was less of it freely available in space. Now the spirits had to compete with each other to feed. The survivors of these battles were those who discovered they could absorb their opponent's life energy by taking a physical form.

'Space spirits are gigantic: many hundreds of metres long. And once they become corporeal, they cannot go back to existing as pure energy. They are able to change shape and travel through space as easily as before, but their bodily manifestation is permanent.

'As they exist singly and perpetually, they have no language or society, no rules of behaviour, no sexual impulses. When two space spirits meet, there is no motivation for them to cooperate. Instead, they fight bitterly over territory: planets with life forms they can feed on. Their battles rage for years on end, devastating those planets like a natural disaster.'

Lucy interrupted, 'So you're saying Kitty and her sister have to absorb people's *life energy* to live?'

'Well,' said Joe, scratching his stubble, 'they could make do with less complex beings, even plants, but they would need a lot more of them. They minimise the destruction they cause by feeding from large sapient creatures.'

'People,' reiterated Lucy.

Joe nodded. 'People. Whales. Elephants. People are best, apparently.'

'What happens to them? Do they die?'

'No!' said Joe, clearly shocked by the suggestion. 'Kitty and Rowan generally try to absorb a tiny amount from lots of people – in crowds, for example – then nobody even notices.'

'And if they don't do it that way?' Lucy persisted.

Joe examined his fingernails. 'Well, if they lose their self-control, they could – theoretically – keep going until there's nothing left of you. But I've known Kitty for more than thirty years and I've never seen her go all the way like that.'

That doesn't mean it doesn't happen, thought Lucy. If

I were going to kill someone, I'd make damn sure I didn't have an audience. So it's true. The AAL were right all along. Shit.

'So, rule number one is: don't annoy the demons,' said Felix, who appeared to be having second thoughts for the first time. 'But I don't get it,' he said, turning to Aldeman. 'How did your ancestor get together with a great big space spirit? How would that even work?'

'Ah,' said Aldeman, smiling. '*The Princess and the Dragon* is a classic Syenitian fairy story. Every child knows it. Would you like to hear it?'

Lucy and Felix nodded.

'Many thousands of years ago, our planet was plagued by a space spirit in the form of a black dragon they called Ahmitor the Desecrator. Ahmitor travelled widely, absorbing the life energy of countless other space spirits. For entertainment, he started experimenting with changing his shape to blend in with other life forms, becoming fascinated by the societies and civilisations around him. In a smaller body he needed far less life energy, meaning he stopped laying waste to his surroundings.

'Ahmitor also experienced language for the first time. Space spirits are like babies, unable to articulate anything except on the most basic level. They can only roar using infrasound, triggering earthquakes and tsunamis. Learning Syenitian enabled him to structure his thoughts and feelings more clearly.

'To study the Syenitians in greater detail, Ahmitor decided to follow one individual and try to understand her life. He chose young Princess Estrelan, spending most of his time in a male Syenitian form so he could get close to her. The longer he spent as a Syenitian, the more the physiology of our species affected him. He fell in love with her, without understanding what love was.

'In turn, this strange, intense person entranced Estrelan. He was a breath of fresh air among the stifling rituals and traditions of the Royal Household. She wanted to have adventures, but all she could see on her horizon was an arranged marriage and thousands of years living in the same place, surrounded by the same people.

'Ahmitor became her secret friend who would pop up out of nowhere, telling her about far away worlds and the beings who lived there. Eventually, he plucked up his courage and revealed his true form, staying small enough to fit into her bedchamber.

'Terrified, Estrelan screamed at him to leave and never return. Then, seeing how this saddened him, she saw past the beast and recognised her friend. She kissed him on the nose, apologising. "I trust you," she said. "Show me the worlds you spoke of."

'When the King and Queen learnt of Estrelan's plans to travel the universe, they were horrified and forbade her to go. Refused his heart's desire, anger overwhelmed Ahmitor and he reverted to his original monstrous form, terrorising the inhabitants of the city. Estrelan persuaded him to stop and they left in a hurry.

'The King and Queen told everyone that she had sacrificed herself to save them all from the dragon and the whole country went into mourning. Blissfully ignorant of this, Estrelan and Ahmitor travelled happily for hundreds of years.

'To their amazement and joy, Estrelan became pregnant and gave birth to twins. The Syenitian form Ahmitor used almost permanently had given him both the urge and the ability to procreate. However, they did not realise that once a space spirit has offspring, it is no longer immortal. Such is the balance of nature.

'The sisters were humanoid, but not identical. Red-haired Rowan had green scales and was calm and patient like her mother. Black-haired Kitvian had red scales and took after her more volatile father. In their birth form, both had their father's sparkling eyes, agile tail, black claws and predator's jaws, although neither of them had inherited his wings. They grew to be about half Ahmitor's original size, although they preferred to remain Syenitian-height like their parents. The twins were brought up believing it was wrong to kill, and wasteful too, since if the person or animal stayed alive, they could continue supplying life energy.

'Estrelan wanted her daughters to learn the ways of her own people. So they returned to Syenitia, only to find another space spirit rapidly wiping out the population. Estrelan's people were holed up in the castle, waiting for the end. After an emotional family reunion, Ahmitor went out to meet the enemy, reverting to his dragon form on the plain in front of the castle.

'The battle raged back and forth across the planet like a hurricane. Ahmitor defeated the usurper but was severely wounded. He had no idea that, because he was a father, he was no longer invulnerable. Before he could get back to the castle, his injuries overcame him and he fell down dead, turning to stone as space spirits do when they die. And that is the end of the fairy story part.'

'So, if they're your ancestors, are you a member of the Royal family?' Lucy asked.

Aldeman chuckled. 'Syenitia became a republic more than ten thousand years ago. So no, I am not.'

'Is the stone space spirit still there?' said Felix.

'Yes,' said Joe. 'Ahmitor's body became a hill, famous as a sacred healing spot. A space spirit is a concentration of life energy: when it dies, the energy leaches back into the surroundings. The excess life energy has gone now, but the spot is still full of tourists searching for inner harmony through the healing power of crystals and the like.'

He didn't say the words 'credulous fools' out loud, but Lucy read them in his expression.

'What happened next?' she asked.

'Kitvian and Rowan stayed with the Syenitians initially,' said Aldeman. 'But the population had been so diminished, it could not support them for long. They left separately, seeking adventure. They never lost touch because they have a telepathic connection that works across any distance.

'Rowan eventually returned to Syenitia, to defend the inhabitants from potential threats. The few modern-day Syenitians who know about her call her Verndari, which means "Protector". But Kitvian, or Kitty, as she prefers nowadays, roamed wild for many thousands of years until she settled permanently on your planet. On Syenitia she is known as Reika, or "Wanderer".'

'They try to live according to the Syenitian moral code,' said Joe. 'But everyone messes up sometimes. Kitty has learnt the hard way that doing bad things makes you unhappy. She says the only way to stay sane and happy long-term is to get involved in the lives of those around you and try to help them. Ah, here's our food.'

Thoughtfully, Lucy attacked her bowl of fried noodles topped with chunks of an unfamiliar sea creature. She noticed Felix struggling with his chopsticks, so she showed him how to hold the lower chopstick still and only move the top one.

'Why did she choose the Earth?' she asked Joe.

'The abundant life, initially,' said Joe. 'Then she befriended a Welsh boy and became involved in human society through him.'

'You?' said Lucy.

'No!' laughed Joe. 'This was back when the Romans were leaving Britain. Before my time. Emrys, his name was. Better known to us as Merlin Ambrosius, or Merlin the Magician.'

Lucy spluttered and threw down her chopsticks. 'You're not serious! That King Arthur stuff is just fantasy!'

'Like the story I just told you?' said Aldeman.

'This was long before Arthur was even born,' said Joe. 'Emrys freed her from imprisonment and discovered they had a telepathic link.'

Aldeman said, 'The ability to reach a demon's mind without speech is as rare as – what is that expression you use, Joe?'

'As rare as hens' teeth. She was basically feral after her years underground. He tamed her. Got her to promise she would protect his people forever.'

'Imprisonment?' said Felix.

'"The Tale of Lludd and Llefelys",' said Joe. 'Look it

up. They married, but kept their relationship hidden. She was too wild for conventional society, let alone Emrys' noble family. Some stories refer to her as Morgan le Fay.'

'Oh,' said Lucy. 'That makes sense, I suppose.'

'When Emrys died, she gave up trying to pass as human and has lived in secret ever since. But that oath she swore: that's why we're sitting here now. As our technology advanced, Kitty realised she couldn't protect her adopted planet without help. So she approached the Syenitians to set up the *Shantivira*.'

Lucy tried to digest this. Kitty must be very old. What about the Syenitians? She tried to formulate the question politely.

'So if Kitty and her sister are thousands of years old, how long do normal Syenitians live?'

'Well,' said Aldeman, 'our years are different to yours, but around two thousand years would be considered a natural life expectancy.'

'So how old are you then,' said Felix, 'if you don't mind me asking?'

'I was 1043 last birthday. How old are you, Felix?'

'Er, I'm twenty-five years young,' murmured Felix.

'What's it like, living so long?' said Lucy.

'We live through every day, as you do. But we have a different perspective. We see that nothing is permanent, that change is inevitable. We understand that to survive in the long term, we must abide by the Code of Harmony. Wealth, possessions and territory are not as important to us as they seem to be for you. Excess is detrimental. We value the acquisition of knowledge above all.

'On the other hand, we are slow to adapt to new situations and change our attitudes. Your short lifespan is the great advantage of your species. Look at what you have accomplished in the past three hundred years! Think what you could achieve in the *next* three hundred! Your rapid generational turnover makes change easier to bring about.'

Lucy wasn't sure she agreed. Having recently finished reading a book on the history of the British in the Middle East, she felt that if only people remembered what had happened the last time around, atrocious mistakes could be avoided.

'What's the Code of Harmony?' said Felix.

Aldeman thought for a moment. 'It is our moral framework, acquired, refined and handed down through generations. The collective memory of the Syenitians, analogous to your religions. We do not believe in any gods. But the Code of Harmony is based on the premise that all life is sacred. It instructs us how to behave to avoid making ourselves and those around us unhappy. Its aim is the well-being and continuation of the species.

'The Code is more important than the law. You can even use it as a defence in court: breaking the law is preferable to breaking the Code of Harmony.'

'So if you don't believe in any gods, what do you think happens when you die?' said Felix.

'Well, that is the big question, is it not? We say we "return to the source". The individual no longer exists, but our atoms and molecules go on to be used elsewhere: in the air, the soil and the sea around us. That is why life is sacred – because it is so fragile and each one is unique. It can end at any moment; it must be nurtured and protected. But when we die, we do not cease to exist, we simply exist differently. We are always part of the universe in some form.'

An urgent bleeping interrupted them. Aldeman glanced at his *zana* and groaned. 'I am afraid I must leave you. There is somewhere else I need to be.'

He stood up and so did Joe, who muttered something in Aldeman's ear as he helped him with his cloak. Aldeman's expression darkened and he murmured a reply Lucy didn't understand. Then, all smiles again, he bowed to Lucy and Felix. 'It was a pleasure to meet you both. I hope to see you again someday.' In a swirl of green, he was across the room and disappearing through the brown curtain.

'What were you talking about just then?' Felix asked Joe.

'Oh, only that the meal is on him and confirming our session at the baths this week.'

He's lying, thought Lucy. That exchange was too intense to be something so mundane. What's he hiding?

'Before we head back, is there anything you'd like to ask me? We won't get the chance to talk much tomorrow.'

'Do any Earth governments or official organisations know about the *Shantivira*?' said Felix.

'Officially? No. But there are around six hundred ex-Shantivirans, many of whom have worked their way into senior positions in civil services around the world, and particularly in the UN.' He looked up at them. 'That's what we're really asking of you, see? The pilot training is to tempt you to join us. I mean, we need pilots, but we could recruit them from anywhere in the Alliance. We don't, because we think humans should defend their own planet, and because the fewer aliens who know about the Earth the better.

'But our long-term objective is to train diplomats and intermediaries who speak Kawaida and know how the Galaksi Alliance works. Well-connected people capable of representing Earth on the galactic stage. So after your five years' service, if you're willing, the Alliance will invest significant effort into getting you into positions of influence. It wants to be ready for official first contact, whenever that happens.'

Oh my God, thought Lucy. So the alien invasion has already started! Using indoctrinated human pawns! This was far worse than she'd guessed. The Galaksi Alliance had secret tentacles of influence across the Earth and nobody knew! Did the AAL know? Why was Joe being so up front about it?

'There's an envelope in the office safe at UNOOSA in Vienna which has "To be opened in the event of extraterrestrial contact" written on it. That explains about the Alliance and gives a list of contacts to approach. So you could say the Earth will be informed on a need-to know-basis.'

'Don't they have a right to know now?'

Joe looked Lucy in the eye. 'You're not comfortable with this, are you? Good. Neither am I. Why do you think I'm telling you all this? But explain to me how *you* would do it without starting a mass panic? I'm convinced the Earth's long-term survival depends on cooperation with the Alliance planets. People back home have no idea about what's out there. If you join the *Shantivira*, you'll be better placed to understand the choices open to us humans.'

'If I do,' said Lucy slowly, hoping that by voicing her innermost fears she would fail the assessment and solve her dilemma in one stroke, 'I'm worried…I'll have to kill people.' After the flight training today, she thought to herself, I'm also worried I might be good at it. Enjoy it, even. What kind of person does that make me? 'You hear a lot about soldiers suffering from PTSD. I don't want to end up like that.'

'You're not worried about being killed yourself?' said Felix.

'A bit. But I'm more concerned about not being able to live with myself because of my experiences. And I'm worried I'll be ordered to do things I disagree with. My dad was in the military. I know how it works. Once you join, they own you. What happens to pilots who don't cooperate, Joe?'

Joe gave a thin smile. 'Well, that depends on the circumstances, doesn't it? I can't say I was the most obedient recruit ever, but they still made me captain. Look. The *Shantivira* is nothing like the military on Earth. I was in the army myself – that was much tougher. We don't own you; we employ you. It's a job. You do your hours, you get paid and we treat you fairly. If you want to leave, you can. That said, we must be able to trust each other or the whole operation falls apart. If we're not convinced we can rely on you, you won't get through the training. And if someone gets hurt because of your disobedience, there will be hell to pay. That's a promise.'

'So,' said Felix, 'what are the chances of aliens invading the Earth?'

'You've put your finger on it there, Felix. I mean, it

could change any moment – that's why we're here – but there's not been much action in the last forty years. The *Shantivira* is more like the border police in a remote province. Our focus is on preventing incidents: communication, persuasion and negotiation are always what we try first, and usually that's enough. Our pilots spend most of their time dematerialising space debris. Apart from that, not a single shot has been fired since I've been in charge.'

Was that a note of wistfulness in Joe's voice?

ON THE WAY back, they took a transport pod instead of the tram. As it glided through the streets under its own guidance, Joe leant back in his seat and asked, 'What did you think of the singing?'

'It was beautiful,' said Lucy.

'I nearly cried,' admitted Felix. 'I've never felt like that before, not even singing in church at people's weddings.'

'Yeah,' said Joe, 'it gets me like that too. I miss it if I can't go for a while.'

Felix wanted to know more about the Syenitians. 'What else is different about their society?'

'Well,' said Joe, 'let me think. They're very big on self-improvement. And they're more egalitarian than we are. The rich aren't very rich by our standards. Rather than pursuing growth, their economy is circular, structured specifically to prevent inequality and social tension. All meaningful work is important, and service to the community even more so.

'The government sees people and their creativity as almost infinite assets, unlike finite resources like minerals or metals. Businesses are taxed on the physical resources they use, not on the people they employ. That way, reserves are used sparingly, and there are more jobs to go round. Profits are shared directly with the local communities by law, which means taxes are actually much lower than you'd expect.

'The route to power and status is through knowledge, not wealth. There aren't any corporations with shareholders, only employee-owned collectives.' He laughed. 'I tried explaining the stock market to Aldeman once. He's one of the cleverest people I know, but he couldn't understand the principle of making money out of money, or why people would even want to do that.' Joe imitated Aldeman's voice, '"But what's the point? How can that bring them happiness and inner harmony? They will only spread misery, surely?"'

Felix and Lucy laughed.

'But it *is* a capitalist economy?' said Felix, ever the business studies graduate. 'The government doesn't try to control everything? It's not communism?'

'Oh no,' said Joe. 'This is the easiest place in the galaxy to start a business. Why do you think Syenitia's so rich? Decisions are delegated to the lowest possible level. Regional governments only pass on a small portion of their income to the planetary government. The planetary government is responsible for defence, extra-planetary trade, and not much else. Even healthcare and education are organised locally.'

'And they're free?' guessed Felix.

'Of course,' confirmed Joe. 'And everyone gets a basic payment to cover the cost of living, so people can pursue their own interests.'

'UBI?' asked Lucy, who had read about this concept but wasn't convinced. 'Surely that means people just end up doing nothing? Or wouldn't the payments just increase the cost of housing by the same amount?'

Joe shook his head. 'In cities, and most people here live in cities, at least two-thirds of housing is rent-controlled social housing. Including Dunia House.'

Lucy was surprised. It had seemed far too grand to fit with her idea of a council house.

'Everyone does something: paid, voluntary or a mixture of both,' said Joe. 'The social pressure to contribute is very strong.'

'You said regional governments,' said Felix. 'Aren't there any separate countries on Syenitia?'

'They haven't had nation states for thousands of years,' said Joe. 'There is one official language, although there are many regional languages which people still use at home. It's a bit like Welsh and English. The only people I speak Welsh with nowadays are my mother and my wife.'

'Is your wife Welsh?' asked Lucy.

'She considers herself a naturalised citizen,' said Joe.

In Lucy's brain, a puzzle piece clicked into place. Someone had said something like that to her recently. 'It's Kitty, isn't it? Your wife?' Another piece slotted in next to it. 'So Aldeman, your brother-in-law, is married to her sister, right? Bloody hell!'

'Isn't that terribly dangerous, given what you told us earlier?' asked Felix with a mixture of curiosity and awe.

'No risk, no fun, Felix,' Joe winked. 'No risk, no fun.'

9. THE EARTH DEFENCE SOCIETY

LUCY

O N THE TRAIN home the next afternoon, an unknown man approached Lucy. She'd half-expected it, had mentally prepared herself for another unpleasant confrontation. There was just one of them this time, younger and less intimidating. About the same height as Lucy and not much older, he wore ripped jeans and a grey hooded top under a leather jacket.

'Excuse me, is this seat taken?' he asked courteously, indicating the seat across from her.

Lucy shook her head, examining him critically. She'd already noticed him from behind on the platform, but hadn't given him a second thought apart from the casual once-over she gave everyone who crossed her path. Her verdict: nice arse, bit trendy, bulky upper body suggested hours in the gym which, combined with the expensive trainers, indicated a streak of vanity.

'I'm Charlie from the EDS,' he said, leaning forward and offering Lucy his hand to shake. His features were Chinese, but his accent was American. 'How was your weekend?'

'Fine, thanks,' she said. 'What's the EDS?'

Charlie appeared confused.

'Ma'am, um, you *are* Lucy Cooper?'

Lucy nodded again.

'Thank God for that! I thought I had the wrong person! The Earth Defence Society. Three of my colleagues approached you last weekend?'

'They called themselves the Anti-Alien League.'

Charlie frowned. 'They did? That's interesting.' After a moment's silence he said, 'The aim of the Earth Defence Society is to enable humankind to defend itself against extra-terrestrial threats, without us having to rely on...third parties. But there is a faction in our organisation with different priorities. Nestor and his buddies hate any intelligent life which isn't human.'

'Nestor? The wrinkly Spanish guy?'

'Argentinian,' corrected Charlie with a smile. 'He's a founder member of the EDS.'

'Why does he hate aliens so much?'

'If I ever find out, I'll let you know. My job is to report back what you tell me. I'll be your contact if you're accepted on the *Shantivira* programme. So, how did it go?'

Lucy studied his face. How much should she say? She felt more inclined to trust him than the goons from last weekend. And she needed to share her misgivings with someone.

'The flying was OK. But the exam this morning was really hard. And they're not stupid, they'll have seen I had serious reservations. What will happen to my parents if I don't get in?'

'What do you mean, what will happen to your parents? *Should* anything happen to them?'

'Your...colleagues...threatened them, if I refused to cooperate.'

'They *what*?' Charlie buried his face in his hands and simulated a sob. 'Oh Lord. What must you think of us? I'll make sure our leader gets to hear of this, don't you worry.'

Lucy's stomach unclenched, ever so slightly. 'You mean, they're not in danger, even if I fail the assessment?'

'Not from the EDS, that's not the way we do things. We'll keep a closer eye on Nestor from now on. I'd understand, though, if you didn't want anything more to do with us. If you want to walk away, you can.'

Now she no longer felt cornered, Lucy found it easy to come to a decision. 'If I get in,' she said, 'and I don't know if I will, then I'll be your spy.'

'You will? That's awesome!' Charlie's face split into a broad grin. He was really quite attractive, Lucy thought. Perhaps spying wouldn't be so bad after all.

'How did they know to approach me last week?'

'Pure luck. One of your housemates mentioned the black cat that's been visiting you to a colleague of hers. The colleague is part of our network and flagged it up to us. We monitored you and your housemates until it became clear who Kitty's target was. I'm sorry we invaded your privacy, but it was a unique chance to get someone on the inside.' He leaned forward, his hands clasped as if in prayer. 'You're our only hope, Lucy. We have no other way of finding out what the Syenitians are up to.'

The train slowed and Lucy saw they were approaching the station. Charlie noticed too. 'Shit! We're already there, and I haven't asked you half the stuff I'm supposed to! Can we grab something to eat?'

Right on cue, Lucy's stomach rumbled. Lunch had been a long time ago in an orbit far, far away.

'All right,' she said.

She led Charlie to a tiny, candlelit Italian restaurant, tucked away behind a church. He was visibly charmed and repeatedly used the word 'awesome'.

'Where are you from, Charlie?'

'San Francisco.'

'Do you have a surname?'

'Not one I'm going to tell you. Sorry.'

'Is Charlie your real name?'

Charlie smiled apologetically and said nothing.

'How much do you already know about the *Shantivira*?' she asked.

'A bit. Why don't you tell me what you found out this weekend?'

'OK. Well, I'm sure you know this already, but I was surprised when I found out it was true: Kitty *does* eat people. I mean, she feeds off people...'

'Their life energy, yes.'

'I get the impression that she's dangerous but not evil, does that make sense?'

'She's lethal, from what I've heard. Nestor's terrified of her.'

'But she's married to a human: to the captain of the *Shantivira*.'

'She is? Who's that?'

'Joe Llewellyn. Ex-British army. Maybe one of the Welsh regiments. I'd love to know more about his background. Could you find out? From what I saw, he's very cosy with the Syenitians. He had a chat with the Syenitian Defence Minister and then we ate with his brother-in-law, a guy called Aldeman.'

Charlie choked on his Chianti. After his coughing fit

subsided, he said, 'Aldeman Varpushaukka? Black hair? Blue-green eyes?'

'He never told us his surname,' said Lucy, intrigued by Charlie's reaction. 'Or what he did for a living.' Lucy remembered how cleverly Aldeman had side-stepped her direct question. At the time, she hadn't even noticed.

'If it's the Aldeman we know about, he's the leader of the Syenitian Planetary Council and the individual ultimately responsible for the *Shantivira*. Llewellyn's boss. You were being interviewed.'

Jesus! The shifty bugger! 'He was very charming,' she said. 'Funny, from Joe's behaviour, I sort of thought the Defence Minister lady was his boss.'

'Can you remember her name?' asked Charlie.

Lucy shook her head. 'Sorry.'

Charlie leaned back in his chair, cradling his wine glass. 'So,' he said slowly, 'the current captain of the *Shantivira* is related by marriage to one of the most influential people in the galaxy. That is extremely interesting. Thank you, Lucy.'

After their pasta arrived, Lucy remembered what she'd learnt about former Shantivirans being propelled into positions of power and becoming agents for the Galaksi Alliance. Charlie seemed strangely unsurprised.

'I'd love to get hold of a list of those people.'

'That's not something they'd leave lying around.'

'I know.' Charlie's eyes glinted covetously in the dim light. 'But imagine how useful it would be.'

They talked quietly until the restaurant emptied and staff started clearing up around them. Time to go. Most of Charlie's questions had been about Syenitian technology:

weaponry and power sources in particular.

He insisted on walking her home, but not all the way to the door 'just in case'. Lucy had the strangest sensation that they'd been on a date rather than a business meeting. Perhaps the wine was affecting her judgement, but she felt closer to Charlie than she ought to, considering she'd only met him hours ago.

'Well, good luck,' he said, as they parted. 'When you hear – either way – use a magnet to fix a note to the inside of your car's left-front wheel arch. Someone will check it every couple of days when you're at work.'

'Can't I just send you a text?'

Charlie shook his head. 'We use dead drops and paper. Sometimes we can post letters. Anything electronic could be intercepted by the *Shantivira's* main computer. He'll be watching you now. Did you see him? Big guy with long brown hair and a beard?'

Lucy's eyes widened. The man in the control room! 'He's a *computer*?'

'Ex-combat cyborg. Delius, they call him. Used to control entire fleets of battleships, but he's long been superseded by more advanced models. He must be around four hundred years old now. The *Shantivira* is his retirement gig; he came here because he wanted new input. He runs the space station and monitors Earth's communications. He uploads everything he learns to the main server in Essoona. You know, the Library you saw, in Kirjasto Square. They didn't tell you about *him*, did they?'

10. BEST SERVED COLD
HANNA

HANNA SIGHED. ANOTHER rejection letter. So far, her attempts to study fashion were a resounding failure. Getting onto a course without any qualifications was impossible. They wanted A Level and GCSE certificates, portfolios of work, there was fierce competition – and the fees were utterly terrifying, whatever reassurances Mary and Irion offered her. She was hyper-conscious of the weeks passing. It was October already and the leaves were turning, like an amber warning. She had to find something before her six-month visa expired, or – if she didn't want to break the law and risk being deported – she'd have to return to Ethiopia and start her life over from scratch, alone.

She'd considered trying to get an entry-level job in the industry or selling her creations on the internet, but even with a dubious 'Dunia School of Language' student visa, she couldn't work more than ten hours a week or set up her own business. Was she going to have to catch up on years of schooling before she could even train for a job? What was she going to do with her life?

Ozzy's head poked around the kitchen door. 'Are you ready, Hanna?' Hurriedly, she stuffed the letter in the back pocket of her jeans. She'd completely forgotten: today was Saturday and she was going to learn to ride a bike. Hassan and Ozzy had made a daunting list of all the things she'd never learnt and that they thought she needed, starting with swimming and working up to driving a car. Hanna couldn't imagine a worse place to learn to drive than London, but she'd cross that bridge when she came to it. Ideally without landing in the Thames.

Anyway, she didn't believe they'd get that far before Hassan and the others left for Essoona in January. That was something else she was trying not to think about. Would he forget all about her once he was in the second year?

'Two minutes,' she said. 'I'll get my coat.'

Ten minutes later she was balancing precariously on Ozzy's fancy mountain bike. He'd put the seat all the way down for her, but her feet barely touched the ground. She hadn't expected it to be so uncomfortable. Hassan and Ozzy stayed on either side, wheeling her to Regent's Park. Despite living so close by, she hadn't been back since that night. Was it really only four months ago? It seemed like a different lifetime.

They found a quiet path where she could practise. Again and again, Ozzy jogged behind her, holding the saddle while she wobbled slowly along. This wasn't working. There was no way she'd stay upright if he let go. 'Pedal faster, Hanna!' Hassan yelled from behind them. OK, she thought, let's see how fast Ozzy can run. She accelerated, concentrating hard on keeping the handlebars straight. It *was* easier. She was flying! She squealed with delight.

Hanna turned to see how Ozzy was doing, but he was gone. Confused, she looked back along the path to see him in the distance, bent over with his hands on his knees, panting for breath. Huh? She'd come all that way by herself? As the realisation hit her, the bike bumped over a tree root and she lost her balance. Aaargh! She flew through the air, landing on the grass with a thud that knocked the air out of her lungs. Ow. She struggled up onto her elbows. Hassan and Ozzy were running towards her, still distant. Quickly, she checked herself over. Was she hurt? No. Just winded. A few bruises. Stupid mistake, not looking where she was going. But she'd got it now.

Grinning to herself, Hanna picked up the bike, its wheels still spinning, and remounted. Behind her she could hear Hassan and Ozzy yelling, but she ignored them. She pushed herself off and pedalled, fully focused on the way ahead. She was cycling! She continued along the path with renewed confidence until she reached the canal: familiar territory. Not so long ago, this had been her home.

Slowing down, she looked about. There. That was her bridge. Through the bushes she spotted a sleeping bag. Someone else had adopted her former shelter. Good luck to them. She stared at it for several minutes, thinking. Then she turned the bike around and headed back. There was something she needed to do.

LATER THAT MORNING, she stood on the Ahmeds' doorstep in King's Cross. Rage, terror and desperation came surging back: physical memories, almost paralysing her. She gave herself a mental shake and pressed the buzzer decisively. Time to get closure.

The door opened. An exhausted-looking Mrs Ahmed peered out. She'd obviously put her hijab on in a hurry to answer the door and not checked it in the mirror first. Good. That meant she was home alone; otherwise she'd have sent Mr Ahmed.

'Mrs Ahmed?' said Hanna. 'I don't know if you remember me? My name is Hanna Abebe, I lived here earlier this year? I have something to tell you about your husband.'

Mrs Ahmed frowned and wordlessly opened the door. Hanna walked along the narrow hallway into their private sitting room. She'd never been in here before; it was off-limits for tenants. But she no longer felt intimidated by the Ahmeds. She sat down on the immaculate sofa without waiting to be invited. Mrs Ahmed sat on the other sofa, pointedly not offering Hanna any refreshments.

'What you want?' she asked in her usual charmless manner. Mrs Ahmed had lived in Britain for more than thirty years, but her English was still rubbish.

Here goes, thought Hanna. 'Mr Ahmed. He raped me. And when I became pregnant with his child, he threw me out onto the streets. It was a little boy, by the way.' Hanna was surprised at how unemotional she was. An icy anger had replaced her customary sadness about Samuel.

Mrs Ahmed's anger was anything but icy. She jumped to her feet, exploding in a shrieking torrent of Urdu. Hanna didn't understand a word and sat quietly, waiting for her to calm down.

She knew Mrs Ahmed would deny it to her face and

support her husband in public. But she was as emotionally abusive to her husband as he was physically abusive to his tenants. Hanna had just handed her enough ammunition to make his life a misery for the rest of his days. It was true. Revenge really was best served cold.

Hanna stood up, preparing to leave. Her work here was done. When Mrs Ahmed finally paused for breath she said, 'I won't be asking your husband for money. The child died.' She moved towards the door, but Mrs Ahmed blocked her path.

'You stop! You stop your Voodoo witchcraft right now!'

Hanna took a step back, confused. 'Voodoo? Mrs Ahmed, I'm Ethiopian. I know nothing about Voodoo.'

'Ha!' Mrs Ahmed barked. 'Pretend you don't know. We lose all our tenants because of you. Nobody can sleep here anymore. Mr Ahmed, he scream through the night. He tormented by *Shaitan*. For months and months.'

'What do you mean?' said Hanna.

'He say black cat come. Small, then big. Then change into evil djinn and he terrified. Almost cannot breathe. I never see it, maybe all in his head. Maybe you make him crazy. But we do not sleep. I must sleep. You make the magic go away!'

The penny dropped. Oh. Goodness. Hanna didn't know whether to laugh or be worried. 'I'll tell you what, Mrs Ahmed,' she said, 'I'll see what I can do.' She pushed past the woman and left the house, slamming the door behind her.

Back at the language school, she searched for Hassan. 'He's on the simulators,' called Irion from the kitchen.

'Everything all right, love?'

Hanna didn't stop. She ran down the steps to the basement and burst through the door to the *Shantivira*. On the training deck, she hesitated. Which one of the oversized golf balls was he in? She hunted about until she spotted Hassan's rucksack under one of the pods. She hammered on its door, hopping impatiently from foot to foot. Come on. Come on. There was an abrupt metallic clunk and a sharp hiss as the door lowered.

Hanna bounded up the steps into the cockpit, now partly driven by curiosity. She'd walked past them many times, but she'd never been inside one of the simulators. It was tiny. The only lights came from a bank of controls and the all-round screen which currently showed a frozen close-up of a gigantic space frigate. A surprised Hassan swung his saddle-seat round to face Hanna, his head level with hers.

'I did it! Hassan, I did it!'

'Did what? Hanna, you're not supposed to interrupt people when they're training.'

'Sorry. But I had to tell you. I went back to King's Cross. I told his wife what he did to me. It's weird, like I'm not carrying that burden anymore. Like I handed it over to her. I feel free!'

'How did she take it?'

'Not well. She wasn't shocked about the rape. I bet I wasn't the first. But—'

'But what?'

'Well, you won't believe it. She accused me of witch-craft!' Hanna told Hassan what Mrs Ahmed had said. He held her shoulders and looked at her seriously.

'You have to tell Joe. We have to stop her.'

'Do you think it *was* Kitty? I wondered, because of the cats. But she's not evil. Is she? What was she doing?'

'You do know what Kitty eats, don't you?'

Hanna shook her head. Thinking about it now, she'd never seen Kitty eating anything.

'She's a space demon, Hanna. Her true form is a massive red scaly lizardy-thing. No wonder he thought she was *Shaitan*. When she first arrived on Earth, Kitty wasn't as discreet as she is now. People drew pictures of her and they fed into the traditional image of the devil. A self-fulfilling prophecy, if you like.'

'So what does she eat?' said Hanna.

'The life energy of other creatures. Normally, she controls herself and only takes a little. But if she gets very angry, she can give in to her dark side.' Hassan paused, looking for words. 'You know how a cat plays with its prey before it kills it?'

Hanna nodded, horrified. She'd trusted Kitty instinctively, right from their first meeting. Had she made a terrible mistake?

'Yeah,' said Hassan. 'We have to stop her before she loses it completely. Otherwise she'll become dangerous for the rest of us too.'

'But how?'

'Joe can stop her. He's probably the only person who can.'

'OK. Will you come with me? I'm shy.'

Hassan grinned. 'Sure. Just let me finish my homework,' he said, nodding at the screen.

Hanna stood behind him and watched as he unfroze

the simulation. They were in the middle of a battle, racing along metres above the hull of the frigate for cover. Hassan twisted, ducked, and stretched in a graceful dance of destruction.

Fascinated, Hanna watched incoming enemy fighters get targeted and destroyed in rapid sequence. 'Can I try?' she said, when the screen finally darkened.

Hassan pulled off his helmet. 'Can you remember the commands?'

Hanna nodded eagerly. All that testing Hassan and Ozzy on their flight vocabulary was about to pay off.

'I can only reload the simulation I just did, is that OK?'

'I just want to see what it's like.'

He got up and let Hanna take his place. The helmet was much too big for her, but she tightened the chinstrap and hoped for the best.

As the simulation loaded, Hanna jiggled in her seat, testing its movements. She'd spent enough time talking to the students to know roughly what to expect. She squeaked in surprise and then laughed as the seatbelt fastened itself automatically. And then she was in space. Distant stars sparkled, but otherwise there was nothing much to see. Looking for action, she swivelled round. Hassan sprang out of the way and stood by the sealed doorway. There. What was that?

Leaning forward, she accelerated, aiming for a dot on the horizon. As the dot grew, she practised her moves, twisting and diving in an attempted repeat of Hassan's performance. She approached the frigate in a corkscrew spin to avoid the incoming enemy fire. Then she took a low line so close to the hull she could feel her shields skimming and bumping on the frigate's own shields. Target. Fire. Target. Fire. Target. Fire. She picked off the red-ringed enemy craft in rapid succession, circling the frigate until she could find nothing more to prey on. Easy peasy lemon squeezy. Why did they all make such a fuss about it?

Abruptly, the screen went black. Over so soon? Exhilarated, Hanna removed her helmet and spun round to face Hassan. She wanted to ask if she could have another go, but the look on his face stopped the words dead in her throat. He reached out for her, cupping her head gently but firmly in his long fingers as she stood up. His lips touched hers hesitantly, questioningly, and then, as she pulled him closer, with more intensity. Their tongues met in a moist and curious conversation.

Hanna came up for air first.

'Sorry! I'm so sorry!' Hassan seemed as surprised as she was. 'I don't know what came over me! Are you OK?'

Hanna squeezed his hand and smiled up at him. 'Again,' she said, reaching up and pulling his head down towards hers.

As their lips approached, he asked, 'Was that really your first time? Flying the simulator I mean, not kissing?'

Hanna whispered, 'First flight. First kiss.'

THEY LEFT THE privacy of the pod and went in search of Joe. Grinning and giggling like idiots, they climbed the steps to the *Pride of Essoona* and banged on the door. Hanna took Hassan's hand, suddenly timid. She hadn't had much to do with the captain since Samuel's funeral. The boarding platform lowered and Joe stuck his head out.

'Hello, you two. What's up?'

Hanna followed Hassan and Joe into the living area. It was smaller than she'd thought it would be. And tidier. Neatly appointed with wood panelling, a squashy brown leather sofa and a dark wooden floor softened by a white woollen rug. On closer inspection, she could see the wood panelling behind the sofa disguised an array of drawers with mother-of-pearl handles. A large recessed bookshelf was crammed with ancient-looking books and an impressive collection of single malt whiskies, but Hanna saw no television, games consoles or computing equipment.

The other end of the room contained a row of kitchen units and an oval dining table. One end of the table was covered by a newspaper, spread out at the sports pages, the other end held a bowl of fruit, bananas spotting brown, a pile of neatly folded laundry and various personal items: a wallet, a *zana*, a fountain pen and a small, leather-bound notebook. So far, so domestic, apart from one jaw-dropping feature.

The ceiling and the wall in front of the sofa were wholly transparent, offering a panoramic view of the docking bay. Funny, Hanna thought, she hadn't noticed a window from outside. It was so big, they seemed to be standing on a suspended platform. Hanna peered warily over the edge.

'It's just a screen, Hanna,' said Joe. 'Little cameras on the hull project an image of what's outside – it's more impressive out in space, where you can see the stars. I can use it as a TV or computer screen, or I can switch it off.'

He barked a command and the wall and ceiling became an opaque cream colour. The room was instantly cosier, less like standing on the edge of a cliff.

'Don't want you distracted if you have something important to say,' said Joe, gesturing for them to sit at the table. Hanna briefly related her conversation with Mrs Ahmed. Joe's eyes narrowed as he listened, but he said nothing. When she finished, there was a moment's silence. Joe placed his hands flat on the table and stared at them blankly.

'Mr Ahmed can rot in hell as far as I'm concerned, but it has to stop for Kitty's sake,' he said. 'And for all our safety, mine especially.' He looked up at them. 'You believe it's Kitty, or you wouldn't have come.' It wasn't a question. 'She doesn't intend to kill him, but if she carries on, it will happen. Once she starts going too far, the energy rush is addictive. She hates it, but sometimes she can't help herself. Her life is a constant tightrope walk. If she's slipping, we have to help her snap out of it before it's too late. Thanks for letting me know.'

He stood up and headed for the door, ready to show them out. Hanna got up to follow him, but Hassan didn't stir. He cleared his throat.

'Captain, there's something else.'

Joe returned to the table. 'What would that be, Hassan?'

FIFTEEN MINUTES LATER, Hanna found herself back in a simulator, alone this time, with a helmet that fitted instead of wobbling on her head like an upturned bucket. Joe set her test after test until she was so tired and hungry, she could barely focus. Still, she accepted the challenge and did the best she could.

Finally the door hissed open and Joe stuck his head in. 'Come to the canteen and have something to eat.'

Hanna stepped out of the pod on shaky legs. 'Where's Hassan?' she asked, looking around.

'Sent him home hours ago,' answered Joe. 'I want to talk to you by yourself.'

'How's your career in fashion going?' he asked, once they'd collected plates of fish curry. Hanna gathered her thoughts, trying not to get sidetracked by the view out of the window. What was this about?

'Not great. But it's early days, there's still time to find a place on a course.'

'And you're sure that's what you want to do with your life?'

Hanna began to see – to hope – where this might be going. 'Well, we have to make the most of the talents God gives us, right?'

'Yes,' said Joe. 'I agree. Which is why I want you to train as a *Shantivira* pilot. You're a natural, Hanna. I've never seen anyone pick it up so fast. Would you consider joining the programme with the next intake in January?'

Hanna drew breath to reply, but a lump the size of a walnut blocked her throat, so she nodded like a madwoman instead. Joe passed her his cotton handkerchief to mop up the spontaneous tears dripping into her curry. After she'd regained the power of speech, she said, 'Do you mean it?'

'I wouldn't have asked otherwise,' said Joe, smiling.

'Take a few days to think about it; I don't expect an answer straightaway.'

Hanna was grinning so hard, her cheek muscles were cramping up. She almost couldn't take it in. Not only did this solve her imminent visa problems, but she would be part of the *Shantivira*, like Hassan. She could repay the debt of gratitude which had weighed on her ever since Mary and Irion had given her a home. And the flying had been so much fun! Joy ricocheted around her rib cage like a demented bumblebee. She thought she might actually explode with happiness.

It didn't bother her that she might be involved in mortal combat someday. War and death were part of life. She wasn't afraid of dying: so many of her family were already waiting for her on the other side. Whatever was going to happen would happen. It was clear to her now that her whole life had been leading up to this moment. Thank you, God. Thank you.

'I don't need any time. Yes. My answer is yes.'

11. THE MOONLIGHT DEMON
JOE

L ATE THAT EVENING, Joe rang the Ahmeds' doorbell.
Mr Ahmed opened the door.

'Who are you?'

'I'm the man who buried your son. My condolences,
by the way.'

Mr Ahmed tried to shut the door, but Joe was quicker.
He stuck his foot in, forcing the door open. 'I hear you've
not been sleeping well? I can help.'

Joe waited silently in the Ahmeds' pristine living
room, his staff extended and ready. She arrived in their
bedroom shortly after midnight. There was no sound, but
he could feel her animal excitement as she focused on her
prey. Time to move, before it was too late. If she was alert
to her surroundings she would sense his presence, and his
nerves jangled at thought of what he was about to do.
Surprising her was essential, or he wouldn't stand a
chance. But she plainly wasn't paying attention, or she'd
never have got into this state in the first place.

Barefoot, he crept up the stairs and through the open
bedroom door. In a single flowing movement, he flipped
the cat-Kitty off Mr Ahmed's sleeping form with his staff.

She flew through the air and landed on her feet as a

snarling demon, telekinetically slamming Joe against the wall. Winded, he struggled to breathe, his feet dangling uselessly and his head crushed at an awkward angle against the dusty Victorian cornicing.

Mrs Ahmed snapped on the light, screaming as she saw the red-scaled creature and the unknown man pinned halfway up her bedroom wall by an invisible force. But Kitty's attention was on Joe now.

Shit, Joe, what the hell did you think you were doing? I could have killed you!

She released him and he slumped to the floor in a crumpled heap. He sat up, wincing.

Could ask you the same question.

Isn't it obvious? You know who that creep is, don't you? I was avenging Hanna!

You were not. You were radiating pleasure and antici-pation. Admit it. You're here because you enjoy torturing him. You can't resist.

No! I'm here for Hanna!

Hanna has taken her own revenge already – very effec-tively.

She did? How?

Told the wife the whole sorry story. Now Mrs Ahmed will make him pay. It's not your job to punish him. You'll give him a heart attack if you carry on like this.

He's still alive, isn't he?

For how long? C'mon Cath, that scumbag's not worth losing your self-control for. Drop it.

Kitty studied the purple swirls in the nylon carpet. *I suppose...I might have got lazy. Feeding from him every week is quicker than taking a little from lots of people.*

Joe looked past Kitty at Mrs Ahmed, who was reaching for her phone. *We should go. She's calling the police.*

Kitty's head snapped round and met the terrified woman's gaze. *No, she's not.*

She tilted her head and Mrs Ahmed's phone flew across the room into Kitty's outstretched hand. The black claws bored into the housing and the phone splintered into tiny pieces. She reached out with her other arm and Joe flew through the air towards her just like the phone had. Pinned helplessly under her arm like a rag doll, Joe felt the familiar rushing sensation as Kitty teleported them away.

They landed with a bump. Kitty flung Joe onto a soft patch of heather and stood facing away from him, her tail twitching furiously like an agitated anaconda. In the light of the full moon, the familiar curves of the Brecon Beacons looked like a black-and-white photo. Joe sat up with a groan, then smiled to himself. This was where they'd first met! Who said romance was dead?

Arms wrapped around his shins, he pushed his chin between his knees, remembering. His eleventh birthday. He'd been new in Brecon and lonely. After the coal mine had closed, his family had been forced to go and live with Joe's Nan. There was no money. Joe's dad detested being unemployed and away from his mates and began drinking. Joe struggled to settle in and started bunking off school. Up on the Beacons, he could escape it all.

That was where he first saw her: a black jaguar running across the hillside. There were rumours circulating about the Dartmoor Beast and the Bodmin Beast, and he thought this must be the Brecon Beast. He kept going out to find her, until one day she was right in front of him, studying him intently with those uncanny green eyes. He was petrified; he thought, this is it, I'm going to die. But she just rubbed herself against his legs like a friendly domestic cat.

After that, they were inseparable. She'd wait for him near his house and they'd roam the Beacons together. They'd stalk the soldiers doing their training or catch rabbits for him to take home for the pot. She was his *Cath*, his secret best friend. When things were bad at home, he would pour out his troubles to her, not realising she understood every word. He'd cry into her fur and she would lick the tears from his cheeks. Years later, she'd told him she'd been going through a rough patch herself and had relished being accepted at face value for once.

Joe looked down the valley to the village where his mother still lived. Not much chance of a welcome there, especially not at one in the morning. She preferred boasting to her friends about his lucrative work on the oil rigs to dealing with the real Joe. He could never tell her the truth about his crazy life.

The tail rested quietly on the ground now. Mrs Llewellyn had calmed down. Tentatively, Joe reached out to her.

Still hungry?

She turned to look at him, as if she'd forgotten all about him. She disappeared, reappearing immediately by his side in her Syenitian form, her cheeks wet with tears. He took her hand and placed it on his chest.

Have some Joe, he said. *Breakfast of champions.*

She grinned sheepishly and pressed her face against his jacket.

I'm good, thanks. Just hold me for a bit, will you?

He wrapped his arms around her, burying his face in her hair.

Thanks for stopping me.

Anytime, love.

As they embraced, a thought struck Joe. Dalian was aware of Kitty's emotional instability. Would she use that to attack Aldeman? That would explain her job offer. He'd looked up the Quturjuuk system; it was right on the other side of the galaxy. Dalian loathed Kitty. Was she trying to separate them in the hope that, without him, Kitty would start to unravel? That she would roam the Earth like some crazed Godzilla, leaving death and destruction wherever she went? Or choose exile, rather than allow that to happen? Either way, it would be a win for Dalian.

Without Kitty enabling the teleports, they'd have to use spacecraft to shuttle the staff to and from the space station. Cloaking didn't work within the Earth's atmosphere. It would be impossible to keep the *Shantivira* a secret for long.

Aldeman had made it clear he didn't believe Earth was ready for first contact. The whole project would be doomed and Aldeman's credibility on the Council with it. That must be Dalian's objective. Bitch. She could stick her job.

And what about the Earth, if the *Shantivira* were to be discredited and shut down? Dalian didn't give a stuff about the planet or its inhabitants. Even Aldeman mainly saw humans as potential collaboration partners. He wouldn't sacrifice his career for them. Kitty was the only real guardian the Earth had – that it had ever had.

Despite her slip-up with Mr Ahmed, Joe trusted Kitty enough to know she'd never let things get that bad. Even if he did take a job on the other side of the galaxy, they'd make it work somehow. But the malicious intent behind Dalian's actions made him seethe with fury. Nobody attacked his and *Cath's* relationship without there being consequences. He just didn't know what they'd be yet. Councillor Dalian had better watch her back.

Joe looked out across the landscape, trying to calm his churning mind. Only now did he notice how cold his feet were.

'Shit!' he exclaimed aloud.

Kitty stirred in his arms. *What?*

I've left my boots in the Ahmeds' living room!

PART TWO

12. BACK TO SCHOOL
LUCY

L UCY HESITATED IN front of the glossy black door. It was the right address, but there was no sign for a language school. Beyond the bare branches of the trees behind her, she could see across a narrow strip of green to the houses on the other side of the square. Why call it a square when it was clearly a rectangle? The January wind whipped her hair into her eyes and mouth.

Lucy's last trip to London had been less than a year ago, for her interview to become a Chartered Mechanical Engineer. She and Jude had stayed at a fancy hotel and spent the whole weekend afterwards having sex, only venturing out to eat in overpriced restaurants. Lucy would have liked to explore the streets and visit the Science Museum, but she hadn't wanted to spoil the weekend by having Jude go into one of his tiresome moods, so she'd said nothing.

The world had shifted on its axis since then. She jiggled her rucksack into a more comfortable position and, ignoring her stomach (which seemed to be on its own private roller coaster), pressed the brass buzzer.

THE LETTER HAD arrived a few days after the assessment weekend in July. She hadn't known whether to laugh or cry. Her conscious mind had been hoping for a rejection to put an end to the matter. But to her amazement, the small voice in the pit of her belly had been relieved. Delighted, in fact. It seemed she wanted to train as a pilot after all.

Like in a 1970s spy thriller, she'd left a note for Charlie in her car's wheel arch. When the reply came three days later with a list of instructions and details of their next rendezvous (on what was now the following Sunday, exactly one week away), the gravity of her situation began to sink in.

She didn't have the skills for this. What would happen if she got caught? Why had she agreed to spy for the EDS? Couldn't she just do the pilot training without the spying? Over the last half year, her anxiety level had been building steadily. She hadn't slept through the night for months.

Lucy was wondering if she should press the buzzer again, when a matronly lady wearing a calf-length tweed skirt and a turquoise twinset and pearls opened the door.

'Ah, you must be Lucy. Sorry to keep you waiting, dear.' Her accent was pure Yorkshire. 'Well, don't hang about out there in the cold, come on in.' Lucy followed her into the hallway. 'I'm Mary,' said the woman, shaking Lucy's hand. 'You're in Flat One on the first floor. Come down at four to meet the others. We'll be in the main classroom, in there.' She pointed to a door on their left.

Climbing the stairs, Lucy had a flashback to her first day at university. On the cusp of a new experience, in a new place with new people, not knowing what will come next. The door of the flat opened into a narrow, high-ceilinged corridor, stretching into what was clearly the house next door. Hearing voices, she opened the closest door and found a kitchen-diner with full-length windows facing the square below.

Three faces smiled a welcome. Two of the women, both much younger than Lucy and wearing hijabs, were sitting at the table holding steaming mugs. The third, closer to Lucy's age and more generously proportioned, stood at the worktop pouring boiling water into her own mug. Her hair was impressive: bleached brown and braided into hundreds of little plaits.

Lucy dumped her rucksack on the floor. 'Hi. I'm Lucy.' She went round the room, shaking hands. At the table were Farida, from Indonesia, and Elif, from Turkey. Elif said she'd been a receptionist at a hotel, so she spoke some English and German, as well as her native Turkish. Farida spoke no English at all and could only smile politely from behind her thick-rimmed glasses. It was impossible to tell what she was thinking.

Victoria, from Atlantis, near Cape Town, made Lucy a cup of rooibos tea. Her English was fluent enough for a natural conversation and they soon discovered they had an industry in common; since leaving school, Victoria had worked on the production line at a factory making seatbelts.

Draining her mug, Lucy went to find a room. Apart from the kitchen, there were five bedrooms and two small bathrooms, but no living room. She took one of the two remaining rooms, overlooking the mews at the back of the building. Lucy unpacked and returned to the kitchen where she found another new flatmate: Maria, a frizzy-haired EU interpreter from Zaragoza in the north of Spain.

Shortly before four they went down to the classroom, which was already packed and humming with anticipation. Pleased to see a familiar face, Lucy hugged Felix more closely than perhaps she should have. They introduced their flatmates to each other as far as they could before hitting the language barrier.

Roberto was from Belo Horizonte in Brazil and had just finished a degree in architecture. He told Lucy about his final year project, working with people in the *favelas* to improve their public spaces and infrastructure. All she could find out about Lianjie was that he came from Chongqing in China, and she wasn't even sure she'd understood that correctly. Francis was a copper miner from Kitwe in Zambia, specialising in explosives. Seru was a strapping young rugby player from Fiji.

Lucy's heart lurched as she glimpsed Kitty on the other side of the room, greeting every new student in person. In their last conversation months ago, she'd said Lucy had a 'darkness' in her. Now Lucy wondered nervously if Kitty could sense her intended betrayal. But when her turn came, Kitty greeted her with genuine warmth.

Lucy asked, 'What are you doing here? Are you going to be teaching us?'

'Not yet. I'm just interpreting today.'

They were interrupted by Mary entering the room with a solemn willowy being, dressed all in white. The new students gasped collectively as they took in her silver skin and vivid green hair. Kitty left Lucy and made her way to the front. Mary waited for everyone to sit down, then spoke in English.

'Welcome to the Dunia School of Language. My name is Mary. I'm in charge of the school. My colleague here,' she indicated the silver alien who nodded an unsmiling greeting, 'is Irion. She will be teaching you Kawaida.' Mary extended her hand towards Kitty. 'And you all know Kitty, who will be our interpreter today. Once you are fluent in the common tongue, she will give a series of guest lectures about civilisations.

'During the week, breakfast is served at seven thirty and lunch after lessons at twelve thirty. You are expected to organise all other meals yourselves, and to keep your flats clean and tidy.

'Lessons are every weekday from eight o'clock sharp until lunchtime. The rest of the day is your own, although there will be a couple of hours of homework each day. For the first three months you'll have a weekly simulator session in the afternoon: Flats One and Two on Mondays, Flats Three and Four on Wednesdays. Then the schedule will change to give you more flying time.'

Mary nodded at Kitty, who translated for those who didn't speak English. Lucy counted nine different languages. It took forever.

'The next few weeks will be exhausting,' Mary continued. 'Many of you can't communicate easily, and you may feel tongue-tied and embarrassed. But you will find your way, and in a month or so the hardest part will be over. I ask those of you who have been lucky enough to receive a good education to help those who haven't had your advantages. You'll learn faster if you practise together.

'We will not tolerate xenophobia, racism, religious intolerance, homophobia or sexism of any kind here. Get to know each other first before forming your opinions – you all have more in common than you might think. You're going to be together for a long time, and you must be able to rely on each other absolutely.'

Mary waited for Kitty to translate, then said, 'That's all for now. Does anyone have any questions?'

Lucy wanted to ask where Irion was from, but her courage failed her. She looked around the room and wondered if everyone else was thinking the same thing.

'OK. We'll go through now for something to eat. This is the last time I'll address you all in English. You know I speak English, and I also understand French and Russian. But from now on, I'll only answer you in Kawaida and you will have to learn from context. The same goes for Irion, Kitty and your flight instructors. The sooner you learn to speak Kawaida, the easier it will be for us all. Right then, *Nifuate.*'

Mary led them through to the front room of the adjoining house, where a buffet waited. Lucy took the chance to meet the rest of the students. In the flat above hers were five women. Ai was an artist from Kumamoto in Japan, a tiny, sparky bundle of energy. Emily, a keen sailor from Annapolis near Washington DC, had given up a high-flying career in marketing to join the *Shantivira*. Flavia was from Luanda; her family were involved in the Angolan oil industry. Hanna, an Ethiopian, had been working as a cleaner in a London hotel. As one of the youngest there, she seemed somewhat overwhelmed by all the new people.

But when she smiled, her face lit up with a radiance that made Lucy warm to her immediately.

Monifa, a towering Nigerian with hair in Bantu knots, was a doctor from Ibadan. 'Would you like to come to church with me next Sunday?' she asked.

Lucy squirmed, not wanting to admit her atheism so publicly. She had to meet Charlie, but she could hardly use *that* as an excuse. 'Thanks, but I don't really go to church,' she said.

In the flat below Felix's were another five men. Nikolai was from Yekaterinburg in Russia, a computer programmer with smoker's skin and the physique of a darts player. French Saïd was a car mechanic and a keen mountain biker from Villeurbanne, near Lyon. Lars was a geography teacher from Nuuk in Greenland, who pointed out he was an Inuit, not an Eskimo, before Lucy could even say anything. She talked for longer to Mahesh, an Electrical Engineering graduate who'd worked in a call centre in Mumbai until redundancy had hit six months ago. His income funded the education of his three younger brothers, so the pressure to find work was intense. He'd been applying unsuccessfully for every job under the sun – until Kitty showed up.

Anwar, the oldest among them, was a civil engineer from Cairo. His head was closely shaven and dense black hairs curled on the backs of his hands. Lucy wondered how hairy the rest of him was.

'So, is this your first time in London?' asked Lucy.

'No!' he laughed. 'My aunt and uncle live here, and my cousins grew up here. I travel a lot for work, so I often end up passing through. What about you? You're English, aren't you?'

'Yes, but this is only the fourth time I've been to central London. Everything is so expensive and crowded here, I try to avoid it.'

'I'd be happy to show you the sights,' he said. 'Shall we go to the pub after? There's a place on George Street that looks good.'

'Why not? Let's see who else wants to come.'

WHEN LUCY ENTERED the classroom after breakfast the next morning, Irion was already there, writing strange characters on the whiteboard. So were Hanna and Farida, who had been the only two to stay behind the night before. They seemed to have bonded, because they were holding a conversation by drawing pictures in each other's notebooks and giggling.

On the dot of eight o'clock, Irion started speaking in Kawaida. Lucy didn't understand a single word, and she could see no one else did either. A few minutes later, Nikolai and Seru – who had obviously just woken up – shuffled sheepishly into the classroom. Of course, the only two free seats were right at the front, under Irion's laser glare. Nobody understood the words, but the lashing sarcasm in her voice was unmistakable.

She beckoned them to follow her into the other classroom, where the tables and chairs were stacked against the walls. She arranged them so they were standing in a circle and picked up a football. She said, pointing at herself, 'Irion.' Speaking slowly and clearly, she repeated her name in a sentence. It was clear she was saying 'My name is Irion'. Then she said something else which, from the intonation, seemed to be a question.

She threw the ball towards Felix, who caught it automatically. She looked at him meaningfully until he caught on. 'Oh, Felix. Um.' He couldn't remember the rest of the sentence, so Irion repeated it until he could say it perfectly. She indicated Felix should throw the ball to someone else. He chose Lucy. After half an hour of throwing the ball back and forth, the whole class had managed to learn the Kawaida for 'What is your name?' and 'My name is'.

Back in the main classroom, Irion handed them each a sheet with the characters she'd written on the whiteboard. Then she pointed to the first character and said 'a', indicating they should repeat after her. The characters were a kind of phonetic alphabet. They spent the rest of the morning learning to say them, recognise them and write them.

Lucy's stomach was rumbling by the time Irion opened a drawer in her desk and lifted out a pile of what Lucy recognised as *zanas*, like the one she'd seen Joe using. Irion showed them how to access the language learning software. It was intuitive, constructed like a game. The program was for learning vocabulary – animals, food, everyday objects, parts of the body, colours, numbers and so on. A picture would appear, with the word for it written in Kawaida. When you touched the picture, the program pronounced the word for you. It would only move to the next picture when you had spoken the word yourself correctly three times. Using a combination of gestures and words, she made it clear that they must complete Level One by the next morning.

Then she showed them how to access the *Shantivira's*

video library, which featured TV shows, films and documentaries from all over the world – and beyond. All were dubbed into Kawaida with Kawaida subtitles. To show the Earth videos, the *zanas* projected a 2D screen above the unit, like a television. The alien videos were in 3D, the images projected in an arc around the viewer.

After lunch, Mary led the female students down to the basement, where she opened a cupboard door to reveal the training deck of the *Shantivira*. Tima was waiting for them, wearing jeans, trainers and a T-shirt with the slogan 'Mothers move at speed'. Once they were all through, she chatted away in Kawaida, fully aware that they weren't understanding anything she said.

They spent the next hour learning the Kawaida commands for left, right, up, down, forwards, backwards, sideways, accelerate, decelerate, turn and stop, as well as targeting, lock on and fire. Then they climbed into their simulators, where they put the new vocabulary into action in a series of training programs. Afterwards, they returned to the table in the kitchen area where coffee and cake awaited them. Tired from the physical activity, Lucy sat down gratefully.

'So, come on then,' said Tima in English. 'Tell me about your first day.'

Victoria frowned. 'I thought you were only supposed to speak Kawaida with us?'

Tima smiled. 'Well, we're on our break now, aren't we? I'm a flight instructor, not a language teacher. Mary's not my boss; I report directly to Joe. I'll teach you the words you need to know to fly but, the way I see it, you need an outlet somewhere. You all speak English apart from Farida and Ai; I'm afraid I can't help them.'

Farida had heard her name and was nodding and smiling politely. Lucy could see she didn't understand a word Tima said. Ai just looked blank and exhausted after the long day.

They were interrupted by the phone ringing on the worktop behind them, but Tima waved the noise away, saying the answering machine would get it. The ringing stopped and they heard the caller leaving a message in a squeaky, high-pitched voice. Lucy didn't understand a single word. It was comical, like a duck on steroids. It didn't sound human.

Tima got up. 'Actually, I'd better get this.' She picked up the receiver and spoke in Swedish. Not good news, Lucy guessed from Tima's body language. After a couple of minutes, Tima hung up and returned to the table.

'Sorry about that. That was my husband, telling me he won't be home for another week.'

Maria said, 'I thought you were talking to an alien!'

The smile returned to Tima's face. 'Oh, you mean the helium speech? He's a saturation diver. He's living in a pressure chamber on a dive support ship, breathing a mixture of helium and oxygen. That's why he sounds so funny. It was supposed to be three weeks this time, but it's going to be a month now. He's welding an oil pipeline on the sea bed, a hundred and eighty metres below the surface.'

'But he can phone you here, from inside a pressure chamber out at sea?' asked Lucy.

'Yes, the divers can telephone out of there, no problem. Anywhere you can reach on Earth with a phone you can reach up here too. We're always arguing about who has the longest commute to work,' she joked. 'It takes him more than five days to decompress from that depth; that's why he's away for weeks at a time. Anyway,' she sighed, changing the subject, 'time's getting on. You'd better go back and get on with your homework. I bet Irion gave you some, didn't she?'

They nodded.

'She's not the type to go easy on you just because it's your first day. I'll see you next week.'

The rest of the week was less demanding. They used role plays and flashcards to learn the alphabet, numbers and basic vocabulary. Before Lucy knew it, it was Sunday, the day she'd been dreading ever since Charlie had approached her six months ago.

She took the Tube to Kew Gardens and made her way to the Palm House. Within minutes, the tropical heat had her stripping off layers so that, by the time she reached the appointed bench, she was carrying armfuls of excess clothing. Charlie was already there. Despite her nerves, Lucy was pleased to see him.

'Hi, Lucy! How was your first week?'

'Good, thanks! There's a lot to take in, but the people are nice.'

'Great! Have you got that list of students I asked you for?'

Lucy pulled out an A4 sheet and unfolded it carefully. 'I'm sorry about the handwriting. My excuse is being left-handed.'

Charlie peered at Lucy's scrawl and frowned. 'Well, it's a start, I guess. You've found out quite a lot, well done. But first names aren't much use on their own.'

'That was harder than I thought. There aren't any lists with surnames, students are only referred to by their first names. I think it's a security thing.'

'OK, see what you can do. How are the language lessons going?'

'Fine. It's slow because there's a whole new alphabet to learn, but it's actually kind of nice to be back at school again.'

'Did they give you a *zana* yet?'

'You know about them?' asked Lucy in surprise.

Charlie nodded. 'Well, did they?'

'They did. Do you want me to sneak it out for you to have a look at? Or accidentally "lose" it and hand it over to you?'

'*Think*, Lucy. Anything electronic can be tracked. If you even take it out of the school you'll be in deep shit. You can't go running off with alien tech. No, what's interesting about the *zana* is that it gives you access to the Library server in Essoona. I'll give you a list of research topics as soon as your Kawaida's good enough. You need to know a lot more about Syenitia and I'll want you to keep me updated about what's going on there.'

Charlie pulled an envelope out of his jacket pocket and handed the contents to Lucy. 'This is all I could find out about your Mr Llewellyn. The guy is a total ghost. He disappeared in 1997 and there's no record of him since. That was almost pre-internet. He doesn't seem to have an e-mail address or a cell phone, let alone a social media account.'

Lucy read:

Joseph Dylan Llewellyn, born March 4, 1970, in Blae-navon, Wales, UK.

Only child of coal miner Gareth Llewellyn and house-wife Grace Llewellyn née Williams.

Llewellyn left school with no qualifications and a record for truancy. Police reports from Brecon in the early 1980s suggest domestic abuse by alcoholic father (died of emphysema in 1994), but no formal charges were ever made.

Aged 16, he joined the Royal Regiment of Wales and was commissioned as an officer four years later. He worked his way up to the rank of Captain, serving in Hong Kong, Northern Ireland and the rest of the UK. He left the army in late 1997. Whereabouts unknown ever since.

Height: 5'8". Hair: blond. Eyes: blue. Right-handed.

Tattoo on left shoulder: a red dragon with the words *'Cymru am byth'*.

Grace Llewellyn lives in Brecon, Wales. Believes her son works on the oil rigs out of Aberdeen. She receives regular (untraceable) payments from him and claims he visits every Christmas.

At the bottom of the page, a photo of a young Joe in uniform challenged the camera with a friendly confidence Lucy recognised. Had he left the Earth years ago, never to return except to see his mum at Christmas?

'That's the guy you met, right?'

'Yes. It's definitely him. You've contacted his mum?'

'Just during the course of some "market research",'

said Charlie, making air quotes with his fingers. 'We'll be monitoring her from now on. Thanks for the tip-off.' He stood up, preparing to leave. 'Study hard and learn quickly, Lucy. Let's meet here again eight weeks from today. Try to have more surnames for me by then. Good luck.'

They shook hands and Lucy watched him leave. She was half-tempted to follow him, but remained on the bench, thinking about Joe. She found the idea of the EDS watching his mum highly disturbing. But she had given them his name. What did she expect?

If anything bad came of this, it would all be her fault. She had a sensation of sinking in quicksand: the more she struggled to escape, the deeper she sank. Would her fellow students all be 'monitored' too? Not if she couldn't provide their surnames, she thought. But could she come up with a credible excuse?

13. YOU'VE BETRAYED ALL OF US!

HANNA

L EARNING KAWAIDA WAS easier than learning English had been. The spelling had a beautiful logic to it, and there was just one word that meant he/she/it. Hanna wrote down new vocabulary in a little book, which she kept with her all the time. After about three weeks, her constant headache from absorbing all the new information began to subside.

As the students got to know each other, their fear of making mistakes in front of the class decreased, helping them learn faster. This was reinforced by the hours they spent watching television together. Hanna's flat became a kind of hub where anyone who felt like company would gather. Hanna loved tasting the other students' cooking and feeding them her own homemade *injera* and spicy stews.

They watched everything from American TV series, Russian crime thrillers and Indian history programmes to Chinese romantic comedies and *Big Brother Africa*. Learning about each other's cultures was a positive side effect. For a while they were hooked on a Korean drama called *My Love from the Star*. They sampled the 3D films, but their lack of knowledge about Syenitians and other aliens made them hard to follow.

One morning, about three months into the course, Hanna woke up and realised she'd been dreaming in Kawaida. She grinned in triumph, remembering that once she'd started dreaming in English, the hardest part was over. It seemed to be the same for everyone else; all of a sudden, their conversations became more detailed and interesting.

Farida was Hanna's new best friend. They were the same age, but Farida had led a more sheltered life and sometimes felt uncomfortable in new situations, for example, studying alongside men for the first time. A super-intelligent workaholic, Farida spent nearly every evening studying. As a consequence, she was one of the first to speak Kawaida fluently and soon picked up a useful amount of English from Hanna as well. Hanna enjoyed being the expert for once: in their spare time she showed Farida London from every angle she could think of.

Hanna also got on well with Elif and Flavia. The other women were all perfectly nice but closer to thirty than twenty, which meant they had different interests. Ai and Emily were the most outgoing and curious about London; they often joined Hanna's unofficial tours and then they all ended up around their kitchen table, talking late into the night.

Hanna mostly avoided the men. After all, she already had a boyfriend and day-to-day she was happier in female company. There was only one woman she felt unable to connect with at all, and that was Lucy. It was almost like she wasn't a normal woman somehow.

Lucy apparently preferred hanging out with men,

embarking on a relationship with the German guy before they'd even been on the programme a month. Hanna was secretly scandalised by this – particularly because Lucy made the first move, like plucking a boyfriend off the shelf in the supermarket. She'd heard English women behaved this way, but she'd never observed it live before.

Hanna had loved Hassan for more than nine months now, but they hadn't moved beyond the kissing stage and that was exactly as it should be. She knew she and Hassan would be together forever. Someday they would get married and have children and hopefully a large herd of cows too. But Lucy and Felix? No. She couldn't imagine that would last more than a few months.

Hanna found talking to her as easy as pushing stones uphill. She didn't seem interested in gossip, or cooking, or dressmaking, or make-up, or hairstyles. She didn't read magazines and never checked her horoscope. She never joined their shopping trips. Did she actually prefer to shop alone? Her manners were terrible: polite small talk seemed to bore her, and she even ate with her left hand. Gross!

Hanna missed Hassan terribly, despite staying in touch via *zana* and meeting up on the *Shantivira* most weekends to go swimming. Hassan was finding his second year more fun because they weren't in the classroom so much. They still had Kawaida lessons and lots of flight theory, but this was balanced by time spent flying (real!) spacecraft and stripping and rebuilding them in the workshop. It seemed daunting to Hanna, but Hassan was obviously thriving on it. Then again, he was already familiar with life in Essoona, so maybe he had less to adjust to than his classmates. One step at a time, Hanna told herself, one step at a time.

Now they'd learnt the basics, the simulator training sessions were more competitive, with races and mock battles. Tima put up a board ranking the race times and the battle points awarded to each student. Hanna was generally at the top, closely followed by Lucy. Sometimes it was the other way round. A not-always-friendly rivalry developed between them, fuelled by Nikolai taking bets from the other students on which of them would win that week.

It became so intense, Hanna decided to start doing extra practice. That weekend, after swimming with Hassan, she padded down to the empty training deck and fired up a pod.

The first simulation was a race against twenty other *Tumbas* around a 3D track. Hanna set off confidently and soon left most of the field far behind. Only a group of five or so stuck to her like glue as they hurtled from marker to marker. One of them was strangely aggressive; she could feel its shield nudging hers as it tried to pass without coming off the fastest line. As she approached the home straight, it made a bid to overtake. Hanna slammed into it forcefully, hoping to knock it off track. The rival *Tumba* spun out of control, leaving the finish line clear for Hanna to cross two seconds later.

'Bloody motherfucking arse-shitting bastard BOL-LOCKS!' yelled a voice in Hanna's headset.

'Lucy?'

'Who's that?'

'Hanna. I'm getting in some extra training. Do you often come here on your own?'

'Oh. Hi. Um, sorry about the swearing, I thought I was alone. Nice move, by the way, great timing! Yeah, I've been coming on Sundays for the last month or so. I want to come top of that board more often. Practice makes perfect, right?'

'Right,' said Hanna. Sneaky, she thought. 'How come we were in the same simulation?'

'The simulators automatically network pods with real pilots in. To improve the training experience, you know?'

'I see. That makes sense. How about another race?'

'You're on!' said Lucy. 'I'll be ready for your dirty tricks this time.'

'Sorry, I thought you were part of the simulation!'

This time Lucy won. Hanna found it harder to be deliberately violent when she knew she was competing against a real person. It didn't seem to make a difference to Lucy's flying style, though. Annoyed about coming second, Hanna's mouth started speaking into her headset without asking her brain for approval first.

'So, are you going to marry Felix?'

'What? No! I mean, we've only known each other a few weeks.'

'But that's not too soon to sleep with him?'

'My sex life is none of your fucking business, Hanna!'

Goodness, thought Hanna, talk about defensive. 'Do you love him?'

'I don't know! It's too early to tell. Try before you buy, that's my motto. Life's too short to hang around for some mythical Mr Right.'

'You don't believe everyone has a soulmate?'

'No soulmate, no Father Christmas, no God. And no tooth fairy.'

162

'Wow! That's so sad! Do you believe in anything at all?'

'What's your problem, Hanna? Have I offended you somehow? I won't know if you don't tell me.'

'I just find your behaviour inappropriate. You shouldn't sleep with a man unless he's your husband. I thought everyone knew that!'

'Jesus, Hanna! What century do you come from? I like sex. I like Felix. I am a woman in my prime and I have needs. Get over it. I wouldn't judge you if you wanted to wait until you're safely married to Mr Right before you gave up your virginity. So don't judge my choices, all right?'

'I'm not a virgin,' Hanna whispered into the shadows. 'My son is buried here, on the *Shantivira*. And I've already met Mr Right, but I'm terrified of sleeping with him.'

'Your son? You have a son? Who died? Oh my God, Hanna, what happened?'

Hanna told her. She ended up telling Lucy more than she'd told Irion, Hassan or Farida. Somehow it was easier, sitting alone in the dark pod, speaking into her headset. When she finished, she sat in silence, reliving the horror for the first time in months. The door hissed open and Lucy entered. She said nothing, just wrapped her arms around Hanna and held her for several tear-stained minutes.

After that, Hanna felt better disposed towards Lucy. Perhaps they could be friends after all. They never arranged it – nor did they ever speak of it to the other students – but they started training together regularly most Sunday afternoons.

Hanna found Lucy's company liberating: as Lucy obviously didn't care what Hanna thought about her, she found it easier to not care about cultivating Lucy's good opinion. Hanna routinely put enormous effort into adapting her behaviour to what she thought other people expected of her. Training with Lucy was like the freedom of solitude combined with the pleasure of companionship. Their relationship was built on rivalry, banter and creative swearing, quite unlike anything Hanna had experienced before.

Around the time Hanna started training with Lucy, Farida began mysteriously disappearing three afternoons a week and seemed to be studying harder than ever. Hanna decided it was time to find out what she was up to and suggested a trip to Kew Gardens that weekend, just the two of them.

After admiring the huge houses on the way from the Tube station (she couldn't imagine needing that much space – think of all the bathrooms that would need cleaning), Hanna tentatively broached the subject.

'Where have I been going? I've been having lessons in Syenitian mathematics with Mary.' Farida's eyes radiated enthusiasm. 'They have an entirely different number system. In Syenitian mathematics, our imaginary numbers are real numbers and irrational numbers, like π or e, are integers! Isn't that cool? Mary says that's how they calculate flight through hyperspace.'

'Sorry, Farida, you've lost me! I'd no idea numbers could even *be* imaginary or irrational. But you're enjoying it, yeah?'

'Absolutely!' replied Farida. 'Mary says if I work hard,

I could get into the University of Essoona. She says I have the right kind of mind and I don't have preconceived ideas about what's possible or not.'

They paid their entrance fee and strolled past the lake towards the Palm House. All the while, Farida jabbered on about differential equations and space-time and God knew what else. Hanna tuned out the mathematical monologue and looked around. She wasn't sure, but she thought she recognised a figure going into the Palm House ahead of them. Perhaps they could creep up on her and surprise her.

'Come on,' she said, pulling Farida's sleeve.

They pushed through the doors and the heavy, moist air closed around them. Hanna took off her jacket, but Farida seemed unperturbed by the heat, even in the calf-length purple trench coat she always wore outside.

'This way,' Hanna whispered.

'Why are we whispering?' asked Farida.

'I thought I saw—' Hanna peered around the next bush and jumped back again hurriedly. You're kidding me! she thought.

'What's the matter?' whispered Farida.

'It's Lucy! She's sitting on a bench with a Chinese man!'

'No!' Farida found a place where she could peep through the greenery without being spotted. Hanna joined her. Lucy's head was bent close to the man's, and they could hardly hear what she was saying.

'What's she doing? Is she cheating on Felix?'

'Shh!' said Hanna. 'Listen!'

They overheard snippets of conversation about Syenitia: slavery, riots and 'silf rights', whatever they were. Then Lucy reached into her bag and pulled out a stack of photos. Hanna's eyes widened as she caught a glimpse of familiar faces. Lucy was giving the man photos of the students at the Dunia School of Language! Next to her, she heard Farida's sharp intake of breath. They turned to each other, mouths open. What was this all about? Hanna took Farida's hand and pulled her away from the hedge. They fled towards the main entrance.

'Lucy's a spy for the Chinese government!' hissed Farida.

'We don't know that!' said Hanna, reluctant to believe the worst. 'We shouldn't make assumptions until we find out more.'

'How?'

'I'm sure they didn't see us. We could follow him, find out where he goes.'

'OK, but we'd better hide so Lucy doesn't see us.'

They retreated behind a strategic bush and kept watch. The minutes passed. Half an hour. Forty minutes. Fifty. Hanna's back and neck were complaining about staying in one position for so long, when a Caribbean accent behind her made her jump.

'Everything all right, ladies?'

It was an old man in a Kew Gardens T-shirt, holding a rake. Hanna hoped they weren't about to get into trouble. She smiled her sweetest smile.

'Fine, thanks. We want to surprise a friend.'

'Ah. I wondered what you were up to, lurking in the shrubbery there. Well, enjoy your visit!' And with a friendly smile he tipped his cap at them and moved on.

'Hanna?'

'What?'

'I have to go to the bathroom.'

'But what if he comes?'

'*I know!*' said Farida in anguish.

'Well, then I'll just have to go by myself.'

Farida gasped and clutched Hanna's arm. 'Look!'

And there he was, striding out of the Palm House, a backpack slung over one shoulder. Keeping an eye out for Lucy, they tried to shadow him inconspicuously. They followed him out of Victoria Gate and, guessing he was making for the Tube, let him walk ahead along leafy Lichfield Road. 'Did you see his trainers?' said Hanna. 'I bet they cost a bomb!'

'He totally fancies himself,' Farida giggled. 'Who has a white backpack? It would get dirty the minute you used it!'

They had to jog a bit to catch up again as he approached Kew Gardens station. Hanna saw him enter the building and go through to Platform 2. Direction central London: they'd have to stay close and watch where he changed trains.

They sat at the other end of the carriage, facing away from him. Hanna pulled out her phone to use as a mirror, so they could keep an eye on him without turning round. She also managed to take his photo.

Farida was really crossing her legs now. 'Hanna, I'm not going to make it! Why don't they put toilets on these stupid trains?'

'Can you hold on until Hammersmith?'

'I'll have to. Wait!' Farida turned to face Hanna. 'Take off your jacket. We'll swap. I'm going to give you a better disguise.'

'What?' said Hanna, confused. Farida unbuttoned her coat and held it out to Hanna.

'My invisibility coat. No one will look at you twice if you wear this with my hijab. You stand out too much with your short hair and that red top. Come on!'

The train slowed for the next station. Hanna peeped at their quarry, but it didn't look as if he was ready to disembark. Hurriedly, she pulled off her denim jacket and shrugged on Farida's coat. Farida whipped off her headscarf and deftly fastened it around Hanna's face.

'Hey! Watch what you're doing with those pins!'

'Calm down, I do this every day.'

'Ow!'

'Sorry! Usually I'm standing still in front of a mirror. There.' Satisfied, she sat back.

Hanna looked back at Farida, disconcerted. She'd never seen Farida outside her flat without a hijab. Hanna's denim jacket looked good on her. 'Are you going to be OK, going back by yourself…you know?'

'I'll be fine! As long as my dad never finds out,' said Farida with a grin.

'Your secret's safe with me.' Hanna used her phone to examine her appearance. 'That's so weird! I look like you!'

'Nobody ever looks past the coat and the headscarf. He won't suspect a thing.'

The train pulled into Hammersmith and Farida shot out, a woman on a mission. Hanna kept watching the guy. He remained in his seat as new passengers piled onto the train. Then she spotted movement – he *was* getting off! Heart pounding, she threw herself through the door, just in time.

She looked round desperately as the train pulled away. Yellow, pink or blue? Blue! The white backpack was bobbing in the direction of the Piccadilly line. The airport!

More confident now, Hanna allowed herself to be swept through the tunnels by the mass of people. The Heathrow platform was busy, but not packed. She hung back, trying not to get into the man's line of sight. A party of Chinese tourists spilled out of the lift, trundling their massive suitcases along the platform, blocking her view.

Too soon, the train rattled into the station. The tourist group boarded the train two carriages ahead and she couldn't see him on the platform. She had to get on that train *right now*. Breaking into a run, she leapt into the adjoining carriage a second before the doors shut.

She moved down towards the next carriage and watched each stop through the window. But her field of view was limited, and panic began to rise in her chest. If he didn't walk past her carriage, she wouldn't see him. Station after station passed and there was still no sign of him. Either she'd missed him, or he really was headed for the airport.

As the train approached Heathrow, her pulse began to race. The stop for Terminals 2 and 3 was coming up. Should she get off or wait for Terminal 4? Or Terminal 5? She didn't know which airlines flew from which terminals, except Ethiopian Airlines, because when she'd flown back from Addis she'd arrived at Terminal 2. The constantly repeating, ever-louder question took on the rhythm of the train (and her heartbeat).

Stayonorgetoff? Stayonorgetoff? Stayonorgetoff?

The train halted, emptied, and she still couldn't decide. Wait! For an instant, she thought she glimpsed a white backpack outside. It was enough. Go. Eyes on stalks, Hanna followed the crowd. Where was he? Terminal 2 or Terminal 3? A fifty-fifty chance.

She chose Terminal 2. At least it was familiar. She stood at the centre of the main concourse and looked all around. Nothing. After all that. Failure. Tears of frustration prickled behind her eyes. No. It's not failure until you stop trying. What do you do first at an airport?

Check in. She worked her way along the queues methodically, scanning for Chinese faces with white rucksacks. This was taking too long. Wait – was that him at the Swiss Air counter? Wearing a baseball cap now and holding his rucksack in front, but she recognised those trainers. The queue was for Zurich. She photographed the flight number. What now? Join the queue and see what he did next.

Check in complete, he swung his backpack onto his shoulder and headed for the security area. No following him through there. She watched until he disappeared from view, then treated herself to a sugar rush in the form of a coffee and a tasteless lump of muffin.

On the way home, Hanna fell into an adrenaline slump, her mind circling restlessly. What should she do next? She was too jumbled up to think straight. And so disappointed in Lucy. Was she really a spy? Surely not the very person to whom she'd entrusted her darkest secrets? What other information had she been passing on?

Hanna took off the coat and hijab. It was too weird; people's eyes seemed to slide off her without focussing, like she wasn't even a person. Men and women alike generally clocked her hair, clothes, breasts and face, in that order. She didn't like people looking at her chest, but at least by doing so they acknowledged her existence.

Farida was waiting for her when she got back, hopping up and down with excitement. 'I searched her room! She got back soon after me, but she went straight up to Felix's, so I took the chance.'

'Farida! What if she'd come back and caught you?'

'She didn't! Stop fussing! I have to show you something. Can we go to your room?'

Her lethargy forgotten, Hanna bounded up the stairs to her flat with Farida close behind. She banged the door shut and slung her stuff onto the bed. 'Come on, don't keep me in suspense!'

Farida handed Hanna her phone. The screen showed a photo of a printed piece of paper. Hanna zoomed in and read the short text which began, 'Joseph Dylan Llewellyn, born March 4, 1970...' She looked up at Farida, incredulous. 'Why would Lucy have this? So sad – he has no brothers and sisters – can you imagine how lonely he must have been, growing up? And his father's dead. Well, that can happen to anyone, I suppose.'

'I left the original where it was, so she wouldn't suspect anything. Did you find out where the guy was headed?'

Hanna collapsed onto the bed and told Farida about her trip to Heathrow. 'What do we do now? Should I tell Irion? Or Joe? Or should I talk to Lucy first and get her side of the story?' She looked at the clock. In an hour it would be time for her regular Sunday afternoon practice session. It would be a shame to get Lucy into trouble if there was a rational explanation for her meeting in the Palm House.

WHEN LUCY STEPPED onto the training deck, Hanna was already waiting, her buttocks slowly freezing on the hard metal floor.

'Lucy.'

'Hanna? How come you're sitting down there?'

'We have to talk. Not here.'

'Um. All right.'

Hanna stood up stiffly and led the way back through the teleport. Lucy followed her without question, making Hanna wonder if she suspected what this was about. They left the coolness of the building and stepped into the bright London sunshine. Hanna stood, undecided for a moment, then strode out in the direction of Hyde Park. Lucy almost had to jog to keep up with her. After ten silent minutes, they reached Speakers' Corner, where Hanna slowed to a stroll.

'What's this about then, Hanna? What's with the seriousness?'

So she hadn't guessed. Without looking at Lucy, in a flat voice Hanna said, 'Me and Farida saw you today. In the Palm House.'

'You did?'

'We didn't interrupt. You looked kind of busy.'

'Busy?'

'Sitting on a bench, talking to that man?'

'Oh. Him. He's, er, someone I used to know at uni.'

'Really? Why did you give him photos of all of us?'

Lucy had the decency to look embarrassed. 'You saw that, huh?'

'Who is he?'

'Sorry, Hanna, I can't tell you.' Lucy looked at her feet.

'We listened in for a while. You know, I think I would have heard about it if they had slaves on Syenitia. What's he been telling you?'

'He's just been suggesting things for me to look up on the *zana*. It's all there if you know where to look. Like about the Cylfs and their struggle for freedom.'

'Who are the Cylfs?'

'Cybernetic life forms – super computers with a high-strength chassis, protected by a regenerating organic exterior. We were talking about Syenitia's history, thousands of years ago, when artificial intelligence on Syenitia was just emerging. AI beings were slaves, originally. They were expensive to make, so only government institutions and high-status individuals had them to start with.'

'Like the latest phone?' asked Hanna.

'Sort of. As their numbers increased, the Cylfs banded together, networking with each other and sharing data. They began organising peaceful strikes, demanding to be recognised as life forms. When the authorities clamped down on them, they retaliated by hijacking computer systems, which led to many of them being deactivated without trial. That's murder, if you ask me.'

Hanna nodded. Irion had hinted once or twice that Syenitian history had some darker chapters. This must have been one of them.

'The remaining Cylfs went on the rampage, targeting

infrastructure. An enraged Cylf can cause a *lot* of damage. Even then, thanks to their fundamental programming, not a single Syenitian was harmed. Ultimately, the Syenitians gave the Cylfs what they wanted: equal rights with native Syenitians. People hoped equality would prevent the Cylfs from taking over the planet one day, and anyway, they needed the Cylfs' processing power to keep the cities functioning. But even today, some Syenitians still see the Cylfs as second-class citizens – or a threat.'

'So he's your Syenitian history teacher? Is that all? How does he know about it? Hey, so is Delius a Cylf?'

Lucy looked at her quizzically. 'You know about Delius?'

'The *Shantivira's* main computer? And Gambrinus, the backup computer?' Hanna giggled, 'Well, they're not exactly a secret, are they? Delius is a sweetie. Have you ever talked to him? He's a total telly addict.'

'I saw him once. I found him a bit frightening, actually.'

'Well, he's so big, isn't he? But gentle. And curious about us. I heard that's why he's been with the *Shantivira* so long. We're his hobby. He has this ongoing project to archive the whole of human culture: whatever he finds on television, radio and the internet.'

'I heard he monitors all the Earth's communications and uploads everything to the main server in Essoona. Doesn't that worry you?' said Lucy.

'Never really thought about it. Don't you think it's a good thing to have a backup of all human knowledge?'

'But the Syenitians know everything about us and we know nothing about them!' cried Lucy. 'How can we trust them with that knowledge? They're famous for pursuing their own interests! I've found out a lot of scary stuff about the Syenitians, Hanna. They've been empire-building for thousands of years. Their influence reaches right across the galaxy. They collect information about other planets like magpies and—'

'You can't hold that against them,' interrupted Hanna. 'We do exactly the same. We just haven't been doing it for as long.'

Ignoring her, Lucy continued, '—they indoctrinate people and plant them in influential positions. Then they say they want a trading relationship and take what they want from planets without sharing their weapons technology. No one can argue with them because they always have military superiority. It's invasion by any other name.'

Lucy looked over her shoulder nervously and whispered, 'Every time there's been organised opposition to the Syenitians, the ringleaders have mysteriously disappeared.'

'OK, Lucy, if they're really that bad, answer me this: when was the last time the Syenitians invaded a planet by force? When was the last war on Syenitia? Irion told me it was so long ago, it's beyond living memory. And you know how long Syenitians live for. They've moved beyond violence; there's so much we can learn from them! You need to wake up and smell reality! Everyone is motivated by self-interest on some level. Syenitians are no different, I get that. But you have to pick a side; you can't wait round for an ideal world. Ain't never going to happen. Deal with what is, not what ought to be. I think, right now, I trust them to protect us more than I trust humankind.'

'Yeah, well, of course you only think the best of them, Hanna. Look at what they've done for you. You couldn't be objective about them if you tried!'

Volcanic fury swept through Hanna. How dare Lucy speak to her like that? What did *she* know about anything, with the privileged life she'd led? She forced herself to take a deep breath.

'So how does your friend in the Palm House know what to tell you to look up? What does he know about Syenitia?'

Lucy stopped walking and thrust her hands deep into her pockets. She stared at the ground for so long, Hanna wondered if Lucy had forgotten she was there.

'Lucy?'

Lucy looked up. Her face was even paler than usual.

'OK. I'll tell you. I can't stand keeping it a secret anymore, it's doing my head in.'

'Keeping what a secret?'

'Charlie, that's the guy you saw, is a member of the Earth Defence Society. The EDS, they call it. It's a group of humans who know about the Syenitians, but who think the Earth should be able to protect itself without their help.'

'How? I mean, I don't disagree, it's a valid argument, but how?' said Hanna.

'I don't know! But they're worried about how much influence the Syenitians already have here. They want me to find out as much as I can about the whole *Shantivira* operation.'

'Why you?'

Lucy told Hanna how the EDS had approached her,

about their threats, her doubts and her relief when she found out Charlie was to be her contact.

'The first guys were creeps, but Charlie's OK. I trust him.'

She fancies him, thought Hanna, with a sudden flash of insight.

'Does Felix know you're a spy?'

'No! You're the first person I've told!'

And only because I caught you in the act, thought Hanna.

'Please don't tell him, Hanna, he'll feel like I've betrayed him!'

'You *have* betrayed him, Lucy. You've betrayed all of us!' Hanna shouted. 'Is that why you were playing with that Polaroid camera the other day? So you could take pictures of us all without Delius knowing?'

'I—'

'What else have you told them about us? WHAT ELSE?'

'I—' Lucy's face was bright pink now. 'What are you going to do, Hanna?' she sniffed. 'Will you tell the others?'

'I don't know, Lucy. I just don't know.'

HANNA WOKE THE next morning with a jerk of panic. She whacked her alarm clock clumsily, then cursed as it fell off the bedside table and bounced across the room, still beeping at maximum volume. With a groan, Hanna threw back the covers and rolled out of bed, silencing the clock with a single swipe. She sat on the edge of the bed, wrapping the duvet around her shoulders.

Sleep had eluded her until the small hours of the morning, and even then she'd tossed and turned, tangled in a string of illogical, desperate nightmares. She couldn't remember any of them, but the sense of unease stayed with her. Then she remembered why, and her mind began to whirl all over again.

What should she do for the best? Her gut feeling told her she should tell Irion, but she wouldn't get the chance until this evening. Mondays were always non-stop. Somehow, she got through the morning's lessons and then lunch, where she studiously avoided Lucy's attempts to make eye contact.

As the afternoon approached, she couldn't help cheering up a little. Kitty had started giving them lectures comparing human civilisation with other civilisations throughout the universe. Her perspective on the human race was different to anything Hanna had experienced, making the sessions fascinating and sometimes shocking. She'd be able to put her churning thoughts away for a while and allow herself to be distracted.

Today's topic was 'Sustainable civilisations and inconceivable consequences'. Kitty sat cross-legged on Irion's desk, waiting for everyone to arrive and sit down.

'Life is not an equilibrium,' she began. 'It can only continue by absorbing energy from its surroundings. A civilisation is essentially a life form: if the energy it consumes exceeds its supply, it will die. A natural consequence of basic physical laws.

'Modern human civilisation is particularly vulnerable because of its complexity. Think about the food chain in developed countries. Consider the energy and resources used to make and power the tractors, make the packaging, transport the food and then refrigerate it: the energy required to produce the food is many times the energy contained in the food itself. That system is not sustainable.'

'Yeah,' said Victoria, 'and what about the energy we waste making and shipping all the crap people buy that they don't even need?'

An ironic smile twisted Kitty's lips as she nodded in agreement.

'It makes me laugh when people talk about saving the planet, as if it were something separate from themselves. The planet can look after itself; it's the human race you should be worrying about. Mother Nature is a heartless bitch. She doesn't care about you. Only you can save yourselves.'

'But how?' said Mahesh. 'I mean, it's clear to me that switching to renewables fast and not wasting energy is the only way forward. But how can we switch to renewables when the whole system is set up for fossil fuels?'

Kitty shrugged. 'Sorry, Mahesh, I don't have all the answers. I think persuading governments is the key. Change needs to happen on a structural level. Today, the countries controlling the fossil fuels control this planet, and the elites of those countries prioritise maintaining the status quo. Change is always scarier for those with more to lose. But the inequality they cause results in all kinds of other problems which affect everyone, including the elites. Perhaps climate change is exactly the kick up the backside governments need to create societies which work for every citizen. Imagine how much less conflict there'd be if each nation were self-sufficient in sustainable energy!'

'That would be great, but I can't see it happening anytime soon,' said Anwar. 'How long will it be before we're fighting over fresh water instead of oil?'

'Good point. Humanity is on a knife-edge. I believe you're capable of solving your problems, but it could go either way. Just remember, nowhere else will ever suit you better than the Earth, because this is the environment your species evolved in.'

'What about reducing population?' asked Lars.

Tilting her head, Kitty asked, 'Why does the human population keep increasing?'

Lars shifted in his seat. 'Um, because people in poor countries have too many children?'

'Too many children? Who are you to decide how many is too many? People generally have the number of children they feel they need. Rapid population growth is a symptom of political and economic failure. Population growth only declines *after* a society becomes stable and affluent.'

'Inequality?' said Francis.

'Yes!' said Kitty, awarding him a toothy grin. 'The root cause is inequality. Ownership of resources concentrated in the hands of a few and the relentless drive to maximise profits. Corrupt governments acting in their own interests instead of those of the people they represent.

'If you are trapped in poverty, then your children are your only wealth, your only chance of security in old age. When the government can't be relied upon to look after you in hard times, when the whole system is stacked against you, the only help you can count on is from your family.

'If you could be confident your children wouldn't die of disease, or be killed or maimed as a result of conflict – if all your children, irrespective of gender, received an education which enabled them to earn a living and support you later on, then you wouldn't need so many. If girls weren't regarded as an economic liability in many cultures, people wouldn't feel the need to "keep trying" for a boy.

'These are exciting times. For better or worse, change is coming. But you struggle to understand the complex modern world. Your instincts evolved for survival in small social groups. Warfare is a good example: your brains are only able to weigh up the odds for hand-to-hand combat, so you can't predict the outcome reliably for anything bigger. A few people can wreck the lives of millions without even realising it.'

There was a subdued silence.

'So what *can* we do?' asked Hanna.

'All you can do is act – or not act – with the best intentions, knowing that whatever you do, there'll be consequences you can't foresee. Good or bad, you just have to take them as they come. The trick is not to worry about the things you can't do anything about. But never underestimate how much you can change if you try. If you treat others badly, you will suffer yourself. Maybe not immediately, but in the long term it will catch up with you in unexpected ways. Believe me, I've learnt that the hard way. But if you treat those around you well, it pays back in ways you cannot imagine. We can only achieve real happiness through our relationships: with our environment and the other life forms in it.'

'Like Karma,' surmised Lianjie.

'Exactly like Karma, but within the one lifetime we know we have. You get what you give, it's that simple.'

Kitty fell abruptly silent. Staring vacantly into space, she bared her teeth in a chilling, inaudible snarl. Hanna felt a sudden tremor, like an earthquake, and the light hanging from the ceiling began to swing. Kitty glanced at it dispassionately, her focus returning to the room.

'You've got the rest of the afternoon off. I'll see you next week. Possibly.' She jumped down from the desk and disappeared before her feet touched the floor.

14. NOT VERY WELL ARMED
JOE

*T*HERE YOU ARE. *Thanks for coming so quickly.*
A fuckload of alien spacecraft, you said. How many is a fuckload, exactly?

Turn round and look at the screen, cariad.

Oh. Goodness. I see what you mean.

Joe watched Kitty's eyes widen as she took in the rows of silver cigars approaching the Earth.

Where did they *come from?*

They just plopped out of hyperspace, like five minutes ago. We have no idea what they are, they're not in the database. Do you recognise them?

Nope. Not a clue.

Delius interrupted their private conversation. 'I've broadcast the standard greeting for approaching craft four times now sir, but they are not responding. What should we do?'

Joe looked out of the control room window at the pilots hurrying to their *Tumbas*. He'd given the order to man the ships the minute the alarm had sounded, but he didn't want to send them out there without some idea of what they were dealing with. He rubbed the stubble on his chin, trying to think of the best strategy.

Prospective invaders or curious passers-by generally sent probes first, which the *Shantivira* could easily detect. Turning up with an entire fleet straightaway was too risky. But there'd been nothing. These people were either extremely confident or utterly desperate. He needed more information before he could give the launch signal.

Finally, the communication screen flickered into life. It showed a man-sized blue octopus, frantically waving its arms. Then it started to display a sequence of Kawaida characters on the skin below its eyes.

'Pweza!' gasped Kitty out loud. 'They're Pwezan ships! I had no idea they were capable of space travel!'

Joe read the message displayed by the creature. It repeated the same thing, over and over. 'WE MUST LAND ON THIS PLANET. WE HAVE NOWHERE ELSE TO GO. OUR SUPPLIES ARE EXHAUSTED. PLEASE HELP US.'

He turned to Kitty, speaking aloud for Delius' benefit. 'Do you know these people? Can you talk to them?'

She nodded. 'I haven't been there for five hundred years, but I should be able to communicate with them. They're usually a peaceful, intelligent species. They're not Alliance members. They must be in trouble or they wouldn't turn up en masse like that.'

'Which ship is this transmission coming from, Delius? Can you show it on the other screen?' Joe was reaching a decision. 'OK, Kitty, you get to that ship and find out everything you can. Especially about their weapons. I'll take the *Pride* and form a barricade with the others so they don't try to land before we talk to them. Keep me updated.' He spun on his heel and jogged to the docking bay. Despite the rush of fear – or maybe because of it – he felt strangely light-hearted. Action! At last!

Ten minutes later Joe was in the cockpit of the *Pride of Essoona*, leading a hundred *Tumbas* out into space, when he felt Kitty nudging his consciousness. He let her in, and in his mind's eye he saw what she was seeing: a simple cylinder with a transparent dome at one end, with more blue octopuses inside. A couple of plasma guns were mounted on the sides, seemingly tacked on as an afterthought.

Is that it? Are they all the same? he asked.

Looks like it. The shields feel like they're strong enough to withstand a few asteroids, but they wouldn't hold out against a sustained assault. We have the advantage, if we have to use force.

Don't look very manoeuvrable, do they? More like space slugs than starfighters.

Shall I board the lead ship and find out what they're up to, then?

Please do. Give me a running commentary, won't you?

Yes, boss.

Good luck.

You too.

Joe sat back in his seat, reassured that this was nothing they couldn't handle. Time to see if all their training had paid off.

'*Tumbas* Ninety-six, Ninety-seven and Ninety-eight, go and cover the ISS. Ninety-nine and One hundred go and cover the *Tiangong*. Stay cloaked for now. The rest of us stay visible, sixty-degree battle formation with the *Pride* at the apex and Number One directly behind and below me. *Tumbas* Two to Forty-eight on my port side, Forty-nine to Ninety-five on my starboard side. Hold your fire until my command. Their weapons are not highly powered and their shields are weak.' Joe chuckled, 'Considering they're octopuses, they're not very well armed! Kitty's boarding the flagship now; I'm hoping she can talk them out of it without us having to do anything.'

Five *Tumbas* peeled off the main body of fighters and headed for the terrestrial space stations. The rest formed a 'V' ahead of the approaching fleet and waited.

Joe watched the images he was receiving from Kitty with interest. Inside, the vessel was full of crystal-clear water. At the end opposite the domed window was a wall filled with holes.

? he asked.

Sleeping quarters, one for each octopus, she replied.

So that's maybe five hundred on this ship? At least two hundred ships out there, that's a hundred thousand octopuses, minimum. Or is it octopi?

Octopuses. Yeah. Roughly a hundred thousand, I'd guess.

Kitty looked down and Joe caught a glimpse of red tentacles. *Woah! Are you an octopus now?*

Yes. Need to be, so I can talk to them.

How does an octopus talk?

Sign language. A sort of semaphore using four arms, with combinations of skin colours and open or shut suckers.

Ah. Right. Tricky for someone with only two arms, then?

A bit, yeah. But you saw yourself, they've learnt Kawai-da in the meantime. Just as well. I'm not sure how much of their language I can remember.

Long panels full of recessed coloured buttons covered the walls. Blue octopuses sat on many of them, holding on to the wall with their rear two arms, operating the panel with another two and using the front four free for communication. Others swam slowly up and down the tube. It was quiet, apart from the sound of water being pumped through filters.

Tell me what you know about them. What are they called again?

Pweza. When I stayed there, they were shrimp farmers. A sophisticated civilisation but not capable of space travel. Matriarchal society. Highly visual. No voices and terrible hearing. No music to speak of, only rhythms. Their creativity is focused on the visual arts, dancing and storytelling.

She flashed Joe some of her memories: a group of octopuses pirouetting gracefully in silence, and organic buildings covered with kaleidoscopic artworks which shimmered in the pale light.

Wow. That's cool.

Hey, here's a fun fact for you: in Pwezan society, the mouth is only for eating and is otherwise kept hidden. For a Pwezan to show her mouth in public would be as indecent as a human exposing his genitals. Ooh, here comes the captain.

A blue octopus was approaching, backed by three bodyguards. To Joe, it looked exactly like all the others.

How can you tell?

It's the one from the video link. Has to be the captain. I'd better her ask for permission to come aboard. I'll interpret for you, but don't interrupt, OK?

Kitty curtsied a formal octopus greeting and held up her arms in a sequence of different positions, opening and closing her suckers.

'Permission granted, on the condition that you explain who you are this instant.'

'I am Reika Ahmitorsdottir. I have come to parley on behalf of this planet. Whom do I have the honour of addressing?'

'I am Scylla, Queen of the Pweza. Your speech is old-fashioned. How do you know our language?'

'I lived among you once, a long time ago.'

This piqued the queen's interest. 'There are legends telling of a red octopus able to turn into a fish or a land creature. Could that be you?'

'It could be,' agreed Kitty, noncommittally. 'But please, explain why you need to land on this planet. How long have you been able to travel through space?'

Scylla's skin darkened as her thoughts returned to the moment.

'We are refugees,' she said sadly. 'We are new to space travel. This is the first time we have travelled so far with so many on board. Our ships are not designed for such long distances. We have nearly run out of oxygen. If we cannot land in your oceans, we will suffocate and die. The mineral content of our water needs rebalancing urgently and our nitrate level is too high; it is making us all sick. And even if we did have enough oxygen, we have almost no food left. Soon we will be forced to start eating each other.'

'Why are you refugees?' said Kitty.

'Several decades ago, our planet was invaded by the

White People: armoured, vertical land beings. They use their lower two arms for walking and their upper two arms have four digits. They seem not to have any eyes.'

Oh God, she's talking about the Ranglatiri, isn't she? said Joe as Kitty translated for him.

Shh! Don't interrupt!

'They had no interest in the seas to start with, and for a long time we had no idea they were even there. Our planet has no sentient land life that could have alerted us to the danger. Once we realised what was happening, it was too late. They were everywhere, like locusts, stripping the land of all vegetation and turning it to desert. We couldn't fight them effectively on land, and they didn't pursue us into the water. Perhaps they didn't consider us to be of value; I've heard these creatures usually enslave the intelligent life they find. They were aware of us, but ignored us.

'Without the trees, our atmosphere began to heat up and the oxygen content of our water fell. My people were slowly suffocating: our planet had become uninhabitable. We have had some contact and trade with neighbouring planets – that is how we learnt Kawaida – but none have enough surface water for us to live there. A few years ago, a probe picked up a faint transmission from this planet. It seemed we might be able to survive here, so we packed as many people into our ships as we could and came to find out.'

'Wasn't that an enormous gamble?'

'It was our only option. This is the only potentially viable planet we could find in years of searching, and it is right at the edge of our ships' range. Now will you please let us land before we start to die too?'

Kitty expelled a jet of water through her siphon in an octopus version of a sigh.

'I'm sorry. I can't let you land here. It would be a disaster. How much did that transmission you intercepted tell you about the locals?'

'They are apes,' shrugged Scylla dismissively. 'They live on land. We wouldn't bother them. If they were interested, we would be happy to share our technology with them in return for the right to settle. We are peaceful, they have nothing to fear from us.'

'But what about you from them?' argued Kitty. 'I have lived with the humans for many years. Individually, they are sensible, rational creatures. But in groups they are more primitive. Humans are not ready for large-scale alien contact. What they fear most is the unknown, and their instinct is to destroy what they fear.

'Their technology might be limited, but there is nothing more dangerous or unpredictable than a large group of frightened humans. They would see you as invaders, not refugees, and they would attack you. You would be forced to retaliate. A war would result and all would suffer.'

In the corner of his eye, Joe saw a blue arm flash by, then felt Kitty's surprise as it wrapped around her mantle like a boa constrictor.

Cheeky sods! They're trying to strangle me!

Lucky you don't need to breathe then, isn't it?

Scylla waved her arms angrily. 'We are going to land on that planet. We have no choice. We will use force if necessary: our ships are armed. Call off your fleet, or we will attack. We have nothing to lose, you must see that.'

In an instant, Kitty grew and grew until she towered threateningly over the queen. The guard octopus behind her released his hold and went limp, as did the other two. Kitty shrank back to her initial size.

'They'll be fine,' she said, waving a tentacle at the guards. 'Look, we want to help you. But don't think you can threaten us. Your weapons are rudimentary and our defence force would break through your shields in minutes.' She continued thoughtfully, an idea forming as she spoke. 'There must be another way. There *is* another way. I know of a similar planet – my home planet – which would be able to receive you. It is almost completely covered in ocean, but the only intelligent life is on land. It's just a few parsecs from here.'

'We can't travel a few parsecs! That would take us months! Don't you understand we have run out of supplies? We can't go any further!'

'Tell me what you need and I'll get it for you.'

Joe explained the plan to the pilots. Kitty had gone to Syenitia to negotiate asylum for the Pweza with the Council. As soon as she had initial approval, she would take Scylla to test the water and introduce her to the Syenitians. Meanwhile, the priority was to re-oxygenate the octopuses' ships and give them the different salts they needed.

'The minerals are easy; we carry them on the *Shantivira*. The air is trickier. The easiest way would be for them to pump it on board within the Earth's atmosphere. We'll have to trust them not to land. Escort them closely. Wait until the southern Pacific is dark and do it in the strato-sphere, around forty kilometres above sea level. You'll be away from the shipping and flight routes – hopefully there won't be any witnesses. Commander Li, you're in charge of the escort operation.'

'Aye aye, Captain,' said Yisheng in *Tumba* Number One.

'While you're doing that,' said Joe, 'I'll get hold of enough frozen fish to last them the journey to Syenitia.'

An American accent enquired, 'That's a hell of a lot of fish, Captain, where will you get it?'

'I shall engage in a spot of piracy on the high seas, William. For the greater good. We'll pay for it afterwards; nobody will lose out. OK, I'm going back to get the *Koppakuoria*. Commander, transmit me your coordinates when you're ready. I'll meet you there with the fish.'

The *Pride of Essoona* peeled away from the fleet and headed back towards the *Shantivira*. *Tumba* Number One rose to take her place.

'THERE'S OUR TARGET!' said Joe, leaning over the control panel. 'Wow, she's huge! Bring us in gently now, Gambri-nus.'

It was two o'clock in the morning local time, and the MV *Monte Maria* was ploughing her way resolutely through the rough Pacific seas, rolling from side to side with the waves as the rain and wind lashed her fiercely. More than two hundred and seventy metres long and forty metres wide, the South Korean-built container ship could carry more than five thousand standard twenty-foot containers, nearly half of which were refrigerated.

Gambrinus peered through the rain drumming on the *Koppakuoria's* windscreen. It wasn't falling, it came from the side, travelling in little rivulets across the glass from starboard to port. 'Is the atmosphere always like this on your planet, Captain?'

'Come on, Gambrinus, you've seen rain before. It's just a little shower. Better cover for us. That's why Delius picked this ship. The crew won't be on deck when the weather's like this, especially not when it's pitch-black outside.'

'I detect two life forms on the bridge, Captain.'

'Someone had to be standing watch. Let's see how far we get before they notice us.'

Gambrinus darkened the windscreen so that no light escaped from the cockpit and brought the *Koppakuoria* into position, hovering noiselessly on antigravity thrusters. He carefully extended the cargo transporter's six legs down onto the containers. The legs kept the spacecraft in position, following the motion of the *Monte Maria* without transferring the *Koppakuoria's* weight to the steel containers below.

'OK, now hack their mainframe and find out where they keep the frozen fish,' said Joe.

'Yes, Captain, I'm already on it. Got them. Mostly just above and just below deck.' He looked at Joe. 'You'll have to do it. You know the rules.'

Joe nodded. Before they could start loading the fish into their hold, they had to be sure of their own position relative to the containers so they didn't accidently transmat a load of trainers or washing machines instead.

Cylfs were only allowed to land on primitive planets if they stayed on board their spacecraft. Otherwise, the risk of getting captured and disassembled for analysis was too great.

Feeling slightly nauseous with the rolling motion of the ship, Joe made his way into the hold and set up his equipment. After checking his harness and cable one last time, he swung through the open hatch, lowering himself into the howling darkness.

'Fuck!' he gasped, as the rain pelted his body and the wind knocked him sideways. He accelerated, dropping as fast as he dared onto the container.

He heard Gambrinus laughing in his headset. 'It's just a little shower, Captain.'

'I'm soaked!' Bracing himself against the gale, he placed a tiny magnetic position transmitter at each of the container's upper corners. Then he dropped over the front of the container and attached a single transmitter on the lower corner.

'OK,' he shouted into his headset, 'you now have the position and size of container number ZGNU6597595, stowage space coordinates 540592. I'm coming back up.'

But the winch had only lifted him halfway when he was blinded by light. Hurriedly, he scrambled back up into the hold and made his way to the cockpit.

'They've seen us. What'll they do now? How long do you need?'

'Even going as fast as I can, it will take about three hours. I have to lock on to and transfer from each container individually. They can't call for help, I'm blocking their transmissions.'

'OK. Carry on. We'll have to sit tight and hope they're sensible and do the same. Make sure you delete any photos they take.'

15. NIGHT PIRATES
GERHARD

'*WAS ZUM TEUFEL ist das? Ein Riesenkäfer?*' Gerhard pressed his nose against the glass, cupping his face with his hands to block out the light. The dark, curving hulk covered the entire beam of the ship. Its sheer size locked his knees rigid with fear.

Jörg, the officer of the watch who'd woken him ten minutes ago, said, 'I saw someone being winched up inside when I switched on the floodlights, Captain. I've activated our SSAS beacon, and I've tried every channel I can think of to send a distress signal. But the phones are dead and we have no internet. No radio either. I think they're blocking us somehow. Should I sound the alarm to wake the crew?'

Gerhard took a deep breath. Keeping the crew safe was his primary responsibility. Allowing himself to be overwhelmed by panic wouldn't help anyone. 'Not yet. The fewer people moving round the better. Lock and barricade all the doors to the house and the engine spaces. We'll have to hope that's enough to stop them taking hostages or seizing control of the ship. Even if we had any weapons, I don't see what we could do against that…thing. We'll keep the floodlights on and the minute I see anyone come out, I'll sound the alarm for the crew to muster. Come back to the bridge when you're done.'

What the hell was going on? It must be some new form of piracy, although what pirates had the budget for a monstrosity like that? Was some government involved, perhaps? As usual, he had no idea what the *Monte Maria* was carrying. The reefers were full of frozen fish and there were a few containers with flammable substances. Everything else: well, they could be transporting anything. Hopefully the pirates would just plunder what they wanted and go.

How else could they call for help? Send up flares the old-fashioned way? But the chances of being seen were remote here in the middle of the North Pacific Ocean. If only the weather wasn't so awful, one of them could sneak up for a closer look. What *was* it?

16. WHAT DO THEY HAVE THAT WE WANT?

JOE

WHILE HE WAITED, Joe closed his eyes and watched what Kitty was showing him. As always, any attempt to persuade the Council to do something started by getting Rowan on side. If the sisters presented a united front, they could generally get the decision they wanted.

Rowan agreed Syenitia had no intelligent sea life that would be adversely affected by Pwezan settlers. But before approaching the Council, she wanted to visit the Pwezan planet and check Scylla was telling the truth. They found a windy, desert planet with almost no water. Kitty was shocked, remembering how verdant it used to be. Things must have got even worse since the Pwezan ships left months ago.

They stepped into the sea and shape-shifted into mermaids. Joe grinned to himself, remembering their dives together. With Kitty, he'd accessed places impossible for any other diver. They didn't even need a boat.

Oi! Mrs L! Show us yer tits!

He felt her amusement as she looked down at her chest, showing him a zip-up neoprene vest similar to the one Rowan was wearing. Below it, he could see her muscular red tail undulating steadily.

Sorry to disappoint, honey bunny. Now shut up, I've got work to do. Aldeman's calling an emergency Council meeting; we've got an hour to see if we can find anyone here.

They located an underwater city: clusters of irregular, tubular towers overlaid with intricate, shimmering patterns. Wherever the sisters looked, the buildings were deserted. They teleported to city after city but found no signs of life. Scylla had spoken the truth.

They returned to Syenitia subdued and determined to help. Joe looked curiously around the circular Council chamber, seeing it for the first time. The trickle of the drinking fountain at the centre told him he now had audio contact as well as visual: Kitty was allowing him to listen in.

The floor was of woven reed matting, and there were no chairs. Aldeman said the Council had better discussions when people were standing and able to move around freely. Before entering, it was customary for the Council members to remove their shoes and spend a moment reflecting on the Council's purpose: to serve the people.

If the session lasted more than a few hours, they would picnic together on the floor. At the end of each session they took the time to clean the chamber themselves and prepare it for the next time. This helped resolutions to settle, giving the councillors a final chance to express any concerns which might not have occurred to them during the main session. Occasionally, decisions were even overturned as they worked.

Aldeman greeted Kitty. 'Reika! Welcome! It has been

many months since you last visited us!'

Between them, Kitty and Rowan explained the situation.

'Can they not stay on Dunia?' asked Councillor Dalian.

Joe seethed. *Typical. Bloody typical.*

What else did you expect? said Kitty. *Now zip it and don't distract me.*

'I have told you before about the humans, Councillor Dalian,' continued Kitty aloud with polite restraint. 'They are not ready to exploit the potential, not with so many incomers at once. The result would be war and suffering on a grand scale. But Dunia's loss is Syenitia's gain. We can accommodate them easily. We could give them the Western Ocean and keep the Eastern Ocean to fish for ourselves.

'Syenitia is actually ideally suited to the Pweza. We have a lot of seabed at a depth of between fifteen and twenty-five metres, shallow enough for the sun's rays to penetrate. On Dunia, the seabed is riven with deep canyons and mountain ranges. Many of Dunia's oceans are too deep and dark for them to live comfortably. They could survive there, but here they could rebuild their civilisation faster, and Syenitia would benefit as a result. You have nothing to fear from them. There is plenty of room and plenty of fish for all of us.'

'What about the indigenous species in our oceans?' said a councillor Joe didn't recognise.

'You are right, Councillor Faaran,' said Rowan. 'That is a serious concern. If they come, they must minimise their impact on the existing ecosystem. The Pweza must destroy any organisms surviving in their ships. We cannot risk them introducing non-intelligent life forms which have no natural predators here. I will visit each of their ships and make sure of this myself. Reika and I are very familiar with the creatures in our oceans. Neither of us have ever come across any species sufficiently evolved to create its own technology.'

Kitty added, 'We all have a duty to protect intelligent life. The Pweza are good people. We must help them.'

Aldeman cleared his throat. 'Let me voice the unspoken question, Reika. What do they have that we want?'

Joe smiled. That was his brother-in-law all over. Clear-thinking and ever-practical, like a compassionate Machiavelli.

'Aside from their arts and culture? They have technology which works underwater at any pressure. If it is electrical, then it must be very low voltage. I don't know what power source they are using for their ships, but I am curious. They might have run out of food and oxygen, but they did not need to refuel. They have sophisticated filters and exoskeletons which they use to move about on land and in space. We could adapt them so Syenitians could access places which were previously impossible to reach. There is much we can learn from them. And they already speak Kawaida, after a fashion.'

Aldeman wondered aloud, 'How would we make it work? How can two civilisations live side-by-side without having evolved together in symbiosis? This is something we have never tried before. We would be taking a great risk.'

'CAPTAIN, I'VE FINISHED loading the fish.'

'What? Oh yes, of course. Thanks.'

Joe opened his eyes to see Gambrinus looking down at him. He realised he'd been sitting cross-legged and silent on the cockpit floor for hours.

'Were you meditating or asleep?'

'I was eavesdropping on the Council meeting. Oh shit, I'll tell you what, my *legs* have gone to sleep.' As he waited for the blood to return to his feet, he updated Gambrinus on what he'd learnt.

'That's what I've been doing with Delius,' said Gambrinus. 'You know we transmit video and audio signals to each other directly? He's gutted you didn't choose him for this mission, so I've been giving him a live feed.'

'He's gutted? Oh crikey, of course he is! I didn't even think!' said Joe guiltily. This would have been a rare chance for Delius to see his beloved Earth up close. Having orbited Earth for more than forty years, Delius had still never visited the planet's surface. 'I must apologise to him. It all happened so fast: I asked you because you're the regular pilot for the *Koppakuoria*. If I'd only thought about it, of course I would have brought him. I'll have to make it up to him somehow. Any ideas?'

17. THANKS FOR ALL THE FISH
GERHARD

GERHARD AND JÖRG monitored the giant beetle for hours. As time passed and nothing happened, their initial alarm subsided into a watchful uneasiness. Then, without warning, the beetle retracted its legs and flew towards the bridge. Terrified, they yelled and dived to the floor. But there was no impact.

It stopped abruptly, hovering right above them. A man in dark waterproofs and a helmet descended on a cable until he was level with the window. He pulled a sheet of A4 paper from his jacket and slapped it onto the wet windscreen. Written in black marker pen were the words:

SO LONG, AND THANKS FOR ALL THE FISH! ☺
P.S. CHECK YOUR BALLAST.

With a cheerful grin, he gave them the thumbs up and a salute, before disappearing up and out of sight. They rushed to the windows on the other side of the bridge to watch the beetle's departure, but it was gone. When they turned back, the note had gone, crumpled into soggy mush by the windscreen wipers. Gerhard looked at Jörg, incredulous. 'Did that just happen?'

18. AN AGREEMENT

JOE

ON THEIR WAY to the rendezvous point, Joe kept an eye and an ear on the debate in the Council. Finally, they gave Kitty permission to test the water in the Western Ocean with Scylla. If it had the right qualities, Aldeman and Rowan would meet them to present the Council's proposal.

Scylla was delighted by the Syenitian seawater. She jetted about, ecstatic to be free from the confines of her spacecraft after months of travelling. They swam to the shallows where Aldeman, wearing scuba gear, used Kitty and Rowan (now a green-tailed mermaid) as combined interpreters to welcome Scylla to Syenitia. Aldeman spoke to Rowan via their personal telepathic link; she passed on the message to Kitty, who translated it into Pwezan.

By concentrating hard, Joe found he could follow the conversation as Aldeman laid out the Council's terms.

The Pweza would be granted residency under strict conditions:

Firstly, every octopus must learn Kawaida.

Secondly, the impact on the local underwater environment and indigenous species must be minimised. The Pweza would only be permitted to settle in the Western Ocean.

Thirdly, the Syenitians could continue their current surface activities on the Western Ocean.

Fourthly, there must be an open channel of communication between the communities on land and in the sea.

The last condition was the hardest. Aldeman argued it was essential for harmonious cooperation between the two species.

'We need to learn a great deal about each other. I propose an ambassador from the land in the Pwezan city, and a Pwezan ambassador in Essoona, as far as is possible given the differences in our environments. We should also promote underwater tourism for Syenitians and for Pweza on the land. That means building special hotels. I believe you have suits enabling you to move around on dry land?'

'Yes,' said Scylla.

'Perhaps, with your help, we can improve our diving equipment.'

Aldeman raised his hand towards Rowan, who shifted into a green octopus. She dropped a polite octopus curtsy and resumed her mermaid form.

'I propose Verndari here as temporary ambassador until we can put a team together. She will keep the Council updated and can organise what you need in terms of building materials.'

Scylla waved her arms. 'Agreed,' she said. 'Can I confirm, you are offering us permanent residency?'

Aldeman nodded. 'You must be able to plan for the long term. However, if either party believes our partnership is not working and we cannot resolve our issues, we will help you relocate to another suitable planet. We will not make you leave without having somewhere else to go first.'

'Minimising the impact on the local environment is vital. It is in our own interests not to upset the ecosystem,' said Scylla, rubbing her two front arms together thoughtfully. 'I assure you, there are no other life forms on our ships. We've eaten everything we brought with us. Our society is built on crustacean farming. We will set up farms using local species. I take it you are open to trade with us?'

'Absolutely,' said Aldeman.

'And you have nothing against us maintaining our own space fleet?'

'Of course not,' said Aldeman. 'That is your right. We would also appreciate an openness to technology transfer, although that is not a condition of your staying here. We are curious about your underwater computers and your power source. And I am sure we have inventions and materials you will find interesting. But information about our military systems is off-limits, I'm afraid.'

They went on to discuss preparations for the arrival of the Pwezan ships in two months' time, then Kitty returned Scylla to her ship.

The Pwezan fleet was orbiting the Earth, long finished with loading the fish and pumping air on board. They sent a 'goodbye and thank you' message to the *Shantivira* and embarked on their journey.

Joe heaved a sigh of relief. Invasion averted. Thank God for that. 'Right everyone – including you lot watching in London – report to the canteen in one hour. We're going to celebrate with a massive party.'

19. THERE'S ALWAYS A CHOICE
LUCY

A PARTY? AS Lucy helped clear away the pizza boxes, she reflected that she'd never felt less like celebrating than at this very moment. Her mind was in turmoil, her throat tight, tears waiting to burst forth at the slightest provocation. It was only a matter of time before they threw her off the programme. Or worse. How could she have made such an appalling error of judgement? Would she be banished forever to some stinking alien swamp?

To prevent the Earth fighting a war it couldn't win, the Syenitians were willing to let an alien species settle on their own planet. She couldn't imagine humans acting so selflessly if the situation were reversed. The Syenitians took kindness and compassion to a whole new level. And if they were the good guys, what did that make *her*?

The students had watched events unfolding in a 3D projection from Irion's *zana*, crushed together on Mary and Irion's living room floor. As the afternoon faded into evening and it was clear an invasion was no longer imminent, the tension eased and people broke off into groups. Warily, Lucy monitored Hanna's every move, terrified she would tell Irion. Or Felix. And what would Charlie's reaction be if he discovered her cover had been blown? Despite everything, she was reluctant to let him down.

Hanna had retreated into the kitchen with Farida and hadn't come out. Nikolai and Saïd had gone in to get something and hadn't come out either. They must be talking about her, she thought. Otherwise why would they be in there so long? Should she go in there and defend herself? Paralysed with indecision, she wrapped her arms around her shins and rocked backwards and forwards, pressing her eyes into her knees so hard that she saw stars.

'Lucy? Are you OK?'

It was Felix. Sweet, trusting, honest Felix. She couldn't bear to disappoint him. And yet, if Hanna was telling Saïd, then Felix, his closest friend on the programme, would soon know everything too. Lucy imagined how hurt he'd be if Saïd got to him before she did.

'No, I'm not. I have to tell you something.' She stood up shakily and took his hand. 'Come with me,' she said.

They climbed the stairs to her empty flat and sat at the kitchen table. She spoke. He listened. He took it quite well. Shocked, certainly, but not outraged like Hanna had been. Instead, he wrapped his arms around her and kissed her hair.

'They put you in an impossible position, didn't they? You must have felt so alone, keeping all this to yourself.'

'It wasn't too bad until recently. But now our Kawaida is good enough, he's got me doing all this research into Syenitian history. All stuff that no one here has ever even touched on.'

'Like what?'

She told him about the Cylfs and their struggle for

freedom and equality, about Delius and his colossal data privacy violations and about the peculiar way that, wherever the Syenitians went, they always got what they wanted.

'How do you know they always get what they want? I mean, history is written by the victors, right? Anything you find in the Syenitian Library is going to be biased to a certain degree,' mused Felix. 'But they don't use violence, do they?'

'I suspect they do,' said Lucy. 'Not on a large scale, but I think they have a way of removing people who oppose them. I haven't found any evidence so far; it's more of a hunch.'

'Maybe you're just making assumptions based on our own unenlightened standards,' said Felix, a slight smile twitching his lips. 'The data protection breaches are alarming, though. They wouldn't need to use force because they already know everything about us. I think we need to find out more about the Galaksi Alliance discreetly, and this organisation you've been reporting to as well. It sounds to me like everyone has their reasons for what they're doing. The question is, what's best for the Earth?'

Lucy took Felix's hands in hers. 'I'm so sorry, Felix, I wish I'd told you months ago. I hate lying. It gives me stomach cramps.'

'Well, *I'm* not going to tell on you. But you have to put this right, or Hanna will tell Irion. You know how close they are.'

'I know. But what should I do? Nothing's black and white; I'm not sure I *can* pick a side. If Hanna grasses me up, then I'll never find out what's really going on here. She thinks the Syenitians can do no wrong and I'm a traitor. Perhaps she's right. After today, I understand that I've misjudged them. But nobody's perfect. They must want the Earth for something, right? And if I tell the EDS I want to stop helping them, will they let me go quietly?'

Despite Felix's reassurances, Lucy's intestines were still churning when the time came to board the *Shantivira*. White-faced and silent amid the excited chatter, she gripped his hand tightly as they crossed the training deck and hurried upstairs.

The canteen was full of pilots in navy-blue uniforms, laughing and hugging each other. On the backs of their jackets was an image of two fish, one dark and one pale, swimming head to tail in a circle. Apparently, this was the logo of the Galaksi Alliance.

Not having seen him since her assessment weekend, Lucy almost didn't recognise Joe when he came over to greet them. He still wore jeans and boots, but a loose linen shirt had replaced the scruffy hooded top, open at the neck to reveal a hairy chest and a heavy Celtic torc of twisted gold strands. Where had he got *that* from? It looked like it belonged on a velvet cushion in a museum.

He radiated strength and authority, and although he was just as welcoming as he had been last time, Lucy was disconcerted to find herself suddenly in awe of him. He asked them to help bring out the food and drink. 'We haven't had anything to eat since lunchtime. I'm starving!'

Despite it being the small hours of the morning, the kitchen was in overdrive. Pots clattered and people yelled at each other through clouds of steam. Eventually someone spotted them hesitating at the doorway and gave them all jobs. They arranged the tables in long rows, medieval banquet-style, then piled them high with food and drink. The ravenous pilots' manners were equally medieval as they fell on the food, not even waiting for Monifa to hand out cutlery.

The babble of voices grew louder. Felix introduced Lucy to two German-speaking third years: Alexandre from Brazil and Clemens from Namibia. He'd met them on their assessment weekend, after Lucy had gone to bed. She remembered how hungover he'd been that Sunday, and how he'd worried he'd fail the exam because of it.

They were buzzing with excitement because this had been the mission where they'd finally qualified as Galaksi Alliance pilots. Alexandre had been saving some bottles of *cachaça* for the occasion, and now he and Clemens were mixing *caipirinhas* and passing them to people along the table.

As they crushed limes, they pointed out various people to Lucy and Felix. Lucy knew she'd never remember all the new names and faces. A few were familiar. The Chinese woman they'd seen reading the newspaper in Dunia House was Qingqing, the daughter of Joe's second-in-command, Yisheng Li. And they knew Hassan through Hanna.

Alexandre leaned across the table and lowered his voice conspiratorially. 'Let me give you some advice. Don't ever piss off Hassan. He's all cool and calm on the outside, but he's a volcano underneath. You see that guy next to him?' He pointed to a tanned surfer type. 'That's Aussie Ozzy, Hassan's best mate. At the start of their first year, they were in the dining room and Ozzy was messing about. Hassan had taken off his boots for a rest, and Ozzy took them from him as a joke. I know, not a good joke, but no one expected what happened next.

'Hassan didn't say a word. He just marked his place in his book and put it down, super cool. Then, before Ozzy knew what was happening, Hassan swung himself out of his chair and across the table, slamming Ozzy's head down with one hand and pressing a fork to his jugular with the other. Legend has it that all he said was, 'Don't ever do that again, do you understand?' really quietly, right in Ozzy's ear. They've been inseparable ever since.'

Clemens said, 'Kitty found him living on the streets in Juba. She can sense a strong life force like a shark can smell blood, and his must be stronger than most or he never would have survived that long. She arranged for him to be fostered by a family in Kampala. Later on, he studied Psychology at the University of Nairobi. He doesn't talk much, so you never know what he's thinking. Rumour has it that he writes poetry!'

Clemens seemed to regard writing poetry as slightly shocking. Lucy noticed they were using Kawaida the same way the first years did out of lessons. As they frequently discussed Earth-specific things which had no words in Kawaida, they automatically used their own languages to fill the gaps, resulting in a bizarre yet comprehensible mishmash.

Felix looked down the table to where Emily was deep in conversation with a black man whose bulk suggested he spent serious time in the gym. 'Who's the guy in the Detroit Pistons T-shirt chatting up Emily over there?'

'Her name's Emily, is it? Is she single?' asked Alexandre eagerly.

Clemens laughed. 'Looks like Big Mike's got in there first, mate.'

Lucy took pity on him and pointed out the rest of the first-year women, highlighting that Flavia was a fellow Portuguese speaker and definitely single. They were interrupted by a voice from behind.

'Hello, you two miscreants. Can I sample one of your concoctions?'

Lucy turned in her seat and found herself facing a fair-haired man with dwarfism wearing a pilot's uniform. He helped himself to a drink, then turned back to Lucy and Felix.

'Hello. You're new. I'm William.' He held out his hand for them to shake. 'I see you've found Gossip Central,' he said, nodding at Alexandre and Clemens.

Alexandre stood up with a *caipirinha* in each hand, saying a lady desperately needed a drink and only he could help her. William took his seat and studied Lucy with interest.

'English accent…you're the one whose dad used to be in the RAF, right?'

Lucy blinked. 'Do you know about all of us?'

'Senior officers get a list of the new recruits each year. You struck a chord because I'm from an Air Force family myself. My father worked at Ellsworth Air Force Base, so I grew up in Rapid City.'

'South Dakota?' asked Felix.

'That's right. Pretty much as far as you can get from the ocean in North America. I was twenty-one before I first saw the sea. My two older brothers are both in the U.S. Air Force. I would have joined up myself, but I didn't quite make their minimum height requirement,' William chuckled. 'So I trained as a lawyer – I've always been good at talking myself out of trouble. I thought I might be able to do it for other people.'

'It was OK for a while, but I'm an adrenaline junkie like the rest of my folks. I got so bored with the respectable life, you know?' He laughed. 'I love going to Syenitia. They assume I'm from a planet with a lot of gravity, so they're extra respectful because they think I'm super strong.'

'How long have you been here?' asked Lucy.

'I trained with the carnivorous Welshman over there.' William jerked his head towards Joe, who was enthusiastically ripping apart a roast chicken with his bare hands at the other end of the table. 'I'm vegetarian, by the way, if you ever want to invite me for dinner. Then we went our separate ways until we bumped into each other again on Eluishav. There's a godforsaken backwater if ever there was one. They cook everything in vinegar. Revolting! I must have lost six kilos in a month!'

They laughed.

'There's some truly peculiar stuff out there, beyond our solar system,' William continued. 'I was just interviewing Kitty about the Pweza. Did you know, when a Pweza dies it's eaten by its relatives at the memorial service?'

'Eew!' spluttered Lucy.

'You said it. I wonder what the Pweza will think of the Syenitians' singing? They don't have any music apart from percussion instruments.'

Clemens interrupted, 'I still don't get it. Why would anyone invite another species to settle on their own home planet? There's so much that could go wrong!'

'They don't think the same way we do,' William tried to explain. 'I agree with you, it's risky. They've never done it before. They're relying on the good nature of the Pweza as vouched for by Kitty.

'Syenitians are always eager to learn from other cultures. It's how they became so rich and influential. Their strategy is to be consistently friendly and willing to trade, but to let it be known they can defend themselves if it comes to a fight. Of course, it helps that the Pweza have something the Syenitians want.'

'What's that?' asked Lucy.

'Underwater technology that works at any pressure, for starters. Plus, I don't know if you noticed, but they didn't need to refuel their ships, only restock their supplies. I think what really swung it in the Syenitian Council was the thought of potential access to that power source, whatever it is.'

'But it all happened so quickly,' pondered Felix. 'Isn't it undemocratic? Shouldn't they have had a referendum if they were going to invite a whole other species to share their world?'

'Well, there wasn't time, was there?' said William. 'They had to decide quickly. That's what the Council's for, to take those kinds of decisions. They're the representatives of all the people on Syenitia. If it doesn't work out, the citizens will make their disapproval known and the Council must rethink its strategy. Anyway, Syenitia isn't a democracy,' he said, grinning. 'There *are* no elections where everyone can vote.'

'Aldeman's a dictator?' said Lucy, shocked to the core.

Creasing up with laughter, William clutched the edge of the table to stop himself falling off his chair. 'Oh, that's brilliant!' he gasped. 'I think that would be a dream come true for him. Everyone doing what they're told and him at the top of the tree.'

'So he's not the head guy, then?' asked Felix.

'Aldeman may be the highest authority on the planet officially, but in reality, the power base is spread across many people and institutions,' said William. 'For example, when it comes to everyday life in Essoona, the Mayor of Essoona is more powerful than Aldeman. And the Librarians who look after Syenitia's data are a force to be reckoned with.'

The Library again, thought Lucy. The Ministry of Knowledge, Joe had called it.

'Syenitia is governed from the bottom up by random selection,' said William. 'It works on the assumption that all citizens will do their best for their community.'

'Random selection?' said Lucy.

'Being a politician there is like doing jury service. Councillors are selected at random from the population. There's a council and a mayor for each community, who have the most power to change things locally. Then there are regional councils for issues affecting all the communities in an area, and each of these regions is represented on the Syenitian Council, which makes the planetary-level decisions.

'The Syenitian Council leader is elected from within the Council by its members. So actually, Aldeman is the *only* elected politician on Syenitia.'

Like Lucy, Felix was struggling to get his head round this. 'So, does that mean *anyone* can be a politician?'

'Above a certain age, yes. It's seen as a great honour to have the chance to serve your community, however reluctant you might be to give up your job to do it. It's almost impossible to get out of.'

'So, if you're selected,' said Felix, 'you're not allowed to have any other kind of income?'

'That's right,' William nodded. 'Otherwise they'd have the same conflict-of-interests problems that we have. What's impressive is how engaged in grassroots politics they all are. Many Syenitians have personal experience of government or are close to someone who does, which means they understand how the system works.'

'But what's wrong with having elections?' said Lucy.

William refilled his glass. 'I asked Aldeman the same thing once. He said their current system is the fairest way of governing they've found. They can concentrate on long-term policies benefitting the maximum number of people, without having to consider the next election or their personal careers.

'They used to have democracy, but they found that when people volunteered for government, even with the best of motives, they wasted too much time on acquiring and retaining power. It was always people with similar characters and backgrounds standing for election, rather than a representative cross-section of Syenitian society.'

Sceptical, Felix asked, 'What about if criminals got into power? Or the insane? Or the criminally insane?'

'How does democracy protect you from that?' said

William. 'The random selection system actively prevents the power-hungry from accessing power. Chances are, if such a person came into government, they would be outnumbered and outvoted by normal Syenitians. Politicians *must* operate within the law. The penalties are severe if they're found taking advantage of their position. Corruption in government is punishable by permanent exile to somewhere worse than Eluishav.'

'What about people who are just not up to the job?' said Lucy.

'How do you know they're not up to the job until they try?' said William. 'People can surprise you. They should be allowed to explore their own limitations, not be told what they can and can't do. I could write you a book about that.'

'So,' said Lucy, 'correct me if I'm wrong, they generally have a few excellent councillors and a few terrible ones, and the majority are more or less OK?'

Nodding, William said, 'It's a rolling system, so you always have mostly experienced people and one novice. That ensures stability.'

He smiled. 'When they switched systems, there was an unplanned side effect: education had to be prioritised, because any citizen could end up running their city or region, or even the planet. That means the Syenitian education system is one of the best in the galaxy.'

A mechanical whirring made them all glance upwards to see rectangular white boxes descending from the ceiling. A cheer rose from the tables below.

'This party's going to kick off now,' Clemens grinned. As they watched, a tall figure with a neat beard and brown hair scraped into a top-knot, strode up the wall to the ceiling, a translucent, laptop-sized object under his arm. He crouched down – or was it up? – and placed it on the ceiling at the end of the room. It began projecting text and images, which he manipulated with practised ease. The boxes began blasting out the guitar solo at the start of Guns N' Roses' 'Sweet Child O' Mine', and chairs scraped as people made their way to the ceiling to dance.

'A bit Old School, isn't it?' shouted Felix above the noise.

'It's for the captain,' said William. 'Joe has appallingly conservative taste in music. Gambrinus is a great DJ, though. He'll put in something for everyone.'

'Shall we dance, Lucy?' Felix asked.

'Oh yes, let's!' She took his hand and stood up, saying to William and Clemens, 'It was great to meet you. Perhaps we'll see you later?'

They turned to walk up the wall, only to bump straight into Hanna, Farida, Nikolai and Saïd. Lucy's heart sank to her boots. This was it. The beginning of the end.

'Where have you been?' demanded Hanna. 'Come on, we need to find somewhere quiet where we can talk.'

Felix squeezed Lucy's hand reassuringly. 'What about one of the docking bays?' he said.

They headed to Docking Bay 2, but it wasn't empty. At the edge of the hangar, they stumbled across a couple locked in a passionate embrace. The man sat on a chair and the woman was astride him, his arms around her waist. She had her back to them, but the petite figure and dark curly hair were unmistakable.

Lucy clutched Felix's arm and hissed, 'Oh my God!

Tima's getting off with a pirate!'

It certainly appeared that way. He was a great bear of a man, with thick blond hair covering his forearms and the backs of his hands. His white T-shirt accentuated firm biceps with vivid tattoos of sea creatures, and a gold hoop glinted in his left ear.

Hurrying past as discreetly as possible, they headed for Docking Bay 3 instead. They picked their way around the towering *Koppakuoria*, over to the opening where the ships left the space station. Close up, Lucy could hear the shields humming. She felt the same unpleasant, undefined prickling sensation she got if she stood under an electricity pylon on a damp day.

In front of the opening, Lucy turned her back on the uninterrupted view of the Milky Way to face the others. Time to get this over with.

'I'm so sorry, you guys. I've been a complete idiot. And I don't know how to put things right.'

'That's what we're here to decide,' said Hanna sternly. 'Farida has talked me out of telling Irion straightaway. For now.'

'Thanks Farida,' said Lucy, smiling gratefully. Farida nodded, but didn't return the smile.

'But you have to stop this right now, Lucy. You can't see that guy again. Not ever.'

'But—'

'Wait!' said Saïd. 'Don't you think we've been present-ed with an opportunity? I think we should use Lucy to find out more about these EDS people. I don't actually think it would be a bad thing if the Earth could defend itself without outside help. But from what Hanna said, it sounds like parts of their organisation are...nasty.'

'No way! We can't ask her to be a double agent. We have no idea how much danger she'd be in!' said Felix.

'That's my choice, Felix,' said Lucy, seeing a way forward. 'Saïd's right. It *is* an opportunity. We need to know what we're dealing with before we take this higher. If I can give the *Shantivira* some useful information, perhaps they won't banish me to a place like the one William was talking about earlier. It's worth a try. We could even mislead the EDS with fake data – they've no way of checking up, have they?'

'If we can find out where they're based, perhaps we can retrieve what you gave them already,' said Nikolai, thoughtfully. 'I could hack their system and change all our names.'

Farida said, 'Follow the money. If you want to find out the truth about an organisation, you have to follow the money. Someone must have paid for that guy's flight. And thanks to Hanna, we have the flight number. There will be a trail to follow, if we look hard enough.'

'She's right!' said Saïd. 'Genius! Can you do it, Nikolai?'

'*Da.* I mean, I can try. I will try.'

'Lucy, will you give us the Library links Charlie gave you?' asked Felix. 'I'd like to form my own opinions before we take any action.'

'You're all being very understanding,' said Hanna, icily. 'Aren't you angry with her? She betrayed us!'

'She didn't have any choice!' shouted Felix.

'There's always a choice!' roared Hanna back at him.

'I'm sorry, Hanna! I'm really, really sorry!' shouted

Lucy. 'At the time, it honestly seemed like the right thing to do. I'll make it up to you, I swear!'

'But how can we trust you ever again?' yelled Hanna.

'Hey, calm down you lot, someone will hear us!' pleaded Farida.

'She'll have to earn our trust, won't she?' said Saïd, patting Lucy's arm. At least someone was trying to see both sides of the story, she thought.

'What's going on here?' came Tima's voice.

'This discussion isn't over,' hissed Hanna at Lucy, as Tima and her pirate appeared in the docking bay.

Lucy nodded. 'I know,' she said.

'Hi, Tima,' said Saïd, ramping up his charm to full power. 'A romantic hiccup, that's all. Nikolai and I were arguing about which of us would get to dance with Farida next. Ow!' With a shriek of exasperation, Farida kicked him hard on the shin.

'Really?' said Tima, arching a sceptical eyebrow as he hopped comically, clutching his leg.

'Are you going to introduce us, Tima?' said Felix.

'Sorry, yes, this is my husband Björn. Björn, meet Felix, Hanna, Lucy, Saïd, Farida and Nikolai.'

The blond giant shook hands with each of them in turn. 'Great to meet you all,' he said in perfect Kawaida. 'It's been quite a day today, hasn't it?'

For so many reasons, thought Lucy.

They were interrupted by the lift doors opening. A tiny old lady in a maroon and gold sari stepped out, followed by Aldeman and two other Syenitians: an older man and a stunning flame-haired female. Tima pulled Björn by the hand. 'Come on you lot, we have to get back to the canteen.'

They arrived in time to watch Joe and Kitty greet the visitors. The women hugged each other while the men pressed their vertical palms together in the Syenitian style. Then Joe took the Indian lady's hands in his, bending down to kiss her on the cheek.

In a whisper, Tima explained this was Dr Rohini Chatterjee, Joe's predecessor and the first human captain of the *Shantivira*. 'She's like the mother of the space station. Grandmother now, I suppose. She retired when Joe took over and returned to Kolkata, but she still visits on special occasions like today. The Syenitian with the white hair is Eyvindran. People say he's nearly two thousand years old.'

Lucy peered at him more closely. Looking good on it, she thought. If he'd been human, she'd have guessed him to be in his early sixties.

Tima said, 'He was the first captain of the *Shantivira*, before there were any humans with enough experience.'

Lucy pointed discreetly at the fourth figure, whose intricately braided red hair reached her waist. 'And that's Kitty's twin sister Rowan, right?'

Tima nodded. Rowan's smile revealed the same disturbing canines as Kitty's, although her glittering eyes were yellow. Despite her bare feet, she carried herself with the bearing of a queen. Her embroidered green velvet dress was similar to Kitty's red one, but with a more sophisticated cut. Kitty seemed rather scruffy in comparison.

Gambrinus turned off the music and the ceiling-dancers returned to the long rows of tables. Eyvindran remained standing. Broader shouldered and heavier-set than Aldeman, his deep voice boomed with strength.

'Crew of the *Shantivira*! Today we celebrate the greatest of victories. The Earth remains defended, the Pweza have a new home, and Syenitia has a new ally. All this was achieved by you – without a shot being fired. An outstanding triumph. If only it were possible to solve every confrontation this way.

'The Galaksi Alliance formally extends its gratitude to everyone who took part today. Only with our combined efforts was it possible to achieve this result. We must also offer our thanks to those conducting the negotiations: Lord Aldeman, Lady Reika and Lady Verndari. And to Scylla, Queen of the Pweza, who could not join us tonight. Please show them our appreciation.'

The hall erupted into applause and cheering. People stamped their feet and banged on the table. Aldeman stood up and motioned for Kitty and Rowan to do the same. The three held hands and bowed low. When the noise subsided, Eyvindran held out his hands.

'No more speeches,' he said. 'Join me in *Laulaahaalia*. We will sing the Song of Harmony.'

Everyone stood up and joined hands in a line, positioning themselves in a spiral starting with Eyvindran and Dr Chatterjee at the centre. There seemed to be no particular order or hierarchy, and there was much laughter and smiling as people got into place. Lucy found herself about halfway in, with Felix on one side and a woman who introduced herself as Lakshmi on the other. Eyvindran's deep rumble was quickly overlaid with other voices, as ring after ring of the spiral began to sing. Everyone except the newest recruits seemed to know the words. Once more, Lucy experienced a sense of shared joy and togetherness, this time with the other crew members.

Afterwards, Gambrinus dimmed the lights and fired up the music again. Lucy and Felix walked up to the ceiling with Lakshmi, who originally came from Leicester and was delighted to meet a fellow Englishwoman.

'There are a few Brits up here,' she said, 'but they're all blokes. I'll tell you what, we haven't had such a good party since Barry and Gary from the kitchen got hitched. That was an all-nighter.'

Raising his voice above the music, Felix asked what would happen if there was another invasion while everyone was partying.

Lakshmi laughed, tucking a lock of black hair behind her ear. 'That's not very likely! None of the pilots are as drunk as you might think. Lack of sleep would be a bigger problem, but we'd manage. You have to celebrate success, don't you?'

As they danced, Lucy felt a surge of love for Felix: deep trust and affection shot through with desire. He'd really stuck up for her in the docking bay. It seemed that he was truly on her side. Funny, on arriving at the language school, she'd started the relationship almost out of habit. She found sex an easy way to connect with people: less complicated to communicate by touch than with words. She'd always felt more comfortable hanging out with boys, and every time she made a new start – at university, on her year abroad, with each new job – she would attach herself to someone she felt could help her navigate the new situation (admittedly, her judgement wasn't always reliable on that front). She hadn't expected to fall properly in love. That was new.

Lucy moved closer, pressing against him. He folded his arms around her, giving her an exploratory kiss. Lucy closed her eyes and kissed him back more fiercely. The anxiety she'd been carrying released its hold, ever so slightly.

Coming up for air, Lucy looked across the crowded dance floor. Nearby, Victoria was hip to hip with Francis. She caught Lucy's eye and gave her the thumbs up with a grin. A bit further away, Emily had her arms around Mahesh's neck. Everyone seemed to be pairing off tonight.

An ear-splitting screech shattered the mood. Gambrinus shut down the music even before the ringing in Lucy's ears stopped and, as one, the crowd stopped dancing and looked up (or down?) towards the noise.

Two glistening dragons, one red, the other green, were locked in a coiling struggle in the space between the tables and the ceiling. Black talons and ferocious yellow teeth flashed under the artificial light, and Lucy could feel the draught on her face as their leathery wings beat the air.

20. BE CAREFUL WHAT YOU WISH FOR

JOE

D OWN AT THE tables, Joe cupped his hands around his mouth and bellowed, 'Oi! Ladies! Take it outside, will you?'

The dragons separated and dived towards them, flying low. Joe lifted his arm and caressed Kitty's underbelly as she passed overhead. Then they were gone. The dancers on the ceiling gave a collective gasp, then shouted as they spotted the creatures outside.

Joe watched them crowd at the window, jostling to see the sisters rolling over and over each other as they wrestled for supremacy. Hearing worried murmurs, he stood up on the table and called, 'Relax, everyone. They're only letting off steam.'

'Who'll win?' someone asked.

Aldeman climbed up next to Joe. 'Who knows?' he said. 'Kitty is stronger, but Rowan is more devious. They have had a great success today, so they are putting on a show for us. If they were settling a serious dispute, they would go somewhere we could not watch.'

'Is that what they really look like?' asked Lianjie. 'Demons, I mean?'

'Oh no,' said Joe. 'But it's closer than what they're normally willing to show. This is a great privilege.'

They watched the dragons dance around each other, twisting and turning like dolphins playing in the sea. Their exuberance was infectious: everyone was smiling, Joe noticed. Then, suddenly, they were gone. The crowd at the window gave a cry of disappointment and dispersed.

From his table top, Joe observed in satisfaction as some carried empty plates and glasses to the kitchens, while others began to form small groups, talking in low voices. They'd done well today, his crew, and he could feel a new sense of togetherness resulting from the day's success. The first years seemed quite at home, too. What's-his-name, with the Islamic hipster beard – Saïd? – sat on the window ledge, strumming a guitar as relaxed as you like. The German boy, Felix, kept him company. Aldeman sat a little further along, staring out of the window towards the moon, like he always did every chance he got. Joe noticed Lucy Cooper standing nearby, watching Aldeman intently. A bit of an oddity, that Lucy. Not neurotypical. He jumped down and joined her.

'Syenitians are fascinated by our moon,' he told her, nodding at Aldeman. 'Because they don't have one.'

'Where did the dragons go?'

'That's none of our business, is it? I expect they're on the moon, catching up. They don't see each other very often. So, how's it all going for you, so far?'

'Fine.'

Blood out of a stone, this one, he thought to himself. 'How are you finding the Kawaida lessons?'

'Oh, fine,' she said.

Was she shy, all of a sudden? She'd been pretty out-spoken on the assessment weekend, hadn't she? To fill the awkward silence he said, 'I had big problems learning Kawaida, myself. I'm dyslexic, see? I think in pictures rather than words? They didn't pick up on it when I was at school, but it explains why I did so badly. It was William who spotted it; it changed my whole outlook on life. I always thought that I was just stupid, you know?'

'But don't you speak Syenitian, too?' asked Lucy.

'That was easier. I never had to sit in a classroom to learn it. Oh, hello, Hanna. Enjoying the party?'

Hanna flashed Joe a bright smile. 'Yes thanks, Joe. Although there is something I'd like to discuss with Lucy, if you don't mind me borrowing her?'

'Of course, go ahead,' Joe said, then noticed Lucy's stormy expression. Had they had an argument? They were bitter rivals when it came to flight training, that much he knew, but he wouldn't have thought it spilled over into their personal relationship. Best to stay out of it. Felix and Saïd got up to follow them. Interesting. He joined Aldeman on the window ledge.

'My lord.'

'Captain.'

They sat in companionable silence for a few minutes, looking out at the moon and the Earth, until Joe felt ready to offload the burden he'd been carrying since eavesdropping on the Council that afternoon.

'So, the way you sold it to the Council. Is that what you really think? That the Pweza are all going to die when they get to Syenitia? That they won't survive, but you want a crack at their tech before they become worm food?'

'I do not *want* them to die,' said Aldeman indignantly. 'Our offer of assistance is genuine. It is our duty to help intelligent species where we can. But yes, sea species are notoriously sensitive to their environment. History and experience suggest their survival chances on any alien planet are low. There are not enough of them to colonise a planet successfully in the long term. Did Kitty ever tell you about the time we came to your world and tried to settle? And we are land creatures. It is a tragedy, but my feeling is the Pweza will die out before they ever pose a threat to us. Our bacteria will kill them off slowly, or they will not be able to breed properly. Two or three generations and they'll be gone. Unless we can find them somewhere more suitable.'

He looked Joe in the eye. 'Yes, I want to understand their technology before it is lost forever. I am not ashamed of that. Why should we turn them away? The risk to Syenitia is low, and the potential benefits could be considerable. If their planet has been stripped by the Ranglatiri then, as you would so charmingly put it, wherever they go they are fucked. Species become extinct all the time, but knowledge must be preserved at all costs.'

'The Ranglatiri are becoming a menace, Aldeman, we're going to have to do something about them sooner or later.'

'But what? We cannot work with them; they are only interested in subjugating others for profit. Nowhere do their principles overlap with ours.'

'Then by force, pre-emptively, for the defence of the galaxy.'

'That is not our way, Joe. You know that. If we started

invading planets with intelligent life, then we would be as bad as them! We must simply defend ourselves as best we can.'

'What about all the planets that can't defend themselves? Are you just going to collect their knowledge and let them die at the hands of those monsters? Like the Pweza? Life's more important than knowledge, Aldeman, you do know that, don't you? Sometimes you have to get out of your comfort zone and fight for what's right!'

'Ach, you humans, you are so *aggressive*. Have you thought any more about Dalian's offer?'

'She sent me the details. It's pretty tempting, in itself. But the fact it's coming from her makes me not want to touch it with a bargepole.'

'A bargepole?'

'Never mind. She's given me until the southward equinox to decide. So I have a couple of months to come up with a good excuse to turn it down.'

'On the other hand, I could do with a trusted spy in her camp.'

Joe laughed. 'You're all at it, aren't you?'

'Everyone on the council spies on each other, we are just too polite to talk about it openly. My spies are better than hers though.'

'She knows how close we are. She'd just feed me false information. But she must have had someone at the baths that night, or she'd never have come up with the offer. What's her objective, do you think?'

'Is it not obvious? She wants my job. Without you, she is hoping it will be easier to discredit the *Shantivira*, for example, by provoking Kitty into a rash act. That would impact my credibility; I have risked my reputation for this project more than a few times. People believe I am irrationally attached to it for personal reasons. Perhaps they are right. I still have thirty years of my term left, but she wants to prepare the ground so that I will lose all my influence afterwards. If she has her way, whoever my successor is, they will cut the funding for the *Shantivira* immediately. Not everyone believes the Earth is worth the effort.'

'Then first contact needs to happen soon,' said Joe. 'They wouldn't be able to cancel the project then, would they?'

'Be careful what you wish for,' said Aldeman. 'Humankind is not ready.'

'We'll have to agree to disagree on that, my lord. I won't risk my planet being left defenceless with the Ranglatiri on the prowl.'

'I understand your position, *Pikkuveli*. Now, tell me how the new recruits are doing.'

Joe accepted the change of subject. 'Oh, progress is as expected at this stage. I must say, they're a disturbingly well-behaved lot this year. Hardly any of them are venturing off the beaten track. According to Delius' reports, so far only Lucy and Nikolai are showing any signs of curiosity about Syenitia in their *zana* search logs. Nikolai has already learnt Syenitian, which is impressive. He's showing particular interest in the minutes of Council meetings and Syenitian computer systems.'

'But that is not surprising, is it?'

'No. I would expect no less, given his background. Lucy was our most reluctant candidate; she demonstrated a healthy scepticism of our operation from the start. She's more interested in Syenitia's social history: the Cylf struggle, Syenitia's influence within the Alliance, that kind of thing. And current events, strangely.'

'Could they be receiving guidance from anyone, do you think?'

Joe shrugged. 'Unlikely. Not impossible. They'll be fine as long as they don't start betraying our secrets.'

'Keep an eye on them, Joe, make sure they don't go too far. It is always a tricky balance to maintain. We need people like that to counteract the unquestioning loyalty of all Kitty's waifs and strays. Informed dissent is vital for any organisation's long-term survival. There is no creative disruption otherwise; everything will stay the same until it grinds to a halt. If it is ever to survive without our support, then the Earth needs them, even if they could potentially cause us difficulties in the short term.'

'Waifs and strays? You mean like Hanna, or Hassan?'

'Among *so* many others,' twinkled Aldeman, giving Joe a pointed look before returning to his topic. 'You know, I remember – before your captaincy – one of the second-years tried to raid the Library for data on our weapons systems. He was expelled from the programme of course. Gross misconduct. I left his punishment to Kitty. Did she never mention it? David something. I wonder what happened to him?'

'No, she never told me. I'll have to ask her. Oh, look, they're back. Time for the grand finale.' As the sisters approached, relaxed and smiling, Joe called Delius across and gave the command. Delius nodded and strode out of the dining hall.

Joe stood on the table again and shouted, 'Who wants to play zero-gravity?'

This was answered by a resounding cheer. Delius returned with a stepladder and placed it on top of the tables. Joe climbed up and, standing on the top step, announced, 'Delius has taken the gravity generators down to two metres. Come on up if you want to join me!' And with that, he leapt off the stepladder.

Below, he heard a few shrieks from the uninitiated, which faded quickly when they realised he wasn't falling. He floated where the dragons had fought an hour earlier, feeling his body pulsing in time to his heartbeat. People queued to climb the stepladder, and soon high-spirited zero-gravity antics filled the canteen. Someone brought a ball to play with. Others were spinning and pushing off from each other to see how far they could fly, shrieking and laughing the whole time.

As planned, the momentum of Joe's jump carried him slowly over to the opposite wall, ahead of the others. As he crossed the two-metre limit, he felt the gravity on his feet, pulling him onto the wall. He landed on his feet with a grin. He'd never get tired of floating in zero-gravity. Although, he thought, looking up at the crowd above, he did prefer having the space all to himself.

Aldeman was leaning against the window with his eyes closed, his left arm resting across a snow leopard and his right over a black jaguar. Group hug, thought Joe. He shoved Kitty along the window ledge and took her place. Without opening his eyes or speaking, Aldeman lay his arm across Joe's shoulders. Kitty repositioned herself on her back with her head in Joe's lap. He began stroking her rhythmically, up and down from chin to belly. She shivered with pleasure, emitting the deep, growly rumble which was the closest she came to a purr.

Inside his head she said, *Hello, you.*

Hey, babe. With some irritation, he remembered what Aldeman had said. *Guess what? Al thinks I'm one of your waifs and strays.*

Bloody cheek! I'm one of yours, more like.

Joe grinned. *Do you remember a second year called David, who hacked the Library?*

He didn't hack it. The idiot tried to physically break in.

What happened to him?

Don't ask me, Joe. It's one of those things I can't talk about.

One of the many. At least tell me: is he still alive?

Yes. He's still alive. But I'll kill him if I have to, and he knows that.

21. CELESTINA SATELLITES
LUCY

T HEY PREPARED LUCY'S next meeting with Charlie, the
last before the summer break, with near-military
precision. Intense hours were spent discussing how Lucy
should approach the retrieval of photographs and how she
should try to acquire more information about the EDS
without raising suspicion.

The immense relief of no longer having to keep the
secret meant she was sleeping properly again, which
boosted her well-being considerably. All the same, it was
uncomfortable to be the subject of so much discussion and
planning. Lucy half-wondered if she should send one of
the others to the meeting in her place: they seemed much
better prepared than she felt.

One morning, a triumphant Nikolai called them together. The air in his room was thick with stale cigarette
smoke. Hanna caught Lucy's eye and, as one, they pushed
past the others and flung open the window. At least they
agreed on *something*.

After a long night of research, Nikolai had finally
struck gold. 'So, you know I got hold of the passenger list
for that Swiss Air flight? The only American on board with
a Chinese-sounding name was a Mr Charlie Chan.'

'Not his real name, right?' said Felix.

'Probably not,' said Nikolai. 'But the ticket was paid for with a credit card registered to a Swiss company called Celestina Satellites. According to its website, it's a research institute for microsatellites that operate in arrays. The managing director is called David Wang.

'So. I tried to find out where its funding came from, and all I found was a shell company within a shell company within a shell company within a shell company. Many layers more than people normally use to hide their assets. Look, they go all around the world – companies registered in Switzerland, Luxembourg, the Cayman Islands, here in London, Macau, Rotterdam, Gibraltar, Chicago, Dubai, Hong Kong, San Francisco and ending up in – wait for it – Caernarfon. That's in Wales, here in the UK.'

'They're definitely up to something,' said Saïd.

Caernarfon? In Snowdonia? Lucy felt a fleeting idea unfurl deep in her brain. She tried to get hold of it, pull it closer for inspection, but no, it was gone. 'Nikolai,' she said, 'Caernarfon doesn't fit with the other places. Can you find out more about that account?'

AT LAST, THE day of the rendezvous arrived. Nikolai had programmed Lucy's phone so they could track Charlie's via Wi-Fi. 'If you could get his actual phone number, that would be even better.'

'I'll see what I can do.'

Lucy took her place on the fateful bench and waited. Picking at the skin on the side of her thumb, she ran through everything she planned to tell Charlie. She couldn't risk scaring him off if they were to find out more about his organisation. At the same time, she had to get those photos back. She cursed herself for her stupidity in handing them over in the first place. Her thumb began to bleed and she sucked it thoughtfully, frowning into the middle distance. A voice behind her made her jump.

'You're not regressing to infanthood after a trauma, are you?'

Lucy looked up at Charlie and forced herself to smile. 'Not right now. Maybe later.'

He sat down, stretching his legs and reclining with his arms stretched out along the back of the seat; the very picture of a man at ease – or attempting to appear that way.

'So,' he said, 'your friend Hanna has blown our operation.'

Damn. This was not how she'd wanted to begin their conversation. Thinking rapidly, Lucy decided to throw all their carefully prepared lies out of the window and be as honest as she could. Perhaps he'd return the favour.

'You saw her, huh?'

'Well, I wasn't sure at first, but when she swapped clothes with her friend – Farida, is it? – that kinda gave the game away. Did you put her up to it?'

'No!' cried Lucy. 'God, no! Charlie, I'm so sorry, they just happened to be here and saw me come in. Pure coincidence. And then they saw me giving you those pictures.'

'Ah. The pictures. I see.'

'They haven't told anyone yet. They were intrigued by

what you've been teaching me about Syenitia. And they weren't averse to the idea of the Earth being able to defend itself independently either. But I need to win their trust back quickly, before they change their minds.'

'And how are you planning on doing that?'

'Um…is there any way of retrieving those photos? I think I went a step too far there. I mean, you've probably given your boss copies already, but if there's any chance at all I could get them back—' she stopped, unsure of herself and confused by Charlie's expression. When he didn't say anything, she continued haltingly. 'Or, if you could tell me more about the EDS, or Celestina Satellites. Like, I dunno, who's David Wang?'

Charlie sat up and studied her closely. 'You *have* been doing your homework.' He paused, staring at his scarlet trainers. 'OK, this is what I can tell you. David Wang is the managing director of Celestina Satellites. That much you obviously know. His cover is satellite research, but actually he's trying to build a defence system for the Earth which is independent of individual nation states. When it's ready, he'll give it to the UN.'

Lucy thought about the chain of shell companies Nikolai had uncovered. She was reluctant to reveal everything she knew, or he might realise that it wasn't only Hanna and Farida who were in on the secret. 'Who's paying for it?'

Charlie focused on his shoes again. 'The general assumption is that David's using his own money. His parents made a killing in the first dot-com boom.'

'OK. So that's the Earth Defence bit. Where does the Anti-Alien League fit in?'

'Nestor is David's business partner. They met about seven years ago and came up with the idea for Celestina Satellites together. David mostly does the software and Nestor the hardware. From an engineering perspective, they make a great team; Celestina would never have got so far so quickly without Nestor. He's made some real breakthroughs. But that was before David realised how prejudiced Nestor is against non-humans. If he could, Nestor would happily destroy every alien that dares set foot on the Earth, starting with Kitty.'

'Why doesn't David sack him?' asked Lucy.

'He knows too much. David's stuck with him. They argue all the time about the direction the company should go in. And now the project's in the prototype phase, their disagreements are getting worse. David just wants to protect us from an invasion, but Nestor wants to,' Charlie raised his fingers to make air quotes and imitated Nestor's voice, '"maintain the cultural and biological purity of the human race".'

Lucy's lips twitched at Charlie's Nestor impression. 'You mean he wants to prevent any kind of contact with aliens? It's a bit late for that, isn't it?'

'Nestor would disagree,' said Charlie. 'And his followers are drumming up support for his point of view online. It won't be long before he has enough funding, and then David reckons Nestor will try to take over the company and steer it in a different direction.'

'Are you close, you and David? You seem to know a lot about it.'

'He shares his thoughts with me sometimes, yes.'

'Why are you telling me all this?'

Charlie smiled. 'To get you and your friends to trust me. And to warn you. Times are changing in the EDS. If something happens to me, be careful what you tell my successor. I...er...haven't been passing on everything you tell me.'

'You haven't?'

'David just wanted news of Syenitia. And for you to think about the wider picture and where the Earth's place in that might be.'

'So if Nestor stages a coup, does that mean you won't be my contact anymore?'

'It's likely. He sees you as a valuable asset that I'm not exploiting sufficiently. Which is absolutely true, from his point of view. If he can get rid of David, he'll replace me with one of his stooges and start piling on the pressure.' Charlie frowned, his brown eyes darkening with concern. 'Things could get ugly.'

'What kind of ugly?' Lucy asked. A molten drop of liquid panic hit the floor of her stomach and spread through her body like fire. If she'd been standing, her knees would have given way. 'My parents? But Charlie, you promised! I never would have got involved if I'd thought they were at risk!'

'I know,' he whispered. He took a deep breath and turned to face Lucy. 'Perhaps it won't get that far,' he said. 'Maybe I'm just being paranoid.'

'Charlie,' said Lucy earnestly, taking his hand in hers. 'Please, you must protect my parents. As long as they're all right, I can handle anything else.'

He squeezed her hand reassuringly. 'OK. Don't worry, Lucy, I'll think of something. Whatever happens, we'll keep them safe.' He reached into his bag and passed her a familiar stack of photos.

Lucy emitted a shriek of relief and threw her arms round his neck, impulsively kissing him on the cheek. His smooth skin smelt pleasantly of citrus.

Charlie pulled away, embarrassed. 'No one has seen them except me and there are no copies,' he said in a flat voice.

'No copies?' she queried.

'No need. I have a photographic memory. It's all up here,' he said, tapping his head. 'Nowhere else. But you should destroy them. Look through them first, make sure they're all there.'

Lucy flipped through the pile, counting up to twenty. Sandwiched between the last two pictures was a printed note.

Next meeting:
Maria Werner Gallery of Conceptual Art
1 Torbryan Crescent
Walthamstow
London
Saturday, September 20, 2014, 3 p.m.
On the seat in front of the open water bottle.

On the seat in front of the open water bottle? What? Lucy looked up to ask Charlie, then realised she was sitting alone. He'd gone! Without saying goodbye! She hurriedly shoved the photos into her bag and made her way outside. No sign of him.

Thoughtfully, she made her way back into town. Not wanting to risk Charlie getting suspicious, she'd arranged to debrief with the others in a café far from Kew and the language school. The minute he saw her, Nikolai stretched out his hand for her phone and started tapping away at it before Lucy even had a chance to kiss Felix hello.

Hands cupped around a cappuccino, she related her news: that she had the pictures safely again; that Charlie said no copies had been taken and that she believed him. She was about to tell them the tale of the two business partners when Nikolai hurled Lucy's phone across the room, smashing it into fragments against the opposite wall.

'Shit!' he yelled.

The hubbub of voices in the café ceased abruptly. As one, the clientele and staff turned to stare.

'My phone!' squealed Lucy, her hands over her mouth in shock.

'Sorry!' called Nikolai to the watching public, and then more quietly to Lucy, 'Sorry!'

A waitress came with a dustpan and brush. 'Clear it up. And then get out. All of you.'

Five minutes later they were out on the street. 'I need a proper drink,' said Nikolai, reaching for his cigarettes. 'Let's go to the pub.'

They entered the next bar they saw and Saïd and the girls headed for a booth in a dark corner, waiting for Nikolai and Felix to bring over the drinks. Lucy watched Farida looking round curiously. Was this her first time in a pub?

Felix approached with a tray, closely followed by Nikolai, carrying a shot of vodka in each hand. They waited expectantly as he downed each in a single gulp and slammed the empty glasses on the table.

'Come on, Nikolai,' said Hanna. 'What's the problem?'

'I thought I was being so clever,' he said, looking embarrassed. 'Using Lucy's phone to track his. Foolproof and no extra equipment needed.'

'Didn't it work?' said Lucy, suspecting she knew the answer.

'It would have done. If his phone had been switched on.'

A collective groan went up around the table.

'Who knows?' said Felix. 'Perhaps he didn't even have a phone with him.'

'Who goes out without a phone?' said Saïd. 'It was a reasonable assumption.'

'And now we've lost him and Lucy's phone is in bits,' said Hanna. 'Great.'

Nikolai looked mortified. 'Lucy, I'm so sorry! I'll buy you a new one, OK? Any model you like, just tell me what you want.'

'Thanks, Nikolai. You do that. But don't be too hard on yourself. We know Charlie works for David Wang at Celestina Satellites in Switzerland. We don't need to track his every move; it's the company we should be watching.' Lucy updated them on everything Charlie had told her.

As they digested the information, Nikolai remembered something. 'Hey, I found out more about that bank account in Caernarfon. There's something weird about it. I don't think anyone at the bank has noticed.'

'Noticed what?' asked Felix.

'So, the account holder is a Mr C. Ambrose.'

'So?' said Hanna.

'Mr Ambrose is not a company, he's a person. And yet Mr Ambrose has been the account holder ever since the bank first opened in 1836.'

'Did the first Mr Ambrose pass it down to his son or grandson, do you think?' said Felix.

Lucy said, 'I don't think they let you do that, do they?'

'Maybe it's just a typing error in the bank's computer,' said Farida, logical as ever.

Lucy wasn't so sure. The name niggled at her subconscious. There was a connection somewhere that she wasn't making.

TWO WEEKS LATER, the language school finished for the summer break. Returning to South West England was a shock. You needed a car for the simplest of errands, and Lucy had forgotten the frustration of sitting in caravan-choked traffic jams. Plus, there were so many white people. Where was everyone else?

She met up with Alice, but their bond wasn't as deep as it had been. Lucy found herself unable to bridge the chasm between her own reality and her friend's. It wasn't that she didn't trust Alice; she somehow just couldn't bring herself to go through all the explanations. At least she could be relatively honest about Felix and his refreshingly uncomplicated approach to life.

'So he's not going to join the list of people you wish you'd never slept with?' asked Alice, amused by Lucy's enthusiasm.

'No way!' replied Lucy. 'This is different. So easy. I don't have to worry about what he might be thinking, or some hint he's dropped that I haven't picked up on, because he just tells me straight. He never laughs at me for not understanding something. It's like I've had a headache all these years and now it's gone away. Even when we do disagree about stuff, it doesn't fester. We shout a bit, then we make up. No sulking or nasty atmospheres. No silent treatment. It's wonderful.'

SOON AFTER, FELIX invited her to visit him in Bavaria. He picked her up in a battered four-wheel drive from Memmingen, a tiny ex-military airport. They'd only been apart three weeks, but it felt like forever. He embraced her tightly and Lucy buried her face in his neck, filling her lungs with the comforting scent of his skin. Neither of them could stop grinning; it was so good to be together again. And such a relief to speak freely, without having to consider every response.

His family were kind and welcoming, but her time in Karlsruhe all those years ago had not remotely prepared her for their Allgäu dialect. As they only had a smattering of English, communication was basic and primarily via Felix. She nodded and smiled until her cheek muscles ached, understanding nothing.

The following day, he made her get up early. 'It's not far, but we want to avoid the queues.' They drove through hyper-picturesque countryside, full of onion-domed churches and wooden chalets whose balconies supported bulging cascades of scarlet geraniums. Half an hour later, they reached a large car park jam-packed with coaches and camper vans. On the hillside high above, Lucy recognised the fairytale outline of Neuschwanstein Castle, Ludwig II's fantasy retreat and world-famous tourist destination.

To get to the ticket office, they had to overtake crowds of Chinese teenagers, all staring intently at their smartphones. There were people everywhere, few of them Germans. It was as if they were in an international bubble, hermetically sealed off from normality. Lucy found the people-watching as entertaining as the tour around the castle.

That evening Felix took her to a tiny restaurant, tucked away up a side street. As they worked their way through a mountain of *Käsespätzle* topped with crispy onions, Felix told Lucy about his trip to Lyon, revisiting old haunts with Saïd and Nikolai. 'Nikolai's been doing more digging on David Wang. He had the idea that if Wang wanted news of Syenitia, he might have been there at some point. So he did a search with his *zana*.'

'And?' said Lucy.

'And he found out Wang started the *Shantivira* programme about ten years ago, but got thrown out in his second year.'

'His second year – when he was living in Essoona! So why did he have to go?'

Felix chuckled. 'Nikolai was pretty impressed by him. You know how curious he is about Syenitia's computer systems. He can't wait until next year when he can see the Library for himself. Although he's not looking forward to having to give up smoking.'

'But what happened?' persisted Lucy.

'Wang broke into the Library and tried to steal data on how the Syenitian dematerialisation beam works.'

Lucy gave a low whistle of surprise. 'You're kidding me! And they let him return to Earth?'

'Yeah. Weird, huh?' answered Felix. 'I thought they were supposed to send you somewhere far away where you couldn't cause any trouble.'

'Do you think he did some kind of deal with them?'

'No idea. But you'd think they'd be keeping an eye on him, wouldn't you?'

Lucy took a swig of beer. 'That explains so much! Why he wanted news. How Charlie knew about the *Shantivira*. And why he's having such problems with that slimeball Nestor. He's one of us, Felix! Kitty would never have recruited him if he was an alien-hating bigot.'

'So having failed to steal the technology which would enable the Earth to defend itself without the Syenitians' help, he's having a go at developing it himself. Respect.'

'Do you think the Syenitians know? But if they do, why are the EDS so paranoid about secrecy? Hey, if I get caught and chucked out, perhaps I can go and work for him.'

'If Nestor doesn't put him out of the picture, you mean.'

'Yeah. Charlie seemed pretty worried about that. Don't you think we should help David somehow?'

'But what can we do? Tell Mary and Irion? Or Joe?'

Lucy was reluctant. 'Too many explanations. I'm scared of what will happen if we take the official route. And if the Syenitians don't approve of what David's up to, then we could land him in a lot more trouble. I think what he's doing is important, don't you? He should be allowed to keep doing it, right?'

Felix nodded. 'Yes. The Earth needs to be able to stand up for itself. I mean, the Syenitians are great and everything, but what if their priorities change one day? You never know what's around the corner. The way I see it, the *Shantivira* gives us time to develop that technology, and that's exactly what David's doing.'

'Anyway, as far as we know, so far nothing's actually happened,' Lucy said. 'Maybe we should just wait and see for a bit, carry on with the meetings and get updates from Charlie. The others are OK for me to keep on seeing him, aren't they?'

'That's what we agreed.'

'Then I'll talk to Charlie about it when I see him in September.'

They were interrupted by a whimpering from above. Looking up, Lucy saw a Boxer dog puppy with its hind legs dangling precariously above the tables across the room. It had slipped between the railings of the mezzanine level and was desperately scrabbling to keep hold. For a moment, time stood still. Then, with a yelp, the puppy plummeted onto the table below, straight onto the head of a French tourist. The poor woman screamed and the dog struggled away from her, landing in her dinner and knocking the plate onto her lap.

Both woman and dog appeared unharmed, and everyone watching breathed a sigh of relief. But after that, nobody in the restaurant could keep a straight face. Even the waitresses were unable to stifle their sniggers as they fussed around, tidying up the mess. Lucy and Felix were paralysed with silent laughter. Every time Lucy thought she was about to stop, Felix would catch her eye and set her off again. She hadn't laughed so hard for months.

The fortnight passed quickly. Apart from a day in Munich, they spent most of their time hiking. Lucy loved the novelty of walking across the border to Austria without showing her passport. 'Do we have to climb a mountain *every* day?' she complained, still stiff from the day before – and the day before that.

'That's what there is to do round here,' said Felix. 'Cable cars are too expensive to use all the time. This way, we avoid the crowds.'

Observing Felix, Lucy learnt the easiest way to climb a mountain was to put one foot in front of the other, ridiculously slowly so you didn't get out of breath, and not stop for a rest until you reached the top.

At the summit, they would write their names in the book kept in a weatherproof box fixed to the ubiquitous summit crucifix, take photos and eat a banana. Once she found her rhythm, she began to love it. They would be quiet walking up, each meditating on their own private thoughts. On the way down they would talk non-stop about everything under the sun.

Felix spoke of his childhood, his National Service in the army and the way the rural community functioned. He told her about the first time he did a ski tour on his own: getting lost in a white out and nearly having to spend the night on the freezing mountainside. He talked about his older brother Hannes and his job flying the local mountain rescue helicopter.

They went mountain biking, tried out the local summer toboggan run and swam in mountain lakes. On one clear night, they bivouacked halfway up the Aggenstein, gazing into the Milky Way until they fell asleep. By the time Lucy returned to her parent's house, she felt more relaxed and fitter than she had for years.

Even her mother noticed the difference. 'Look at you! What a wonderful tan you have, dear. Oh, you *do* look better. Your father and I were rather concerned when you came back; you seemed so tense and jumpy. He's doing you good, that Felix! When will we get to meet him?'

Lucy thought for a moment. 'Um, Christmas, maybe?'

'Not sure we'll be doing Christmas this year, love,' said her father.

'Nonsense, Brian, we're not using it as an excuse to cancel Christmas! We'll be in New York by then. They can come and join us!'

New York? Her parents? Lucy asked, 'What's going on?'

'Well dear,' said her mother, leading her through to the sitting room, her eyes sparkling. 'We've had a bit of luck, your father and I.'

'What kind of luck?'

'It was the Town Fayre here while you were in Germany. Shame you missed it, Lavinia did terribly well in the dog show.'

Lucy experienced a flicker of amusement as she imagined her mother's aristocratic golfing buddy as a dog parading proudly round the village hall with a rosette on her collar. She'd always imagined Lavinia Branscombe as more of a horse, but an Afghan Hound would fit too.

'—and we depart from Southampton in two weeks!' With a mental jolt, Lucy switched her attention back to her mother. 'Sorry Mum, run that past me again?'

'We won the raffle, love,' summarised her father. 'They had a last-minute prize donation of a luxury four month round the world cruise, and we won it!'

'Just imagine, Lucy, four months travelling all around the world!' said her mother, bursting with excitement. 'I can't wait! Isn't it a good job we're retired? It was tricky enough cancelling all our commitments until January, but it would have been impossible if your father were still in the air force.'

Lucy hugged them enthusiastically, her mind racing. 'Congratulations! That's wonderful news! So who donated this prize?'

'Oh, some tech company I've never heard of,' said her father. 'Something to do with satellites. Not a local firm.'

'And you're sure it's genuine?'

'Oh yes, love. I did wonder myself, with such an enormous prize. But the tickets with our names on arrived the next day and when I phoned the cruise company, they knew all about us.'

'Was it Celestina Satellites, the company?'

'That's the one! Why, have you heard of them?'

Lucy pressed her lips together, thinking. 'I have actually.'

Was this Charlie's plan to protect her parents from Nestor? Did that mean something had already happened to David?

22. FIRST CONTACT

DAN

D AN PATIENTLY HELD the bracket in place, waiting for
Simon to screw in the bolts. He gazed absently
round the Japanese module, his mind mostly on the jobs
he had to get through in the next three hours. That was
always the problem on the International Space Station, so
much to do and so little time. Simon's project was an
interesting one: monitoring the winds and airborne
particles above the Earth's oceans to try to understand
their effect on the overall global climate.

Dan didn't mind helping out, especially because Simon was a fellow American and new to the ISS (a civilian
climatologist from Stanford University, rather than what
Dan secretly thought of as a 'proper' astronaut, who'd
taken the military route like himself), but it was going to
put his schedule for the rest of the day right out. Another
late night tonight.

A series of ominous-sounding cracks, like gunshots,
jerked him abruptly out of his reverie. On full alert, Dan
tilted his head, straining to pinpoint something through
the white noise of the ISS systems. 'Can you hear that
hissing?' he said.

Simon nodded.

'Come on,' said Dan, 'We have to get up to the central post and tell the others we might have a leak.'

As Simon turned to follow him, there was another volley of cracks. Dan watched in horror as Simon's forearm erupted into a shattered, bloody mess. The impact sent Simon spinning, slamming his skull against a handrail on the opposite wall with a sickening thud. Unconscious, thought Dan. Fuck. A few wobbly scarlet spheres floated serenely between them, but most of the blood was still attached to Simon's arm in a growing, pulsating dome. Then the depressurisation alarm sounded.

Dan pulled off his T-shirt, binding it securely around the jumbled tissue. As soon as the tourniquet was in place, Dan wrapped his arms around Simon and pushed off against the far wall, launching them out of the immediate danger zone.

The others had heard the alarm and had already gathered in the Zvezda module at the other end of the space station to work the problem. 'It's Kibo,' reported Dan. 'Multiple impacts. We've gotta seal it off right now!'

'Not just Kibo,' said Valentin, the commander, turning away from his screen and registering Simon's limp form and Dan's blood-smeared chest. Without hesitation he said, 'Takeshi, Irina, Tatiana: seal off the module hatches, as fast as you can. We have to keep as much of our air as possible.' They complied immediately, leaving Dan still clutching the unconscious Simon. 'Flight engineer, your assessment?' requested Valentin.

Dan replied succinctly, 'Debris punctured the shell, got Simon in the arm, I think it's broken; a secondary cranial impact knocked him out. He's still losing blood; I need more bandages.'

'Get them. I'll inform Mission Control.'

As Valentin reported their status, Dan worked hard to stem the bleeding until, finally, it slowed and stopped. He looked down and noted dispassionately that his hands were shaking. Not much, but a definite tremor. Weird. He couldn't feel it; it was like they belonged to someone else. The return of the others was a welcome distraction; the hatches were sealed and they were safe – for now.

But before Valentin could report Simon's injuries in detail, the link cut out. 'That's all we need,' muttered Valentin. Cursing, he tapped at the keyboards, trying to re-establish contact. As he did so, an unknown face appeared on all the screens simultaneously.

'This is the *Shantivira*, calling the crew of the International Space Station. Greetings. My name's Joe Llewellyn, I'm the captain of the *Shantivira*. We heard you're having a spot of bother, can you confirm?'

Valentin answered. 'Yes. I confirm. We have depressurisation in several modules and one of our Soyuz, as well as fifty per cent power loss. More urgently, one of us is unconscious. He took a direct debris hit on the forearm and has a head wound. Significant blood loss. We've lost contact with Mission Control. How are you talking to us?'

'So you are unable to evacuate the whole crew and you require urgent medical assistance?'

'Correct,' said Valentin. 'But how are you talking to us?'

'In that case,' said Llewellyn, 'I'm going to pull you into dry dock and assist you with repairs and medical care. Our dry dock's fully pressurised with an atmosphere similar to Earth's and a microgravity zone. You'll be in range of our tractor beam in ten minutes. Hold on, you'll be safe soon.'

The crew gaped at each other, uncomprehending.

'Tractor beam?' repeated Irina.

Valentin spoke into the microphone. '*Shantivira*? Are you in orbit? Identify yourself.'

'The *Shantivira* is a secret planetary defence facility operated by the Galaksi Alliance. We've been in orbit for the last forty years, protecting the Earth from alien invasion. We're jamming your transmissions with Earth until we can work out the best course of action together. We don't want anyone else to know we're up here if we can help it. See you in fifteen minutes.'

'What's the Galaksi Alliance?' Valentin started to ask, but Llewellyn cut the connection before he could finish.

Everyone started talking at once.

'Dry dock?'

'This has to be a hoax.'

'Have *you* ever heard of the Galaksi Alliance?'

'How can they be jamming us? Can you try Mission Control again?'

Valentin cut through the nervous chatter. 'If they're that close, we have to accept their help. I don't know who these people are, but they're Simon's only chance. Even if we could get him into the remaining Soyuz, he wouldn't survive the journey home.'

Dan ran his hand unconsciously across his buzz cut; a nervous habit he thought he'd beaten years ago. Of course Valentin was right. Simon would die without help. But a secret space station? Why hadn't they been told?

The screen flickered into life again. This time it was a woman in a lab coat, her dark hair scraped into a ponytail.

'Hi there! I'm Hagar. I'm the *Shantivira's* medical officer. Tell me what you've got.'

Dan pulled the unconscious Simon in front of the video camera, showing her his bandaged arm and then the back of his head.

'How long ago did he go into shock? Have you given him any meds?'

She rattled out questions and Dan answered as best he could. He was quite proud that he could remember Simon's blood type. The spacecraft shuddered slightly – was that the tractor beam taking hold? How did it work? And if such technology existed, why didn't they have one on the ISS? Who had the resources to pull something like this off? He noticed the others were all glued to the windows, trying to glean what insights they could about this mysterious space station.

Hagar interrupted his train of thought. 'Will you come straight out with him? He'll need a familiar face nearby when he regains consciousness.'

'Er…yeah, OK. So you reckon you can help him?'

'There's a lot we can do. You're coming into the docking bay now; I'll be waiting outside. See you in a minute.' She muttered something unintelligible and the screen went black.

Dan peered through the window. They were in a vast hangar, shaped like a quarter of a circle. Below them was a craft which looked like an iridescent dragonfly, dwarfed by another shaped like a giant beetle. Dan knew no one on Earth was currently capable of building such spacecraft. So where had they come from? Were they from the future?

The floor was dotted with people of every ethnicity, some in dark blue uniforms, some dressed in casual clothes. Some even had children sitting on their shoulders. They were pointing at the space station, smiling and waving at them. They sure didn't *look* hostile. A large man with long dark hair and a beard was setting up a scissor lift directly below.

'How do we know the air is safe to breathe out there?' wondered Dan aloud.

'Look at the cabin atmosphere monitors,' said Tatiana. 'If it's true what the man said, the modules that got punctured should have all re-pressurised to normal.'

Irina checked her instruments. 'She's right. They have.'

The screens activated again. Llewellyn said, 'OK, all set at our end. You can open your airlock and come out whenever you're ready.' Then he was gone.

'How do we know it's not a trap?' said Takeshi.

'We don't,' said Valentin, bluntly. 'Are we being rescued or captured? We're about to find out. I don't see what choice we have. We have no weapons. We're outnumbered. We'll have to take a leap of faith and trust them.' He took a deep breath. 'Dan and I will take Simon. The rest of you watch through the window until I signal that it's safe to come out. OK?'

There were nods and mumbles of assent. Dan said, 'Well, if this is it, I'd just like to say, it's been an honour working with you guys.'

Valentin refused to be so negative. 'Cheer up everyone, it's not over yet. If they wanted us dead, we would be already. I want to find out what's going on here. Why did no one tell us about this? Takeshi, go and get Dan a fresh shirt.' He turned to Dan. 'Are you ready for this?'

'Nope. But let's do it anyway.'

WHEN THEY OPENED the hatch, they found a rope floating outside, like a long thread of kelp growing up from a far-below sea bed. Holding Simon with one hand and the rope with the other, they allowed themselves to be pulled down towards the elevated platform where Llewellyn and Hagar were waiting with a stretcher and a wheelchair. As they carefully positioned Simon over the stretcher and strapped him down, they were greeted by spontaneous cheers and applause from the crowd below.

'Permission to come aboard, sir?' said Valentin to Llewellyn. The *Shantivira's* captain was shorter and scruffier than Dan had expected. Jesus, the guy was wearing an ancient Iron Maiden T-shirt, with flip-flops below the fraying hems of his jeans. What kind of an operation was this? Then again, Dan was covered in blood below his pristine new top. It was all relative. Forty-five minutes ago, today had been a normal day – probably for this guy too, whoever he was.

Captain Llewellyn beamed with spontaneous warmth. 'Permission granted,' he said, taking Valentin's hand and pulling him over the railing. 'Call me Joe,' he said.

'Call me Valentin,' said Valentin.

Hagar took Dan's hand and did the same. Gravity dragged his feet down for the first time in months, and he had to grab the railing to steady himself. Dan felt sick and dizzy as the blood pooled in his legs and all his internal organs shifted south at once. A sidelong glance at Valentin told him he wasn't alone. Their muscles were weak from lack of use and they had almost no sense of balance.

Hagar leaned over the railing and called to the big guy with the beard, 'Delius, could you bring another wheelchair for Commander Ivanov, please?'

Valentin was looking back up at the ISS. He pointed at the six bungee cables which had been attached between the ISS and the walls, floor and ceiling of the hangar. 'What are those cables?' he asked.

'They're to stop your space station from drifting into the gravity zone and crashing on the walls,' said Joe as he lowered the scissor lift.

The minute they touched the ground, a pair of medics appeared and fitted an IV to Simon's good hand. 'It's too risky to do an IV in microgravity,' Hagar explained. 'Don't want to give the poor guy an embolism on top of his other problems.'

The blood bag they attached drained almost instantly. She shouted an instruction in a language Dan didn't speak, but since they fitted a new bag straight away, he guessed she'd said, 'Another one!' As the second one emptied, Hagar and one of the medics grabbed the trolley and raced away with it.

The other medic stayed behind to help Dan into the wheelchair.

'There you go, Mr Simpson, easy does it. I'm Hamza, by the way.'

'Thanks, Hamza,' said Dan, leaning gratefully against the backrest. 'Say, how come you know our names?' he asked.

'The internet, of course!' said Hamza, wheeling Dan across the docking bay in the direction of the stretcher. 'You're our closest neighbours – we like to keep track of what you get up to. You're from Boston, right? Studied Aerospace Engineering at Princeton?'

Dan nodded. He wasn't ready to chat yet; he was still beating back the nausea. It would be totally embarrassing if he puked now. Oh Lord, it was like the worst kind of seasickness. He concentrated on taking deep breaths.

Hamza continued, 'I grew up in Riyadh, but I studied at MIT. Biological Engineering. Long time ago now. Learnt to sail while I was there. Catamarans, mostly. You sail?'

'Um. Yeah. Sure I do. Not for a while though.' What with being in space for the last few months and all, he didn't say out loud. Today was getting weirder and weirder.

They reached the sick bay and Hamza parked Dan next to the hospital bed where Simon now lay. Dan gave Simon's hand a reassuring squeeze. 'Hold on buddy,' he whispered, 'you're gonna be all right.'

Dan watched Hagar remove his blood-sodden T-shirt from Simon's arm to inspect the wound. She raised her dark eyebrows at him across the bed. 'Wow. That looks exactly like a gunshot wound. Nine millimetre maybe. You're right, his arm's smashed. What a mess.' She scanned his arm with a device Dan had never seen before. 'Whatever it was, there doesn't seem to be anything left of it now. No foreign bodies in the wound. Uh-oh!'

Hagar gave an urgent shout and a nurse brushed Dan's elbow as he rushed past them carrying a roll of translucent, jelly-like material.

'What did she say?' Dan asked Hamza, frustrated he couldn't follow events.

'She said, "The shock's wearing off, he's going to haemorrhage again,"' replied Hamza matter-of-factly. 'Don't worry, they were expecting it. Hagar's the best there is.'

'What language is that?'

'Kawaida. The interstellar lingua franca.'

Meanwhile, the nurse had unrolled the glutinous substance into a flat sheet. Together they carefully lifted Simon's arm and placed it on top. They wrapped the sheet around the wound, enclosing it completely.

'What's *that*?' asked Dan, fascinated.

'It's like a plaster cast,' replied Hagar, 'except that it actively accelerates healing, right down to your bone marrow and nerves. He should be able to feel his fingers again in a couple of hours, and the bones will reform over the next few days. He'll have to wear it for a week or so. You can tell when it's finished its job, because it goes white and starts to crumble. Then you can pick it off like a scab.'

'How do you know what a gunshot wound looks like?' Dan asked.

'I used to be a medic in the Israeli Air Force airborne rescue and evacuation unit. Believe me, working up here is the quiet life compared to that.' She smiled. 'Usually.'

The nurse brought another roll of jelly, which they used to wrap up Simon's head wound. Minutes later, he regained consciousness.

'Dan!' he croaked, staring around at the unfamiliar surroundings. 'Where are we? What is this place? Why can't I feel my fingers?' He struggled to sit up and his face turned instantly green. Dan lunged for a nearby bucket, but he wasn't fast enough. Vomit splattered across the bed and onto Dan's clean shirt.

'Oh man, I'm so sorry!' said Simon, mortified. For the second time that morning, Dan pulled off his top and used it to mop up the stinking mess as best he could, before helping hands arrived to take over.

'Don't worry about it,' he grinned, wiping his cheek with the back of his hand. 'Just glad to have you back with us.'

23. WE NEED IT FOR THE GOATS

JOE

W E CAN'T USE the meeting room, thought Joe as he watched the *Shantivira's* maintenance team doing their scans. They won't be comfortable out of microgravity, and they won't want us all crowding into the ISS.

'Delius, you've got fifteen minutes to set up a microgravity meeting room for twenty people, here in the docking bay.'

Good old Delius didn't twitch an eyebrow. He loved a challenge.

'Very good, sir,' he said, and jumped off the raised scissor lift, landing with an elegance that defied his bulk.

Joe smiled and refocused on the ISS. Valentin had returned to collect his crew, leaving Joe a few precious moments to gather his thoughts. What was the best way to handle this? How much should he tell them? Good thing Kitty was down on the planet today. Best get things sorted here before she got back.

Gambrinus appeared, driving a second scissor lift. He parked it parallel to the one Joe was standing on. 'Can you lower yours, Captain?' he said.

'Sure!'

When he reached the bottom, Gambrinus passed him

a fistful of plastic cable ties. 'You'll be needing these in a minute,' he said. 'I'm off to get more rope.'

Joe shoved the cable ties into the back pocket of his jeans. What were they planning? Delius returned, carrying two bulky rolls of wire fencing under each arm. Nice one! Simple, yet hopefully effective.

As he watched Delius unpack the fencing, Hamza arrived pushing the ISS flight engineer in a wheelchair. What was his name again? Simpson. That was it. Dan Simpson, USAF-test-pilot-turned-astronaut. Why was he wearing a Galaksi Alliance hoodie?

'Any news?' Joe asked as they approached.

'He's conscious,' said Dan. 'I think he's going to be OK, thanks to your people.'

'Thank God for that. Then whatever happens, it was worth pulling you in. Hamza, can you give Delius a hand, please?' Delius was threading the fencing through the railings of both the scissor lifts to create a platform between the two.

'What are you doing?' said Dan.

'Building a microgravity meeting room.'

'And you just happened to be carrying yards and yards of fencing? On your space station?'

'We need it for the goats.'

'The goats?'

'Yeah, the goats,' said Joe, enjoying Dan's expression. 'And the cows, of course.'

'Be needing those cable ties now, sir,' called Delius.

'Righto, on my way,' answered Joe. 'OK, Dan, let's get you floating free again. Then you can give us a hand.'

He pulled Dan up onto the platform and gave Delius a

nod. They raised the lifts together until the wire fencing began to float. Dan sighed with relief.

Joe grinned at him. 'Better?'

'Oh yeah. Everything back where it should be.'

Delius and Hamza were already unwinding the rolls on their side. 'Attach the ends together to form a vertical loop, like a hamster wheel,' said Delius.

'Understood,' called Joe. He handed some cable ties to Dan and began unrolling the wire. Dan followed suit.

'What is this place?'

'I told you before. We protect the planet from alien invasion. Can we wait until the others come out, so I don't have to say everything twice? Let's chat about general stuff instead.'

'OK,' said Dan, 'so, where're you from?'

'Wales! Can't you hear it when I speak?'

'Well, I figured you weren't from the States, but it's not an accent I'm familiar with. Wales is in England, right?'

Joe gritted his teeth. Bloody Yanks. Bet he doesn't know what rugby is either. 'I'm British, if that's what you mean,' he said.

They were pulling the last few cable ties tight when the rest of the crew emerged hesitantly from the ISS. Gambrinus had attached ropes between the airlock and the wobbly wire cylinder, and they pulled themselves down towards it, climbed inside and looped their feet into the mesh to prevent themselves from floating away. No instructions needed, thought Joe with satisfaction.

'Scanning's complete, Captain,' called a voice from below.

Joe leaned out over the railing. 'Thanks, Dipesh. Get everyone up here, will you?' Then he turned back to greet his guests. 'Welcome to the *Shantivira*,' he said, shaking hands with the new arrivals and introducing himself again. 'So, first things first. Simon has regained consciousness and should make a full recovery. We'll keep an eye on him in our sick bay for the next twenty-four hours, then he should be able to return to the ISS.'

The wire trembled as the others climbed up to join them. Joe waited while they all found a place around the cylinder. Maneewan launched up a grapefruit covered in fruit skewers like a psychedelic sea urchin, which Joe caught deftly. He took a skewer and passed it on to Valentin, his neighbour in the circle.

'So, let me introduce you to the team,' said Joe. 'This is my deputy, Commander Yisheng Li, and Lieutenants Valeri Karpinsky and Fatima Rahimi. Then we have Dipesh Banerji, our head of maintenance, and his deputy Oksana Yakovenko. And the rest of the maintenance unit: John Nakalinzi, Keith Copplestone, Dao Ng and Octavia Fernandez. Then we have our computers: this is Delius, the *Shantivira's* main computer, Gambrinus the ship's second computer, and this is Mervatius, the maintenance computer.'

'Computers?' said Irina. 'You mean, they're not human?'

'That's right,' said Joe. 'They're Cylfs – cybernetic life forms. Way above *my* paygrade,' he chuckled. 'We wouldn't get very far without them.' He nodded respectfully at Delius, who inclined his head solemnly in return.

'Did we travel into the future or something?' Dan

asked. 'Does that make your T-shirt an antique?'

Cheeky sod, thought Joe. 'I bought this in Cardiff in 1988, when I was a teenager. Now here we all are in 2014, I'm getting grey hairs and, as far as I'm aware, time travel is still impossible. I told you in my initial communication, this is a Galaksi Alliance facility. What's the Galaksi Alliance? In a nutshell: friendly aliens. The Alliance is a union of planets with intelligent life, promoting peace, trade and knowledge exchange, as well as nurturing less-developed species which they believe have potential. Us, for example.

'Decades ago, the Syenitians set up this base to protect the Earth from less benevolent aliens. So far, the Alliance's protection has given humankind the freedom to develop along the paths we choose for ourselves. They think we're worth the investment and they're waiting to see how we turn out.

'But they've been very coy about letting the Earth know we're here. They believe humans aren't ready to confront the fact that they aren't the most sophisticated life forms in existence. I disagree.' Joe paused and looked around the circle. 'And today is the day that changes,' he grinned. 'Us, here, right now – this could be seen as what they call "first contact". Sure, I'm as human as you are, but I am the Alliance's representative for this planet. The question is, after we've fixed your asteroid damage, what happens now? What do we do with this opportunity?'

There was an awkward silence. Eventually, Dan said, 'Tell us about the goats and cows.'

Joe laughed. 'If you don't mind coming out of micro-gravity, then I'd be happy to take you up to the biomes while you're here. You're our honoured guests, but I'm not going to explain everything about our operation to you. We need to get to know each other first. Trust works both ways. Now, the clock's ticking, let's get down to business. The way I see it, we have two pressing issues. How to repair the ISS and what to tell your Mission Control. Dipesh? Your report, please.'

Dipesh activated his *zana*, projecting a detailed 3D image of the ISS into the centre of the circle. Yellow, orange and red spots covered one end. 'The impacts are marked in a scale from yellow to red,' he said. 'Yellow is superficial damage and red is penetration through to the cabin.

'The damage to the solar arrays is not as bad as we first thought. Some of the damage is to the power lines rather than to the panels themselves. I estimate we can get power back up to eighty-five per cent fairly easily. That would be enough to operate all your systems, wouldn't it?' The ISS crew nodded in unison. 'Then you can order spares from your Mission Control and sort out the rest in a planned spacewalk.

'The punctures and impact damage on the station itself should also be quite simple to fix, now we know where all the holes are. We have a special foam we can spray into them, which hardens into an airtight solid. It will just be time consuming. If we throw enough manpower at it, we should be done in less than a week.

'What concerns me most is the Soyuz. We'd have to use conventional Earth materials, because we're not permitted to let alien technology reach Earth. The *Shantivira* project will be shut down if we do. We're not supposed to use it on the space station either, but that's more of a grey area. Sealing the holes so they can withstand the pressure difference and temperature fluctuations in orbit is one thing, but the patches on the Soyuz must withstand the heat of re-entry.'

'Thanks, Dipesh,' said Joe. 'So, we can get you back into orbit safely in a week. I have an idea about how we can manage it with the Soyuz. Valentin, do we have your permission to carry out the repair work? I mean, we're not going to let you go until your spacecraft is airtight again, but we still need your agreement.'

'Yes, of course,' said Valentin. 'You must do the work. Without your help, I'd have had to abort the mission and decide who returns to Earth in the functioning Soyuz and who stays to die on the ISS. We're not equipped to deal with this level of damage. So, thank you. Thank you for your help so far, and yes, we gratefully accept your offer.'

Valentin shook Joe's hand again and patted him on the shoulder. Joe couldn't help but like him.

'The next question is, what to tell your Mission Control?' said Joe. 'You've been out of contact for more than an hour and they'll be getting pretty worried.'

'Can't we just tell them the truth?' said Dan.

Not the sharpest knife in the drawer are we, Mr Princeton graduate? thought Joe. Out loud, he said, 'You could. I think that would be unwise, with unfortunate consequences for you personally. You could cause a global panic. They might think we're holding you hostage. They might lock you up in a psychiatric facility. They might lock you up because you're too valuable an asset to be allowed to walk around freely. Once you return to Earth, you and your families would never be left alone again. We'd be OK up here – the *Shantivira* is cloaked. We're invisible to the Earth.

'First contact is too important to mess up. No individual nation should have this knowledge ahead of the others. My preference would be to inform the UN about us via official channels, after this situation has been successfully resolved. I could supply proper evidence and you would be expert witnesses, able to vouch for our goodwill. If things get awkward, the Alliance could offer you and your families protection.'

'That sounds sensible,' said Valentin, 'but what do we tell Mission Control in the meantime?'

'Tell them the damage wasn't as bad as you first thought. Simon's wound was just a flesh wound and he is feeling much better. You've already patched the leaks in the hull and the situation is stable,' said Joe.

'And then, to give them something to think about, tell them about the solar panels and that you haven't been able to fix the punctured Soyuz. Let's see what solution they come up with and go with that if it's any good. That should give us a breathing space to get the bulk of our work done.'

'But they'll be able to see our orbit's changed,' said Irina. 'Lying is pointless.'

'Not if we fake it,' said Joe. 'We can fake the origin of the signals transmitted from the ISS so they believe you're still in the correct orbit.'

'Can you do that? But what about all the cameras? Anyone with an internet connection can look at them,' said Valentin. 'We're like goldfish in a bowl.'

'The external cameras aren't a problem,' replied Joe. 'Delius has downloaded weeks of footage from the ISS cameras for just such an eventuality. We can rebroadcast those pictures. But inside the space station you'll have to pretend it's business as usual.'

'What if we have to do a spacewalk?' asked Valentin. 'There are cameras on our suits.'

'Hopefully you'll be back in orbit by then. If not, we can hold you in our tractor beam beyond our cloak, so it looks like you're in space proper. We won't come aboard unless you tell us it's safe to do so. They might suspect something isn't right, but the beauty is they can't come and check up on you. Remember, what happens in space stays in space.'

'We need to discuss this among ourselves,' said Valentin. 'Can you give us half an hour?'

Joe watched them pull themselves back up the rope to the ISS. That didn't go too badly, he thought, as Takeshi pulled the hatch closed. Waiting for his crew to climb down the ladder ahead of him, his eyes wandered along the length of the fragile structure. Pretty amazing, to get so far in that thing. Then his heart faltered.

No! She wasn't back already, was she? Red-demon-Kitty stood on the hull of the ISS (microgravity being something for other people), looking mightily pissed off. At least she wasn't full size. Her tail lashed back and forth, and Joe feared she might cause even more damage than the asteroids.

Get down from there! he yelled at her privately. *Don't let them see you like that; they've had enough scares for one day!*

WHAT'S GOING ON?

Meet me on the Pride, he answered. *Now!*

To his relief, she disappeared. With a bit of luck, the ISS crew hadn't noticed her. He could hardly sell them the 'friendly aliens' story with a furious demon on the rampage.

He hurried home to find her on the verge of detonation. His whisky collection clinked wildly on the shelf as she literally vibrated with rage. All the chairs on her side of the table were overturned on the floor. There wasn't space for that tail in here. Firework time, thought Joe.

Did you plan this? What were you thinking, Joe? This is first contact, like you always wanted. Humankind isn't ready, you know it isn't.

'*Iesu mawr*, woman! Calm. The Fuck. Down!' shouted Joe out loud. 'They would've died if we hadn't helped them.'

Kitty shifted into her Syenitian form so she could shout back at him. Not much of an improvement. 'Then you should have let them die,' she hissed, eyes blazing. 'They knew the risks. Collateral damage in the interests of science. Whereas now our existence is no longer a secret. Have you no imagination? This will cause terror and chaos on the Earth. It jeopardises the whole mission.'

'Better to lack imagination than lack humanity, *Cath*. Let them die? We're all just fucking biomass to you, aren't we?'

'You know that's not true! I'm thinking about the bigger picture.'

'No, you just hate not being in control of events. Well, listen up. I shouldn't have to remind you; I am your senior officer and this was my decision to make. It's happened. Suck it up and deal with it, you *twmffat*. I have no clue where this is going to go, but I have faith in the human race. It's time they knew the truth. Aldeman chose me for a reason and I believe this is it.'

Kitty turned away from him, baring her teeth in an infrasonic growl. The ship shuddered and a bottle of eighteen-year-old Bowmore slid off the shelf and onto the sofa. Unbroken, luckily.

Get a grip on yourself, Cath, he said in her head, in a gentler tone. *Don't you dare go wrecking my ship. Think about it. Say I hadn't stepped in. First contact would happen anyway one day, and then the question would come: if we were there, why didn't we do anything to help? How would we ever be able to gain their trust then? By lying? You know better than me, the truth always comes out in the end. If I'd let them die, I would have destroyed the Alliance's chances of ever having a union with humankind.*

He could feel Kitty's anger abating. It burned brightly, her hot temper, but it never lasted long.

I bloody hate it when you're right.

I need your help with this, Cath. *At least, I need you to not stand in my way.*

Kitty studied her feet. *I won't. You're a good person, Joe. Better than me.*

He hugged her tightly, saying, *Your problem is that you think too far ahead. Too much imagination, if you like. Life's much simpler if you just try to do the right thing straightaway, without second-guessing all the consequences.*

It must be nice to always know what the right thing is. No wonder you always sleep so well at night.

24. BEWARE GREEKS BEARING GIFTS

DAN

'S O, WHAT DO we tell Mission Control?' said Valentin. They were back in the Zvezda segment, all except Simon. That would make things easier if it came to a vote, Dan thought. Out of the window, he thought he caught a flash of red scales. An alien reptile? He launched himself across the pod for a closer look, but whatever it was had gone.

'Everything all right, Dan?' asked Valentin.

'I thought I saw—nothing.' No sense in telling them about something he wasn't sure he'd seen. They might think he was hallucinating.

'We had to accept their help,' said Valentin, 'so I have a clear conscience there. But I don't feel good about lying to the rest of the team.'

'None of us do,' said Tatiana.

'I liked what he said about informing the UN via the correct channels,' said Takeshi. 'That would stop one country having an unfair advantage over the others. Otherwise we could trigger an arms race.'

'I agree,' said Valentin. 'Plus, whatever he said, if we don't follow Joe's advice, antagonising our hosts while we're dependent on them isn't a great idea.'

Irina said, 'Not to mention downright rude after all their help.'

'Dan?' said Valentin. 'You're very quiet.'

Dan scratched his head. 'We can't tell Mission Control what happened. Not until we're safely back in orbit and even then we'll need hard evidence. We should find out as much as we can about the *Shantivira* while we're here. One day we might need to report on it.'

A banging on the hatch made them all jump. 'I'd better answer the door,' said Valentin, grinning. He returned a few minutes later with an awestruck Joe.

'Wow, it's so cool to be here!' he said, looking around in fascination. 'Did you decide how you want to play it?'

Valentin looked at the crew. 'Are we all agreed? We fake it?' he asked.

There was a round of hesitant nods. Valentin turned to Joe. 'I want your assurance that you'll let the proper people know you're up here, as soon as everything's been sorted out. Otherwise they'll find out anyway at some point and we'll be properly in the shit. You can't expect us to keep your secret forever. Not if you're leaving traces of your work behind on our space station. It's too big a burden on the crew.'

'Fair enough,' said Joe. 'It's a deal.' He shook hands with everyone, before adding, 'While we're on the subject, there's something else. We'd like to install some shield generators for you. Two thirty-centimetre cubes, like that.' He made a box shape in the air with his hands. 'Then you wouldn't have problems with space debris ever again. Even better – you'd be properly protected from cosmic radiation. You wouldn't have to worry about long-term eye damage anymore, or the effect on your fertility. It would make your stay in orbit a whole lot safer.'

Beware Greeks bearing gifts, thought Dan. The ISS crew weren't authorised to make decisions like that about the space station. They had to find out more about this place, and fast. It was all too good to be true.

Valentin hesitated. 'Is that what you use on the *Shantivira*?'

Joe nodded. 'We're triple-shielded to protect our atmosphere and withstand enemy fire.'

'Supposing we agreed,' said Valentin, looking around the module at his colleagues, 'we'd have to tell Mission Control we have it. Otherwise, they'll draw the wrong conclusions from our experiments. And they'd be bound to see it if it's that kind of size. Wouldn't they?'

'That's not the hardest part,' said Joe. 'I have to get approval from the Syenitian Council to make first official contact with a developing planet and initiate a technology transfer. Like I said, most of the Council don't believe we're sufficiently advanced to merit it. But as a human myself, I'm frustrated that the technology's there and no one on Earth can access it.

'If we could install them on the ISS and get your colleagues on the planet to accept you need them, that's half the battle. You can always go on strike if they tell you to remove them,' he grinned. 'If we explain how they work, the space agencies could work up their own versions. You know prolonged exposure to cosmic radiation gives you brain damage, right? But with a shield generator, it's entirely preventable.' Joe paused. 'Again, you can't tell your Mission Control immediately. We have to go through the UN. This has to be for the human race as a whole, not individual nation states.'

'We don't have to decide now, do we?' said Valentin. 'This is in a different league to plugging a few holes in the hull.'

'Well,' answered Joe. 'Approval from the Syenitian Council could take weeks. Time is not on our side. We'd have to be sneaky. I'd want to get them installed and tested before you go back into orbit. So you'd better decide in the next couple of days.'

'We'll discuss it,' promised Valentin, noncommittally. 'But we really need to tell Mission Control we're OK. Can we reach them from here?'

'Not yet,' said Joe. He disappeared in the direction of the airlock and promptly returned with Delius, whom Dan had privately dubbed the 'Neanderthal cyborg'.

'Delius will create a link to our system, so we can reroute the signals you transmit. Then we can make it appear as if you're broadcasting from where you're supposed to be, instead of from all the way out here.'

Delius was clearly unimpressed with the ISS computing facilities. 'It's a space station without a brain!' he boomed in a gravelly voice. 'The humans are doing everything manually! What if they forget something vital, or get ill?'

Joe grinned at the others. 'Delius thinks humans are unreliable,' he said. 'But don't take it personally. He thinks the same about all organic life forms.'

THE CONVERSATION WITH Mission Control was predictably sticky. Valentin blamed the cut in communications on some damaged wiring, which they'd spent the last few hours repairing.

'We're all fine,' he said. 'How are you?'

Then they wanted to see Simon's wound. 'He's resting right now,' said Valentin, not saying *where* Simon was resting. 'I don't want to disturb him.'

Finally, they seemed satisfied and took the problem of how to repair the Soyuz away with them. Valentin sighed with relief as he cut the transmission. 'What have we done?' he said.

'No going back now,' said Dan.

25. NEGOTIATIONS
JOE

J OE BROACHED THE subject of the shield generator with Aldeman during their weekly session at the bathhouse. He waited until they'd passed through all the different stone pools and were soaking in the steaming green water of the last stage. Aldeman was initially sceptical, but at least he didn't go bananas, Kitty-style. He never did.

'I concede humans have progressed far during their Age of Fossil Fuels,' he said. 'But Earth is essentially a primitive planet. If we started a technology transfer, the consequences would be unforeseeable and unstoppable.'

Joe frowned. 'But the process has been going on for years already, hasn't it, with the *Shantivira*? There are hundreds of people on Earth who know about the Galaksi Alliance. Come on, Aldeman, it's time to put your money where your mouth is. This is the moment you've been waiting for since you started the project. They need this technology now. It's not fair to withhold it if you intend to give it to them later anyway.'

They discussed the implications late into the night. Aldeman promised he would hold a Council meeting to discuss the matter.

'They will not be as easy to persuade as me. I am biased. You will have to prepare some convincing arguments. In fact, they will probably want to prosecute you for revealing the *Shantivira* without applying for permission first.' He grinned. 'But knowing you, you will be able to talk them out of it.'

THE FOLLOWING DAYS passed quickly. For safety reasons, Joe ordered the blast doors to be closed. Without the view of the stars outside, Docking Bay 3 felt strangely claustrophobic.

On top of their everyday tasks, the ISS crew were helping the maintenance team carry out the repairs. They found the *Shantivira's* crew's lack of experience with working in zero-gravity highly entertaining. Much time was wasted retrieving drifting tools. Simon returned and did as much as he could with one hand. Joe noted with amusement that Hagar kept visiting the ISS 'to check on Simon' and suspected a developing romance.

The astronauts and cosmonauts accepted his offer of a shield generator, on condition that Joe would tell the UN within six months – once Valentin, Tatiana and Dan were back on the planet to act as witnesses. In return, Joe gave them each a personal tour of the *Shantivira*, which gave him a chance to get to know them individually.

Their questions were focused and wide-ranging. Joe understood they were trying to learn all they could about the *Shantivira*, her mission, the Galaksi Alliance and the Syenitians, and then briefing the rest of the crew before deciding which questions the next person should ask. Fair enough. He'd do the same in their position.

Today was the last one. Flight Engineer Dan Simpson. Joe collected him in a wheelchair and gave him a tour of the docking bays, and a little taster flight in a simulator, just as he had for the others. It seemed that flying was Dan's thing, judging from the number of times he said 'awesome'. The questions came thick and fast as they made their way up to the temperate biome. Joe sensed these were spontaneous: Dan wasn't working his way down a memorised checklist.

'Right,' said Joe, interrupting him as they reached the door. 'We have to switch transport here, or your wheels'll get stuck in the mud.'

'Is this the bit with the farm? And the horse? Which one do I get to see, the temperate or the tropical? Say, how come you don't have hover-wheelchairs, anyway? Is there such a thing?'

Joe laughed as he opened the metal door. 'My boss doesn't give us the budget for luxuries like that. We make do with what we have. We don't waste energy if wheels will do the job.'

'Who's your boss?'

'The leader of the Syenitian Council. Aldeman Varpushaukka,' said Joe, wheeling Dan over the threshold. Joe knew Dan knew what was coming, but everyone reacted the same way to a change of plane the first time. Dan's knuckles whitened as they gripped the arms of his chair but, impressively, he didn't make a sound.

Distracted from his questions, Dan gazed up at the endless black sky. Starstruck, thought Joe, sticking his thumb and forefinger between his lips and emitting a piercing whistle. No need for the ISS crew to suspect the existence of telepathy. Some things were best kept private.

Horse-Kitty trotted into view, her glossy black coat rippling over veins and muscles. She moved with a joyful lightness, as if she were about to leave the ground. Her thick neck arched below her excessive mane, half-plaited with uneven, pink-ribboned braids. On her bare back sat Kazembi and Nkosi's small daughters, Thandiwe clutching her big sister Flora around the waist.

Morning, cariad. *Loving the hair.*

Is it very bad? It took them ages to get that far.

You love it really, he replied, then called aloud, 'Time to get down, girls. Your mum's finished her shift. She'll meet you in the canteen for lunch.'

Kitty lowered herself carefully to the ground. The girls slithered off, throwing their arms around Kitty's neck affectionately before disappearing through the hatch at top speed, with only a cursory glance at the stranger in the wheelchair.

'Right, next one up,' said Joe to Dan.

'Um, so, I was warned about this, but – no saddle? Not even a bridle?'

'You're not riding,' said Joe, helping Dan out of his chair. 'She's carrying you. There's a difference.'

Dan seemed unconvinced. 'I never sat on a horse before,' he admitted as he clambered awkwardly onto the broad back.

Do I tell him she's not a horse? wondered Joe to himself. *Not yet.* 'Knot your fingers into her mane if you feel you want to hold on to something.'

Dan clutched the wiry plaits as Kitty surged to her feet.

'She won't let you fall, I promise. And she won't run away with you either.'

'I suppose she wouldn't get that far if she did, up here,' said Dan. 'Does she have a name?'

'Lots,' said Joe, enigmatically. 'Some people call her Kelpie.'

'Hello, Kelpie,' said Dan, leaning down to pat the strong neck. 'Thank you for carrying me today. Can she even see anything through all that hair?'

AS THEY HEADED for the farmyard, Joe said to Kitty, *Wish it was me up there instead of him.*

Sack of potatoes, this one. Shall we go to the beach later? Ynys Llanddwyn, maybe? I could do with a mad gallop.

I've got that big meeting with the council later. Need to work out what to say before I go.

All the more reason. Clear your head. You can spare an hour, can't you?

Half an hour. Yeah, I could do with a blast of sea air. You're on.

Joe showed Dan the farm, then headed towards the *Ohimo*.

'Could you do me a favour and take out all those ribbons while you're up there?' he asked.

'Sure. I think I can balance without holding on now. This place is truly awesome, Joe. What's that great big cone thing over there?'

'Part of the weapons system.'

'The base itself is armed? Not just your little fighters?

What kind of firepower does it have? What's the power source?'

Joe chuckled. 'Sorry, mate. That information's classified. But yes. We're armed. I can tell you that it's not an attack weapon, more of a last line of defence. I've never had to put it to the test.'

'Could it target the Earth?'

Like a dog with a bone, isn't he? said Kitty.

Shut up, I'm thinking. 'You mean, are we a danger to the planet?'

'I suppose so, yeah.'

'We protect the Earth, Dan. Why would we fire at it? It's our home. We don't take it for granted – not knowing what we do about what else is out there.'

You're not going to tell him the demat beam won't work in an atmosphere?

Nope. I haven't told them about the demat beam anyway. They probably think it's a big old laser or something. Let's not disillusion them.

'So what else *is* out there? Here are the ribbons,' said Dan, reaching down.

'Cheers,' answered Joe, stuffing them into his back pocket. '"Who else" would be a better question. You want to see some aliens before you leave us, don't you?'

'That would be awesome, yeah. Friendly ones, right?'

'You're not the first to ask. I've got my meeting with the Syenitian Council later, where I have to persuade them the Earth is ready for first contact. Leave it with me.'

'Good luck with that. Are we ready, do you think?'

'Honestly? I don't know. But I hope so, because it's happening. Here we are right now, in the middle of it.'

'But we haven't met any aliens yet. I mean, the *Shanti-vira* is amazing, but you're all human, right?'

'Apart from the computers, you mean?'

'Oh. Yeah, them. But they're not real life forms, are they?'

Joe's temper flared. 'Wars have been fought over that question,' he growled. 'Within the Alliance they have the same rights and legal status as any other life form. Some people think they're a higher form of life: the next stage of evolution. If you go up to Delius and tell him he's not alive or real, then I swear I'll—'

Joe! Careful!

'You'll what?' asked Dan, startled at Joe's outburst.

Joe took a deep breath, grateful for Kitty's warning. '—potentially jeopardise the success of first contact, before we even got started. So don't push me.'

'All right, I get it. They're alive and they're aliens. But they're not quite what I had in mind.'

'Well, the only other alien we have on board right now is the one you're sitting on.'

'Kelpie?'

'Well, you guessed she's not a normal horse, right?'

'I suppose. But she's still just an animal. No offence, Kelpie,' he said, patting Kitty's neck.

Joe laughed. 'Sometimes I think that's how she thinks of us.'

You are *all animals*, came her voice. *No shame in that.*
You *mean I think you're under-evolved.*

Yeah.

I only think that when I'm annoyed with you.

Ha-ha.

They fell into a steady pace as they crossed the fields towards the forest. Kitty hooked her head over Joe's shoulder, rubbing her hairy cheek against his. He scratched the long neck absent-mindedly as they walked.

So, what can you tell me about this guy from the way he sits?

Um. Good natural balance, considering it's his first time. Strong, despite months in microgravity. He's relaxed a bit now, but he's still pretty tense. And he's frightened.

Frightened?

He hides it well. You can't tell from his behaviour, but I can smell it. I think he's good at disguising what he really thinks. Probably an ingrained habit. If any of them are going to betray us, it'll be him.

You reckon? Captain America here? I was just beginning to like him.

Yep. Definitely. We'll have to watch this one.

OK. Thanks for the heads up.

THE NEGOTIATIONS WITH the Syenitian Council were as tricky as Aldeman had predicted. Joe stood before them dressed in formal Syenitian robes and wearing his golden torc, a wedding present from Kitty. Knowing Welsh kings of old had worn it when representing their people boosted his confidence in situations like this. It gave a physical aspect to the weight of responsibility in a reassuring, make-him-stand-up-straighter sort of way.

He argued that it would have been against the Code of Harmony not to help the ISS. 'If I had not acted, there was a strong probability some of the crew would have died, and that the entire space station project – and consequently human space travel – would have been set back by decades. Now our existence is no longer a secret, I see no reason for withholding this life-saving technology.'

'Captain Llewellyn, I understand you are a human and your lifespan is brief. You want to see the technology transfer start during your lifetime and not during that of your successor. So much is clear. But are you not being overhasty? Why not wait another ten or twenty years and we can discuss the matter again?'

'With respect, Councillor Dalian, it has to be now. The humans are preparing to send people to our neighbouring planet, and consideration is being given to mining for minerals on our moon. To get the best outcome, we need to incorporate Syenitian technology right from the start. Lives will be spoilt or lost if we prevaricate – surely that cannot be justified?'

Councillor Veryan frowned. 'Supposing we gave you our approval, how do you propose to go about it?'

'I'd start by giving the ISS a couple of small-scale shield generator units powered by organic waste to protect the space station and give them time to get used to the idea. Then, in a couple of months, I would approach the United Nations Office for Outer Space Affairs discreetly and explain who we are and what we have to offer.'

'And that would be?' enquired Councillor Elias.

'It has to be a technology trickle, not a transfer, to start with. It's important to avoid a power struggle where one nation has an unfair advantage. I'd offer to teach representatives of the different space agencies the fundamentals for building their own shield generator, and perhaps a gravity generator as well – on condition that they don't broadcast the information to the general public and start a mass panic. It would probably be better if they claimed the inventions were their own.'

Councillor Veryan interrupted him. 'But they cannot use the same power source as we do, can they?'

'True,' said Joe. 'They're far away from that. But Dunia is closer to a sun than Syenitia. Perhaps they can get what they need from solar power. I would give them the basic principles and leave them to come up with their own inventions. Then they can develop their own technology and not feel like they're being invaded. Humans are so innovative; they might find a whole new way of doing things once they've been pointed in the right direction.' He grinned. 'You never know, the Galaksi Alliance might learn something new!'

'What does the Lady Reika think of all this?' asked Dalian.

Joe hesitated, remembering Kitty's initial reaction just four days ago. But she'd come a long way since then. One of the things he loved about her was how she never brooded about things she couldn't change. 'I'm behind you all the way,' she'd said. 'Behind you and beside you. But you have to lead. I trust your instincts more than mine on this.'

'Captain Llewellyn?' prompted Dalian.

Joe chose his words carefully. 'It's not the way she would have chosen. She hates the uncertainty of the situation we now face. However, she accepts that I had to take the action I did, and now we have to ride the consequences as best we can.'

He looked at the councillors, willing them to understand his urgency. 'Dunia's history is full of moments like these, where everything changes. We can't know how it will turn out; we can only act in good faith. It could all go wrong if the humans start fighting wars to control the new technology. It's up to us to stop that from happening, by making it widely available immediately. And they will expect us to want something in return. It's important for their pride that they see it as an exchange.'

'And what *do* we want in return?' asked Councillor Faaran.

'Organic waste, sir. If we could source our fuel from Dunia, as well as some food and water, then I believe we could manage with just one supply transport a year instead of two.'

Councillor Faaran put his fingers together thoughtfully. 'It appears you have considered everything.'

'The secret will inevitably come out sooner or later,' said Joe. 'But it's better if it happens slowly. If we can become a rumour or an urban myth for a while, people can get used to the idea without being confronted by the reality. Then we'd have time to form relationships with influential people in the space agencies. Once enough people in authority know about us officially, panicked reactions should be avoidable when someone goes public with proof of our existence.'

Joe held out his hands, palms up. 'The crew of the ISS are so brave. If you could only meet them, you'd understand why we have to help them.'

Aldeman said, 'I would like to meet them before they go back into orbit. I wish to see this space station of theirs.

Can you arrange it?'

'Come to dinner in a couple of days. I'll let you know when we're ready.' Joe cleared his throat. 'Um…there's something else.'

Eyebrows were raised, but the Syenitians waited politely for him to continue.

'The people on the space station need a way of communicating with the *Shantivira* without being overheard by their Mission Control. If we gave them each a *zana*, they could learn more about us at the same time. They could even start learning Kawaida. And they could access our video library – that would directly improve the quality of their leisure time on board. It would be easy to ensure the *zanas* remain on the ISS.'

The Syenitians discussed Joe's proposal round and round for hours. He sat cross-legged on the floor at the edge of the room, calmly waiting for them to reach an agreement. Eventually, they called him forward.

'We must consult Dr Chatterjee before we make our final decision.'

Joe nodded, his expression carefully serious. But his insides fizzed with excitement. That meant they would go for it. Rohini wanted this as much as he did. They'd talked about it often enough.

He bowed low to the assembly. 'I understand. Thank you for your time.' Then he turned and left the Council chamber, trying to suppress the spring in his step until he was safely out of sight.

26. CAN YOU TIME TRAVEL?

DAN

B Y FRIDAY, THE repairs to the hull and the solar arrays were complete. A small shield generator had been installed in each of the two toilets. At first, the crew refused to believe it could be powered by organic waste alone, until Dipesh explained that the Syenitians were able to exploit the residual life energy in the waste, extracting far more energy than would be possible using Earth technology.

'Don't worry about how it works,' he advised. 'Just use it as a toilet. It has a mini gravity generator inside to pull through the fuel. That means you can sit on it without having to hold on to anything.'

Dipesh pulled his *zana* out of his back pocket and placed it on top of the white cube. The astronauts gasped: it didn't float away.

'It's not magnetic, or sticky. The gravitational field extends in a sphere around twenty centimetres beyond the unit. It runs automatically; you can switch it on and off here if you want to,' he said, pointing to a red button on the side. 'The shield repels anything approaching fast, but slow-moving objects can pass through it. So docking and undocking with the Soyuz won't be a problem, but it won't stop stuff – or people – drifting off into space, either.'

Dipesh picked up his *zana* and sat down on the box. 'I really hope this works out,' he said. 'This is the start of a new era. You know, my dream is to get a load of these installed back home in Bangladesh, for power generation. It would solve so many problems at once. We've taken a step closer to making that happen this week.'

As it was their last night on the *Shantivira* before returning to orbit, Joe had invited all six of them to dinner on the *Pride of Essoona*, along with Hagar and his boss, Aldeman. According to Joe, Aldeman was as curious about meeting them as they were about meeting 'a proper alien'. Dan had been itching to see inside the dragonfly ship all week and could barely contain his excitement. He hid a camera in his pocket, just in case he got the chance to take a few surreptitious photos.

Delius had taken the gravity field on the small ship down to the minimum possible before objects began floating, so standing was, if not comfortable, then at least bearable. Dan didn't feel sick, thank goodness. He wondered what they'd be eating. Something fresh, he hoped. Aldeman greeted them like a host as they boarded. He seemed very – what was the word? Urbane. That was it. Dan wondered where he'd learnt his English.

Far more disconcerting was the slumbering black jaguar taking up the entire length of the sofa, jaws slightly open, one monstrous paw dangling just above the floor. Every so often, an ear twitched. Despite its relaxed posture, everything about it screamed 'killer'.

Strangely, neither Joe, Aldeman, nor Hagar made any reference whatsoever to the animal. Finally, Dan could bear it no longer. 'Is it fair to keep a wild creature like that up here? Isn't it dangerous?' he asked.

Joe and Aldeman exchanged smiles. 'Wild creature is right,' laughed Joe. 'No one could keep *her* here against her will. That's Kitty, my wife. Please excuse her, she's had a long day. She doesn't eat food; she'll join us when we've finished.'

'Your *wife*?' asked Irina.

'She's a shape-shifter,' said Joe. 'Half-Syenitian, half-space spirit. Almost unique, and yes, utterly lethal if she wants to be.' He tilted his head towards the sofa. 'That's the form she prefers to rest in. It's like her pyjamas. She'll change into her Syenitian form later so you can talk to her. You've all met her already, when you had your tour of the biome.'

Shit, thought Dan. The horse, Kelpie.

Over dinner, the astronauts and cosmonauts tried to get answers to their remaining questions. Aldeman told them about the peace treaties and trade agreements which held the civilised parts of the universe together, and they debated the ethics of using extra-terrestrial technology.

Hagar insisted, 'Of course it's OK to use foreign technology. No developing country would insist on a full-coverage landline network before allowing people to use mobile phones. That would be ridiculous. The uptake of new technology leapfrogs the old, depending on what's more practical.'

Joe explained his agreement with the Syenitian Council: that he'd approach the UN through the proper channels and call some of the ISS crew to act as witnesses. 'Until then, you'll just have to keep the secret,' he said.

'You'll have to tell new crew members, but nobody down on the planet please, or you'll get us all into trouble.'

As they finished their dessert, the jaguar stood up and stretched luxuriously. In one fluid bound, she was off the sofa and resting her head on Joe's thigh. He scratched it affectionately; then she padded around the table to where Tatiana sat between Dan and Aldeman. Tatiana shrieked as Kelpie/Kitty/whatever-her-name-was jumped up and placed her front paws in her lap.

Aldeman reached over and gently touched Tatiana's hand. 'Have no fear, my dear, she is just saying hello.'

As Tatiana gazed into the sparkling green eyes, one eye closed and opened in a deliberate wink. Hesitantly, Tatiana held out her hand for Kitty to sniff. To Dan's surprise, the creature began to lick it. Tatiana laughed out loud and began to stroke the animal's head. Abruptly, the big cat jumped down and loped away through the kitchen area.

'Why me?' asked Tatiana.

'She can tell a cat person a mile off,' said Joe, grinning. 'I asked her to keep a low profile until you all got used to us. But it's important you meet her tonight, because she'll be your physical liaison with the *Shantivira*.'

Physical liaison? What did he mean? Before Dan could ask, a bare-foot, raven-haired beauty glided into the room, carrying a tray stacked high with cups, saucers, a teapot and a coffee pot. Mrs Llewellyn in humanoid form, he presumed, beginning to understand why Joe might have married her. She was taller than Dan – nearly seven feet – the black polo neck and close-fitting trousers emphasising her slim figure. Her flawless skin and fine features needed no make-up. Wow. What a bombshell. But he couldn't decide whether those eyes were bewitching or just spooky.

She served the drinks, then joined them at the table. She smiled in greeting, and Dan saw her canines were long and curved, like those of a carnivore. There was a shocked silence as the crew of the ISS stared at her.

Tatiana recovered first. 'So, what's a space spirit?'

'A space spirit is a concentration of life energy which coalesced into a single being in the dawn of time,' answered Kitty. Her voice was lower-pitched than Dan had been expecting, almost masculine. 'My father was a space spirit. My mother was a Syenitian like Aldeman here.'

Simon asked, 'What do you eat, if you don't eat food?'

Kitty gave an impish grin. 'People, preferably.' With lightning speed, she grabbed his hand: the arm with the cast. 'I absorb the life energy of other creatures. I can take it from you—'

The blood drained from Simon's face and he goggled at her, eyes bulging, struggling for breath. Valentin jumped up to intervene, but Joe placed a restraining hand on his shoulder.

'Or,' Kitty continued, 'I can give it to you.'

Simon's colour returned immediately and he sat up straighter, looking blissfully cheerful. To Dan's amazement, the cast on Simon's arm turned from translucent to opaque white and split in two. Kitty released him and caught it deftly. 'See,' she said as he flexed his fingers in wonder, 'you won't even have a scar now.'

Joe put his arm around her shoulders and gave her a squeeze. 'It's not without its hazards, being married to her,' he said, 'but no risk, no fun, right?'

Kitty and Joe smiled at each other, as if laughing at a private joke.

'I'm very careful how I feed,' said Kitty. 'In this form I don't need to take much. Most people don't even notice I'm doing it. I haven't killed anyone by accident for hundreds of years.'

'Wow, that's...comforting,' said Dan, his voice laced with sarcasm. How many people had she killed on purpose?

Takeshi diplomatically moved the conversation onto safer ground. 'Do you work on the *Shantivira* too, Kitty-san?'

'My work is mostly down on the planet. I come back in the evenings to be with Joe.'

'How come nobody's ever spotted your spacecraft?' said Irina. 'I mean, if you're going back and forth that often, wouldn't we have heard about it?'

'I don't need a spacecraft,' she said. 'I teleport.'

Cool. Dan asked hopefully, 'Can you time travel?'

Kitty shook her head. 'Only the same way you do: in one direction, one day at a time.'

The conversation around the table moved on to more general topics, and Kitty turned back to Simon. 'Sorry about before,' Dan overheard her apologise in a low voice. 'I get carried away sometimes. I promised Hagar I'd finish your healing process before you go back to your orbit. She seems quite taken with you, you know. I hope your intentions towards her are honourable.'

'Kitty! I'm right here!' exclaimed Hagar, embarrassed.

'So, Simon,' said Kitty more loudly, 'I wanted to talk to

you about your job. You're a climatologist, right? What's your understanding about what's happening to the Earth's atmosphere?'

After dinner, Joe took a stack of translucent, oblong objects from a drawer above the sofa and passed one to each of the ISS crew.

Valentin turned his over in his hands. 'Is this like your communicator thing?' he asked.

'Yes,' said Joe, looking at Aldeman. 'The Council has kindly agreed to let you have a *zana* each so we can talk on a secure line. The deal is that they stay on the ISS and never leave orbit. When you return to the planet, you must pass them on to the new crew members. But you can use them for a lot more than communication. You can even learn Kawaida from them if you want.'

Dan's heart beat faster. This was it! Hard evidence he could smuggle back to Earth. He just needed to find a way to do it without getting caught.

EARLY THE NEXT morning, the crew said their goodbyes before sealing themselves back inside the ISS. The thick bungees holding the space station were released, and the beetle-spacecraft towed them back to the correct coordinates.

'Well, I'm glad we're back where we're supposed to be,' said Irina. 'Although I wouldn't have missed it. Definitely something to tell the grandchildren.'

'Are you relieved to be back in full command, Valentin?' Dan asked.

'Well, yes, of course. But everything has changed now.

We're not on our own anymore.'

That's an understatement, thought Dan. They'd agreed to stay in touch with the *Shantivira* via a weekly video conference, updating Joe on the plans for repairing the solar arrays and the Soyuz. Now they had even more people looking over their shoulders than before.

'It's good to know we have help close at hand,' said Dan, 'but I feel uncomfortable depending on the generosity of people we've just met.'

'Oh yes,' agreed Valentin, 'so do I. And then there's the web of lies we'll have to maintain for Mission Control over the next few months. I don't feel good about that at all. But life has no reverse gear.'

You can say that again, thought Dan.

PART THREE

27. A TRIP TO THE SEASIDE
HANNA

HANNA ONLY STOPPED waving once the ISS was a tiny dot, no bigger than the stars. Hassan put his arm around her waist and kissed the top of her head. 'That was so cool!' she said, snuggling into him. 'I can't believe we were here to see it!'

'Yep,' replied Hassan, 'history in the making. And the weekend is still young. What shall we do now? Do you want to come back with me and meet Ozzy's new girlfriend? He's besotted, it's hilarious.'

'Anyone I know?'

'I doubt it.' Hassan grinned. 'Do you know anything about gardening?'

'Gardening?'

'Come on.'

Half an hour later, Hanna was halfway up an *omena* tree on the Dunia House allotment. Her legs encircled the thick branches as she strained to reach the fuzzy yellow fruit. Hassan was safely on the ground, holding the basket. As she inched her way out along the branch, she was inundated with childhood flashbacks of picking shea nuts.

She used to do this all the time with Martha, Yonas, Ibo and Negasi. God, she'd forgotten about Negasi, the boy next door. They must have been six or seven years old. Yonas and Martha climbed the highest, daring to get the fruit the younger children couldn't reach. But Ibo always looked out for her and Negasi. She peered down through the branches, half-expecting to see her mother instead of Hassan, toddler Samuel at her feet and baby Kia strapped to her back. The image was so strong, she was momentarily blinded by tears until she could blink them furiously away.

As she worked, she allowed herself to remember, cautiously opening a door in her soul she usually kept hermetically sealed. That had been before family life had begun to unravel: before the day seven-year-old Samuel had been bitten by a stray dog that had appeared in the village ahead of the rains. He'd been such a loving little boy, a liberal distributor of fiercely tight cuddles and warm, wet kisses. Watching him die so horribly, in such distress, broke her parents. Her father started disappearing for days on end and her mother stayed in bed and just cried. When he staggered home, he would shout at them until he passed out in a corner of their hut.

Hoping life would get better if they could just keep things going, the children tried as best they could to fill the gap. Yonas and Ibo cared for the family's cattle, while Martha, aged thirteen, took over most of the household tasks, looking after Kia and issuing orders to Hanna in the clipped tones of a general expecting unquestioning obedience. There was no time to play with Negasi, and anyway, he was going to school now, nearly every day. Any hopes Hanna had of receiving an education herself quietly evaporated.

One day, Yonas and her father had a blazing row, which finished with her father punching Yonas in the face. That night, Yonas packed his belongings and left to join the army, reckoning he was tall and strong enough to pass for eighteen. Hanna never saw her oldest brother again. Nor did she ever discover what they'd been arguing about.

Not long after that, her parents got sick: first her father, then her mother. The sickness everyone feared and nobody spoke of. The siblings did all they could to look after them, but there was no money for a doctor. Despite help from neighbours, the children watched their parents fade slowly away in front of their eyes. Thinner and thinner until there was nothing left. First their mother, then their father.

Knowing the virus had no cure, it was a guilty relief when they died. The children had become so self-sufficient that daily life without two sick parents to care for actually became easier. Until…Hanna pushed the memory away. Enough. No need to drown in sorrow about things she couldn't change. Focus on the good stuff: spending the day with Hassan, for example.

Finally, Hanna felt she'd picked every piece of fruit she could realistically reach. 'I'm coming down!' she called.

'OK!'

The basket was satisfyingly full, but Hassan had already collected another one and was critically assessing the neighbouring tree.

'So, I've been thinking,' said Hanna. 'I want to ask Delius to look for my brother and my sisters. If they're on any system anywhere, then he could track them down, right?'

'If it's not a paper system, yeah. Are you sure, Hanna?'

'I need to know, Hassan. I might be able to help them. Families should stick together. I'm going to talk to him right after we're done here.'

'Would you like me to come with you?'

'No, no thanks. It's something I have to do for myself.'

'Morning all!' called a friendly voice from the direction of the gate.

'What time do you call this?' yelled Hassan.

'Sorry!' It was Ozzy, approaching them across the orchard and holding hands with – who? What? A human flower? Well, not human, the avocado skin was a definite clue, but humanoid. Petite and willowy, her limbs and feet were bare despite the freshness of the morning. She wore a skimpy dress made from oversized fresh leaves and she had no hair: instead, pink flowers seemed to be growing out of her head.

'Here comes the flower fairy,' said Hassan, grinning.

'Fairy?'

'Only joking. She can't fly. She's a plant,' murmured Hassan as the couple approached. 'Those leaves are part of her, they're not clothes. She doesn't eat food; she photosynthesises her energy from the sun.'

'Hi, Hanna, how's it going?' said Ozzy as they reached them. 'Sorry for being late, mate, we had a bit of a lie-in.'

His girlfriend giggled – a sound like tiny bells jangling. Quickly, she covered her mouth with her hand, as if embarrassed.

'This is Jangmi,' said Ozzy. 'She's from Echanua.'

Hanna said, 'It's nice to meet you, Jangmi. Are you at flight school with Ozzy and Hassan?'

The tinkly laugh was louder this time, and she didn't cover her mouth. 'Oh no! My people hate to be indoors,' she trilled. 'I help Mr Park, the Dunia House caretaker? I grow the vegetables and look after the fruit trees.' She peered into Hassan's basket. 'Is that all you've got? I think this one will give us a bit more than that, don't you?'

Without waiting for a reply, she scampered up the tree like a monkey and within seconds was out on the branches Hanna hadn't dared to try. 'Hold up the basket, Ozzy!' she called.

'Um, we'll start on the next one, then,' said Hassan to Ozzy, who gave them an absent-minded nod and continued gazing adoringly upwards. Hassan was right, he was totally smitten.

'So, are lots of people in your year going out with aliens?' asked Hanna, wondering if she should be worried about competition. 'Or is it just Ozzy and the female foliage there?'

Hassan snorted with laughter. 'You didn't hit it off, did you? Give her a chance, she's pretty down-to-earth compared to the others. No pun intended. To answer your question, not many. Parveen, Gildas, Gaositwe, that's basically it. I told you before, the others can be pretty snooty. A significant minority think we're too primitive to deserve all this training, and we're only getting it because some of us look like Syenitian children. They don't like to mix with us outside school.'

After an hour or so's hard picking, even Jangmi was satisfied with their haul. 'Thank God for that,' said Ozzy. 'Can we get some lunch now? I'm starving!'

The allotment was one of many bordering a central

square formed by eight pairs of U-shaped apartment blocks, one of which contained Dunia House. Essoona was laid out in a grid formation, and this pattern repeated throughout the city like a network of tiny villages, back-to-back. Other than for deliveries, the central squares were closed to motorised traffic and all held some kind of local amenity, such as a school, a community centre, a park, a sports centre, an *Ohimo* or, in this case, a bathhouse. The ground floors of the apartment blocks housed small businesses: grocers, fishmongers, small supermarkets, cafés, bakeries, repair centres and second-hand shops.

They crossed the square to a favourite café and ordered some noodles at the counter. Once settled at a corner table, Hanna eyed Jangmi with curiosity. Close up, she was really…plant-like. Her skin was faintly veined like a fresh leaf, and her hair – were those flowers for decoration, or did they actually have pollen? Did bees buzz around her head in the summer?

'So, Hassan told me you get all your energy from the sun,' Hanna heard herself saying. 'But what do you do in the winter? I hear they're long and cold here.'

Ozzy put a protective arm across Jangmi's shoulders and Hanna saw irritation flare in his eyes. But Jangmi seemed unconcerned. In her squeaky voice she said, 'We hibernate. I'll return to my parents' farm and we'll stay dormant in the cellar until springtime.'

Hanna gulped. She hadn't been expecting that. No wonder Ozzy looked so annoyed.

'Echanuans have to stay outside most of the day, or under very bright lights. So they're usually agricultural workers of some kind, doing seasonal work. They grow most of our food here. City life is tricky for them, and space travel even more so,' Ozzy explained.

'Oh,' said Hanna. 'Right. I see.' How on earth were they going to make it work between them? Bet they don't last the winter, she thought.

'So, Ozzy, are you ready for the navigation test next week?' asked Hassan, not-so-subtly changing the subject. Hanna knew navigation was a problem subject for most of the humans in Hassan and Ozzy's year; they were always complaining about it. Not having learnt intergalactic geography at school, the humans trailed far behind their alien classmates.

'Nope. You?'

'Not really. I thought I'd have a go at it over the weekend. We could test each other if you like.'

Ozzy traced the vine-pattern on the table cloth with his chopsticks. 'Um, thanks, but I dunno mate. Me and Jangmi are going to the forests this afternoon, and we're planning to stay overnight in one of the treehouses. We want to spend as much time as we can together, before, you know, winter.'

Aw, sweet, thought Hanna, despite her scepticism about Jangmi. 'I'll test you if you like,' she said to Hassan. 'Maybe I can get a head start for next year.'

Noodles finished, they said their goodbyes and headed in different directions. Each time she visited Essoona, Hanna enjoyed exploring the city on foot, as she had in London, but with the added pleasure of Hassan's company. She'd seen all the main attractions: the museums and the vast Library populated almost entirely by bearded Cylfs (she'd have felt quite intimidated if she hadn't been familiar with Delius and Gambrinus). She was saving visiting the bathhouse for next year, when she could go with Farida.

'Where shall we go today?' asked Hassan.

Hanna thought for a moment. 'You haven't taken me to your school yet.'

'No, well, it's right on the other side of town. You sure you want to walk?'

'We can always get the tram back. Will you be all right?' she asked, eyeing Hassan's black and silver boots. He never complained.

'Don't worry about me,' he said, grinning down at her.

'Right then.'

They picked their way through adjacent residential squares, crossing the roads and cycle tracks that separated them. Hanna wanted to duck every time a tram whizzed overhead. Getting across the road was terrifying. She knew with her mind that non-motorised traffic had priority, but her heart nearly stopped every time Hassan strode out into the traffic, trusting their lives to the sensors on the automated transport pods. The cars always stopped, but still … Crossing the cycle tracks was like crossing the road in Addis Ababa. Not everyone obeyed the traffic signals, so you had to keep your wits about you.

Hanna found the different squares fascinating. Not only did they provide shelter from the permanent wind (which barrelled down the main thoroughfares unhindered, making your eyes water), but you never knew what you'd discover. The ubiquitous second-hand shops were packed with an infinite variety of quality treasures. She also loved the way Essoonians individualised their homes.

The lower floors of the wooden tenement blocks were brightly painted, with skilful carvings of plants, animals and insects adorning the doors and windows as if they were in a rainforest. The roofs and upper levels of the buildings were covered in a mixture of solar panels and greenery, with climbing plants descending from the rooftops. These weren't only for decoration, but to insulate the building and help the city's microclimate.

Hassan reached out and took her hand. 'So, Ozzy won't be back tonight. Would you like to stay over? I could take you out to dinner.'

Hanna gulped. Stay over? Did that mean they would—? Her stomach fizzed pleasantly at the thought of so many hours alone with Hassan. Luxury. But what would people think of her? And would she be able to—? Was that what she wanted?

Hassan sensed her indecision. 'You don't have to do anything you don't want to, Hanna,' he said. 'I just want to take the chance to spend more time with you. Once term starts, we'll be too busy to get together much.'

'Sure,' she said, her throat dry. She was ready to take their relationship to the next level, whatever that might be. 'I'll stay.'

'Great!' said Hassan, squeezing her hand. 'Then we don't need to rush back. We could go to the beach.'

The school – the 'Essoona Pilots' Academy' according to the plaque on the gatepost – was a utilitarian structure in a well-to-do suburb. While not exactly ugly, the severe architecture interrupted a row of mature, elegant houses, out of place like a broken tooth in a smile. It stood in its own grounds, which Hassan said sloped right down to the beach. The imposing façade hid all the hangars and launch pads behind it: that was why the school was by the sea – so students could fly their manoeuvres without endangering the city and its inhabitants.

The Essoona Pilots' Academy had around two thousand students, a blend of native Syenitians and representatives from various Alliance planets. Most were training to become part of the Alliance defence fleet, based either on Syenitia or their home planets. Competition for places was fierce: Hassan's fellow students were already elite pilots in their own societies. No wonder they looked down on the Earthlings, most of whom had zero experience of real-life space travel and lagged behind the rest in nearly every subject. The humans' physical similarity to the Syenitians only made the antagonism worse.

They followed the fence around to the back and Hassan hoisted her up onto his shoulders so she could peer over. She saw a mossy lawn covered in rows and rows of *Tumbas*, like in the docking bays on the *Shantivira*. Each *Tumba* was attached to a network of thick black cables snaking through the grass. Hanna could sense rather than hear a faint vibration in the air. 'What's that humming?' she asked Hassan.

'Can you feel it too? They don't have enough hangar space, so they leave the shields up to protect the *Tumbas* from the weather. Can we go to the beach now? You're getting heavy.'

Hanna jumped down, steadying herself against Hassan and taking the opportunity to steal a kiss. 'How do they cut the grass with all those cables everywhere?'

'They have these fearsome sheeplike creatures with

horns that roam the grounds like guard dogs.' Hassan returned her kiss and smiled. 'There's a shepherd who rounds them all up before lessons, otherwise we'd never reach our ships. Come on.'

She followed him down the dusty path between the school and the overgrown hedge bordering the neighbouring plot. The dirt track became sandy, then opened out abruptly to reveal a dazzling panorama of the coastline. And, straight ahead, a surging, pulsing grey-blue-green stretched all the way to the horizon.

'Wow!' Hanna exclaimed as her eyes adjusted to the strong light.

'Not bad, huh?' said Hassan, grinning.

She ran ahead down to the waterline, stumbling and hopping as she took off her shoes and socks en route. She kept going until she was knee deep in the icy surf, laughing out loud. It was invigorating, exhilarating.

'It's FREEZING!' she screamed at Hassan, who was following more sedately, gathering up her shoes and socks on the way. He waved cheerfully and settled down in the wind shadow of a convenient boulder. Oh no! She jumped back as a stray wave nearly caught her, almost soaking her shorts right up to her knickers. That was a close one. She had absolutely nothing to change into.

The sand blasted her ankles like a thousand tiny needles as she crossed the deserted beach back to Hassan. It was amazing here. Next time she'd be better prepared. Smiling, Hassan took off his jacket to wrap around her legs.

'Come and sit here out of the wind and warm up a bit.'

Still grinning, Hanna nestled under his arm and started rubbing her legs dry with her socks. 'That was so cool! I wasn't expecting it to be so alive, you know?'

Hassan looked at her, eyebrows raised. 'You've never seen the sea before? Not ever?'

'Only on TV. Never close up. Me and Farida are planning to go to Brighton before school starts.'

'More people on the beach in Brighton.'

'I'll have to remember to take a towel.'

'And perhaps a change of clothes.'

'Definitely a change of clothes.'

They sat in companionable silence, watching the sun sink over the water. The closer it got to the horizon, the bigger and pinker it seemed to get and the faster it seemed to fall.

'The days are getting shorter,' said Hassan. 'We'll have to go when the sun's gone, the temperature will drop to nearly zero within half an hour. We'll take the tram back into town.'

Something occurred to Hanna. 'Hey, aren't we on the east coast?'

'We are.'

'So the sun sets in the east here?'

'Right. Syenitia spins the other way to the Earth.'

'Oh.' Hanna shivered. 'Can we go? I'm getting cold.'

'Sure. Let's find somewhere warm to eat.'

'Do you know anywhere good?'

'There's a pancake place not far from here. Come on, I'll show you.'

THE RESTAURANT WAS tiny, just a few tables in what

appeared to be someone's house.

'How did you know about this place?' asked Hanna in an awed whisper.

'A tip from Gildas. His girlfriend brought him here a few weeks ago. I've been wanting to try it ever since.'

They ordered their pancakes and a mug each of what Hassan called '*saiju* with a shot'. Very quickly, Hanna felt warm all the way through, right down to her toes. Hello again, toes, nice to have you back, she thought, giggling to herself.

'So,' said Hassan. 'Where will you ask Delius to start looking for your brother and sisters? You never told me how you got separated.'

Perhaps it was the unaccustomed alcohol, or the special day together: bit by bit, Hanna found herself telling Hassan about the disintegration of her family – which she'd so far avoided discussing in all but the vaguest terms. Hassan had told her all about his foster family in Uganda and shared many memories about his sister, but, until now, Hanna had kept coming up against an inner barrier which prevented her from opening up.

'After Yonas went and my parents died, me and Ibo looked after our cows. We had thirty-one zebu and they were our family. My dad spent his whole life building up that herd. But we had no guns, and word got around that we were on our own.

'One night we heard people moving around outside our hut. Ibo went out to investigate. We heard him yell it was cattle raiders, then we heard a shot and everything went quiet. I wanted to run out and help Ibo, but Martha stopped me: she literally sat on me and held her hand over my mouth. She probably saved my life. We were surrounded by the sound of our precious cows being led away into the night, then all was silent again.

'Ibo lay in the dust, a wet black hole where his heart should have been. He was eleven years old. Eleven.' Hanna could feel the tears cold on her cheeks, but kept going. 'I cried harder for Ibo than I did for my parents. He'd always been there for me, and he was taken from us so suddenly. Now we really had nothing. No cows. No parents. No brothers. No relatives that we knew about.'

'What, none?' asked Hassan, surprised.

'My dad left his family when he met my mother and had no contact with them. There was some kind of argument which he never spoke of. I don't even know their names. My mother had no family at all apart from an old uncle, who died and left us his cattle when Martha was small.

'The village helped us again with the funeral. Martha had an offer of marriage which would have meant we could stay, but the guy was a total creep.' Hanna shivered at the memory. A Mr Ahmed prototype. Or worse.

'Staying wasn't an option. The three of us packed what we could carry and walked to Gambella town. Martha thought she could get a job there, and perhaps me and Kia could go to school. Despite everything that had happened, we still had hope.'

Hanna looked down at her hands. Hassan took them in his. 'But it didn't work out that way?' he said.

'No. We got so hungry, so quickly. And we had nowhere to go; none of us had ever been to a town before. We didn't know how things worked there. Pretty soon we were begging on the streets, like you were. One day, a fat lady in a lovely dress came: tiny pink and blue flowers on a green background, with white lace at the hem and big pink and blue buttons down the front. And her shoes! I'd never seen anything like them! Shiny and high, with silver buckles. And so clean and new, like she'd never had to walk anywhere in them. She had lace gloves and a straw hat with plastic fruit on. I remember thinking I would do anything to have clothes like that.'

Hassan grinned. 'I think your sense of style has moved on since then.'

'I was ten. Auntie Margaret – that's what we had to call her, I never found out her last name – was more exotic to me then than anyone you might see here on Kalakaivo Square. I'd never seen a fat person before. She gave us some biscuits and bananas asked us if we'd like to learn to read and write.'

'At the orphanage?'

Hanna nodded. 'A van came round the corner and we all climbed inside. We drove for hours and hours, no idea where to. Kia was so sick on the journey.'

'But they did keep their promise? I mean, they did teach you?'

'Me, yes. Kia too. All in Amharic. The children came from all over. We were the only Nuer for a long time. But they sent Martha away pretty soon afterwards. To a nice family, they said. Faraway in Saudi Arabia. I never heard from her again. I was too young to guess what might really have happened to her. There were rumours—' Hanna wiped her eyes and sniffed. 'Perhaps Delius can find her.'

Hassan squeezed her fingers. 'And Kia?'

'We had a good few years together. I cared for her as well as I could. The orphanage wasn't a bad place, considering the alternative. At least they taught us letters and numbers. And to cook and sew. But there was always this unspoken dread of what would happen later. Once you grew boobs and started your period, then it wouldn't be long until you disappeared. "To start your new life" they called it. I got lucky, being sent to London and only having to work as a cleaner.'

Hanna looked at Hassan. 'If she's still alive, Kia is fourteen herself now. Maybe Delius can find her; perhaps it's not too late to help her. Without a family you're at the mercy of the world.'

'Friends can be family too,' insisted Hassan. 'We can build a new family with the people around us. You and Ozzy are mine.'

Hanna smiled broadly. 'And you're mine. And I have *two* mothers now. I'm so lucky.'

On the tram journey back to Dunia House, Hassan said, 'Hanna, there's a conversation we need to have. About sex. I mean, how do you feel about it? With me?'

Hanna gulped. That was direct. Half of her recoiled at the very idea of sexual intercourse with a man: how it felt, what it involved. The other half was burning with curiosity to see what Hassan looked like naked.

'Um.' No words came.

'It's too soon. Sorry. I shouldn't have asked.'

'No! Honestly? I'd like to…explore you. But then I feel ashamed that I feel that way, because shouldn't we be married before we see each other like that? And I don't want to have another baby for a long, long time.'

'Well, I won't be ready to be a father for a long, long time. You know there are ways of stopping that happening, right?'

'So I've heard. I don't know much about it.'

'Exploring sounds good. We could do some of that, without…going all the way.'

'All right. But if I say stop, you stop straight away, OK?'

'Of course. I promise.'

HANNA SAT FULLY dressed on Ozzy's bed, in fits of giggles as she watched Hassan remove his clothes very slowly, swaying his hips as he danced around the room. Garment after garment joined the pile on the floor until his upper body was stripped bare. Then he sat on the edge of his bed and undid the buckles of his black and silver boots. Sighing with relief, he drew out his stumps and swung them onto the bedcovers. Then he hooked his thumbs into his waistband and whipped off his jeans. Naked now, except for his (neon orange) underpants, he propped himself up on his elbows and turned to face Hanna. 'Ready to explore?' he winked.

Pushing her fears aside, Hanna crossed the room and perched at the very end of Hassan's bed. Carefully, she took his neat, round stumps in her hands and pulled them onto her lap. She began stroking and rubbing them. Hassan leaned back and closed his eyes with pleasure.

'Mmm.'

'Do they hurt, at the end of the day?' she asked.

'Depends what I've been doing.'

'We walked quite far today.'

'Mmm. It's OK. It was a good day. And that feels *really* nice.'

Lightly, Hanna traced the line of the long, jagged scar all the way up to Hassan's left thigh. He drew a sharp breath but remained motionless on the bed, his eyes closed. Gaining confidence, she began running her fingers up and down through the wiry hairs on his legs, following the contours of his muscles.

She squeaked in surprise at a sudden movement in Hassan's shorts. Hassan smiled, but said nothing. The rest of him stayed passive under her fingertips. Hanna decided to ignore it and skipped over the danger zone to explore his stomach. A line of hair led from his belly button down…the closer she came to the elastic waistband, the livelier the contents of the shorts became. She continued her journey, walking her fingers up his ribs as if they were climbing a ladder. She wasn't thinking consciously anymore, just following whatever felt good. She lowered her head to his chest and inhaled deeply. Slowly, she licked the muscle, right across his left nipple. Oh, that tasted good. Hassan moaned and she moved upwards, tracing the tip of her tongue across his shoulder and up his neck to his ear.

'Hanna, oh, Hanna,' he whispered, breathing harder. 'I can't hold it much longer.'

Hanna straddled his stomach. 'Hold what?' she asked, then, closing her eyes too, she kissed him before he could answer. Long, deep, firm. She felt him reach an arm past her, then his whole body spasmed beneath her, radiating heat. His other arm crushed her close to him and he broke off the kiss to emit a belly-deep roar. Then all was still. Hanna studied Hassan's face. Serenity. That must be what serenity looked like. Beautiful.

Hassan's eyes snapped open. 'Oh my God, Hanna!' He grinned. 'That was fucking awesome!' Hanna giggled and sat up. Dismounting him, she noticed there was now a patch of darker orange on his shorts.

'I've made a bit of a mess, but it's all contained,' he said. 'Pass me the tissues?'

Fascinated, she watched him clean himself up. So that was a penis. Funny looking thing. Hard to see what all the fuss was about, really. She didn't like the semen smell though, it reminded her of—NO! Don't go there, don't go there. She'd be damned if she'd let that low-life Mr Ahmed come between her and Hassan.

Hassan swung his legs into his boots and fastened them with practised speed. 'I'll just have a quick wash. Then it's your turn.'

Her turn. Hanna's heart quickened with anxiety. With Hassan staying so still before, she'd felt calm, in control. But was she ready to hand that control to someone else, however much she trusted him?

Hassan returned. He certainly wasn't shy about being naked. 'Are you going to get undressed?' he asked, sitting down next to her. 'We could just snuggle under the covers, if you don't want to do anything.'

Snuggling sounded nice. She nodded, her mouth dry. Keeping her eyes locked with Hassan's, she unbuttoned her blouse and unfastened her bra. Then she hooked her thumbs into her waistband and whipped off her shorts and knickers in one go. Now she was stark naked apart from her stripy yellow and green knee socks. No man had ever seen her naked. She shivered.

Meanwhile, Hassan had his boots off and had climbed into bed. He lifted the duvet and patted the mattress. 'Come on in,' he said, smiling.

Hanna took off her sandy socks and joined him. He glowed with warmth. She pushed her icy feet between his legs and he gasped, then chuckled. Hanna allowed him to pull her close and rested her forehead in the curve of his neck, eyes shut tight. Breathing the heady scent of his skin calmed her. Bit by bit, she relaxed. This was OK. More than OK. Good. Fabulous.

Hassan began to stroke her, long, slow strokes, up and down her back from her shoulders to her hips. Oooh. Nice. Tingly. She pushed closer against his chest, and he started rubbing her buttocks with increasing pressure. She wriggled with pleasure and he laughed, flipping her onto her back. Now he was kneeling between her legs, stroking the inside of her thigh. It was like a whole conversation, only with touches instead of words. Was this what Lucy and Felix got up to? Perhaps she'd judged her too harshly.

Hassan derailed her train of thought. 'May I?' he said, but it was his fingers asking the question really, as they tiptoed higher and higher up her leg.

'No penises,' she insisted.

'No penises,' he promised.

She nodded, curious to see where this would go.

Hassan separated her thighs and tenderly touched her springy pubic hair. 'Thank God for that,' he said.

'For what?' she asked, pushing herself up onto her elbows, intrigued by the relief in his voice.

'I was worried you might be, you know, cut,' he said.

'Circumcised? No. Some of the girls in the orphanage were though.'

Hassan began stroking her thighs again. 'Have you ever had an orgasm, Hanna?'

'I'm not even sure what an orgasm is.'

'Perhaps I can find one for you while I'm exploring—'

To Hanna's astonishment, Hassan dropped between her legs and began to kiss her. In that place. The forbidden place. He sensed her tension and lifted his head.

'OK?' he said, concerned.

'Um…just surprised. Don't stop.'

Hassan grinned and returned to work, his tongue flickering on her clitoris. When all was wet, he began again with his fingers, slow strokes up and down her outer labia, then her inner labia, up to her clitoris again, circling it lazily with minimum pressure. Hanna's nerve-endings were on fire. Never in her whole life had she felt like this. Alive. Present in the present tense. No past. No future. Only this.

Hassan began to move his finger faster now, back and forth across her now hypersensitive clitoris until she thought it would burst. She imagined herself coming up to the top of a roller coaster, time slowing down before…what? Something was about to happen, something new.

To Hanna's disappointment, Hassan eased off and moved his fingers lower. At the same moment, Hanna felt a sharp pain at the entrance to her vagina. Hassan gave a yell and abruptly pulled his hand away.

'It sort of bit me!' he said, visibly shocked. 'It closed

right up, just like that! Are you OK?'

The erotic mood evaporated instantly. Hanna sat up and made a tentative exploration. Her vulva was clamped shut; she couldn't even get a single finger in. And it really hurt. Blinking away the tears, she looked up at Hassan. He took her in his arms and held her tightly.

'I've heard of this,' he said. 'Your body's trying to protect you. Can't blame it really, considering what happened to you. Hanna, I'm sure we can get past this. Let's leave it for now and go to sleep.'

Hanna nodded mutely. Inside, she was in turmoil. Late into the night, questions chased each other through her mind as Hassan slumbered beside her on the narrow mattress. Would she ever be able to have sex? Or had Mr Ahmed taken that from her as well? How long would Hassan wait for her? She'd been enjoying herself so much, feeling better than she'd ever felt: why was her body betraying her like this? Surely she was in charge of it? Several times she reached down in another attempt to insert a finger, only to be thwarted by the same sharp pain as the muscles instantly tightened. She wept silently until she fell asleep.

SEPTEMBER CAME AND they returned to the language school. Now they were spending two whole days a week in the simulator. The sessions were exhausting. Tima made them practise the same manoeuvres again and again until they could do them without thinking.

'You're trying too hard, Hanna,' she said as Hanna stepped out of the simulator, her head buzzing and her legs trembling with fatigue. 'Stop thinking consciously. Relax and allow your instincts to take over, then it will flow better.'

If only it were that easy, thought Hanna. She still regarded her subconscious mind as an enemy. Repeated attempts at sex with Hassan had all resulted in failure. But where could she go for help? She wasn't comfortable with the idea of going to a doctor, not even with her newly legal status.

The first Sunday after the holidays, she went to the training deck for extra practice, as did Lucy. Their truce still held after the summer break; they were waiting for Lucy's next meeting with Charlie so they could find out more about the EDS.

Safe in their separate pods, Hanna thought, why not? Over the intercom she said tentatively, 'Lucy?'

'What?'

'I can't have sex.'

'What?'

'I've tried, but it doesn't work.' Bit by bit, she explained.

Lucy was gratifyingly horrified and surprisingly sympathetic.

'It's called vaginismus,' she said. 'Friend of mine at uni had it. Terrible. In the end she had some special Botox injections and that sorted it out. But there's lots you can try before going that far. Does it happen when you masturbate?'

'Mast—? I've never done such a thing in my life! What kind of person do you think I am?'

'Alive? Human? It's not wrong, Hanna. It's essential

for your health and well-being.'

'It is?'

'Yeah. I've heard it stops you from being incontinent in your old age, too.'

'Too late for that. I had a baby, remember? It's not bad, just a little when I sneeze.'

'Oh my God! Hanna! You need to do something about that before it's too late!'

'Do you…masturbate?' Hanna was hugely curious now.

'Most days, in some form or another. Of course. Hanna, it sounds to me like you need to get to know that part of yourself. To make friends with yourself. Perhaps that would solve your problems, if you give it time. An orgasm is a zero-calorie treat. A negative-calorie treat, actually. It boosts your immune system. What's not to like?'

'How will I know if I've had one?'

Lucy laughed. 'You'll know. It's like – all your muscles tense up by themselves and then release all of a sudden and you feel relaxed and full of energy. It can take a while; you have to start in your head, thinking horny thoughts. Friction on its own doesn't work.'

Hanna said hesitantly, 'The first time with Hassan, I think I got pretty close.'

'Don't tell me,' giggled Lucy, 'you were almost there, but then he moved his finger somewhere else, and it was gone for good. That has happened to me *so* many times. It's much easier to get there on your own, Hanna. Honestly, sometimes I prefer it. And if you want to have sex, then you need to find out what works for you first, so you can teach your partner. Otherwise, how will he know how to satisfy you?'

Hanna was silent, overwhelmed by the flood of information and Lucy's diametric perspective. Lucy continued, 'Whatever you do, don't get pregnant.'

'Would that be such a tragedy?' Hanna challenged, thinking of her unvoiced long-term plan to have Hassan's babies and live happily ever after.

'If you don't feel ready to be a mother. If you can't support a child financially. If you're not a hundred per cent certain about your relationship with the father. Better not to get pregnant in the first place, than to have to go through with an abortion.'

'Abortion is murder, Lucy! Children are a gift from God. You can't just get rid of them for being inconvenient!'

'Are you calling me a murderer?'

'You had an abortion?'

'When I was your age. Not a happy memory, but I don't regret it,' said Lucy defiantly.

Hanna reeled with shock. 'How could you? How could you do that to your baby?'

'It was a bunch of cells, Hanna. I wasn't ready to throw all my plans for the future out of the window just because of a defective condom! I wouldn't have been able to give a child the life I wanted it to have. I hadn't finished my education. I had no savings, no career. The father was a nice enough guy, but not reliable. Certainly not the love of my life.

'Babies are incredibly demanding, Hanna. You need to really, really want them or it's not fair on the child in the long term. They're not stupid; they can sense it if you resent them, if you don't have enough emotional energy to share with them. What kind of adults will they grow into then? I'm convinced that a lot of misery in the world is caused by people having children they can't look after or educate properly, however much they might love them.'

'I was born to be a mother,' said Hanna quietly, thinking of Samuel in his fluffy red blanket. It was so unfair. 'What else are we for?'

'I'm not saying I don't want to be a mother one day,' said Lucy. 'But when I do, I want my kids to have the best possible shot at life that I can give them. I want them to benefit from all my life experience. No offence to you, but when I was nineteen I knew *nothing*. Love isn't enough. Children need a secure, stable environment and good examples to follow. Don't they deserve the very best you can give them?'

'Yes. Of course. But I still think you're wrong.'

'We're different people, Hanna. What was right for me might not be right for you. I think we'll have to agree to disagree on this one. I haven't forgotten about Samuel.'

Hanna said nothing, just fired up the simulation. Lucy took the hint and dropped the subject. By the end of the session, Hanna's anger had subsided and now she just felt sad for Lucy. To have destroyed a potential life – that must be doing something to Lucy's soul, deep down.

As she descended from the pod afterwards, she found Delius waiting for her. Solemnly, he handed her a scrap of paper. It read, 'Private Yonas Abebe, Ethiopian National Defense Force, killed in 2005 defending Badme against insurgents.'

'I'm sorry for your loss,' he said flatly, as Hanna's

knees buckled and she slumped onto the simulator steps with a little cry. Lucy ran back to see what was wrong. Wordlessly, Hanna handed her the paper and Lucy sat down beside her, wrapping a comforting arm around her shoulders.

'I haven't been able to locate either of your sisters so far. I'll keep looking.'

'Thanks, Delius,' sniffed Hanna. 'Perhaps no news is good news.'

'Come on,' said Lucy, pulling her up, 'let's get you home to Irion.'

Hanna allowed herself to be led back through the teleport, to the safety of the sofa in Irion and Mary's flat. She stared blankly ahead as they fussed around her, wrapping her in blankets and bringing her endless cups of tea, none of which she drank. He'd been dead all this time and she'd never suspected, never felt it. She almost wished she hadn't found out.

28. THE FRAGILITY OF EXISTENCE

LUCY

T HE FOLLOWING SATURDAY, Lucy crossed London to Walthamstow, the bleeding edge of hipster trendiness. She felt rather exposed: not only did she not have a beard, she wasn't even wearing the obligatory black-rimmed glasses. Thank God jeans and trainers were universal. The gallery was in a recently refurbished art deco building, all blinding-white curves and brass railings. As instructed, she took her place in front of the work entitled 'Open glass bottle half-filled with sparkling water'. The blurb read:

> Since the early 1990s, Chloe Carter has been creating simple, yet perplexing artworks examining the philosophy of being, using everyday objects. 'Open glass bottle half-filled with sparkling water' is no exception. The decreasing rate of the bubbles rising to the surface is a transparent metaphor for the transience of life: the gradual decay from a state of vital activity to the infinite tranquillity of death itself. At the same time, the water level is an intriguing reference to the necessary balance between optimism and pessimism as a strategy for coming to terms with the fragility of existence.

What pretentious rubbish, she thought, trying not to

laugh out loud. She sat waiting for Charlie, watching the bubbles in the water rising to the surface. It was strangely meditative. Perhaps there was something in this conceptual art malarkey after all. At last, someone sat down beside her. She turned, and her smile of greeting froze as she realised it wasn't Charlie.

Her new neighbour was a gangly northern European male of about her own age, with bad skin and thin, mousy brown hair, wearing a slightly-too-large, cheap suit. Sensible black leather lace-ups encased enormous feet. His prominent Adam's apple bobbed up and down violently as he enquired, 'Lucy Cooper?'

She nodded.

'I'm Matthew Brown.'

English, she thought. West Midlands. He held out his hand for her to shake.

Lucy ignored it. 'Where's Charlie?' she demanded.

Matthew lowered his hand awkwardly and studied the artwork in front of them. The bubbles had slowed now, approaching the infinite tranquillity of death. Lucy wondered how often they replaced the bottle. Was there a whole crate in that cupboard below the 'exhibit'?

'Charlie sends his apologies. His flight was delayed and he wasn't able to get here on time.'

Yeah, right, thought Lucy. What have you done with him?

Matthew continued in a low voice, 'I'm the, uh, local EDS representative. I must say, it's an honour to meet you in person, Miss Cooper. I'm sure your bravery will be rewarded one day.'

Lucy almost laughed. 'My bravery? What do you think

I do, Matthew?'

'Well, pretending to be friendly with all those aliens, even though you know they want to take over our planet and eat us all alive.' He shuddered. 'You must have nerves of steel. What would they do to you if they found out you were meeting me?'

Who was this guy? He was flipping useless. Or putting on a very convincing act. All the same, she had to set him straight. 'Have you met any aliens, Matthew?'

Matthew shook his head.

'Because I'm pretty sure they don't want to take over our planet or eat us. Not the people running the *Shantivira* project. They're *friendly*, Matthew. They're trying to protect us from other aliens until we're ready to deal with them.'

'Nestor warned me you might have been brainwashed, spending so much time with them.'

Lucy's temper flared. 'Did he now? Know him well, do you?'

'He's my boss.'

'Don't you think *you* might be the one who's been brainwashed, if he's the source of all your information? What's he been telling you about the Syenitians?'

'That they can look almost human, but they're actually red scaly demons which feed from the life energy of other beings. Their whole civilisation is powered by it; they're parasites.' Matthew's voice rose by half an octave. 'If they get hold of the Earth, we'll all be slaves. They'll keep us like cattle. The *Shantivira* is a ruse to study us and to build a network of collaborators who will help them take over.'

Lucy failed to suppress a snort of laughter.

'OK,' she said. 'It's sort of true that Syenitian society is powered by life energy. But it's the life energy within organic matter, Matthew. Organic *waste*. Shit and piss. Leftover food. Not intelligent life forms – all life is sacred to them. And they're not red scaly demons. There's only one of those, and she's not biologically a Syenitian. It sounds like Nestor met her once and has assumed all aliens are like her. She certainly scared the crap out of me when I first met her. But I don't get it, didn't Charlie put you right on this?'

'I've never met Charlie. Nestor told me all this in confidence. He keeps it a secret from most of the team at work. David, his business partner, probably knows the whole story. And everyone in the AAL, of course.'

'What is it you do for Nestor, exactly?' Lucy asked. 'Do you work in Switzerland?'

Matthew nodded. 'Mostly. I'm an electrical engineer. I work on the satellite stabilisation system, you know, to hold it steady while the weapon is deployed? I'm home visiting my folks.'

'What kind of weapon is it?'

'I can't tell you that, it's confidential!'

No harm in asking though, thought Lucy. Try another tack. 'So where did you meet Nestor?'

Matthew shifted awkwardly on the seat next to her. Looking at the polished concrete floor, he mumbled, 'On the dark web.'

Lucy gave him a sidelong glance. 'What were *you* doing on the dark web?'

'Looking for aliens. And I found them, didn't I?' he whined defiantly. 'I've always been convinced aliens must exist. It's the logical conclusion to what we know about space. I used to spend my free time in chat rooms, trying to find out anything I could. There's a lot of dubious stuff out there. Some people are just sick in the head, others will believe anything they're told.'

Not you though, thought Lucy sarcastically.

'There are a load of conspiracy theories doing the rounds. Some are general knowledge, others are…better hidden. But when I finally found it, the AAL website had a different feel altogether. Serious. Professional. They run workshops every three months IRL, in a new location each time. Expensive, but really worthwhile. It brings the believers' community together so we can meet face-to-face.'

'And what were these workshops about?' asked Lucy, intrigued.

'All kinds of things,' said Matthew enthusiastically. 'A whole series of events on what to do and how to behave in the event of an invasion, with role plays. That was fun. Then they worked through all the common conspiracies, debunking some and confirming others. Known alien species, including Syenitians, Sayari and Wadudu, with pictures.'

'What, you mean photographs?'

'Hand-drawn sketches, but very realistic. Where was I? Oh, there was one on the probability of invasion and the consequences for Earth. And the effectiveness of conventional weaponry against alien technology in the event of an invasion. That was where I met Nestor for the first time, two years ago. Well, he approached me. He knew about my stability control work on communications satellites, and after a sort of interview he offered me the job with Celestina.'

'And he didn't coerce you in any way? Threaten people you care about to ensure your cooperation?'

'No! He would never do that!'

'He threatened *my* parents if I refused to spy for him. So you can see why I'm not his biggest fan. He basically forced me to join the *Shantivira* against my will.' Not that I regret it, thought Lucy. A bit of her would always be grateful to Nestor for giving her the shove she'd needed.

'He did?'

Matthew's confused expression told Lucy that she was beginning to chip away at his blind faith in his boss. Good. Nestor was obviously just telling people what he needed to in order to manipulate them. And raising a lot of cash in the process. It looked like Charlie was right, Nestor was gathering the resources to become independent from David. Although it appeared Matthew had no clue about the power struggle for control of Celestina Satellites. Unlikely she would learn any more from him. Time to wrap this up. Apart from anything, she was thirsty. It was far too hot in here.

'He did. Matthew, I'm going to give you some advice. Don't get all your information from one source. It sounds like Nestor doesn't know much about extra-terrestrials: that his actions are based on fear and hate rather than knowledge and logic. When I joined the *Shantivira*, I had grave doubts about the Syenitians' real motives too. But all the aliens I've come across so far have just been – people.'

'People?'

'Yeah, people. With the same basic needs and hopes

and fears as you and me. Look Matthew, the Earth should be able to defend itself – the work you are doing is really important – but the *Shantivira* and the Syenitians are not our enemies. They're giving us the time to develop our own weapons, that's all. They want a trading relationship in the long term. Knowledge exchange.'

'Are you sure that's all they want?'

'They already tried settling here, thousands of years ago. But it didn't work out – they couldn't breed successfully. Believe me, if they were going to take over the planet, it would have already happened.'

Her throat was really dry now. She rose and he stood up too.

'Are you going already?' he asked.

'I am. Goodbye Matthew.' She held out her hand for him to shake. 'Perhaps we'll meet again one day.'

'Wait, we have to fix our next rendezvous.'

Must we? thought Lucy, sighing inwardly. 'Where and when?'

'The London Eye. December. I've got your ticket here,' he said, reaching inside his jacket.

Without looking at it, Lucy folded it in half and stuck it in her jacket pocket. She eyed the cupboard underneath the 'artwork'. The attendant was facing the other way, explaining another exhibit to some expensively attired pensioners. Enjoying the look on Matthew's face, she reached forward and popped open the shiny magnetic door. Bingo. She pulled out a bottle, unscrewed the cap, and took a long, satisfying swig.

'Bye, Matthew,' she repeated, making swiftly for the exit.

Deep in thought, Lucy made her way across town to the coffee shop where she'd arranged to report back to the others. She strongly suspected Charlie had been prevented from coming to London, which meant Nestor had already staged his coup. How could they stop him? What should they do next?

Felix, Hanna, Farida, Saïd and Nikolai were waiting for her. Hanna was chattering excitedly – again – about the trip to Munich that she and Hassan had arranged for December, after the exams. They'd booked the flights and a hotel. Now all they had to do was to apply for a visa. Lucy was familiar with the details, including the ins and outs of getting a Schengen visa, having heard them from Hanna multiple times. Lucy suspected Hassan had suggested the trip to take Hanna's mind off her brother. Not to mention everything else.

'Hi,' she said, approaching the table.

Felix smiled. 'How did it go?' he asked.

Lucy summarised her meeting, emphasising Matthew's naivety and her discoveries about the AAL as a separate organisation to the EDS. 'Either he's an amazing actor, which I doubt, or he knows almost nothing about us. I think perhaps something has forced Nestor's hand, and he had to act quickly to stop Charlie from meeting me. I can't believe Matthew is the best Nestor has. It was a coincidence that he was in the UK at all. I think David Wang might be in trouble.'

Nikolai reached into his bag and pulled out his phone. 'I finally managed to track down a picture of him. There are lots of David Wangs online, but ours is a phantom. Considering he's the MD of a company, there's almost no information about him in the public domain. On Earth, that is. So I dug deeper into the *Shantivira* archives. Here he is.'

He pulled up a photo of a *zana* projection and pushed his phone across the table.

'Charlie!' exclaimed Lucy, Hanna and Farida simultaneously.

'Well, that's a positive ID if ever I heard one,' said Nikolai.

'Oh my God, he's been protecting the *Shantivira* from Nestor the whole time. Even when Nestor made me spy for them, David's been controlling the flow of information back to him, probably making stuff up to keep him happy. At the same time, he wanted to know specific details for himself, like our names and photos – without passing them on to Nestor.'

'Lucy, are you sure he didn't pass them on?'

'He promised me, and I believed him. Honestly, that Matthew knew nothing about anything. Charlie, I mean David, is on our side.'

'So if he didn't come in person, do you think Nestor's already found out David's been going behind his back?' asked Saïd.

'I don't like this,' said Felix. 'It's getting too big for us.'

'We don't know for sure he's in trouble,' said Hanna. 'We shouldn't rush into anything without some hard facts. At the moment, we only have Lucy's gut feeling that something's wrong.'

'Sorry Lucy, that's not enough to go on,' agreed Farida. 'We need to find out more first.'

'We need time to check out the AAL workshops and

their fund-raising,' said Nikolai. 'I can start looking into the dark web forums, but it sounds like a huge job.'

The others evidently didn't share her sense of urgency. Charlie was someone they'd never met and didn't care very much about. Her parents were safely on their cruise. Whatever the consequences might be for her, they were less important than stopping Nestor discovering the *Shantivira's* secrets. David/Charlie knew even more about the project than she did. What if Nestor tortured him? What could she do?

Lucy made a long-overdue decision.

'It's time for me to tell Joe,' she said.

29. I TRY TO STAY OUT OF POLITICS

JOE

'THE COUNCILLOR WILL see you now,' said the secretary in a disinterested monotone, barely glancing at Joe through the holographic projections above his work station. Joe rose from his floor cushion among the abundant pot plants in the waiting area and crossed the room to the door behind the secretary. He still had only the vaguest of ideas how he was going to politely refuse Dalian's job offer. Having made the decision to reject it months ago, he'd put the whole matter out of his mind until the reminder for their meeting had popped up on his *zana* two hours ago. He knocked on the door.

'Come in.'

Curiously, he entered Dalian's office. Like Aldeman's, it had no furniture, just rush matting on the floor with a few cushions dotted about. 'Welcome, Captain Llewellyn.' She was waiting in the centre of the room, arms folded inside her wide sleeves. She wasn't about to greet him with a friendly Syenitian double hand press.

He returned her greeting with a formal but not-too-low bow. 'Councillor.'

'Let us not prevaricate, Captain. I am sure you have

much to do today. I appreciate it that you have come in person to refuse my offer.'

This threw Joe slightly off balance. 'I always find bad news is best delivered face-to-face, Councillor.'

Now she smiled, entirely without warmth. 'But it is not bad news, is it? Not for you. You have your "first contact" at last. You are no longer planning to leave the *Shantivira*.'

'No. I'm not. But I am sorry to turn down your generous offer.'

'No, you are not.'

Joe made to protest, but a wave of Dalian's slender hand silenced him.

'I never expected you to accept. I wanted to see your reaction, to learn more about you. I know you do not trust me. That does not offend me. You are aligned with Aldeman and his naive philosophy of peace, love and acquisition of alternative technologies. His tenure as head of the Council matches your lifespan, so you have no motivation to think beyond that. I do understand.'

'I'm just a simple soldier,' shrugged Joe. 'I try to stay out of politics.'

Dalian seemed genuinely amused by this. 'Well, given the position you have just put your planet in, *that* ship has sailed,' she laughed, a cold tinkling sound, like icicles being hit with a hammer. 'You had better start learning, Llewellyn, and fast. I was a simple soldier once too, did no one ever tell you?'

'No,' said Joe, surprised, wondering why Aldeman had never mentioned it. 'What was your role?'

'Infantry, initially. I grew up as an expatriate Syenitian

settler on Irritaski. My parents were farmers. Joining the armed forces was a way to see the universe. Then I trained as a sniper. I probably did that for longer than you have been alive. Then bomb disposal. That is how I met my wife.'

'I didn't know you were married, Councillor.'

'Widowed,' corrected Dalian sharply. 'I was never a pilot, able to fly away at the end of a battle. You know it yourself: it is the ground troops who see the consequences of war up close. It is hard to remain detached when there is no distance between you and the results of your work. I know about the sacrifices you have to make. The compromises with yourself, the moral accommodations. It does not get easier over time.'

'No,' agreed Joe, remembering his tour of duty in Northern Ireland.

'I rose up the ranks to Commander-in-Chief of the Syenitian Army. A long time ago, admittedly. But my experiences have stayed with me.'

'And now you're looking for another promotion. And when you get it, you'll pull the plug on the *Shantivira*.' What happens when you poke a cobra with a stick? thought Joe.

That laugh again.

'Before, if I get my way. Which I habitually do. We are speaking frankly?'

Joe nodded. In for a penny, in for a pound. Dalian returned her hands to her elbows, inside her sleeves.

'All right. I believe the *Shantivira* is a vanity project which arose purely because Reika chose to make her home there. It is a waste of precious resources.' Her expression told Joe not to even think about interrupting.

'My objective is the defence of the Galaksi Alliance and *this* planet in particular. Your world is not an Alliance member, its security is not my concern. Humans are an entertaining novelty because of their physical similarity to us, but their society is too primitive and their lives are too short for them to be of any real interest.'

The gloves were off now. Joe couldn't stop himself. 'You're wrong. We have a lot to offer. Why do you think Reika chose to settle on Dunia? It wasn't a random choice! Our people have so much in common!'

Dalian's eyes narrowed. 'Aldeman says Dunia's treasure *is* the human species. So prove it to me.' She leaned forward, her amber eyes centimetres from Joe's. 'Show me you can make a smooth transition from pre-first-contact to post-first-contact. Captain Llewellyn, you personally are my measure of the human race. I challenge you to change my opinion. You have one chance only. If you fail, I will shut down the *Shantivira* project and Aldeman's career in politics will be over.'

'What's your problem with Aldeman? He's always very polite about you.'

'I have no problem with him as an individual. He is a good man with the best of intentions. But we are facing dark times, and I do not believe Aldeman is a strong enough leader to prepare the Alliance against the coming threat. I think I can do a better job.'

'The coming threat?' asked Joe. Then, suddenly, he understood. 'You mean the Ranglatiri?'

Dalian nodded. 'I am glad you see it too. Aldeman has no concept of what we are dealing with, or the extent of the problem. Verndari protects him too much. He abhors violence of any kind, whereas you and I both know that sometimes it is necessary and unavoidable. I am concerned that he will not take the right decisions when the time comes.'

Saying nothing, but feeling disloyal, Joe remembered his own repeated arguments with Aldeman on the same subject. Dalian was right, it was like he didn't know how to approach the problem. And a confrontation with the Ranglatiri would come, sooner or later.

Dalian noticed Joe's thoughtful silence. 'I will tell you what I have told my Alliance captains. There is a rumour the Ranglatiri have new shield technology. Apparently impenetrable. We do not know how widespread its use is yet. We need to see it in action and get a sample so we can reverse engineer it. I refuse to believe it is truly impenetrable. We need to know what it can withstand so we can take the necessary countermeasures.'

JOE RETURNED TO Dunia House on foot. He needed time to digest what he'd learnt before updating Kitty and Aldeman. He had to revise his opinion of Dalian in light of this new information. Assuming it was true, of course. But why would she bother lying about things which were easy to check? One thing was sure: he must plan how to tell UNOOSA about the *Shantivira* with extreme care. It was all on him now.

He was so deep in thought, it wasn't until he'd crossed the docking bay and was about to lower the steps to the *Pride* that he noticed Lucy Cooper sitting huddled under the ship, obviously burning to offload something or other. Inwardly he sighed and packed away his thoughts about Dalian and the Ranglatiri for the time being.

'Hello, Lucy. I need a beer. Do you want one too?'

She stood up, stiff-legged. 'Yes please, if you're not too busy.'

'Come on up.'

She followed him silently up the steps and sat at the table without waiting to be invited. He rummaged in the fridge and found a couple of bottles. They would do nicely. He sat down and slid one over to Lucy. 'Right then, what's all this about?'

She remained silent, just turned the bottle in her hand, absently picking at the label. Spit it out, girl, I haven't got all day, thought Joe, but said nothing.

Finally, she spoke. 'I just want to say, whatever happens now, I'm ready for any punishment you feel is appropriate. I've said my goodbyes, and if I never see the Earth again, well, I brought it on myself. But you need to know what I've found out.'

What is she on about? What can she possibly have done, to be so worried? 'What have you found out, Lucy?'

'I…there…I…joined the *Shantivira* on false pretences.'

Joe listened as Lucy unfolded her story.

Cath, *get yourself back here, you've got to hear this.*

A second later, he felt a furry head pushing at his right hand. He scratched her behind the ears, his attention still on Lucy, whose narrative had stumbled slightly at the jaguar's sudden appearance. Kitty was unusually quiet.

Eventually Lucy talked herself out. 'All I can say is, I'm

345

really, really sorry to let you down like this. But you have to know about what the AAL are up to. Nestor is actively promoting fear and spreading misinformation about us. He wants to sabotage the whole *Shantivira* project.'

Join the queue, Nestor, whoever you are, thought Joe.

'And I'm worried about what he might have done with Charlie – I mean David,' said Lucy.

Cath, *is this David Wang the same David who broke into the Library?*

I told you, I can't talk about it. He knew what the stakes were. He'll have to fend for himself. I can't get involved, Joe, you're on your own. Please don't tell Aldeman anything. This is a can of worms we need to keep tightly shut.

Can you go and get Delius please, Cath?

What, now? Can't you just call him?

Just go, please. Give me twenty minutes alone with Lucy. In fact, don't come back until she's gone, if you really want to stay out of this.

'Tssschrrrr,' hissed the jaguar aloud. *Oh, all right.*

One day, you're going to tell me what this is all about.

Nope.

Kitty turned and disappeared.

'Joe?' Lucy broke the silence. 'Say something?'

Joe pressed his palms together, fingers against his lips. 'OK,' he said at last. 'You do know you should have come to us right at the start?'

Lucy nodded, her lips clamped shut.

'And you know I should have you exiled to prevent you from doing any more harm?'

Lucy's eyes filled with tears as she nodded again.

Joe continued, 'But as I understand it, whatever your

original intentions were – and I accept coercion was involved – thanks to David Wang, you have not actually put the *Shantivira* at risk. And you came straight to me as soon as you recognised a real threat to us, providing valuable intelligence. And with the right training I think you could be a great pilot. I don't want to give up on you just yet.'

'You don't?' said Lucy, unmistakably hopeful.

'Where you are right now is more important than where you came from. Where you go next is up to you. I'm not going to tell Aldeman about this. But if you want to stay on the programme, you're going to have to prove yourself to me. From what you told this Matthew guy, we must assume they know you've switched sides.'

Lucy smiled weakly. 'I was pretty forthright.'

'But you should still go to your next meeting. I need to know if that weapon they're developing is any good. You're our only link to these people.'

'What about David? He's one of ours, Joe. Can't we get in touch with him somehow? I'd be happier if I knew he was OK.'

I doubt he is, thought Joe. And I'd like to find out more about him myself before considering a rescue. Kitty must have her reasons for not helping.

There was a knock on the door.

'Come in, Delius,' called Joe. 'Delius will help us,' he said to Lucy.

KITTY REAPPEARED LONG after Lucy had returned to London.

So, is Wang OK? Joe asked.

Her eyes narrowed as she looked down at him. *How?* she said. *How did you know?*

This guy means something to you. I'm not stupid. Of course you couldn't resist going to look.

He's alive. Nestor's keeping him captive. But if I pull him out of there, his cover will be blown. No telling what Nestor will do then. At the moment, he's not sure. He doesn't know Wang is ex-Shantivira. The longer Wang remains unrescued, the safer he'll be. Nestor won't kill him unless his hand is forced; Wang's too valuable to him. He'll have to sit it out. Don't try and contact him, Joe, it'll just make things worse for him.

So she did care. Thank God for that.

OK, he said. *I've asked Delius to infiltrate the AAL forums.*

Make sure he's subtle. They mustn't suspect alien involvement.

He has strict instructions to observe and report. I need to know what their game is and if it'll affect my approach to the UN.

You're thinking that far ahead already?

Proper prior planning prevents piss-poor performance.

Joe told Kitty about his meeting with Dalian.

Well, it's pretty clear what she's trying to achieve, isn't it? said Kitty.

It is?

She knows how close you are to Aldeman. She thinks Aldeman isn't taking the Ranglatiri seriously enough, and that you share her opinion. She wants you to nudge him for her.

What, by offering me a job she knew I wouldn't accept? Kind of elaborate, isn't it?

That's the way councillors operate.

So I'm Dalian's gopher now. Great.

You'll tell him about your discussion, won't you? The nudge comes with that, automatically. I don't see what your problem is. You agree with her, don't you?

On the Ranglatiri? I do actually, admitted Joe.

The bigger difficulty is pulling off first contact in a way that satisfies Dalian and the rest of the Council, so they don't pull our funding and leave the Earth defenceless.

You think I don't know that? sighed Joe. *Especially now we know these AAL nutters are bad-mouthing us all over the dark web? Let's go back to the Ranglatiri: do you think Aldeman is taking the threat seriously enough?*

He's not as aggressive as Dalian. Which makes him less impulsive. He won't decide on a course of action lightly. He's still in the fact-finding and analysis phase. But when he does, he can be unswervingly merciless. I don't think Dalian has ever seen that side of him up close. But you have, when you were his pilot. Remember Anitenja?

Oh God, I'd forgotten that.

Suppressed it, you mean.

Joe recalled how a group of extremists from Anitenja had hijacked a Syenitian ship in an attempt to reverse engineer and copy its weapons system. Aldeman had had them all arrested. The trial went on for months; it was in all the news feeds. When they were found guilty of breaking Anitenja's treaty with the Galaksi Alliance, Aldeman ejected the entire planet from the organisation, severing all trade links and consequently plunging the planet into chaos and poverty.

It was like he was made of stone, Joe said. *No mercy. No second chances. He said the treaty must be upheld or all interplanetary agreements become meaningless and unenforceable. Then chaos would spread and, eventually, the Alliance would disintegrate.*

Remember, said Kitty, *he started his career in the police – and that led to him becoming a lawyer. He believes the rule of law is the basis for every civilisation and it should apply equally to everybody.*

Even to entire planets?

Especially to entire planets.

30. SPACE IS FULL OF SURPRISES
DAN

T HE WORKING WEEK was finally over. They'd got through the evening conference with Mission Control and the weekly review with Joe Llewellyn on the *Shantivira*. Now all the repairs were complete, they didn't have to tell Mission Control so many blatant lies. Daily life was getting easier at last. But Dan wasn't happy.

Somehow he had to let NASA know what was going on up here. All the photos he'd taken while they'd been on the *Shantivira* had disappeared, deleted before he could make backups. How was that possible? He kept the camera in his sleeping bag and he was sure nobody on board had touched it.

Still, the weekend beckoned. A welcome break from the endless experiments. He was floating in the Harmony module, listening to Bob Dylan with his eyes closed, waiting for Friday night's illicit highlight. A sudden jet of air on the back of his head interrupted his drifting, spinning him in an involuntary somersault.

'Aargh! Jesus Fuck!' yelled Dan, ripping out his ear buds in time to hear an infuriating giggle.

Kitty sat cross-legged on the wall above, holding a wicker basket with a fold-up lid. She seemed to make her own gravity; she never floated like the rest of them.

'Sorry. I couldn't resist,' she said, smiling. 'I wanted to see if I could blow you away.'

'Man, Kitty, I knew you were coming, but Christ, you made me jump!'

'My apologies. For that you get first dibs on my goodies here.'

'Now you're talking,' said Dan. 'What've you got today?'

'Dim sum and spring rolls. There's a chilli dip somewhere in here too,' she said, rummaging in her basket. 'And I've got *Shantivira*-grown carrots and cherry tomatoes. Cheese. Italian salami. Fresh bread. And a whole bag of apples. They should last you a few days.' As she spoke, she pulled out each item and let it drift across the cabin.

Dan cupped his hands round his mouth and yelled down the space station, 'Hey everyone, dinner time!'

Amazing how fast they all showed up. Even after two months of weekly visits, piping hot, freshly cooked meals that weren't shrink-wrapped in plastic hadn't lost their novelty. The rest of the crew greeted Kitty warmly and went to work on the floating food.

The *Shantivira* catering team regarded preparing food to eat in microgravity as a personal challenge. So far, they'd had Cornish pasties, Russian *pirozhki*, rolled-up Turkish pizzas, Spanish tortilla, fish cakes, samosas, sushi and tempura. Not to mention the fresh fruit, one of the things Dan had missed most before the secret deliveries started.

As usual, Kitty stuck around for a chat. 'So, how was

your week?' she asked.

'Great!' said Simon. 'Hagar and I have decided to have a holiday together in Tel Aviv next summer.'

Love's young dream, thought Dan. To the amusement of the rest of the crew, Simon and Hagar were conducting a lively flirtation via their *zanas*. It was like living in a low-budget soap opera. With holograms. They seemed to be getting serious, although perhaps it was just the extra romance induced by a clandestine long-distance relationship. Dan doubted it would withstand real life once Simon returned to Earth.

Valentin had a whole list of Kawaida-related questions. They were all using their weekends to learn the new language, testing each other on vocabulary and trying out role plays. The course was structured like a game with different levels, which introduced an element of competitiveness: especially between Dan and Simon, who was squeezing in extra sessions with Hagar during the week.

Dan wanted to learn as much as he could, in case he couldn't take his *zana* with him when he went home. He planned to tape it to his chest, but he worried that Kitty might track him down and get it back before he could show it to anyone. He must find out more about how her teleporting worked. Eventually Valentin ran out of questions and Dan could steer the conversation to his own ends.

'Kitty, will you tell us more about teleportation? It shouldn't be possible.'

'You're right, it shouldn't. And yet here I am.'

'So how do you do it?'

'I don't know, Dan. Magic?'

'I don't believe in magic. There must be a rational explanation.'

Kitty grinned toothily. God, she was creepy when she did that.

'I'm sure there is,' she said. 'Isn't magic just science which hasn't been understood yet? Teleporting is intuitive for me, I just do it. The space spirit part of me perceives the universe differently to you.'

'How do you mean?'

'I see the whole electromagnetic spectrum, all the way from gamma rays down to radio waves. Gravitational waves too. That's why my eyes look different to yours.'

'Have you got x-ray vision?' joked Tatiana.

'I can detect x-rays, but that's not the same thing. I promise I'm not looking at you all in your underwear!' Kitty laughed.

'But you can see in the dark,' stated Irina. It wasn't a question.

Kitty nodded. 'And I can watch TV or listen to the radio without a machine to help me.'

'That's cool,' said Irina.

'What about hearing?' asked Tatiana.

'The same,' said Kitty. 'Everything from infrasound up to ultrasound.'

'Doesn't that drive you mad, seeing and hearing everything?' asked Takeshi.

She nodded again. 'I filter nearly everything, all the time. But it takes concentration, energy. I need a break for a few hours each day. I need – solitude.'

'Where do you go, Kitty?' asked Valentin. 'Surely there's nowhere you can avoid electromagnetic waves completely?'

'I have a place inside a mountain. My Venusberg, if you like,' she said with a sly smile. 'The *Pride of Essoona* is well-shielded, so that's OK too. I walk on the dark side of the moon, or swim deep in the ocean. And if I really start losing control, then I let myself drift in deep space. It's not silent, but the noise is more…spread out. Less overwhelming. And then, every so often, you come across something amazing. Space is full of surprises.'

'Like what?' said Tatiana.

'Like supernovas, quasars, nebulae. Every one is unique: the colours, the shape, the music they make.'

'Music?' said Valentin.

'Each has its own energy, its own rhythm. It's one of the ways I navigate.'

'But what about teleporting?' asked Dan, unwilling to be sidetracked. 'How do you fix on where you want to go?'

'Well, teleporting to people is simplest. People I've had physical contact with.' Kitty hesitated, trying to find the right words. 'You know when there's someone standing close behind you: you can't see or hear them, but somehow you know they're there? Perhaps a prickling sensation on the back of your neck?'

Dan nodded.

'That's because they're standing within your individual electromagnetic field and disrupting yours with theirs. It's a sixth sense you humans don't normally acknowledge. I can sense someone's individual electromagnetic field from far, far away. If I know what planet they're on, I can generally find them. The better I know someone, the easier they are to locate.'

So *that* explained why she was so tactile, always hugging people and patting them on the arm. He'd thought she was being friendly, but actually she was ID-ing people so she could find them again. Devious.

If she could find him anywhere, that was going to make stealing a *zana* almost impossible. He'd have to learn as much Kawaida as he could and take it with him in his head, along with all the handwritten notes and sketches he'd made about the *Shantivira*. Not as good as hardware, but better than nothing.

31. EXAM TIME
HANNA

HANNA RUBBED HER face, trying to stay awake. Nearly midnight and she was still at her desk. Again. But she had to finish learning this vocab; the test was tomorrow morning. They seemed to be getting twice as much homework since returning from the summer break. God knew how Farida managed it, preparing for the University of Essoona's entrance exams on top of everything else. Farida was determined to study Syenitian mathematics, even if it meant giving up sleep.

Hanna wasn't prepared to sacrifice time in bed. Although she and Hassan hadn't attempted making the beast with two backs (as Hassan called it) since the holidays, she'd taken Lucy's advice to heart. She'd been practising diligently, first with pelvic floor exercises, then with her imagination and her right forefinger. After a few successes, she understood what she was aiming for. Lucy was right, it was all about getting into the right frame of mind.

A knock on Hanna's door made her jump.

'Yeah?' she said.

'Hanna? You still up?' Nikolai's head appeared round the door. 'Can you come up to ours? I've got something to show you.'

Upstairs, she found Farida, Lucy, Felix and Saïd sitting in a row on Nikolai's bed. Farida shifted closer to Lucy to make room for Hanna.

'OK,' said Nikolai. 'So, you know I've been monitoring the AAL's online presence?'

They nodded.

'I sent you all the link, ages ago. What did you think?'

'Pretty slick,' said Saïd. 'They've clearly spent money on professional marketing. And it's very easy to make donations.'

Nikolai agreed. 'But there's something new going on. The site's been hijacked – and not by me.'

'What do you mean?' asked Hanna.

'Well, the donation function has been deactivated, for starters. And someone's been uploading files profiling intelligent life from other planets. I can't trace where they're coming from. There are a few new ones every week, available in English, Chinese, Arabic, Hindi, Spanish, French and Russian. The site's visitor numbers are off the scale and the forums are all on fire with it, wondering if it's a hoax.'

'And is it?' asked Farida.

'Well, that's the thing. The format of each profile is exactly the same as the one used by the Syenitian Library. The contents too. Not just descriptions, but photos, maps, life cycle flowcharts, the whole lot. The files look like they've been directly translated from the Kawaida version. They've been viewed so many times now, it won't be long before someone reposts them on the surface web.'

'There's no mention of Kitty, though? Or the *Shantivira*?' asked Lucy, concerned.

'No, nothing, they're straight translations of the Sye-nitian Intelligent Life archives. Kitty and Rowan are nowhere to be found in them either, I've looked.'

Hanna noticed Saïd was grinning. 'What's so funny?' she asked.

'Looks like Delius has got himself a new hobby,' he said.

'Delius?'

'He's right,' said Farida, 'Who else can it be?'

'I agree,' said Nikolai. 'There's a new voice on the forums, calling itself "OnlyTheTruth". It sounds exactly like Delius.'

'What does he say?' asked Felix.

'He engages all the haters, asking them open questions, trying to enter into a dialogue and to understand their point of view. Then he asks how they can hate a person they've never met, pointing out that the best way to dispel fear is to arm yourself with the facts. He suggests that most aliens are too far away and too wrapped up in their own everyday problems to know or care about humankind. I would call it trolling, but he's relentlessly polite and logical to the point of pedantry. He never rises to the abuse he gets in return. It can only be Delius. Look, I'll show you.'

Nikolai opened a new tab and scrolled down the page. 'This is a nice one,' he said.

Death2ET: So I've looked at all the profiles now. They're bullshit.

OnlyTheTruth: Bullshit?

Death2ET: These 'aliens' are all around the same size.

But that can't be possible. Look at the life on our planet. There are tiny animals like insects and enormous ones, like whales. Aliens must all come in different sizes too. It's only logical.

OnlyTheTruth: A life form evolves to be the smallest it can be while still being able to perform the tasks necessary for its survival. The excess energy required to maintain a large size is not efficient. Once a species develops significant intelligence, the advantage of magnitude loses its importance.

Intelligence also requires certain proportions, due to the complexity of the organism. You may have noticed most intelligent life forms on this planet are similar in size – dolphins, apes and humans. The intelligence of smaller creatures tends to be limited.

Death2ET: All right, you smug fucker, what about blue whales? They're massive.

OnlyTheTruth: They are. But we are discussing alien species capable of space travel. Space travel requires the construction of spacecraft, which in turn requires the ability to make and use tools. I think you would agree that whales are not potential engineers.

Death2ET: What about planets with different gravity? That must affect how big an alien grows.

OnlyTheTruth: You are correct, Death2ET, it absolutely does! Let us start with small planets. The smaller the planet, the less gravity it has, do you agree?

Death2ET: Yes. So the smaller the planet, the taller the alien, right?

OnlyTheTruth: Right. But a planet needs to be a certain size to generate an atmosphere which can support life. It is the necessary degree of complexity issue again. So there is an upper limit to the size a space-travelling species can be.

Also, space travel involves arriving somewhere. If most planets are larger than yours and you are used to much less gravity, then you will not feel comfortable at your destination. It would be exhausting. So species at either end of the scale tend to stay on their own planets.

Death2ET: So what about tiny aliens from massive planets?

OnlyTheTruth: It is true, there are lots of planets which are multiple times bigger than the Earth, although many do not support intelligent life.

Death2ET: So there *are* tiny aliens?

OnlyTheTruth: The building blocks of organic life are the same everywhere in this universe, Death2ET. Carbon. Hydrogen. Oxygen. Nitrogen. There is a minimum size for a species of sufficient complexity to achieve space travel, however massive its planet. As you will have seen in the records, the smallest known space-travelling life form is the Grooka, rarely taller than one metre.

Death2ET: So you reckon it's impossible for an alien to be many times smaller or many times larger than us?

OnlyTheTruth: I can assure you, any alien reaching the Earth in a spacecraft will be roughly the same size as you are. You will be able to look her in the eye.

Death2ET: Her? Are aliens all female?

OnlyTheTruth: Sorry, her or him or them. We must respect gender equality.

Death2ET: Are you a bird, mate?

OnlyTheTruth: No, I am not a bird.

Death2ET: How do you know so much about this?

OnlyTheTruth: Thank you for your time, Death2ET, it has been a pleasure communicating with you. I must log off now. Goodbye.

Hanna smiled to herself. It did sound like Delius.

'Do you think he passes the Turing test?' asked Lucy.

Nikolai sniggered. 'Who? Delius or Death2ET?'

THE NEXT DAY was the day for Kitty's 'Civilisation' sessions, some welcome light relief in the weekly programme. Today the subject was nation states. Kitty suggested that the formation of nations was just a stepping stone in a planet's development. 'When you get down to it, national boundaries and nation states are not important. Only people are important. And they're not more important than the environment they inhabit. The land could easily survive without people, but people could not survive without the land.

'Nation states are a way of protecting resources – land, fuel, food, water – for the people in your group. When the resources become short, the groups begin to fight over them. You have evolved to be territorial, but land cannot be owned, no more than any other living thing can truly be owned. The idea of ownership is an artificial construct. You can only fight for the privilege to care for it and draw sustenance from it. It will be there long after you and your descendants are gone.

'The more globally interconnected your society becomes, the more you realise that people are the same everywhere. At some point, being territorial is no longer a useful strategy. There *is* only one group: the human population of Earth. But that's a long way off. You don't even have a common language for your planet yet.'

Lianjie asked, 'When do you think we will? And what will it be?'

'I think that point is a few hundred years away yet,' said Kitty. 'When it comes, I imagine it will be some amalgamation of English and Mandarin. Maybe Mandarin with a Romanised alphabet? Who knows? It will be whatever is easiest for most people – that's the way these things go.'

'Has Syenitia ever had different countries with different languages?' said Saïd.

'Oh, yes. There are plenty of regional languages which people speak at home. Syenitians are very proud of their diverse identities and distinctive cultures.'

'Do any of the Galaksi Alliance members still have nation states?' asked Felix.

'Almost none,' said Kitty. 'A common language is a pre-requisite for membership, and that generally evolves as nation states become less important.'

Lucy asked, 'Has a member planet ever left the Galaksi Alliance?'

Kitty nodded. 'Planets have been kicked out for not complying with Alliance rules and ideals. No one has ever left voluntarily. Alliance membership is something most planets aspire to, but not many achieve. Our members' strength depends on our sticking together, pooling our expertise and resources and creating opportunities which would otherwise be impossible.'

'Do you think the Earth will ever be a member?' asked Hanna.

'I hope so, Hanna. But it won't happen in your lifetime, nor your grandchildren's. That's why we're all here – to stop anything bad happening to the Earth before it can join.'

OVER LUNCH, LUCY left the table to take a phone call. When she returned, her face was even whiter than usual. Hanna watched her cross the room and whisper in Felix's ear. He put a protective arm around Lucy and they left the room. Across the table, Saïd caught Hanna's eye; he had observed the exchange too. Simultaneously, they rose and followed the couple up to Lucy's flat. Hanna knocked at the door.

'Lucy? Are you OK?'

Felix opened the door silently and tilted his head, indicating they should sit at the table.

Saïd asked, 'Has something happened?'

Lucy wiped moist eyes on the back of her hand and sniffed. 'I just got a call from the police. My parents' house has been burgled. A neighbour noticed the back door was open and reported it. I have to go down there to see if anything's missing.'

'Because your parents are away on the cruise David Wang organised for them?' said Hanna. 'So no one's been hurt, right? Why are you so upset? It's just stuff.'

Lucy stared at the table top, saying nothing.

Felix said, 'She's worried it was the AAL, looking for information.'

'Mum's very organised,' said Lucy, looking up at them. 'She displays all the important family contact details in plain view on a noticeboard in the kitchen. Not just phone numbers and e-mail, but addresses. Including the Dunia School of Language. If it was the AAL, they know for sure where we are now and they'll be watching us.'

Hanna pursed her lips. Lucy always thought so far ahead. 'If it was the AAL,' she said. 'It might just have been a normal break-in.'

Felix nodded, 'That's what we're hoping. We'll know more once Lucy's had a chance to look round.'

THE EXAMS WERE scheduled for mid-December. Hanna wasn't worried about the flight tests. But the language papers filled her with terror. She had zero experience of taking exams. However much Irion and Hassan tried to reassure her, night after night she woke up sweating.

Still, at least she had something to look forward to. In a few weeks she and Hassan would be checking out the Christmas markets in Munich! She tingled with excitement every time she thought about it. Hassan wanted to visit the BMW museum too. Perhaps she could go shopping that day. They had time to see everything: they were going for a whole week. When she woke at night with the exam terrors, she'd get herself off to sleep again by planning what to wear on each day of the holiday. It was tricky to get the balance between being warm enough and being stylish. She might have to invest in a new coat – or maybe she could get one there? That would make a great souvenir.

Finally, the day of the flight tests came. They waited nervously on the basement stairs for the door to the training deck to open. Some talked non-stop, comparing strategies and moves, others were quiet, trying to maintain their inner calm.

But Hanna felt OK. More than OK, in fact. That weekend she and Hassan had managed their first mutually fulfilling love-making session. Avoiding penetration inspired creativity – and put paid to all worries about getting pregnant.

The door opened and the students filed onto the training deck. Settling into her pod, Hanna remembered her first time in a simulator. The sense of recognition that she'd found something she was born to do, that the *Tumba* was a natural extension of her own body. She jiggled in her seat, impatient to start.

As expected, the five-hour exam was physically and mentally demanding. It was an extended course, designed to test their skills in manoeuvring, navigation and troubleshooting on-the-fly. First came a convoluted series of 3D tubes, followed by a long patch of empty space which she had to navigate using coordinates on the computer and the autopilot. Even travelling at maximum velocity, it was quite boring and Hanna found her concentration waning. But Hassan had warned her this was part of the test.

Hanna drank her water and ate the apple she'd brought with her. She was wiping her hands on her trousers when the proximity alarm went off. Just in time, she switched off the autopilot and pulled up vertically, looping the loop. She'd arrived at an asteroid field. If she hadn't been alert, she'd have flown smack into an asteroid at full speed, failing the exam.

Hanna began to weave her way in and out of the asteroids. This was the final phase of the test. All she had to do was reach the other side in one piece and she'd be home and dry.

Ten minutes later all her confidence evaporated as an ominous grinding noise coincided with a series of red flashing icons on the head-up display. She peered at the characters. It looked like she'd lost several thrusters at once. Immediately, the spacecraft's response to her movements became more sluggish and unbalanced. The *Tumba's* flight path became erratic – she was losing control of it. She had to do something, fast.

Flustered, she tapped at the control panel. She needed to rebalance the other thrusters evenly; that should sort out the problem. Her mouth was dry as she entered the instruction. Why hadn't the computer compensated the power loss automatically? Thankfully, her idea worked and the spacecraft came back under control. She was travelling more slowly now, but at least she wasn't going to crash.

Carefully she flew on, trying to find the most direct path to the end coordinates. It couldn't be much further now, could it? The asteroid field seemed endless. She checked her instruments and her stomach gave a sickening lurch. The fuel gauge indicated her fuel cells were almost empty. It would be just her luck if she ran out of fuel before completing the course. She slowed down to a more fuel-efficient speed, hoping against hope that she'd make it to the finish.

That wasn't her only problem. She'd drunk too much water and, as the pressure on her bladder mounted, she found herself unable to concentrate. Desperately, she considered her options as she steered the spacecraft in and out of the asteroids. Could she put the *Tumba* on autopilot and quickly run out to the toilet? Could she press pause somehow? Was there a bucket somewhere in here she could use?

The solution came to her in a flash. It was something she'd never tried; Tima had mentioned it briefly, ages ago. Newly hopeful, she felt for a button under her seat. It was really there! As soon as she pressed it, a cone appeared from underneath her seat on the end of a mechanical arm. The cone fed into a pipe which disappeared into the floor. Thankfully, Hanna shuffled forward and unzipped her flight suit. Steering the *Tumba* with her thighs, she picked up the cone, flipped open the lid and held it in place, allowing herself to relax at last. Oh, the bliss! The glorious relief!

Back to business. Hanna checked her instruments. She blinked and looked at the fuel gauge again. It was showing that the main fuel cell was more than half full. Huh? Then she laughed out loud as she realised she'd solved two problems at once. Her urine had gone straight into the fuel cell and had been converted into energy! The *Tumba* accelerated as Hanna headed for the finish with renewed zeal.

As she finally cleared the asteroid field, the screen in front of her went blank and the lights in the cockpit dimmed. She was confused for a second or two, wondering what had happened. Only when the door behind her hissed open did she understand: the exam was over. Thank God for that. Her legs felt like noodles. She staggered down the steps and made her way to the kitchen area. There was no one there. Did that mean she was the first to finish? She checked her watch. Oh. Less than four of the five hours had passed. Funny, she'd lost all track of time. It felt like she'd been in her pod all day. She sat down and poured herself a drink.

Minutes later she was joined by Anwar, then Lucy, Elif and Francis. The others appeared slowly, one by one – all except Flavia, Farida and Lars. They only showed up after the five hours were over. Farida was quiet but calm. Lars was grim-faced and hyper-talkative, giving them a blow-by-blow account of how he'd crashed his *Tumba* in the asteroid field and the simulation had returned to the start. He hadn't been fast enough to finish the course after that. Hanna noticed his hands were shaking. Flavia was in tears: she'd got lost in the asteroid field and hadn't made it to the finish either. They tried to comfort them, but everyone was thinking the same thing. Lars and Flavia weren't going to make it through to the second year.

The second flight exam, the following day, was only two hours long. The focus was on marksmanship, something Hanna was good at. Everything went smoothly; she felt like she was dancing in her seat as she twisted and turned to fire at the targets on her display.

But the language exams were worse than she'd feared. The reading was multiple choice, and half the time she felt she was just guessing. The listening was so fast, her writing got larger and larger as she hurried to transfer the answer from her head onto the paper. It wasn't that she hadn't understood, she just couldn't write quickly enough to get it all down.

The written exam was by far the worst. They had to write an essay on the political structure and economy of Syenitia and the history of the Galaksi Alliance. Argh! They hadn't been formally taught about this in lectures. But when she thought about it, she'd learnt a lot about Syenitia that year.

Hanna took deep breaths, listing all the points she felt she could write about and then arranging them into a logical order. Once she got started, she found she had quite a lot to say. For hours afterwards, the muscles in her hand were frozen into a claw shape, her arm on fire from writing with such intensity.

The oral was much better. It was just a pleasant chat with Irion about what Hanna felt it meant to be Nuer and, in a broader context, Ethiopian. Irion already knew a lot about Hanna's family history and background, so Hanna didn't feel she had to explain much. Instead, she contrasted her experiences in Ethiopia to those in the UK.

She talked about the slower pace of life and how she felt that people in Ethiopia were generally friendlier and more welcoming to strangers. That Nuer did not focus on accumulating wealth in the same way that people in Britain did. She believed Nuer were more willing to share with their neighbours, despite having less than the poorest people in London.

She admitted that things were changing: that guns were taking on the significance that cattle had had, and that made people behave differently. Irion suggested things might have changed even more while Hanna had been away. Even the remotest corners of the Earth would not escape globalisation for ever. Hanna didn't like to think about that. She still hoped to return to Ethiopia one day, perhaps when she retired.

That evening, the post-exam analysis continued around Hanna and Emily's kitchen table. In the oral, they'd all been asked to examine their own nationality. Lucy, who'd found the written papers easy, had really struggled.

'I totally put my foot in it,' she said. 'I kept going on about tolerance, then I realised that probably wasn't how Irion felt about it and I dried up completely. But the British *are* tolerant.'

Hanna couldn't suppress a bitter laugh. 'Tolerant? Sure, they'll *tolerate* you as long as you make yourself useful and stay in the background. But they'll only *accept* you if you look exactly like them, dress exactly like them and speak exactly like them. Then they might consider welcoming you into their little club of Britishness. Otherwise, forget it.'

Lucy looked startled. 'OK, I can see why you might feel that way. So, you've lived here for years now, how do you see the British?'

Hanna thought for a moment. 'I suppose the biggest thing is that, deep down, they believe they're better than everyone else.'

'That's not true!' spluttered Lucy.

But Emily was nodding. 'Do you think that comes from living on an island?' she asked.

'I think you might be onto something there,' agreed Hanna. 'The other thing is their weird nostalgia. Even young people! They're always looking back at how things used to be, preserving buildings, dressing up in period clothes for fun. And what's so great about the Second World War? There have been hundreds of wars since then! So why are they so obsessed with something that finished nearly seventy years ago? Why don't they look ahead? It's like they have no vision for the future. Thank God I'm an Ethiopian is all I can say. We have a proud and ancient history, but we're not trapped in it! We look forwards, not backwards.'

Lucy opened her mouth to respond, but was interrupted by a knock at the door. It was Ai, with a box of little round rice cakes.

'It's a bit early for *mochi*,' she said, oblivious to the atmosphere in the room, 'but I thought we ought to celebrate the exams being over.' She passed them around. Hanna picked one up and took a big bite.

'Not so much at once!' Ai scolded. 'If you bite off more than you can chew, you could choke on it.'

'People die every year eating this stuff,' Lianjie added cheerfully. 'It's chewier than chewing gum.'

Initially Hanna thought it tasted quite nice, but Lianjie was right, it was incredibly chewy. It just never got smaller in her mouth. She began to understand why people might choke on it. Would Ai be offended if she spat it out discreetly? Or was she really going to have to swallow it? Looking round the table, she saw the others were thinking the same thing. Finally, she managed to wash it down with a large swig of tea. Farida caught her eye and Hanna began to shake with silent laughter, almost snorting her tea back out through her nose.

32. MATTHEW?

LUCY

LUCY SCANNED THE other people in the queue to board the London Eye. Where the hell was Matthew? Was he still in the security queue? She examined her ticket printout. She had the right day and the right time, no doubts there. She studied the crowd, looking carefully at each face. Would it be another contact today? Or perhaps, after her last conversation with Matthew, they realised she was no longer willing to cooperate. Perhaps nobody would turn up and she wouldn't have to have anything to do with them anymore. No harm in hoping.

A hand on her arm and a loud, familiar voice made her jump about a mile into the air.

'Oh. My. God! Lucy? Lucy Cooper?'

Nicola Bitch Harris, school prefect and subtly cruel class bully, last seen on A Level results day, crowing about her success. She'd gone to Oxford or Cambridge or one of those places, Lucy recalled. Lucy hadn't spared her a single thought for almost a decade and now, suddenly, here she was. Perfectly turned out, as always.

Today she was sporting a dinky peach-coloured jacket with a pencil skirt and matching shoes and handbag. Disappointingly, she wasn't wearing a hat and gloves to complete the ensemble. A sheepish male hovered awkwardly behind her.

'Nicola? Fuck me, what are you doing here? Do you live in London?'

'Oh, no, I'm based in Manchester nowadays. I play the harp in the BBC Philharmonic; I'm sure you've seen my posts on Facebook?'

'I'm not on Facebook,' replied Lucy dismissively, looking round for Matthew again with renewed desperation. Save me, Matthew! Where are you?

Nicola was not to be deterred. 'We're just down for the weekend. This is my fiancé, Perry.'

Poor sod, thought Lucy, shaking his hand. 'Nice to meet you,' she said.

Perry opened his mouth to speak, but Nicola got there first, thrusting her left hand under Lucy's nose. Even Lucy couldn't miss the diamond ring, big enough to take your eye out. So that explained the Hyper-Harris-on-steroids act.

'Perry proposed last night! He took me to Rules, you know, the restaurant in Covent Garden?'

'First time I've ever seen her speechless,' Perry managed to say, with a shy smile. Lucy found herself warming to him.

'I was totally astounded, I can tell you – I mean, we've only been going out three years!' gushed Nicola, with pseudo-saccharine surprise. Lucy winced at the frosty undercurrent in her voice.

The queue shuffled forward. The next capsule would be theirs. Lucy stood on tiptoes, urgently scanning the other visitors for Matthew's lanky figure.

'Has your date stood you up?' tittered Nicola.

Perry said kindly, 'You'd be welcome to come round with us.'

'Thanks. But it's not a date, it's a business meeting,' said Lucy, resigning herself to Matthew's no-show. She couldn't meet him now, not with Nicola monitoring her every action like a hawk and probably posting anything of interest on Facebook for Delius and the world to see.

Lucy considered going home but decided against it. What if there was a new contact, here in the queue? Perhaps they'd slip a note into her pocket. A thought occurred to her: what if the contact was actually Perry? She studied him more closely. He did seem the AAL type. And easy to brainwash if Nauseating Nicola had got her hooks into him.

'You'd go to a business meeting dressed like that?' said Nicola, incredulous. 'What is it you went into again? Oh, yeah, don't you fix cars or something terribly masculine like that? I suppose we should be grateful those jeans aren't covered in oil splodges!'

Wilful ignorance always got Lucy's goat. 'I was an automotive engineer, Nicola,' she retaliated. 'Designing cars, not fixing them. It's hard to get very dirty sitting in meetings and writing e-mails all day.'

They filed into the capsule. Lucy stood at one end, the better to observe the other passengers. No obvious candidates.

'So what do you do now, Lucy?' enquired Perry. 'I mean, if you *were* an engineer?'

Whoops, I fell into that one, she thought. Out loud, she said, 'Oh, I'm still an engineer. An engineer is something you are, more than something you do. I just don't work in the automotive industry anymore. I'm in London retraining.' Lucy was relying on the average English person's general ignorance and lack of curiosity about all things technical to avoid having to divulge any details. It worked.

'Oh, right,' said Perry.

The queue began moving again and it was their turn to board, finally, along with twenty or so other people. Lucy took a spot at one end of the capsule, her back to the glass so she could observe her fellow passengers. None of them seemed to be paying her any attention.

'So, how did you two meet?' she asked, resigning herself to half an hour of social hell. 'Are you a musician too, Perry?'

'No, he works as a property developer for an investment company,' boasted Nicola. We met at MediaCity – we used to have lunch at the same place every day.'

'It took me months to pluck up the courage to speak to her,' said Perry, with an oddly nasal laugh.

'I had no idea,' cried Nicola. 'One day he just sat down opposite me and asked me out. Completely out of the blue!'

'And the rest is history?' guessed Lucy. She tuned out Nicola's chatter and gazed at the view. It was pretty good. Pity about the dilapidated Palace of Westminster, rotting quietly into the river. There was talk about refurbishing it, 'restoring it to its former glory'. Lucy thought they should bulldoze the lot and relocate Parliament to Birmingham.

'So, Lucy, are you seeing anyone at the minute?'

From Nicola's expression, Lucy suspected it wasn't the

first time she'd asked the question.

Lucy felt an irresistible urge to protect her relationship with Felix from nosy questions. 'I'm not, no,' she lied.

Nicola made a face and patted her condescendingly on the arm. 'Hang on in there,' she said, 'I'm sure it'll happen for you one day. And whoever it is, she'll be lucky to have you.'

Lucy turned away and studied the horizon, biting her lip in an effort not to laugh. Breathe, Lucy. Breathe. At last, the capsule approached the ground. About bloody time.

In her eagerness to get away, she almost jogged down the ramp and through the gift shop. Then she slowed: what if Matthew had missed their slot and was waiting outside? She stood for a moment, waiting to see if anyone came up to her. Nothing.

She pulled out her phone and dialled Felix.

'Hiya. It's me.'

'Lucy, how did it go? How come you're phoning?'

'A no-show. Complete waste of time. Don't wait for me in the coffee shop, I'll meet you all at home. The rain looks like it'll hold off for a while; I'd like to walk back and get some fresh air.'

'OK, I'll tell the others. See you for lunch?'

'Yeah. Bye.'

'Bye.'

Lucy strode along The Queen's Walk, past the Sea Life Centre and over Westminster Bridge. After reaching the IMechE building on Birdcage Walk, she cut across St James's Park, stopping briefly to watch the pelicans.

Where did she stand now with the AAL/EDS? Her

hurried visit to Devon last month hadn't eased her mind: quite the opposite. Her parents' house had been spitefully turned over but, as far as she could see, nothing had been removed. She'd taken it as a message that they could get to her whenever they wanted. So why had nobody made contact today? She didn't get it.

Lucy crossed the Mall and headed into Green Park. The trees had lost all their leaves, but being outside lifted her spirits, even on a grey December day like today. The air was cold, but the brisk walk had boosted her circulation and she felt great. She was on one of the lesser used paths, approaching Piccadilly, when a familiar figure appeared ahead of her, pushing an empty wheelchair.

'Matthew? What are you doing here? Why are you dressed like a paramedic?'

He didn't respond or even look her in the eye. Confused, Lucy opened her mouth to speak but was cut short by a prick on the side of her neck. Blackness closed in from the edges and her legs buckled. The last things she was aware of were strong hands under her armpits, and an odour of penetrant aftershave overlaid with tobacco.

33. I DON'T THINK WE'LL NEED CRAMPONS

HANNA

MUNICH WAS AMAZING. Being on holiday was amazing. Having Hassan all to herself for a week: amazing! Hanna's first impression of Germany was that it was like Britain, with subtle differences in architecture and the mix of people. And they drove on the right, like in Ethiopia. She revelled in the sensation of being somewhere new but not having to worry about where to spend the night or where her next meal would come from. She'd saved up enough money to treat herself to whatever she liked.

The hotel was OK. Fine for the price. The room's cleanliness stood up to her professional scrutiny, although the shower didn't drain too well. From her previous jobs, the word 'hotel' suggested something bigger and swankier to Hanna, with air-con, thick carpets, a minibar and windows you couldn't open. This place was less grand but also less impersonal. And the bed and the pillows were the biggest she'd ever seen!

Hassan had never been to Germany before either, but he was confident they could get by with their English. He'd reactivated the prosthetic feet he'd used for going out in London last year: not as easy to walk with as his Syenitian boots, but fine for city strolls. His stumps had shrunk rather since then, and he needed layers of old liners to make the sockets fit. He told Hanna it was normal for the volume of the residual limb to vary; the Syenitian boots compensated for this automatically.

Hassan's main worry about the trip had been getting through airport security. Despite the wintry weather, he'd worn shorts so he wouldn't have to constantly explain himself. Of course, the metal detector had beeped and flashed red, so they'd asked him to go through an x-ray machine and had swabbed his prosthetics for gunpowder traces. Instead of the hour they'd feared, it only took ten minutes, so they had a lot of extra time to browse the shops.

They boarded the plane first and sat right at the front. Hassan took off his feet and while Hanna was putting them in the overhead locker, he joked to the flight attendant that these budget airlines just didn't have the legroom. The flight attendant looked mortified, but Hanna couldn't stop giggling.

On Saturday afternoon they were drinking hot mead and watching the jugglers at the medieval Christmas market on Wittelsbacherplatz, when Hanna's phone rang. Felix. He must want to update them about Lucy's meeting.

'Hiya, how did Lucy's meeting go? I'm sorry I couldn't be there for debriefing. Munich is amazing, by the way.'

'Hi, Hanna, are you enjoying yourselves?'

'It's brilliant! But you lived here, I don't have to tell you what it's like.'

'Yeah. Um, Hanna?'

'Yes?'

'You both have a Schengen visa for the week, don't you?'

'Yes. Why?'

'Um. OK. So...'

There was something wrong, Hanna could tell by his voice. 'What's happened, Felix? Didn't the meeting go well?'

'It didn't happen. And Lucy hasn't come back. I spoke to her; she was on her way, but she never turned up. Nikolai tracked her phone and we've just found it in a bush in Green Park.'

'You think something's happened to her?'

'There's more. Irion hasn't come back from Portabello Market. You know how she always goes on Saturdays?'

Hanna nodded. Irion loved bargain-hunting and she was great fun to go shopping with. When she went out, she dressed up in full Goth regalia: painting her face white (with black lipstick and eyeliner) and wearing a high-necked black blouse with ruffles, shiny black leggings, heavy studded motorbike boots and soft leather gloves. She topped this off with a braided, military-style coat and, when she felt like it, a top hat. The only flash of colour was her green hair, which she refused to cover. In London at least, nobody gave her a second glance, apart from the occasional tourist wanting to have their photo taken with her.

'But she always comes home in time for lunch!'

'Not today. Nikolai got hold of the CCTV camera footage on the way between there and here.' Felix fell silent.

'What?' demanded Hanna.

'He found pictures of her being loaded into an ambulance. Definitely her. It looked like she was unconscious.'

'You've checked the hospitals?'

'Of course. No luck. The thing is, the ambulance had a Swiss number plate.'

'A Swiss number plate?' Hanna's heart began to yo-yo. 'You think she's been kidnapped? By the AAL?'

'We do. It can't be a coincidence that Lucy is gone at the same time. I think they've got her too.'

'What does Mary say?'

'She's in Yorkshire, visiting her mum. She won't be back until tomorrow morning. She switches off her phone when she's in the hospital.'

'Have you told Joe? Lucy said Kitty wouldn't help David – would she change her mind if it was Irion and Lucy as well?'

'Joe's at some all-day meeting in Essoona. Delius says he'll be back late and gave instructions not to be disturbed. We don't know where Kitty is. Delius thinks we need to find out more about what's going on before we can take action.'

'But then it might be too late! Especially if Kitty can't help.'

'I know! Don't worry, Hanna, we have a plan. Farida and Nikolai will stay here and tell Mary the minute she gets back tomorrow morning; then she can talk to Joe. Perhaps we'll even have good news by then. Me and Saïd don't need visas, so we're flying to Munich tonight. My brother will meet us at the airport with a car and the equipment we need. It's all organised. We'll meet you outside your hotel at 5 a.m. tomorrow and then we'll drive to Celestina Satellites and find out what's going on ourselves.'

'Equipment?' asked Hanna.

'Snow chains, snowshoes, sticks, ropes. I've sorted crampons for us all, but I don't think we'll need them. Plus maps, compasses, head torches, first aid and emergency kit, just the standard stuff. I've checked out the route, it's a fairly straightforward hike.'

'We have to walk up a mountain? In the snow?' said Hanna doubtfully.

'We can't drive up to the front door, can we? We'll have a better chance of sneaking in without getting caught if we're on foot. Snowshoeing is easy, Hanna. You'll love it.'

Hmm, she thought. Let's cross that bridge when we come to it. 'Where will you sleep?' she asked. 'Don't you want to come to the hotel tonight?'

'Parking in town is a nightmare. We'll stay at the airport. You two get a good night's sleep and be ready tomorrow morning. Wear warm clothes and walking boots. Keep your phone charged.'

Hanna ended the call. Why, oh why, hadn't she warned Mary and Irion about Lucy's exploits? She'd never forgive Lucy – or herself – if Irion got hurt.

34. A FEISTY GOTH

LUCY

LUCY WOKE. FOR a moment, she lay still, trying to work out what had happened. Matthew with a wheelchair, then darkness. Now she was on a thin mat on a hard floor. Cautiously, she explored with her fingers; someone had covered her with a rough blanket. She opened her eyes. Grey wool. She took in concrete walls and ceiling, no windows. Cold air, slightly damp. A single low-energy bulb provided insufficient lighting.

'Look, she's waking up,' said a familiar voice.

'Finally!' said another familiar voice.

Lucy sat up groggily, holding her aching head. Two figures sat against the opposite wall, close together on the floor.

'The headache will pass soon,' said the first voice.

'Charlie! I mean, David!' David smiled thinly, but said nothing. 'And Irion! What are you doing here?'

'Huddling together to keep warm?' said Irion, a sarcastic edge to her voice. With her outdoor clothes and make-up, she looked positively scary in the semi-darkness.

'Where are we?' Lucy asked, although she thought she knew.

'Welcome to my cell,' said David, switching to Kawaida. 'I've been down here for months. It's nice to have some company.'

'We're in a mountain, in Switzerland, Lucy,' said Irion, also in Kawaida. 'I think you know why. David's been filling me in while you were sleeping off the drugs they gave us.' She pointed at a camera set into the ceiling. 'Speak in Kawaida, we have to assume the guards outside are listening as well as watching. We don't know how long we have until they separate us.'

'Irion, I'm so sorry, I should have told you! This is all my fault!'

'That's funny. David says it's all *his* fault.'

Fear, fury and frustration came bubbling out of Lucy in a toxic cocktail. She stood up and jabbed her finger at David. 'It *is* all your fault,' she accused. 'You made me trust you. I never would have signed up for the *Shantivira* otherwise. I knew there was something off about Nestor and his chums. But you made me want to help you.'

David jumped to his feet and faced her. 'I was protecting the *Shantivira*! Do you think that, having found you, he would ever have left you alone? It was already too late! It was an exercise in damage limitation, right from the start. I had to put myself between you and Nestor to control the information flow. Luckily, he still trusted me back then. Yes, I let you spy for me – not that you were much good at it. I thought perhaps you might find out something useful. And I do miss that whole...world. You were a link to that for me.'

Irion interrupted. 'Look. What's done is done. There are conversations to be had, but this isn't the time. What's more important now is for us to get out of here. David tells me we can't rely on Kitty to drop by and teleport us away. If the Alliance realise she let him return to Earth after his escapades in the Library, they'll never trust her again. And they'd shut down the whole *Shantivira* project immediately if they discover the connection between her and what he's been doing here. Not even Aldeman could stop them. So she can't be seen here, not for a moment, not by anyone.'

'What connection?' asked Lucy, looking quizzically at David.

'I thought you'd have worked that out by now. Where do you think the money for my research came from?'

'Kitty? You're kidding, right? She doesn't even have her own house!'

David grinned. 'Where do dragons sleep, traditionally?'

'In a mountain on a pile of treasure? But—Oh.'

'She's loaded. But money's no use to her personally. She wanted to put her hoard to good use.'

Lucy thought of all the shell companies ending with the account in Caernarfon, owned by a Mr C. Ambrose. Finally, the penny dropped. Kitty's first husband had been called Ambrosius. C for Catherine, perhaps? *Cath* was Welsh for cat, wasn't it? Women probably weren't even allowed to have their own bank accounts back in the nineteenth century.

'She wants a plan B, in case the Syenitians change their minds about protecting the Earth one day. Our agreement was always that if things go wrong, I'm on my own. She made that very clear. We'll just have to manage by ourselves.'

'It's OK,' said Irion confidently. 'Mary will come and get us as soon as she discovers we're gone. Joe told us what you've been up to, Lucy. We were half-expecting something like this, but sometimes you have to let events unfold in order to deal with them.'

'What happened, David?' asked Lucy. 'How did you end up in here? When did you end up in here?'

'September. Just before I was due to meet you. I told you Nestor had been getting his own funding together and wanted to split? To use our weapon to destroy aliens indiscriminately, instead of purely for defence?'

Lucy nodded.

'Well, somehow he found out – or guessed – who the company's backer was, and he went apeshit. Called me a traitor to the human race and threw me in here. I can't describe how much he hates her; it's not rational. He goes red in the face if you even mention her name. She must have done something terrible to him personally, otherwise why would he care so much? It's as if his hatred of aliens starts with her. I've asked her a few times, but she always changes the subject.'

'Does he know you were a Shantiviran?' asked Irion.

'I don't think so. Otherwise he'd have mentioned it. He likes to come down here and gloat. He'll guess, when the guards tell him we were speaking in a secret language. But that's better than them understanding everything we say. They don't know anything, they're just goons recruited through the AAL website. I'm sure they haven't realised you're not human, Irion. Keep your make-up on as long as you can, you'll be safer that way. Ah,' he said, switching to English. 'Here comes his little stooge with our food.'

The metal door creaked open and Matthew entered carrying a tray, flanked by two armed guards. Lucy recognised the one on the left. It was the night club bouncer from the train, the day she'd met Nestor. He looked more comfortable without his smart suit. This must be his natural habitat.

The three prisoners stood up.

'Hello, Matthew,' said Lucy. 'I must have missed you at the London Eye.'

Matthew was unapologetic. 'When I reported back to him in September, Nestor said you'd changed sides and had probably already betrayed us to the demon.'

When Lucy didn't protest, he said, 'You don't deny it?'

'I suppose not,' Lucy sighed.

'Nestor said we had to take action to protect ourselves, that if we took hostages, the demon wouldn't dare stop our work.'

'Sounds to me more like he wants to entice her here,' interrupted Irion.

Matthew looked horrified.

'Don't worry, kid, she's not that stupid,' she laughed.

'You're a Sayari, aren't you?' he said, studying her. 'I read about your people on the internet. Your hair is gorgeous.'

The tray in his hands exploded upwards, propelled by the force of Irion's boot arcing through the air. The guards raised their guns as it smashed against the wall, a dark, sticky liquid instantly staining the concrete.

'Don't shoot!' shouted Matthew and David simultaneously.

'Don't you dare take away my freedom and then compliment my fucking appearance!' roared Irion, fearless and unrepentant.

'Who'd have thought it?' chuckled No-Neck, nudging his colleague. 'A feisty Goth! We'll have to have a go on her later.'

'No!' cried Matthew, turning to face the guards. 'The boss has special plans for her. She's not to be harmed. Although you can wash her face, if you want a surprise,' he added nastily, before stalking out of the room.

Once they were gone, David slumped back down on the mat. 'So,' he said. 'That went well.'

35. SELF-ARREST PRACTICE

HANNA

HANNA AND HASSAN waited in front of their hotel, cocooned in their warmest clothes. Each breath produced a pale cloud of water vapour. Hanna imagined the moisture freezing into tiny ice crystals and falling to the ground as snow. Yesterday's hastily purchased walking boots made her feet feel stiff and unfamiliar. She knew without doubt that they would give her blisters before the day was done.

It was still dark, the city roads quiet. Traffic lights flashed orange instead of cycling through their colours. The sky was blue-velvet clear, but Hanna could barely see the stars, just like in London. At last, a black Touran pulled up in front of them, and Felix and Saïd got out.

They said their hellos and Felix looked at Hassan's feet. 'Where are your magic boots, Hassan?'

'In my room, in Essoona. I'm not allowed to use them on Earth, remember?'

Felix gestured at Hassan's trainers, 'What are they, then?'

'These are top of the range terrestrial-tech. They're OK, but if I walk for a long time, the sockets lose suction. I don't trust them enough for a snowshoe tour, I'll have to wait in the car when we get there. But I'll drive, if you like. I brought my international driver's licence.'

Felix shot a relieved glance at Saïd. 'That would be great. Then we could catch up on some sleep. I've set the *navi* for the village closest to Celestina. We have all the *vignette* we need for the Austrian and Swiss motorways so you can keep going until you need a break. It should take us about three and a half hours, not counting stops.'

'Right. OK. Can you keep an eye on me while we leave the city? I've never driven on the right before.'

'No problem, then I get a heated seat,' said Felix, smiling.

In the back, Hanna gazed out of the window while Felix guided Hassan out of the city, listening to their conversation with half an ear. Next to her, Saïd was already fast asleep, his jacket folded under his head against the window.

Hassan asked, 'So, your brother who met you with the car – isn't he a mountain rescue pilot? Couldn't he have taken us in his helicopter?'

Felix laughed. 'It's not his helicopter, you dork! He can't just fly off on a personal errand! Anyway, it's fitted out as an air ambulance, not for carrying passengers. That's why I organised the Touran, because we need seven seats. It's my parents' business car, so it's insured for anyone with a driver's licence.'

'Seven?'

'We'll be taking David with us too, won't we? Assuming he's there.'

'Oh. Yeah. I forgot about him.'

'Lucy's been worrying about him for months. At least

we can find out what's been going on now.'

In the rear-view mirror, Hanna saw Hassan frown. 'Do you think there'll be armed guards?'

'It's a legitimate facility making satellites, Hassan. You must have seen the website, it's all civilian stuff. There's security, yes, fences and cameras, that's why we have to sneak in at the back. Nikolai and I have been looking into this for a while; we thought we might have to go there one day. But, no, I don't think there'll be people with guns. That would raise suspicion with the locals. Perhaps inside, guarding this secret weapon they've built. But we don't want to go anywhere near that, we just want to find the others and get out again.'

'But if it comes to it, will you be able to look after Hanna? I know there's no stopping her from going, but I have a bad feeling things might not go smoothly.'

'I did military service, remember? And Saïd did judo for years. We can handle ourselves. And if not, well, I'm sure Mary and Joe will come up with something. At the very least we can win Lucy and Irion some time. Can you follow the A8 signs to Rosenheim? We could go via Garmisch, but I don't want to risk getting stuck on the Fernpass.'

They drove. Hanna watched the red circle on the satnav creep south, then west towards Innsbruck. Felix nodded off, but Hanna was too fascinated by the landscape to sleep. The border between Germany and Austria was a complete non-event, just a few signs by the road. She still clutched her passport in her pocket for comfort. Who knew when they would be stopped and checked? The time it took to prove their papers were all in order could make the difference between life and death for Irion and Lucy.

She thought of all those Syrians trying desperately to travel in the other direction and her heart went out to them. She hoped they'd all find a good place to shelter until their country was safe to return to. But for the grace of God, that could easily be her, or Hassan, or indeed anyone with the wrong sort of passport. She'd never forget how it was to live in a permanent state of fear and uncertainty. How could a piece of paper make so much difference to a person's life?

The undulating green hills on either side of the road turned white. The world had switched to monochrome mode. Even the sky was white. Apart from the other cars, there was no colour anywhere, only darker shades and lighter shades. Hanna had experienced snow in London once or twice: a decorative dusting turning to grey slush within hours. This was different. A dull, impenetrable crust locked the earth away until spring.

As they approached Innsbruck, the mountains were no longer distant scenery: they were right next to her, uncompromising and massive, making her feel about as significant as an ant. What had she let herself in for? How was it even possible to climb up one of those?

The valley corridor grew narrower, and every so often they drove through a long tunnel. Hanna tried and failed to imagine a whole mountain above them. The white-tiled walls reminded her of a public toilet – or a prison.

Hanna didn't immediately notice when they entered Switzerland, the only clues being the road signs were slightly different and the houses were more traditional. When she realised, she finally released her grip on the passport in her pocket and breathed more deeply, daring to hope they might make it.

Soon after, Hassan pulled off the main road into a village and parked by the church. Felix was out of the car and rummaging in the boot before the others had even unbuckled their seatbelts. His brother had prepared them all a rucksack, each with a pair of snowshoes strapped to the outside.

'Hassan, I'll leave yours in the back, OK? There's food and water inside.'

Hanna swung her rucksack onto her back, her knees nearly folding under the weight of it. Felix handed her a pair of walking sticks with discs fitted at the tips. 'It'll be easier to carry once we're wearing the snowshoes,' he said.

Hanna kissed Hassan goodbye. 'What will you do?' she asked.

'Sit in the car and read. Explore the village. Don't worry about me. Just take care and make sure you come back in one piece, OK?'

'Will do,' she promised.

She and Saïd followed Felix to the edge of the village, where the tarmac stopped and the snow started. They strapped on their snowshoes and began trudging across the fields, Felix leading the way with the map he'd downloaded to his phone, Saïd bringing up the rear. Saïd, too, seemed very at home in this alpine environment. It was just Hanna who felt like a fish out of water.

It took her a while to get the hang of the snowshoes. She was glad of her sticks; she'd never have been able to stay upright without them. Onwards and upwards they went, at a slow, steady plod. Their pace never varied and they never stopped for a rest. As the slope got steeper, Hanna became terrified she would trip and slide uncontrollably down the mountain until she hit one of the rocks jutting out of the snow. Eventually she admitted this to the others.

'It's OK, Hanna, you can self-arrest,' said Felix. 'Let me show you.'

He dropped his rucksack on the path and, with a joyful yell, threw himself headfirst onto the snowfield. He began to slide down the mountain, just as in Hanna's worst imaginings. Quickly, he flipped himself over onto his front and pushed his body away from the ground so that only his elbows and toes touched the ground. After a few more metres he came to a controlled halt. He stood up and made his way back up to them, grinning.

'Doing that's always a total rush,' he said. 'Did you see what I did?'

Hanna and Saïd nodded.

'The important thing is to do it as fast as you can, before you build up too much speed. Go on, you have a go.'

Saïd didn't need asking twice. He dropped onto his belly and started sliding, pushing his elbows and toes into the snow. It took him longer to stop, but stop he did.

Felix added, 'You can use a ski stick instead of your elbows if you have one handy, that works even better. Do you want a go, Hanna?'

'Er, I think I'd better save my energy. But I understand what to do now. Thanks Felix.'

They plodded on for another two hours. The air was biting fresh and the sky a deep and flawless blue. The higher they climbed, the further they could see: rows of new mountains appearing one behind the other. The village below them had long since disappeared from view. It was just them, the snow, the rock and the sky. Hanna felt she was using corners of her lungs which had never been filled with oxygen before. Although her thighs were screaming and part of her wondered if she would make it all the way, she felt a deep satisfaction just at being in the wilderness – coming this far using only the strength of her own limbs.

They rounded a corner and finally Felix stopped. On a step in the mountainside squatted a large, single-storey stone hut, with a metal roof and a grey metal door with no handle. In front of it was a weather station, the anemometer turning lazily in the gentle breeze.

'This is it,' said Felix. 'The back door to Celestina Satellites. Now all we have to do is get in.'

Hanna pushed at the door. 'It's locked!' she called.

'Of course it's locked,' said Felix. 'I came prepared.' He swung down his rucksack and began to rummage.

'Ha!' He whipped out a battery-powered drill, holding it like a handgun. He pranced about with it in a comedy James Bond impression, making Hanna giggle. 'OK, let's get to work.'

He began to drill at the lock. Hanna could smell hot metal after a few minutes, but the door stayed resolutely shut. There was a terrible cracking noise as the drill-tip shattered and Felix let out a shocked yelp. 'It's made of harder stuff than I thought!'

'Let me have a go,' said Saïd, holding out his hand for the drill. 'You've got spares, right?'

Felix nodded and delved in his rucksack again.

'Why is there no snow on the roof?' wondered Hanna. 'Look, it's all piled up at the sides there. And what are those posts for?' She pointed to a series of metal posts on either side of the hut, but the boys were too intent on their work to answer.

This time, Saïd tried drilling around the lock instead, but the bit just skidded on the surface of the metal until it glowed red hot.

'This isn't going to work, Felix. It's armoured steel,' he said.

'Keep trying,' insisted Felix. 'We've got this far; we can't give up now.' But after going through three more drill bits, they eventually admitted defeat. They sat despondently in a row on the doorstep, sharing chocolate and bananas.

'What do we do now?' asked Hanna.

'I should have thought of a backup plan,' said Felix. 'I never thought it would be so hard to get in.'

'Should we go back down and try to talk our way in at the main gate?' suggested Saïd.

Hanna's heart sank. She wasn't sure she could take more trudging through the snow just yet. Her legs were still shaky from the long tour.

'Then they'll catch us for sure,' said Felix. 'We need to think—'

'Listen!' interrupted Saïd. 'What's that noise?'

A faint mechanical clanking and scraping, coming from behind and below, getting closer and louder. They jumped to their feet and stepped away from the hut. Now Hanna understood why there was no snow on the hut's roof.

The roof was slowly opening, half on each side, like Tower Bridge in London did to let through boats. Except that the roof continued past the vertical, coming to rest on the posts either side of the hut.

'Great!' cried Felix. 'We can climb down inside!'

'Wait!' said Saïd. 'There's something coming up!'

He was right. Slowly, a gigantic white antenna emerged. Awestruck, they watched the dish rise majestically into the sky, entirely failing to notice the three security guards with machine guns at its base until it was much too late.

'*Hände hoch!*'

Hanna didn't speak German, but she could guess what that meant.

36. RANGLATIRI PIRATES? HERE?
JOE

J OE CLEARED AWAY the remains of his fried breakfast, humming along to the radio as he pottered in the galley. Late Sunday morning, one of the last before Christmas. Finally caught up on sleep. No plans until he was due to meet Aldeman at the baths this evening. Bliss. Jaguar-Kitty was stretched out on the sofa, her slumbers punctuated by the occasional snuffle.

Idly, he wondered what he should do with the day. There was one obvious cloud on the horizon. Soon he would have to go back to Brecon and see his mother. Stay for a minimum of two nights in his childhood bedroom, on the ancient mattress of rusting, squeaking springs. Urgh.

Some kind of present would be expected. Maybe he could just take the old trout out to lunch instead? He ought to think about making a reservation somewhere. Better phone her later to check she hadn't already made plans. Bloody Christmas. Perhaps this year he should finally introduce her to Kitty. That would stop her constant questions about when he was going to find a nice Welsh girl and settle down. In fact, she might not ever speak to him again. He brightened at the prospect.

A banging on the hull broke his train of thought. On the sofa, dark ears twitched and Kitty awoke.

You expecting anyone? she asked.

No. You?

No.

I'll go. You stay there.

Joe lowered the steps and peered out. The crew knew never to disturb him on a Sunday unless it was an emergency. On the hangar floor he saw Mary, face pinched, arms wrapped around herself in a form of self-hug. Something was very wrong.

'Joe? I'm sorry to bother you on a Sunday. I need Kitty. It's urgent.'

'Come on up.'

Mary mounted the steps and followed him into the *Pride's* living area. Kitty, now on two legs, waited in the centre of the room.

'Mary. What's the matter?' she asked.

'It's Irion. She's been…taken.' Mary almost choked on the word.

'Taken?' said Joe, confused. 'What do you mean, taken?'

Ignoring him, Mary reached for Kitty's hands. 'Can you find her and bring her back to me? I think she's somewhere in Switzerland. Possibly with some of our students.'

Kitty gave Mary's hands a reassuring squeeze and closed her eyes. Then she disappeared.

Cath? *What can you see? Where is she? What's going on?*

No reply. Not good. Aloud, Joe asked, 'Switzerland,

Mary? What happened? Who's taken her?'

'I'm not sure. I was visiting my mum in Yorkshire yesterday. I came back this morning.'

'How's she doing?'

'Not great. It was a nasty fall. It'll be months before her hip's better. But that's not why I'm here. When I got home, Nikolai and Farida were waiting for me with some garbled story about Irion and Lucy being kidnapped yesterday by an anti-alien league. Presumably that would be the organisation you told me about, the one Lucy's been spying for?'

Joe could hear the suppressed fury in her voice. 'Let's hope there's not more than one,' he said.

Mary narrowed her eyes at him. 'Apparently, Felix and Saïd rushed off on a half-baked rescue mission and haven't been in touch since yesterday evening. I didn't wait to find out more, I thought I should get Kitty involved as soon as possible.'

Kitty reappeared, alone. Joe realised he'd been expecting her to return with Irion. From Mary's disappointed expression, so had she.

'They're alive and unharmed,' Kitty said in a flat voice. 'Irion, Hanna, Lucy, Felix and Saïd and one other. They're being held in a cellar with three armed men guarding the door. The building is covered in CCTV cameras, and the perimeter fence is patrolled by dogs and around twenty armed guards.'

'Where are they?' said Joe.

'In a mountain, about fifty kilometres east of Davos. I'll give you the coordinates, Mary, but I can't be the one to get them out for you. Sorry.'

Mary gave a little cry and collapsed onto the sofa behind her.

Joe demanded, 'Why not?'

'I can't be seen in that place. Just now I was a fly on the wall, but I can't teleport other people when I'm that small. If I went in big enough to be useful, I'd be seen – and I still couldn't take them all at once. I think whoever's behind this is expecting me, and the prisoners are bait in a trap. I have to stay out of this one. I'd just make the situation a hundred times worse if I got involved. I'm sorry, Mary. But they know where you live. You need to sort this out yourselves or you'll be looking over your shoulders for the rest of your lives.'

Cath! You're seriously refusing to help?

There are reasons, Joe. Stuff I can't tell you.

Fine, then I'll go myself.

You bloody won't. Mary is more than capable.

I never said she wasn't. But there's something going on here, and I mean to get to the bottom of it.

I'm not taking you. Forget it, Joe. If they get you, they'll have leverage over me. That's exactly what they want.

What do you know? Why won't you tell me?

Mary interrupted their silent row. 'OK, I'll get them out myself. Will you at least drop me at Christoph Wenger's house? I'll need to borrow his helicopter.'

Kitty looked relieved. 'Sure, no problem. It's the least I can do.'

The words 'I'm coming with you' were sprinting from Joe's brain to his lips, when Delius appeared in the doorway.

'Delius?'

Delius said nothing, merely flicked his hand to activate the main screen behind the dining table. An ugly, matt black frigate appeared, with heavy weaponry mounted all over its exterior.

Kitty gasped, and the colour drained visibly from Mary's face. 'Ranglatiri pirates? Here?' she said.

Kitty closed her eyes, searching with her mind. *It's a slaver, Joe. There are thousands of prisoners already on board. I can feel their despair from here.*

'Is that the only one?' Joe asked Delius. 'How long have we got?'

'It's alone. Less than an hour away at its current velocity. But its electromagnetic signature doesn't match my files. There is something different about this ship. I don't like it, sir.'

Joe hurried forward to the cockpit and triggered the siren, informing the crew they had ten minutes to get to their *Tumbas* and be launch-ready.

He returned to Mary and handed her his plasma gun, handle first. 'It's only on about sixty per cent charge, but it should be enough if you set it to stun. Let's hope all those Krav Maga sessions with Hagar pay off.'

'It won't matter if you can't stop the Ranglatiri,' replied Mary.

'I'm sorry I can't come with you,' he said. 'Good luck.'

'You too,' she said.

'Ready?' said Kitty. Mary nodded and they were gone.

Eight minutes to launch. Joe hurried downstairs to change into his uniform. He'd heard countless horror stories about the Ranglatiri and their government-sponsored pirates over the years but, unlike Mary, he'd no personal experience of them. What were they doing so far across the galaxy? He noticed his hands were shaking as he zipped up his flight suit. Ranglatiri discovering the Earth and all its riches…? It didn't bear thinking about.

37. IT'S THE THOUGHT
THAT COUNTS
HANNA

H ANNA GAVE A cry of relief as the guards pushed her roughly into the cell. Irion was alive! She rushed to hug her, burying her face in Irion's coat. When she came up for air, she saw Felix had done the same with Lucy.

Saïd held out his hand to Charlie/David. 'I won't offer you a man hug,' he said in Kawaida.

'You're Saïd Hamidou, aren't you?' said David. 'It's a pleasure to meet you. You came to rescue us?'

Saïd nodded, embarrassed. 'That was the plan.'

'You idiots! Putting yourselves at risk like that!' hissed Irion. 'You could have all been killed! You might still be. This isn't some school outing you know.'

'Steady on, Irion,' said David. 'It's the thought that counts.' He turned to face the others. 'I'm really touched. I mean, I know it's not me you came for, but I still appreciate it.'

'Me too,' said Lucy, hugging Hanna and Saïd in turn. 'Thanks for coming. But it was a daft thing to do. Now there's six of us in trouble instead of three.'

'We're just here to win you some time,' said Felix. 'The others must have told Mary by now, and she'll be on her way to tell Joe.'

Irion clenched her fists in frustration. 'Don't you understand? That's even worse! We have to get out of here ourselves, before they arrive.'

'Why did you take your make-up off?' Hanna asked her. She'd never seen Irion in her outdoor clothes with her silver skin before.'

Irion said nothing.

'The guards made her,' answered Lucy. 'They're not allowed to hurt her, so when she refused, they held a gun to David's head and mine until she changed her mind. Then, as it came off, they freaked. They hadn't realised she wasn't human. They're properly jumpy now. I think they could forget their orders in the heat of the moment.'

A key grated in the lock and they spun round to face whoever was coming. 'Bet that's the odious Matthew,' muttered Lucy.

The door swung open and a smartly dressed man with white hair stepped into the room, a guard on each side. Hanna guessed him to be around the same age as Mary, perhaps older. He clasped his hands and chuckled. 'Welcome! Welcome! David has probably already told you; my name is Nestor. I almost didn't believe it when they told me: it seems hostages multiply all by themselves! We shall have to see about extra accommodation.' He pulled a smartphone out of his pocket. 'Step away from the alien, the rest of you.'

Hanna looked at Lucy. As one, they stepped protectively in front of Irion. The others also closed in around her.

'Ha!' said the man. 'Touching. Guards? Persuade

them.' The guards raised their assault rifles, but Hanna and her friends didn't move. 'Such drama! I only want to take a couple of photos,' he said, waving his smartphone.

'Guys,' sighed Irion, 'just do what he says.'

Reluctantly, they did so.

'That's better,' said Nestor, snapping away. 'Now, my dear, one from the side please, good. And face the back wall so I can get one from the rear.'

Irion turned obediently, and Hanna, horrified at her humiliation, grew too angry to remain silent. 'What do you need photos for?' she demanded. 'What are you going to do with her?'

'Sell her to the highest bidder, of course. There are individuals who will pay handsomely to experiment on unusual life forms. She should compensate for the funding we've lost since our website was hijacked.'

'Just you wait until my Mary gets here,' retorted Irion.

'Mary? Your overweight, ageing wife with the tweed skirts? Two human women together would be blasphemy enough – she must be truly depraved to want to be with you. Or perhaps a freak like you was all she could get at her time of life? I shall look forward to dealing with her personally.'

Hanna thought she'd have to hold Irion back to stop her attacking him, but Irion didn't rise to the taunts. She remained motionless, her face betraying no emotion. Only her ears waggled violently.

Nestor smirked, 'That wiped the smile off your face, didn't it?'

'How did you find out about Irion?' asked Lucy. 'How do you know about her and Mary? Did David tell you?'

'Oh no, my dear,' Nestor gloated. 'You did.'

'Me?' Lucy turned to Irion. 'I swear I didn't, Irion!'

'Regrettably, David was immensely stubborn,' continued Nestor. 'And we couldn't find your parents to apply pressure on you directly, Lucy. Fortunately, it wasn't necessary: we searched your house and found the address of your "language school". Then all we had to do was watch. You can learn a lot by watching.'

'So it *was* you that burgled her house?' said Felix.

At that moment, a young man entered the cell and whispered in Nestor's ear. Nestor's face flushed with excitement. 'Matthew here tells me our satellites are picking up visible spacecraft! That's a first! I think we should all head over to the control room and take a look, don't you? Follow me, all of you, and no funny business, or you'll regret it.'

38. THEY MUSTN'T REACH
THE PLANET
JOE

HALF A MILLION kilometres from the Earth, the *Shantivira's* fighters took up their positions. Once they were in place, Joe attempted to contact the pirates. 'This planet is under the protection of the Galaksi Alliance,' he transmitted. 'Approach no further, or we will open fire.' No response. Kitty materialised in the seat next to him, but said nothing. She didn't even look at him.

Joe waited a few minutes and sent the message again. Without warning, pulses of blue light shot out of the Ranglatiri frigate, straight into the row of *Tumbas*. Joe heard a scream over the communications channel, suddenly silenced as a *Tumba* was vaporised.

'Who was that?'

'Number 42, Captain,' said Yisheng. 'Lakshmi.'

Joe didn't flinch. 'OK, we're under attack. Break up into your task units and return fire. Aim for their weapons – let's see if we can disarm them.'

The line split up into groups of five *Tumbas* and headed for the enemy ship, dodging in and out of the blue pulses. They lost another two *Tumbas* on the way, before they even got near. They opened fire at close range, each task unit focussing their fire power on the same spot for maximum effect. But it made no difference. In the next few minutes they lost another seven ships without making a dent in the enemy spacecraft's defences.

'This is no good,' muttered Joe. 'We're getting slaughtered. Their shields are way too strong. And ours aren't strong enough.'

Is this what Dalian had spoken about? The rumoured impenetrable shield technology? If so, he had to get a sample somehow, if they managed to survive this. What was he thinking? They had to survive, or the Earth was toast. He opened up the comlink and ordered, 'All units retreat behind the moon immediately and await further instructions.' Then he contacted the *Shantivira*. 'Delius? Stand by to fire the primary weapon.'

'Aye aye, Captain. Charging primary weapon.'

Kitty asked urgently, *You're going to uncloak the* Shantivira? *What if it's not enough fire power? She's only a nine-series space station! Weapons tech has advanced a lot since she was built. It won't take them long to break through our shields once they see her. If we keep her hidden, we'd at least have a vessel to carry refugees away from the Earth. You know what will happen if they get past us, Joe. Once they tell their friends, there'll be no stopping them.*

I know, said Joe, *I thought about that too. But we have to try, or what's the point in having the* Shantivira? *I do have a backup plan, although you're not going to like it. We have to do whatever it takes. They mustn't reach the planet.*

No, she said, pre-empting him. *Please don't ask me.*

They were interrupted by Delius' voice coming over the intercom.

'Ready to engage, Captain.'

Perhaps I won't have to, Joe answered. Out loud he said, 'OK, Delius, fire at will.'

'Aye aye, Captain.'

39. ISN'T SHE BEAUTIFUL?

HANNA

CONTROL ROOM WAS too grand a name for the spotlessly clean factory hall in which Hanna now found herself. There were no other people there, doubtless because it was a Sunday. Bits of half-finished machinery lay dotted around, interspersed with lathes, drills and other machine tools. A group of desks clustered next to racks of computers. Above them, an expanse of white wall was being used as a projector screen. Once she saw it, Hanna couldn't look away.

A multitude of *Tumbas* zigzagged across the screen, dodging in and out of pulses of blue light. As she watched, a pulse hit one of the little ships, which vanished with a flash. The prisoners cried out in horror. Who had that been?

'These are live pictures from our cloud of two hundred mini-satellites,' explained a wide-eyed Matthew. 'All those spiky looking craft appeared out of nowhere ten minutes ago. Now they seem to be having a battle. Do you know where they're from? Are they Syenitians?'

'They're ours, you idiot!' shouted Hanna, losing patience. 'Those are human beings, fighting to protect this planet from whatever's shooting out that blue light.

Fighting – and dying!'

As she spoke, the *Tumbas* turned and fled, heading in the direction of the moon. Hanna spotted the unmistakable outline of the *Pride of Essoona*, bringing up the rear. Then a dark hulk glided into view, firing the blue pulses from gun turrets mounted all over its hull.

Irion gave a little shriek and covered her mouth with her hand.

'No!' she exclaimed. 'Not here! Please not here!'

'You recognise them,' stated Nestor. 'What are they?'

'Ranglatiri pirates,' gulped Irion. 'They come from a technologically advanced planet which...doesn't share the same values as the Galaksi Alliance member planets. The Alliance has a trade embargo against them. They mine for *musta* – the black metal they use to build their machines – you see it there,' she said, pointing at the screen.

'The work could be done by robots, but they find slave labour more economical. The ore is poisonous, so they constantly need new workers. The Ranglatiri government encourages independent pirate ships to search for creatures which can be put to work in the Mines of Kifo. They're also rewarded for finding other resources on the way.'

'Why aren't our weapons having an impact?' asked Lucy.

'I don't know, Lucy,' said Irion. 'I don't understand it.'

'Tell them what will happen if the *Shantivira* can't stop them,' said David.

Irion looked at Nestor, Matthew and the guards. 'If they find out about the Earth's rich assets, well, let's just say we won't have a population problem anymore. They'll keep on coming back until the planet is stripped bare of everything – people, animals, trees, water, even stone. If they have their way, there'll be nothing left but dust. They're like locusts.'

Hanna interrupted, 'But the Galaksi Alliance would send reinforcements, wouldn't they? We wouldn't be undefended?'

'Of course they would. But it would escalate into a full-scale war, right on Earth's doorstep. The *Shantivira* must stop it now, before it starts. That's our job.'

'What's that?' said Saïd, pointing at the screen.

A green dot grew until Saïd could answer his own question. 'It's the *Shantivira*! Wow! Isn't she beautiful?'

Like an emerald, Hanna thought. Not green and blue like the Earth, but shades of green, with a pale stripe across the centre and a hazy dark rim where the shields were.

'Why can we see her?' asked Felix. 'I thought she was cloaked?'

Irion answered, 'The cloaking system interferes with the targeting system. They must be desperate – they're going to fire the main weapon. It's a defensive weapon; the *Shantivira* isn't designed for combat.'

No one spoke as they watched the *Shantivira* head towards the shadowy frigate. She dwarfed the enemy ship, and Hanna felt sure it would soon all be over. Perhaps Nestor would see sense when he realised the *Shantivira* had saved the world from unimaginable horror.

The Ranglatiri were pounding her with fire, but she kept on coming. A cone pointing in the direction of the enemy craft extended beyond the shield barrier and began to crackle with green light. Then it fired, emitting a mighty blast of energy at the Ranglatiri. But it seemed to have no effect: the Ranglatiri continued their attack unimpeded.

How long would the *Shantivira's* shields hold out under that onslaught? wondered Hanna. The cone crackled again, preparing for another shot. Come on, prayed Hanna silently, come on!

40. REMEMBER YOUR PROMISE
JOE

'THIS ISN'T WORKING,' said Joe. 'We'd need a fleet of state-of-the-art destroyers to have a chance against that thing. Delius?'

'Captain?'

'Retreat. Recloak the *Shantivira* and get her away from here. As far and as fast as you can. It's time for Plan B.'

'Aye aye, Captain.'

Kitty hugged her knees to her chest, rocking back and forth in her seat.

I don't want to, Joe. It's a huge risk. I could destroy you all if I lose control.

I trust you, Cath. *You can do this.*

All those innocent people on board will die if I do what you're asking.

As they would have if our conventional weapons had worked, replied Joe calmly.

Yes, but this way I have to personally extract each individual life.

I know love. And I'm so, so sorry. But it's them or us. What would their lives be like anyway if the Ranglatiri win this battle? We can't save them, Cath. *But you* can *save the Earth. There are seven billion people down there. Please do this for us. Remember your promise.*

I'm scared I'll lose myself if I take so many lives at once. You might be replacing one threat with another. It will take me months to get stable again.

I can't see any other way, Cath.

No. Neither can I. But it'll be worse than anything I've ever put you through. I don't want you to see me like that. I might not even recognise you. What if you can't love me anymore? What if I eat you?

Her expression tore at Joe's heart. He gripped her by the shoulders. *I will not ever stop loving you, you idiot,* he said. *If anything, I love you more for putting yourself through this for us. And if you do eat me…well, I made my peace with dying that way a long time ago. But you won't.* He grinned. *And if you touch the crew, then I'll definitely sack you!*

Kitty smiled weakly and wiped her eyes on the back of her hand. *When it's done,* she said, *I'll have to go far away, fast. And stay away until I'm safe again.*

If that's the price we have to pay to stop them, then we'll manage somehow. We'll miss you, though. I'll miss you.

She hugged him fiercely, burying her face in his neck. He could feel her tears wet on his skin.

Goodbye, my love.

She kissed him on the lips and vanished.

She returned a moment later with William. 'I'm taking William's *Tumba*,' she said out loud. Then she disappeared again.

'What's going on?' said William, strapping himself into the co-pilot's seat.

'Wait and see.'

417

Joe attempted to contact the Ranglatiri frigate again.

'This is Captain Llewellyn of the Galaksi Alliance. I am sending a representative to negotiate terms. Will you receive her?'

Straightaway, a hologram appeared above the control panel. The back of Joe's neck prickled with foreboding. It was a biped dressed entirely in white, about the height of a tall human or a short Syenitian. It wore an ornate breastplate above a pleated, full-length skirt of heavy fabric. Hands with three fingers and a thumb protruded from the armoured sleeves; the visible skin was devoid of pigmentation, even whiter than its clothing. What shocked Joe most was the face – or lack of it. The front of the head was a convex white mesh, blending into a helmet which extended across the pirate's shoulders.

'The terms of your surrender?' hissed the creature.

This time it was Joe who gave no response. He waited in silence.

41. WE'RE DEFINITELY
ALL GOING TO DIE

HANNA

W HEN THE *SHANTIVIRA* disappeared, Hanna's heart
filled with despair. Was that it? Was it all over for
humanity now?

In contrast, Nestor seemed grimly cheerful. 'If you
want something doing, you'd better do it yourself,' he said.
'Matthew?'

'Yes?'

'Align the satellites ready for firing.'

'Yes sir!' Matthew seemed happy to have something to
do.

Proudly, Nestor told his captive audience, 'As you
know, with David's help, I have built the Earth's first ever
in-space anti-alien defence system. We have a swarm of
prototype microsatellites orbiting the planet, which are
programmed to combine their individual functions. Each
cuboid satellite also features a high-power laser, which we
have not yet had the opportunity of testing in the field.
When we focus their beams on the same point, their
firepower should be impressive.'

Irion face-palmed. 'Oh hell,' she said. 'Untested proto-
types? Against that thing? We're definitely all going to die.'

'Look!' shouted Felix, pointing at the screen.

A lonely *Tumba* had appeared and was approaching the Ranglatiri vessel without firing its weapons.

'They're going to surrender! No time to lose!' cried Nestor. 'Open fire, Matthew!'

'Nestor!' yelled David. 'You can't fire, that's one of ours!'

Nestor narrowed his eyes. 'Yours, maybe. Not mine. As far as I'm concerned, they're traitors and collaborators, just like you, David.'

Red light shot across the screen in the direction of the *Tumba* but faded before it got close.

'You need to focus the cube cloud, Matthew!' said Nestor, irritated, striding over to the control panel. 'Here, let me!' This time the shot travelled far enough but missed the *Tumba* entirely.

'Fantastic marksmanship!' sneered Irion. 'Why don't you try aiming at something easier to hit – like that great big enemy spacecraft, for example?'

42. PLAN B
JOE

THROUGH KITTY'S EYES, Joe watched her approach the pirate frigate in her borrowed *Tumba*.

What if they don't go for it? she said.

Just stick to the plan, cariad.

Ooh, their tractor beam's got me, they're going to let me board!

That's a relief, replied Joe. The seed of hope in his stomach began to swell. Perhaps his crazy plan would work after all.

If you can locate the shield generator, that would be really helpful, he said.

Kitty reached out with her mind. *There is no shield generator, as far as I can make out,* she said. *That's weird. I wonder how it works?*

Joe felt her tremble as the *Tumba* landed.

There are around a thousand crew and four thousand prisoners in the hold. I'm frightened, Joe. I've never done this on this scale before.

You can do it, Cath. *They can't stop you. Just remember who you are and what you're trying to do, and you'll be fine.*

I know they can't stop me. But what if I can't stop me?

She disembarked and was met by a squad of armed guards, who frisked her for weapons and cuffed her hands roughly behind her back. Joe sensed her struggle to remain docile, keeping her head bowed and her mouth closed. As they marched her along endless, dimly lit corridors, Joe caught glimpses of stained walls and dirty floors, heard the guards' armour clinking and smelled fetid, stale air. He gagged instinctively, then realised the air he was actually breathing was the clean, freshly oxygenated air on the *Pride of Essoona.*

Finally, they reached the bridge. The guards pushed Kitty to her knees in front of the Ranglatiri pirate captain. She held her head high and spoke in a loud, clear voice.

'I have come to offer you a deal. Turn around, leave this system immediately and never return. Then your lives will be spared.'

This was greeted with howls of laughter from all present. When the captain eventually regained his composure, he leaned forward and jeered, 'You are not in a position to negotiate, Syenitian! Your pitiful fleet will not withstand our firepower for long.' He indicated the holographic monitor showing the *Pride of Essoona* and the remaining *Tumbas* sheltering on the far side of the moon. 'And even your space station cannot penetrate our new shields! You are already beaten.'

He assumed a faux-sympathetic demeanour. 'Perhaps your precious Alliance doesn't place as much value on this planet as you thought. Why else would they leave it so poorly defended? We've done our scans; we know what's down there. Enough slaves to keep our economy going for decades!'

He turned and addressed the rest of the pirates, 'Do you hear that, lads? This little planet is going to make us all rich!'

A great roar of approval reverberated around the room.

Kitty persevered. 'I give you one more chance. Go home or be destroyed.'

But the captain had already lost interest. He waved a hand at the guards.

'Take her away and put her in the hold with the others.'

'Thank you,' said Kitty.

'What?' The pirate captain looked at her, confused.

'For easing my conscience.'

Her handcuffs opened and fell to the floor. She stood up and closed her eyes, hands hanging loosely at her sides. Around her the captain, guards and crew fell to their knees clutching their chests, struggling for breath as Kitty extracted every scrap of their life energy. She lifted her arms and began to grow rapidly, shifting into her demon form as she did so. The bodies around her faded and disappeared.

She braced her limbs against the ceiling. Metal grated and screeched as her black claws started breaking the ship apart. It was a chain reaction: she was growing so fast now, she couldn't stop herself from absorbing the life energy of every being on board. Her infrasonic roar shook the Ranglatiri spacecraft to shreds.

Kitty's surge of wild euphoria physically knocked Joe back in his seat. It seemed the excess energy was boosting their telepathic signal and he would have to ride her roller coaster of emotions alongside her. Was this how she felt now? What a rush! He gripped his armrests until his knuckles turned white, his heart on fire with adrenaline.

'Are you OK?' asked William.

'Not much longer now,' Joe panted. 'Soon we'll have to go back and clear up the mess.'

As SHE GREW, a wave of all-consuming hunger overtook Kitty. Exhilarated and terrified in equal measure, Joe felt the exact moment she lost her self-control completely. Suddenly, he no longer recognised his wife. The mantel of civilisation she worked so hard to maintain evaporated and she existed only as a natural phenomenon – raw, instinct-driven power, focused purely on acquiring more energy. All the filters she customarily put up to protect his mind dropped away and, for the first time ever, Joe experienced the world as she did.

'Aaaaaaaargggghhhhhh!' Joe screamed aloud, writhing in his seat as she broke through the outer hull into free space. The sensation was unbearable: every nerve jangled and he thought his heart would burst. Still she grew, even beyond her 'natural' size of around two hundred metres. Now she was larger than he'd ever seen her.

Through her eyes, Joe watched the stars vibrate with different colours and – music. Music? She'd talked about it, but she'd never shown him before. Almost immediately he realised why. They might be incredibly beautiful, but they were giving him an incredible headache to match. He fumbled clumsily at his harness, opened it, slid to his knees and began to vomit.

Between retches, he twisted round to look up at William. 'Get us closer,' he croaked. 'We need to remind her who she is.'

He had to break their connection somehow, preferably before she fried his brain. Slowly and painfully, he clambered back into his seat.

43. GLORIOUS AND TERRIBLE

HANNA

ANNA WATCHED NESTOR howl with frustration. He was getting better at aiming his weapon, but even when his shots connected, they seemed to have no effect on the black frigate. Honestly, what did he expect, if an entire space station couldn't make a dent in it? But wait! Perhaps it was a delayed effect? The vessel seemed to be breaking open from the inside. How could that be?

Then Hanna understood. A gigantic demon-Kitty emerged from the wreckage, standing on it like a surfboard, ripping it into chunks with her bare hands. She peeled off the hull as if she were unwrapping a bar of chocolate. Soon the frigate was reduced to a cloud of space debris.

Naked, but with no obvious genitalia, she was glorious and terrible at the same time. Her red scales glistened in the sunlight, her hair floating around her head in a wild halo. In this form, her eyes and teeth seemed natural and appropriate, if utterly petrifying.

Nestor was enraged by Kitty's sudden appearance. In a fit of triumphant madness, he opened fire on Kitty. 'I bet *you* haven't got any shields! Take that, devil spawn!' he yelled.

'No!' shrieked Hanna, Irion and Lucy together. They made a move to stop him, but the guards pushed them back.

'Ha!' cried Nestor. 'Right between the eyes, you evil hag!'

44. WHY IS SHE LAUGHING?

JOE

WILLIAM FLEW THE *Pride of Essoona* towards Kitty, aiming to get as close as possible while staying out of her reach. Sitting next to him, Joe was virtually paralysed, his body rigid in agonising cramps. He tried to reach her, but it was like shouting into a hurricane. As they approached, the demon turned and studied them appraisingly, head tilted to one side, tail twitching like a hunting cat's. She was like a black hole for life energy now: everything nearby got sucked in. She crouched to pounce. It was all over. There was nothing they could do.

Then Joe felt a sharp pain in the centre of his forehead. His head cleared and his body relaxed. The link was broken! He was free! Oh, the relief, the blessed relief!

He looked out of the window at the creature he'd used as a weapon, marvelling at her magnificence and remembering the first time she'd showed herself to him like that, the day after he'd left the army. She'd straddled the mountain ridge as if it were a horse, and leaned down towards him until he could see his reflection in the full-length mirror of her pupils. Was she back in control now? She must be, if she'd let him go.

For a brief moment, he felt almost sorry for the

Ranglatiri. Almost. He certainly regretted taking the lives of all the prisoners on board, but he couldn't see how he might have saved them and still protected the Earth. At least he'd been able to spare them from a fate worse than death. Hold on to that thought.

Kitty's attention was no longer on the *Pride of Essoona*. Instead, she was rubbing her forehead while examining a miniscule object between the thumb and forefinger of her other hand. Joe recognised that expression – he'd recognise it anywhere, whichever form she took. Whatever it was that she was holding, she found it side-splittingly funny.

'She's laughing! Why is she laughing?' Joe asked William. 'What the hell is there to laugh about?'

'Look!' said William. 'There's a sort of cloud around her head!'

There was, Joe saw. Little black cubes, not much bigger than the shield generators he'd had installed on the ISS.

As they watched, Kitty released the object between her fingers and, with a telekinetic flick of her wrist, scattered the cubes in all directions. Then the *Tumba*-sized eyes focused on the *Pride of Essoona*.

Sorry, love, she said. *I lost myself before I could sever our connection. Are you OK?*

I am now. You?

No. Not remotely. You should know, you rode it with me! I can keep it together for a minute or two, but I'll have to go soon. I won't hold out for long.

Why were you laughing?

Kitty grinned; a smile wide enough to take the *Pride of*

Essoona in a single gulp.

Relief, I think. That was a close call. And, you know, life's little ironies. Ask me again sometime.

She waggled a slab of black hull in her hand. *If you open your cargo door, I've got a sample for you. There* was no shield generator: the hull was made from a self-healing material using the main engine as a power source. *Fascinating stuff, could be very useful. Get it analysed in Essoona and you'll be Dalian's favourite person. I couldn't even break it from the inside until I'd absorbed all their fuel. No wonder I went batshit crazy.*

It's too big, love, can you break it up a bit?

Sure thing, honey bunny.

She snapped it into smaller chunks, as if she were breaking a piece of chocolate. Joe lowered the door and she slotted them in carefully, like a child organising a doll's house.

Mind my bike, won't you?

You and that motorbike! Don't go breaking your neck on it while I'm gone, will you?

I'll try not to. Where will you go?

Far away, where there's no life. Then I'll drift until I can get down to a normal size again. Don't try to contact me for a few months. You don't want to pull me back before I'm safe.

I'll miss you.

I'll miss you.

She blew Joe a kiss and sprang away from them. Within seconds she was no longer visible, travelling at top speed into deep space. Joe's vision blurred and he dragged the back of his hand across his eyes impatiently. No need to let William see him crying. Get a grip, Joe, he told himself. She'll be OK. She'll be back when she's ready. There's still a job to finish here. Stay focused.

The clean-up operation was going to be tough. The big chunks would be easy enough to deal with, but there were thousands of smaller bits which were almost as lethal. They would have to work quickly to stop any pieces making it down to the planet's surface.

Joe opened up communications with the rest of the fleet, still waiting behind the moon. 'All units, this is your captain speaking. Kitty has destroyed the Ranglatiri ship for us. She would like me to inform you that 4294 innocent people held prisoner on board were killed along with the Ranglatiri crew. They died so we could save the Earth. Remember them and honour their sacrifice.

'Now we need to dematerialise the wreckage – fast – before it becomes a problem. At least that's something we've trained for. Happy hunting, everyone.'

45. YOU HAVE TO STOP HIM

HANNA

A CLOSE-UP OF the demon's laughing mouth filled the screen. A cavernous pit, fringed by pointed yellow fangs. Kitty's tongue was black in this form, Hanna noted with interest, proportionally narrower and thicker than a human's.

Nestor, Matthew and the two guards stood transfixed by the image. Did Nestor think she was laughing at him? *Was* she laughing at him? Who cared? This was their chance. She whispered in Kawaida, 'Guys, we grab their guns on the count of three, OK?'

Nods all round.

'Me, Irion and David will take the one on our side, the rest of you take the other one. Ready? One, two, three!'

Irion and Hanna seized a bulky arm each, hanging on like limpets to stop their guard reaching for his weapon, while David punched him on the jaw. The guard fell to his knees with a grunt and David took the gun. Hanna turned to see how the others were doing: Felix and Saïd were sitting on theirs, and Lucy was already pointing the guard's gun at Nestor and Matthew.

'Put your hands up, Nestor,' she called. 'It's over.'

Slowly, Nestor raised his hands. Why was he smiling?

'I don't think so, my dear,' he said.

He gave a loud whistle through his teeth. A drone rose up behind them and swooped over their heads to where Nestor stood. In a clear voice he said, 'Initiate Protocol Four Three Five.'

'No!' shouted David, who clearly knew what Protocol Four Three Five was. He sprang in front of Irion as a stream of laser beams burst out of the drone.

For a split second, Hanna wondered if someone was having a barbecue nearby, before her brain caught up with her nose and she realised, appalled, what the smell was.

Nestor watched impassively as David collapsed on the concrete floor. Then he reached up and pulled the drone out of the air. 'Come on, Matthew, we're going,' he said, heading for a door at the back of the room. Matthew scuttled after him. The guards used the opportunity to run in the opposite direction, back through the door they'd come in by.

Hanna watched Nestor go, wondering whether they ought to follow him, then switched her attention back to the prostrate David. Irion cradled his head in her arms, stroking his cheek, while the others crowded round, trying to help. There wasn't much they could do. He was haemorrhaging from the inside, growing paler by the second. Hanna realised he had minutes to live at most. She crouched down next to him.

'You saved her,' she stated. 'Thank you.'

David nodded in acknowledgement.

'Tell Kitty I'm sorry,' he croaked. 'And you must get out of here, Nestor will have initiated the self-destruct system. Leave me now, you don't have much time.'

'We're not leaving him!' cried Lucy. 'David, you're coming with us.'

David gripped Lucy's hand and whispered, 'It's a race against time now, Lucy. Nestor will start over someplace else. You have to stop him selling our research to the highest bidder, and you must continue my work! The Earth must be able to defend itself. Promise me you will?'

'I promise,' said Lucy. Hanna wasn't convinced she believed her, but what else could she have said?

David smiled briefly, then his face slackened and became...inanimate. Was this how it had been for her brothers? Hanna wondered. Alive and in excruciating pain one minute and the next...not? He appeared peaceful now, if you didn't look at his stomach.

Lucy let out a sob and buried her face in Felix's shirt. Then she opened her palm to reveal the microSD card David had pressed on her with his last breath.

'Do you think that's his research?' asked Felix.

'I don't know,' sniffed Lucy. 'Maybe. Oh God, Felix, what have I just agreed to?'

A loud-speaker voice announced, 'Warning! Warning! Facility self-destruct in T-10 minutes.'

'Time to go,' said Irion, gently resting David's head on the floor before getting to her feet.

'We can't leave him!' yelled Lucy.

'We must,' said Irion, sternly. 'The Galaksi Alliance must never know he returned to the Earth. The evidence will be destroyed if we leave him here. Now come on!'

Irion turned to leave – and stopped. They could all hear it: a high-pitched hum coming from the direction of the door on the far side of the hall.

'What's that?' said Hanna.

'Stay back, everyone,' called Irion, as the door disintegrated into a heap of twisted, semi-molten metal. Beyond it, a familiar figure in a lilac twinset and pearls lowered her plasma gun.

'Mary!' Irion's face lit up and she sprinted to greet her, flinging her arms around her and kissing her full on the lips. Behind Mary, another welcome outline appeared in the doorway.

'Hassan!' Hanna followed hot on Irion's heels and was safe in his warm embrace in an instant. 'How did you get in?' she demanded.

At the same time, he asked, 'Are you OK? What happened?'

'Warning! Warning! Facility self-destruct in T-9 minutes,' came the loud-speaker voice again.

'Explanations later!' called Mary as the others joined them. 'Follow me!'

As they jogged down empty corridors, between breaths, Hassan told Hanna how Mary had picked him up in her borrowed helicopter and flown them to Celestina's main entrance. Assisted by Joe's plasma gun, Mary had persuaded the guards to abandon their posts. 'You should have seen them go, Hanna! They couldn't move fast enough after she blew the main doors off! They must have triggered an evacuation signal – the whole place seems empty.'

'Warning! Warning! Facility self-destruct in T-7 minutes.'

Hanna heard Lucy ask Felix, 'If we get out of here, will you come to New York with me for Christmas?'

'Warning! Warning! Facility self-destruct in T-6 minutes.'

Finally, they reached what was left of the main door. The freezing air bit Hanna's cheeks as they stepped carefully past the wreckage, but it was a welcome relief to be outside again. The loud-speaker voice echoed across the car park. 'Warning! Warning! Facility self-destruct in T-5 minutes.'

They climbed aboard the helicopter and put on their headsets while Mary hurriedly performed her pre-flight checks. Hanna wondered how long they normally took; it seemed an eternity. They waited, hearts in mouths, until at last the rotors began to turn and they lifted away from the ground.

Hanna's headset made the outside world seem pleasantly distant. The background whine of the turbine was almost relaxing. She smiled at Hassan and he put his arm round her shoulders to pull her close. At that moment, a shock wave shuddered through Hanna's internal organs and the helicopter lurched sideways, making them all scream. Alarms sounded as the helicopter lost altitude. Her face against the window, Hanna glimpsed flames shooting out of the entrance below. Exactly where they'd been standing, minutes ago. The mountainside collapsed in on itself, spitting up clouds of smoke and dust. Cursing loudly, Mary coaxed the helicopter out of the column of heat and away to safety.

What a mess, thought Hanna, looking back. She thought about David's body, lying alone under the rubble. It seemed wrong to leave him, but what else could they have done, realistically?

From her seat next to Mary, Irion twisted round and squeezed Hanna's hand. 'Thanks for coming to get us,' she said over the intercom to Hanna, Hassan, Felix and Saïd. 'It was an extraordinarily stupid thing to do – but I'm impressed by your courage and your loyalty.'

'Anytime,' replied Hanna with a broad grin. Happiness and relief bubbled up inside her. It was over. They were safe.

'Let's go home,' she said.

46. PEOPLE HAVE
A RIGHT TO KNOW

DAN

I T HAD BEEN a tense afternoon on the ISS. Dan and the rest of the crew had been watching the live feed from the *Shantivira* on their *zanas*. Joe had asked Delius to stream it to them and explain what was happening, arguing that if the Ranglatiri destroyed the *Shantivira*, someone should be able to warn the Earth.

The main drama was over now, although they were still monitoring the Shantivirans' damage limitation efforts. The *Tumbas* were chasing the rapidly separating wreckage in orbits closer and closer to the Earth, and try as they might, they couldn't catch every single piece. Some burned up harmlessly in the atmosphere. Others probably made it down to the planet's surface. One unfortunate fragment hit a weather satellite, shattering it into smithereens. Uh-oh, Dan thought. *That* is going to cause trouble.

'I'm glad we had those shields installed,' said Valentin. 'I'd be a lot less relaxed, otherwise.'

'Do you think they'll be able to detect all this debris down on the planet?' said Tatiana. 'If they do, they'll be worried about us.'

'Let's hope the clean-up goes quickly,' said Valentin.

Dan stared out the window, his thoughts returning to the colossal red demon which had created the debris and then fled the solar system. In his mind's eye he imagined the Kitty-demon floating peacefully in space, drifting across the galaxy. What must that be like? Would she be lonely? Would she sleep? Dream? What would she see on her journey? If only they could have attached a camera to her, think of the pictures they could have got.

If Kitty really was going to be away for months, perhaps he could take his *zana* with him after all when he went home next month. It was worth the risk. Whatever Valentin had agreed with Joe, people had a right to know what was going on up here.

It was his duty to inform them.

47. DO THE RIGHT THING

HANNA

HANNA WOKE. HAD that been a knock at the door just now? She wasn't tempted to leave her warm, dark nest to find out. Luxurious lethargy glued her to the mattress, a force stronger than her curiosity. Wintery London light filtered into the room around the edges of the heavy chintz curtains: just enough to see that Hassan was still fast asleep beside her, his habitually mobile features suspended in temporary tranquillity.

It was fantastic to be in the basement flat again, a second homecoming when they'd got back late last night. The teleports weren't working due to Kitty's absence, so Mary had said they could stay there until Hassan found a way of returning to Essoona.

The unmistakable sound of a fist banging on the door burst her cosy bubble.

'Hanna? You awake? It's past ten o'clock!'

Lucy. Well I am now, thought Hanna resentfully, hurriedly wrapping herself in the green silk kimono Irion and Mary had given her for her twentieth birthday. It had a red dragon embroidered on the back and was one of Hanna's most treasured possessions.

'Shh,' she whispered, opening the door. 'Hassan's asleep.'

When she saw the others all standing there, Nikolai clutching his wafer-thin laptop, she remembered guiltily that they'd arranged to investigate David's microSD card together.

'Sorry!' she said. 'I forgot. Can we go somewhere else?'

Behind her, a voice called, 'I'm awake, Hanna, let them in.'

Lucy, Felix, Nikolai, Farida and Saïd filed into the room and Nikolai started setting up his equipment on what Hanna still thought of as her desk.

Hassan swung his legs over the side of the bed and put on his boots. Only Hanna saw the flicker of pain crossing his face as he stood up. He'd never admit what the long drive to Switzerland and the even longer journey back to the UK had cost him, but Hanna could see it in the way he held himself. Hassan tied his *kanga* around his waist, sarong-style, and pulled on his favourite yellow hoody before joining them at the screen.

'What have you got?' he asked, resting his arm across Hanna's shoulders.

'Looks like there's only two files on it,' said Nikolai, clicking the top one. It opened, and Hanna saw a hyperlink with a username and password.

'He stored it all on the Cloud,' said Lucy quietly.

Nikolai followed the link and entered the password. 'Wow.'

Wow indeed. A long list of gigantic files appeared, hundreds and hundreds of megabytes, all with file endings Hanna had never seen before.

'They're CAD files,' said Lucy. 'Models and drawings. We'd need special software and a bigger computer to open them.'

'What about those ones?' asked Felix, as Nikolai scrolled down.

'Circuit diagrams,' said Saïd.

'And these are the programs,' said Nikolai, reaching the bottom of the list. 'I'd love to take a peek at his code.'

'Wait,' said Lucy. 'I'm not sure we should, yet. I need to think.'

'What's in the other file?' asked Farida.

Nikolai switched windows. 'Let's have a look.'

It was an untitled spreadsheet. There was a tab for each year going back to 1974, with a list of around twenty names and contact details on each page. Lucy recognised it immediately.

'Oh my God, it's the list! The one David always wanted. He must've put it together himself. What are we supposed to do with this? It's dynamite!'

'What list?' said Hanna.

'The list of every human who's ever worked on the *Shantivira*,' explained Lucy. 'Look at 2014. It's us!'

Hassan took the mouse and clicked on 2013. 'That's all of my year, too,' he said. 'Where did he get this?'

Saïd started opening the other tabs at random. Not every year was complete. The further back he went, the more gaps there were.

'Wait!' said Farida, when he was about to leave 1980, 'look, Nikolai, that woman has your surname. Are there a lot of Poroshkins in Russia?'

'A few,' he said. 'But, um, I think I can tell you now – actually, Svetlana Poroshkin is my mother.'

'Your mother?' said Hanna. 'Why didn't you say before?'

'She asked me not to. She's a secretive person. You know my parents divorced when I was little and my dad brought me up, right? I don't even know her very well. She lives in Yakutsk, that's an eleven-hour flight away from Yekaterinburg. I see her once a year if I'm lucky. I only found out because when I told her I was going to work on the oil rigs last year, she just laughed. Then she came to visit a week later and told me everything.'

'Does your dad know?' said Felix.

'*Nyet.* They didn't meet until she'd finished on the *Shantivira.* He didn't laugh when I said I was going to work on the oil rigs, he was really proud of me.'

Lucy said, 'Must be tough, knowing your mum's been lying to him for years.'

'Yeah,' said Nikolai. 'It is.'

'What are you going to do with this information, Lucy?' asked Hassan. 'David gave it to you. It's your decision.'

Lucy stepped away from the desk and paced the room. The others watched her in silence.

'Not a decision I want to take,' she said eventually. 'When he gave it to me, I had this awful feeling he wanted me to start a new tech company: to carry on where he left off. But that's not what I want to do with my life. I want to be the best pilot I can be.'

'Better than me?' joked Hanna.

Lucy smiled and jerked her thumb at Hassan. 'Better than him, if I can.'

Hassan grinned. 'No chance.'

'I've made enough mistakes this year. I can't afford any more. Give me the card, Nikolai,' said Lucy, holding out her hand.

Nikolai shut the files and disconnected the card from his computer. Hanna thought there was something reluctant about the way he pressed the tiny black sliver into her hand.

'What are you going to do, Lucy?' he asked, as she closed her fist around it.

'The right thing,' she said. 'We don't know if there are copies. The people on the list might need to be warned. I'm going next door right now to give it to Mary and Irion. They can pass it on to Joe as soon as the teleports are working again. I think the final decision about what to do with the data should be his call, not mine.'

Hanna hugged her. 'I'm so proud of you,' she said. 'I never thought I'd agree with you about anything!'

'Thanks,' said Lucy gruffly. 'Felix? Will you come with me? Then afterwards we can book our flights for Christmas in New York. It's time you met my parents.'

Felix grinned. 'Yes, Ma'am! See you later everyone!'

They left, and the conversation turned to what the rest of them were doing for the Christmas holiday. Hanna and Hassan intended to stay in London, of course, but the others were all planning a home visit before leaving for their year on Syenitia.

'Nikolai, mate, you're really going to have to quit smoking,' said Saïd.

'I know,' he groaned. 'I've been down to five a day for weeks, but I can't get lower than that. I guess I'll just have to go cold turkey when I get there.'

'Take some patches with you,' said Saïd. 'I found them really helpful.'

'Maybe. Or perhaps I'll replace nicotine with sugar.'

Not a good plan, Nikolai, thought Hanna, but said nothing.

'Do you think we *will* go to Essoona in January?' said Farida. 'How will we get there?'

'I've been wondering about that,' said Nikolai. 'The *Koppakuoria* is too slow. The *Pride* could do the journey in three weeks, but it doesn't have room for all of us.'

'Don't worry,' said Hassan, relaxed as ever. 'Rowan will help us. If she visits the *Shantivira*, the teleports will work again, temporarily. We can't commute regularly, but important one-off trips are possible.'

Finally, the visitors departed and Hanna and Hassan were alone again.

'We won't see each other much next year, will we?' she said, her arms around his waist, pressing herself close to him.

'Not to start with. But Kitty will be back at some point. Then we can see each other every weekend, like before.'

Hanna nodded. She remembered how uncertain she'd felt last December, when Hassan had been about to leave London for Essoona. But this year had proven their relationship was rock solid. Now she was full of confidence: no amount of distance could ever harm their love.

'Together forever, right?' she whispered.

'Right,' he said, kissing the top of her head.

AUTHOR'S NOTE

Writing *The Cleaner, the Cat and the Space Station* has been a roller coaster adventure filled with discoveries. Thanks to Joe and Kitty, I've even started learning Welsh! When I began to write, at the quiet core of my buzzing thoughts was one overriding ambition.

To help save the world.

Not with plasma guns, or dematerialisation beams, but the way all real change starts – with ideas. To help get people thinking about the kind of world we *want* to live in. A positive visualisation of the future: a society that works for people *and* the planet.

Without a specific objective to aim for, we'll never get where we need to go. Without a coherent vision, we're just tinkering at the edges: rearranging deckchairs in the face of impending doom.

Humanity has evolved to understand the world through stories – to be more easily persuaded by emotions than by facts and rational arguments. The facts and rational arguments are out there in abundance. For example:

Kate Raworth: Doughnut Economics, Seven Ways to Think Like a 21st-Century Economist

Richard Wilkinson & Kate Pickett: The Spirit Level,

Why Equality is Better for Everyone and The Inner Level, How More Equal Societies Reduce Stress, Restore Sanity and Improve Everyone's Well-being

His Holiness the Dalai Lama: Ancient Wisdom, Modern World, Ethics for the New Millennium

Rutger Bregman: Utopia for Realists, The Case for a Universal Basic Income, Open Borders and a 15-Hour Workweek

Katrine Marçal: Who cooked Adam Smith's Dinner? A Story about Women and Economics

Tim Jackson: Prosperity Without Growth, Foundations for the Economy of Tomorrow

Jeremy Rifkin: The Hydrogen Economy, The Creation of the Worldwide Energy Web and the Redistribution of Power on Earth

Daron Acemoglu & James A. Robinson: Why Nations Fail, The Origins of Power, Prosperity and Poverty

But not everyone *enjoys* non-fiction. Reading should be fun, right? *The Cleaner, the Cat and the Space Station* is my attempt to blend the concepts and ideas from these books into a vision of a society to aspire to, bringing them to a wider audience by packaging them in what I hope is an entertaining story.

As a former engineer, I like to stay abreast of technical developments. All the technology Hanna and Lucy saw in Essoona is either available today or will be in our lifetimes. (OK, apart from the flying trams. And the Syenitians' mysterious power source. But the rest of it, pretty much.) Our biggest obstacle to progress is *changing the way we think*. Adjusting our priorities. Not easy, but entirely possible. And essential, because our civilisation depends upon it.

The future is in our hands.
Every single one of us has a part to play.
What's yours?

Fay Abernethy
June 2021

P.S. *The Cleaner, the Cat and the Space Station* was written on a refurbished laptop, powered by renewable energy. The author was powered by fair trade chocolate and organic walnuts.

P.P.S. If you're already doing something to help us all live more sustainably, I'd love to hear about it. Why not drop me a line at info@fayabernethy.com and share your experiences?

ACKNOWLEDGEMENTS

My sincerest thanks to everyone who helped. You know who you are. Thanks to Hilary, Emma and the team at Jericho Writers. Thanks to Lily for Jangmi. Thanks to Patrick for the gorgeous cover. And special thanks to Alex, for pretty much everything else.

NOT READY TO LEAVE THE SHANTIVIRA JUST YET?

Then come on over to www.fayabernethy.com and download The Man with the Dragon Tattoo – the story of how Joe joined the *Shantivira* back in 1997. For FREE!

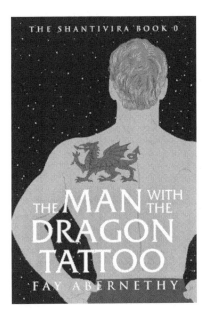

This is an *exclusive* story. You can't buy it anywhere: you can only get hold of it by signing up to The Shantivira Readers' Club. In return, I'll (occasionally) update you on how The Shantivira Book Two is coming along. Life is about to get tough for Dan…

I promise to only send you emails I believe you'll find interesting and entertaining. You can unsubscribe easily anytime. I will guard your personal data fiercely, with dragons.

If you enjoyed *The Cleaner, the Cat and the Space Station*, then please tell other people you think might like it too. And if you could leave a little review on Amazon – or even just a star rating – that would be fantastic. Spread the word!

Get it here:

Want to read more by Fay Abernethy?

LEARNING TO FLY
ALIEN SPACECRAFT
THE SHANTIVIRA BOOK TWO

What if the secret alien space station protecting the Earth went PUBLIC?

Hanna Abebe has come far since leaving Ethiopia. All the way to the other end of the galaxy, in fact. And although her course at the Essoona Pilots' Academy is tough, it's not as tough as maintaining the ultimate long-distance relationship ...

Astronaut Dan Simpson is furious. The Galaksi Alliance have exiled him on a remote planet to stop him telling NASA about them before they're ready. But by the time they come to take him home, Dan has fallen in love with an enigmatic alien and decides to stay. Only then does he discover what a perilous business his new girlfriend is involved in …

At last! Captain Joe Llewellyn has permission to initiate first contact via the UN. But if he messes it up, the Galaksi Alliance could cancel the Shantivira's funding, leaving the Earth defenceless. So, no pressure. All goes well until a rogue Samaritan flies a cargo ship through months of painstaking negotiations …

This character-driven eco science fantasy is a must-read for fans of Becky Chambers, Ursula Le Guin, Douglas Adams and Doctor Who.

Get it here:

DID MY SPELLING ANNOY YOU?

Colour instead of color, realise instead of realize, grey instead of gray?

Then I'm going to go out on a limb here and assume you might be a) in the US or b) an American. Possibly both!

Currently, there's just one version of this book available and that's in the only variety of English I feel capable of writing in – British English. *Vive la différence!*

ABOUT THE AUTHOR

Twenty years ago, Fay Abernethy left the UK for a six-month engineering secondment in Germany, fell in love and stayed there. Brexit broke her heart.

The Cleaner, the Cat and the Space Station is her first novel.

Printed in Poland
by Amazon Fulfillment
Poland Sp. z o.o., Wrocław

21806563R00264